TH
GODMOTHER

An unputdownable psychological thriller
with a breathtaking twist

JANE E. JAMES

Joffe Books, London
www.joffebooks.com

First published in Great Britain in 2024

Cover art by Nick Castle

ISBN: 978-1-83526-413-3

'Best friends tell each other everything, right?' — Jane E. James

PART ONE

CHAPTER 1: ZOE

When I enter the salon and see all the fortieth balloons and banners, my heart sinks. I had deliberately kept this unwelcome milestone to myself since I didn't want to bring attention to the fact that I was now officially old. Admittedly, I was having dinner with my best friend later, *her treat*, to mark my birthday, but that was different because we'd known each other since school and we knew everything about one another. Or *used* to.

I didn't want to share my so-called special day with anyone else. Not even my colleagues, who were all great, but considerably younger than me. But my boss, Angela, who is lovely and normally so understanding, had obviously decided that it was something we should celebrate, so I force a smile onto my face and act thrilled. Even though I'm not.

'Happy birthday, Zoe!' A chorus of female voices chirps, as I'm greeted with scarcely-there embraces and air kisses.

Their various perfumes engulf me and smother my own, as glittering gift bags are suddenly produced from behind their backs. Like magic. *Ta-dah*. Beyond them, on the reception desk, I spy the one thing I didn't want to see — a birthday cake with a number forty candle on it. I can't lie, my smile is waning at this point. Now, even my clients will know my age. Something I'd wanted to keep confidential.

2

'Forty! I can't believe it,' Pug-owning Stacey gushes.

'You look so good for your age,' said unconvincingly by Cat-lover Charlotte. We both know I look exhausted all the time.

'I had no idea you were forty!' exclaims Vegan Victoria.

'Have a lovely day,' oozes Book Club Scarlett.

And finally: 'I know you'd hoped to keep it a secret, but we couldn't let you get away with that.' Expert skier and boss Angela laughs.

It's a bestie thing. Something Maddie and I have done since our schooldays . . . made up nicknames for people without their knowledge. Not in a bitchy, insulting way — that wasn't my style — but just so we'd know who we were talking about in our conversations. Maddie frequently gave her hospital co-workers less than flattering nicknames. But that's Maddie for you, I guess. It was her sense of humour. It's not like she deliberately intended to be mean or anything.

Even though it's only 9 a.m., someone pours warmish cheap Prosecco into paper cups for us to sip and the cake is cut into absurdly small portions because everyone is on a diet and fretting over getting their 10,000 steps in each day. This is hard to accomplish when you spend the entire day standing at a chair foiling women's highlights or parked on your bum applying nail polish. Only I manage to finish my Prosecco. The others leave theirs abandoned in cups. My mind lingers on the bubbly, clear liquid, and I have the urge to drink another.

My *surprise* birthday celebration soon fizzles out, and everyone drifts away. We all have clients to get ready for as the doors open in half an hour. I'm the longest-standing worker at E'lan, which stands for "Distinctive elegance" in French, having worked there for five years, since it first opened its doors. Our team's younger members come and go regularly. It's not that they dislike working here, but they're ambitious and eager to relocate to cities like Peterborough and Cambridge, where the clientele is younger and more adventurous. Stamford is famed for its cobbled streets, designer boutiques, and elite schools, and that means we mostly attract older, middle-class and affluent customers who know exactly what they want, which isn't *change*. Some have had the same hairstyle for thirty years and insist on having the same classy red nail shade every visit.

The high-end hair and beauty salon has a balcony area at the back which overlooks the River Welland. It's used as an unofficial smoking area. I head there now, stealthily picking up one of the forgotten cups of Prosecco on my way. Before I've even finished fishing out my vape from my bag, I've downed the rest of it, not caring that someone else's lipstick is on the cup. As I inhale on my apple mango pod, I glance down at the in-excess-of-a-million-pound, contemporary, architecturally designed houses opposite which have boats moored at the bottoms of their tiered gardens.

Maddie lives in the next-to-last one. Although they don't have a boat, they do have everything else. For her, a red Range Rover Evoque. A black Porsche for Mike. A luxury kitchen that cost three times my yearly salary. Landscaped grounds. A cleaner. A gardener. Each other. *A son*.

She may have everything I've ever desired, but that doesn't mean I resent her for it. Far from it. She's worked hard to get where she is. As has Mike. It's not that I haven't. It's just that some people have more luck than others. They're a wonderful couple, and I count myself lucky to know them. Maddie is like a sister to me. As for their boy Joe, my sixteen-year-old godson, he claims me as his *second mum*. Sometimes I think I have a closer relationship with him than he does with Maddie. The same can be said of Mike occasionally. They can be hard on each other, those two.

Maddie's expensive designer curtains are already open. She's an early riser and is always on the go. She wakes up at 4 a.m. every day, even on vacation. Is it just in my head, or has she been more restless over the past year or so? A bit distant? But when I ask her how she is she always makes out nothing is wrong. I have no choice but to believe her because we tell each other everything, right?

Part of me is riddled with guilt as I think this. I don't want to keep anything from my best friend, but I find it difficult to admit even to myself how much I've turned to booze since Chris and I split up a year ago. I used to only drink at the weekends, but now I drink two bottles of wine almost every night until I black out. I can't bring myself to tell Maddie because I'm so ashamed.

As if lying about that wasn't bad enough, I'm also going through early menopause, which is the last thing I need. Any hopes of getting married and starting a family now are rapidly fading. Self-hatred engulfs me and yet, at least outwardly, I appear as if I have it together. Every day I ensure I'm immaculately turned out for work. A full face of makeup. A perfectly straightened blonde bob. A neatly ironed, soft, grey, salon-issued uniform. And a mint in my cheek to disguise any lingering tobacco vapour.

It occurs to me that what I'm going through could be the cause of the shift I see in Maddie. She might have detected that I'm hiding something from her — she would loathe that — and that's what is making her behave differently around me as a result. If I were to blame for my best friend's anxiety, I would never forgive myself.

CHAPTER 2: MADELINE

Who would have imagined that someone like me — who used to be something of a wild, rebellious teenager who struggled at school and was frequently in trouble with her teachers — would find themselves in my position? A senior nurse at Peterborough Hospital married to a wealthy surgeon. Living in a million-pound house and holidaying at the most luxurious resorts on the planet. I'm also blessed with a darkly handsome, too-clever-for-his-own-good privately educated son. My former classmates from our below-average council-run academy would never believe it of the Madeline Wood they once knew. Not that I interact with any of the old crowd anymore because they don't belong in my social circle. Only Zoe.

It's just gone 9 a.m. After a rushed and silent breakfast, Mike and Joe had left for work and school more than thirty minutes ago. Joe pulled a face at me before following his father out the door as if to plead, "Do I have to go?" but we both knew Mike would have kicked off if there had been any interruptions to his day and nobody wanted that. Now that I work off site two days a week, I get to work from home, which is where Joe wanted to be. But there are no lie-ins for me. I've been up for five hours already.

Although I have a cleaner who comes in for two hours every week, I prefer to stay on top of things, so I write polite little notes to her with smiley emoji requests to remember to iron the Amuse La Bouche tea towels, which she usually forgets to do. In the time it takes me to write these notes I realise I could have carried out the chores myself, but that's not the point. I like things done a certain way and I don't see anything wrong with that. Mike claims that I have obsessive-compulsive disorder (OCD), but with his temper, he can talk. With both of us working in the medical field, it's become increasingly "normal" for us to diagnose each other, so I combat his digs at me by suggesting he has intermittent explosive disorder (IED). Don't even get me started on Joe.

So far this morning, I've spent a couple of hours researching papers on the Royal College of Nursing website as I'm obligated to keep myself up to date on clinical advances. I then pinged off emails to my direct reports inviting them to appraisals next week, and finally got around to wrapping up Zoe's birthday presents. We're seeing her later tonight at our favourite restaurant, The Mad Turk, in St Paul's Street. It's been ages since the four of us got together and I'm really looking forward to it. I've held off on buying shiny balloons, knowing she wouldn't like it.

Impressed with my wrapping skills, and the elegant bird wrap paper, I scribble a huge loopy *With love from all of us* on the tags and place the presents inside a gift bag. A pair of champagne flutes, an Oliver Bonas necklace, a stunning floral green ceramic jug that I fell in love with and ended up buying one for myself as well, and a bottle of Zoe's favourite perfume, Daisy Ever So Fresh. A natural floor dweller when no one else is around, I pull myself to my feet and walk over to the floor-to-ceiling bi-folding doors that open onto the landscaped, tiered garden. It's Mike's pride and joy.

He loves entertaining and has created the perfect outdoor space for it. There's a luxury covered outdoor kitchen, with a barbecue, pizza oven and range, as well as a bar with a hot tub, a rattan sun island and, last but not least, a glass dining pod in the shape of a dome. At the end of the garden, the River Welland's muddied waters flow past. Our neighbours have boats moored at the bottom of their gardens but we're not a sailing family. Neither Mike nor I do well on water. Our first and only luxury cruise around the Mediterranean was a disaster. Being chronically ill with seasickness, we both decided to fly home when the boat docked in Santorini, Greece, for an overnight stop. I think Joe has inherited our fear of water as he's never learned to swim, despite having private lessons.

When the landline phone rings, my whole body tenses. *Is that the school?* Nobody else ever rings us on it, except cold callers. Everyone that we know calls us on our mobiles. I comfort myself with the knowledge that Joe can't already be in trouble because he will only have just arrived at the school gates. Even my problematic teenage boy is incapable of screwing up this early in the day. I decide not to answer it, just in case, because I really can't deal with the stuffy head teacher lecturing me again today, or that awful Miss Crowther, the too-sexy English teacher, who seems to have it in for Joe while claiming to be looking out for his best interests. My honest opinion is to never believe any woman who claims to care more about your child than you do. Because we all know how selfish fathers are at their core, only mothers truly put their children first.

When I catch a glimpse of my reflection in the glass doors, I automatically smooth down my long, glossy black hair. It's what drew Mike to me in the beginning. That and my long legs. In my twenties, I attracted a lot of male attention thanks to my height of five feet ten inches, my expensive white-flashy smile, and my blazing amber eyes that Mike used to say were "on fire". Now that I'm forty (I beat Zoe to that milestone), I no longer cause a ripple of admiration whenever I enter a room, but I believe that's because I mostly ignore the occasional turning of a head or a cheeky sidewards glance from the opposite sex. Mike is the only man I've ever slept with and after eighteen years of marriage to him, that's more than enough for me. In contrast to Zoe, who seems to enjoy sex, ugh . . . gross . . . I can't stand it. I would be more than happy if I never had to open my legs again. Fucking ecstatic actually.

The beauty salon where Zoe works is just across the water. From here, I can see the metal balcony where she sometimes goes to smoke and when I see someone standing on it, I wonder if it's her. It's too far away to say for sure. I told her she shouldn't be working on her birthday, but she just grumbled, 'What else have I got to do?' She hasn't been herself since splitting up with Chris last year.

She will never understand how much I envy her. Although she may not have much money, she does have her freedom and independence. How many hours do I waste each day worrying about my son or my husband? Too many is the answer. You can bet your life they're not thinking of me. I'm the last thing on either of their minds. I may as well be invisible. To Mike, I'm just a body that he attempts to crawl into when he feels like it. Everyone believes that I lead a perfect life, and for the past eighteen years, I've even managed to convince myself of that. I mean, I have everything, right? Haven't I persuaded all those that know us, Zoe included, that I'm the perfect wife and mother? Everybody envies the Blacks. My husband wouldn't have it any other way.

But it's all a terrible lie. I might have the perfect job, perfect house even, but my so-called perfect marriage is a sham. There's something seriously wrong with the men in my life. I don't need my BSc in psychology to know this. I feel it in my heavy heart and my aching bones. Even my friendship with Zoe is less than honest because I can't tell her any of this. If I were to do that, there's no telling what would happen to me, Joe, or Mike. We could lose everything — which is why some secrets aren't meant to be shared — even with your best friend.

CHAPTER 3: ZOE

Having arrived last on purpose, I'm greeted enthusiastically by Mike as soon as he spots me hovering nervously in the restaurant doorway. I watch him cross the room with purpose, a man on a mission, and the other diners sit up and take notice as if they instinctively know he is someone important. He pulls me into a giant hug, in which I can hardly breathe, and smothers me in his delicious aftershave before announcing in a loud voice, 'Well, well, if it isn't the gorgeous Miss Archer.'

I snort jokingly, 'The *Miss* part says it all,' as Maddie and Joe rush to join us. They look incredibly happy to see me, as I am them.

'You simply haven't met your future husband yet.' Maddie glides into my arms, dislodging Mike in the process, who generally likes to linger. She gazes at me with gorgeous orange eyes that sparkle as if she thinks I'm capable of anything. That is why I adore her. My oldest and closest friend.

Joe greets me with, 'My second mum,' as he leans in for a brief hug. I swear he gets taller and better looking every time I see him. He takes after his dad in that way. If I've thought it once, I've thought it a hundred times . . . Maddie is so lucky.

Maddie's face glows with pleasure and a leftover tan from their holiday in the Maldives as she leads me by the hand to our table, which has a carefully arranged stack of beautifully wrapped gifts in the centre of it.

'They're for the birthday girl,' Maddie confirms when she sees me looking. 'Now, sit next to me,' she insists, 'I won't have it any other way.'

'As if,' I chuckle and take a seat next to her. I take the chance to scan my surroundings. The restaurant is furnished with vibrant glass hurricane lights in a typical, rustic ottoman style. We're in the garden room, which is outside and has festoon lights strung throughout. For the first time this year, Maddie and I bare our arms because it's finally warm. It's been a cold June until now. She's wearing a black off-the-shoulder maxi dress with a long split at the side to show off pencil-thin legs and her hair is loose around her shoulders, not a kink in sight. I, on the other hand, am wearing a much shorter, light-blue wrap dress and my bob has been teased into choppy waves, a peace offering from Angela for embarrassing me earlier today.

Having shooed the waiter away with an irritable tut, Mike glugs wine into both mine and his glasses. Maddie never drinks. Not since she threw up all over the boy from three doors down when she was fourteen after getting drunk on whiskey of all things. Joe is obviously underage and wouldn't be served anyway. It doesn't mean he doesn't drink though. He's done so from an early age at home. A glass of wine or two with dinner. A beer with a barbecue. That sort of thing. But Mike wouldn't necessarily want this known, so he orders a jug of 'the finest filtered water you have'. I wasn't aware such a thing existed. I thought water was water, but I don't say so, because Mike is more knowledgeable about such things. He's a real foodie and a connoisseur of wine.

I'm just happy because my glass is filled with chilled white Pinot Grigio. I sip it slower than I'd like because I'm in company and Mike has paid over fifty pounds a bottle for it, according to the wine list, which must mean it's good.

'It should be savoured, like a beautiful woman, to best enjoy the crisp, fruity undertones,' he instructs, swilling wine around his mouth and closing his eyes as if he were approaching an orgasm.

Naturally, I do as I'm told, but I can't help but feel that it doesn't taste any better than the cheap boxed wine I buy.

'What are you having?' Joe wants to know, studying his menu. When I'm around him, I always feel like a teenager again.

'Not sure yet. You?'

'I'm going to start with the harissa chicken wings and then the kofte skewers.'

'You had that last time. Try something different,' Mike barks.

Joe's contorted face tells me that he has been issued an order rather than a request. Poor Joe. Mike and Maddie expect too much of him. They've always treated him like an adult. But he's still a boy.

'Swordfish, that's what we'll have.' Mike nods at everyone as if we actually have a choice. I had forgotten how controlling he can be. It must drive Maddie mad. No wonder she's turned her head away and is secretly rolling her eyes. Despite the fact that Mike is not acting out of the ordinary, *for him*, she seems off with him. This catches me off guard. Should I be worried for my friend? For her marriage?

That idea is dispelled when Mike gently drapes an arm around her shoulders and drums his fingers sensually against her skin — out of ownership or desire, I can't tell. Either way I itch to be touched in this way. To have a man who adores me like Mike does Maddie. When her shoulders tense and she narrows her eyes, I know that something is up. But, judging by the way Mike is acting, the problem doesn't lie with him. He's as smitten with her as ever. My God, is it possible Maddie has fallen out of love with her husband and is having an affair? Then I remember that she doesn't like sex, making this implausible. I know that whatever is going on with her is none of my business and that she'll tell me what's up only when she's ready, but I can't help but worry. They are the only people who care about me. I have no other family. I would be a forty-year-old orphan and alone in the world without them.

'And you, Zoe?'

'What about me?' I ask, puzzled.

'What are you having?' Mike gestures to the menu.

'Oh, I'll have the swordfish as well.'

He beams at that and throws me a saucy wink. 'Great choice.' Then, as soon as he notices the waiter, he snaps his fingers in the air, making Maddie and I cringe. 'We're ready to order now, my man.'

Heads turn to stare at the handsome doctor, whose nose and cheeks are boozy-red. Now I get it. Mike was clearly already intoxicated when they left the house. That wouldn't have gone down well as Maddie has a strong dislike for excess. She practises moderation in everything she does. Whenever she sees me smoking, we usually get into an argument. She'd be devastated if she ever found out that her perfect son habitually smokes marijuana. And that I was the one who introduced him to it.

CHAPTER 4: MADELINE

Choosing the swordfish wasn't such a bad idea after all. You've got to hand it to my husband, he knows what he's talking about when it comes to food. Few people are aware that fish has cancer-fighting and heart benefits, as well as being high in protein and low in calories. As a nurse anaesthetist nutrition is not my speciality. Putting people to sleep is . . . physically as well as mentally, it would seem. That's how boring I've become.

Nobody wants to listen to me. Not Mike. Or Joe. When I see how Zoe is engaging with Mike and Joe at the table and making them laugh, I feel depressingly dull beside her. I could argue it's the drink that makes her light up like that, but somehow over the years, our roles have reversed. I used to be the outgoing, vivacious one, whereas Zoe was reserved.

Mike says I need to "live a little and let my hair down once in a while," but it's not as simple as he imagines it to be, especially in light of our situation. The phone call this morning wasn't from the school but from Joe's therapist, who left a voicemail spikily informing me that my son hadn't shown up for his appointment yesterday. Again! I haven't had a chance to speak to Joe about this yet, what with us all going out for dinner tonight, but come tomorrow I will. I've resolved to drive him there myself next time.

Even though we're paying over sixty pounds an hour for these sessions, the therapist isn't allowed to discuss Joe's mental health with me due to patient confidentiality, even though I'm a nurse. After my son lost his temper and lashed out last year, leaving me with a bruised face that I'm sure most people thought was caused by Mike, Joe was diagnosed with antisocial personality disorder. To be honest, I'd rather them think that it was my husband who hit me than suspect my darling boy, who clearly didn't mean to hurt me. It isn't *his* fault he has a mental illness. *But I do blame Mike.* For setting the wrong example. And for being a bastard.

As I sip my ice water and watch those closest to me eat, drink, chat and laugh around the table, I remember to nod and smile pleasantly so I won't be accused of being *distant*, a word Mike casually tosses around like he does money. It's true I haven't been myself lately, but there is a valid reason for that. In addition to worrying about my son, who the stuffy old head teacher claims is on the verge of being expelled, for good this time, and the therapist urging me to believe that he is a "pathological liar", I'm also worried sick about my husband's affair. Or should I say, another of his affairs? The surprising part of this is that I don't mind if he sleeps with other women. Weirdly, Mike seems more bothered by this fact than I am by his adultery. He wants me to be jealous. To show some passion. Anything but cold, unfeeling, distant Maddie.

Passion, I have in abundance, for my son and my career. Mike, on the other hand, is passionate about young women. And by young, I mean fifteen or sixteen. He knows I'm aware of his infidelities but believes I am ignorant about these underage girls. But I know everything there is to know about my husband. Isn't that the purpose of a private investigator? I can assure you they charge far more than sixty pounds per hour but are well worth the money. I have no intention of divorcing my husband currently but I'm sick with dread at the danger Mike is placing us in. The weight is dropping off me as a result. I haven't been this stick-thin since my twenties.

I wonder how Zoe would feel about Mike if she knew about his preference for younger women. I think she'd be shocked if she knew about the cheating, full stop. She thinks he's amazing. And he is, in so many ways, but he is not the moral man he portrays himself to be, and as a doctor, a surgeon no less, he is risking everything. His career. His reputation. Our lives. He could go to prison if he gets caught.

I keep asking myself, Why don't I just put my foot down with him? Tell him I'm aware of what he is doing and demand that he stop. I'm a nurse which means I have a duty to "do no harm" but I'm also someone's wife, and I love Mike in my own way. He's family. I just don't like him very much. He can be a big-headed, controlling psycho when he wants to be, as well as a serial cheater who is sleeping with underage girls, but he's still my man, and generally speaking, our family sticks together. Besides, it's easy to convince myself that these girls are *almost* women and that they're having consensual sex, therefore it's not a crime . . . and as a doctor, a skilled surgeon no less, who saves lives, he gives so much back to the community, so he can't be all bad. *Can he?*

'You okay, Maddie?' Zoe asks, pulling me out of my head, which is not somewhere I want to be.

'All good, thanks.' I dazzle her with the famous Maddie smile. 'Are you having a nice time?'

'I'm here with my three favourite people in the world.' She shrugs comically. 'You. Mike and "our boy Joe" so why wouldn't I be?'

'*And* you're drinking wine,' Mike chips in, flashing his toothpaste-white grin. *He doesn't know he looks like a loan shark when he does that.*

'*And* I'm drinking wine.' Zoe chuckles in agreement.

'Toast,' I suggest, rising to my feet.

'Toast,' everyone agrees, scraping back their chairs and standing up.

'To my best friend who I love as a sister,' I say, eyes filling unexpectedly with tears, as I raise the glass of water to my lips. 'Happy birthday.'

16

'Happy birthday, Aunty Zoe.' Joe's eyes sparkle with admiration for my best friend and I feel a sharp claw of jealousy scrape down my back.

'Happy birthday, titch.' Mike playfully makes fun of her diminutive size. Zoe, at five feet four, is considered tiny in comparison to my five feet ten.

Even if I do say so myself, my family are stunningly beautiful. All of us are tall and tanned. Fit and trim. We have olive skin and shiny black hair and could easily be mistaken for being Mediterranean. Joe has inherited his dad's well-defined jawbone, alert eyes and symmetrical nose. It's no wonder women fall under the Black men's spell. First Mike, and now Joe, who is so handsome that most of the girls at his school have fallen for him.

But given all that is going on in my life, it's difficult for me to count myself lucky. I should be grateful that we all have good health and that we don't face financial difficulties like so many other people do. Zoe is one of them. I know she struggles to get by on her salary. Hand-to-mouth is how she exists and she's stubbornly independent, so she won't let me help her. She might even try to insist on paying for her share of the meal tonight, but Mike won't allow it. Not for one minute.

I feel even more isolated from them as we retake our seats and carry on with our meal. As Zoe stated in her little speech, while flattering us all with her appreciative gaze, I'm here with my three favourite people in the world, so I should be happy too. I'm not though. On the inside, I'm miserable. That's because, at times, I despise myself almost as much as I do my husband. You see, the real reason I haven't yet confronted Mike about his most recent fling is because I'm scared of what it will do to my son.

Mike is sleeping with Joe's girlfriend.

CHAPTER 5: ZOE

'You could have brought your girlfriend along. I wouldn't have minded,' I whisper to Joe, while Mike and Maddie are preoccupied with the waiter who has brought over the dessert menu. Maddie loves puddings and will have a hard time choosing just one. After a meal, I prefer to smoke, but there's no chance of that with the bestie around.

'That's okay,' Joe shrugs and his cheeks turn red. 'We broke up actually.'

I'm about to tell him how sorry I am when I notice Mike staring wide-eyed at his son. Some form of warning if I'm not mistaken. And all of a sudden, Maddie is more engrossed in twirling her glass in her hand than she is in our conversation. Something is definitely not right, in my opinion. I turn back to Joe, trying to act normal.

'I'm sorry. I know how much you liked her,' I respond while simultaneously realising that I don't actually know that because my godson isn't very open about his personal life. He used to tell me everything, but like Maddie, he has also changed in the last year. Only Mike appears to have remained the same. As always, he is a playful and generous host.

'She wasn't all that hot anyway.' Joe sighs, fixing his eyes on me in an intense way that makes me feel slightly uncomfortable. 'Not like you,' he adds sheepishly.

Giggling uneasily, I teasingly say, 'That's no way to talk to your aunt,' though I'm privately embarrassed by his flattery, which, again, is something new.

'But we're not really related, are we?' he complains in a manner that I find to be overly mature. It shouldn't be expected of a boy his age to feel pressure to become an adult so rapidly. I wish Mike would ease up on Joe.

'Of course, you are,' Maddie interjects now that she's back in the room, so to speak. Her eyebrows knit together as she continues, 'We're family.'

'Some family,' Joe murmurs, while throwing his mum a dark look.

'Am I allowed to open my presents yet?' I clap my hands with childlike enthusiasm, changing the subject. I will stop at nothing to avoid atmospheres because I've never felt at ease in them. "People-pleasing Zoe" is Maddie's nickname for me. It's well deserved.

'Yes, of course,' Maddie has already gotten up and is making room on the table for me to unwrap my gifts. 'Open that one first, I think you'll like it best.'

Out of politeness, I read the gift tag first, although I already know what it will say: *With love from all of us*. Knowing that Maddie is still predictable in some things is comforting.

'Oh, it's gorgeous. I love it,' I gasp when I unravel the wrapping paper to find a box with a necklace made of fresh white and pale blue beading.

'It will look fantastic with your dress,' Maddie exclaims. 'Put it on now so we can see it.'

'Okay.' I jump to my feet. But before I can attempt to do up the clasp at the back of my neck, someone gets there before me . . . Joe.

Similar to Mike's earlier embrace, his insistent hands seem to rest on my skin for an extra second, attracting Maddie's enquiring gaze on us.

'Thanks, Joe,' I gush, deliberately stepping away from him so I can spin around in front of my best friend. I pull at my dress with my fingers, noticing how much shorter it feels now than it did when I first put it on. When both pairs of masculine eyes travel down my legs, it doesn't escape either Maddie or me. *What's got into the touchy, feely, Black men tonight?*

'Will I do?' I ask nervously.

'You look gorgeous,' Maddie responds while smiling dejectedly. 'Doesn't she, Mike?'

Mike pretends to do a double take when he retrieves his gaze from my calves. 'Will you marry me?' He laughs.

We've always teased each other, so I try not to show how depressed I am about being single as I bite back playfully, 'Just name the day, Mike.'

'Dad, you can't have two wives.' Joe fixes jealous eyes on his father. 'Besides, Aunty Zoe is going to marry me when I turn eighteen. Aren't you?'

I wish I could say no to him, but I really can't because of the way he's gazing at me in that endearing "don't say no in front of Dad" way.

'Finally, I have something to look forward to,' I joke, hoping that Maddie doesn't take it the wrong way. It's one thing to have a bit of banter with Mike but no woman wants to witness her best friend flirting with her sixteen-year-old son.

When Joe's face breaks into a smile, I can tell I've done the right thing by him but Maddie on the other hand, well, I can't read her expression. She's gone all distant on us again and is staring into her empty glass.

'Who's up for another bottle of wine to go with dessert?' Mike booms out, oblivious to everyone else's mood, which is typical of him.

I answer distractedly, 'I'm in,' as I watch Maddie cross and uncross her legs next to me. She then spins her engagement and wedding rings on her finger before returning to twirling her glass. I'm familiar with this routine. When we were kids, Maddie had a lot of nervous energy, and as an adult, this energy has turned into anxiety. I'm certain I wouldn't be a bag of nerves if I looked like her or had her money. Or her life. Sometimes, I wonder if she is aware of how stunningly beautiful she is. Even now, she draws attention wherever she goes, but doesn't seem to notice. I've never experienced that. I mean, I suppose I'm attractive enough, but I'm not in the same league as Maddie. There's no point even in trying. So, I don't.

While we were at school, Maddie, being outgoing, adventurous and always up for a challenge, could have easily moved up to the prettier, more popular group of girls in our year if she wanted to, but being fiercely loyal, she chose to stick with me. We didn't need anyone else. We still don't. Now that I'm the rebel out of the two of us, I do everything excessively, including drinking too much, dating too much, and smoking too much. I wonder where my crazy, free-spirited best friend disappeared to. Has her career and motherhood completely engulfed her or is she still in there somewhere? She consistently seems to prioritise others. Mike. Joe. Me. Her work.

For the first time in my life, and for as long as I've known Maddie, I don't envy her. I've learnt something from watching her tonight. She may look like a model in a magazine with her perfect skin, perfect hair, perfect teeth and perfect life but I'm beginning to realise that her family is not as perfect as I originally believed.

CHAPTER 6: MADELINE

During the brief journey home, during which Mike heavily criticised my driving — including my gear changes and how often I glanced in the rearview mirror — Joe seemed glummer and more uncommunicative than usual, and as soon as we entered the house, he went straight to his room.

'Are you all right, love?' I had asked him, and reached out to touch him on the arm, but he forcefully shook me off and then stomped away. After that, I gave up. His actions made me think of the time when he struck me in a fit of rage. I'm a great believer in the theory that just because someone behaves aggressively, it does not necessarily follow that they *are* aggressive, and that is true of my son. Fortunately, Mike was taking a pee at the time and missed seeing Joe's reaction. There's no telling what would have happened if he had, only that I would have two angry men to contend with then, instead of one.

As soon as Mike walks into the kitchen, I surprise him by turning on him. 'You took your time.'

'It was a long one.' His cheek lifts into a grin as he says this.

'I'm not surprised given how much booze you drank.' I chew on my lip as I wait for his response. We both know that I'm spoiling for a fight. It's been brewing for days if not weeks.

'Don't start, Madeline,' he warns, his brow furrowed.

'Me?' I huff. 'Where do you get off perving all over my friend?'

His face wrinkles, perplexed. 'Zoe?'

'Yes. Zoe. There's no need to act dumb.'

'What did I do or say that I haven't said or done a hundred times before?' he asks in the annoying, scientific tone of a doctor that he typically reserves for his patients but occasionally uses on me.

However, he is correct. He has always openly flirted with my best friend and with my approval. Knowing that she was the only woman in the entire world I could trust and who would never betray me by having an affair with my husband, my intention was to make her feel loved and attractive.

Changing tack, I throw my evening bag on the massive kitchen island that runs the entire length of the equally vast room. It feels like I've just challenged my husband to an old-fashioned duel which seems out of place in our ultra-modern, contemporary surroundings.

'Isn't it enough that you're already screwing around?' When I accuse him of this, he has his back to me, but when he slowly turns in my direction and his shoe-polish brown eyes come to rest on me, I can tell he is startled.

'Like you care,' he finally sulks.

As I approach the enormous, shiny black table that matches every single head of hair in our home, I notice his hands bunch into defensive fists at his side as his gaze follows me.

When I don't answer, which would suggest that he's right and that *I don't care*, he moves over to the wine cooler, pulls a bottle of white wine out and then reaches above his head into a cabinet to get a paper-thin glass. He appears to regain his composure as he pours himself a drink.

'Another drink, Mike?' I ask sarcastically. 'Aren't you always telling your patients to cut back on alcohol, saying that they'll feel better once they do and that there is less chance of a heart attack that way.'

'A doctor's mantra has always been "do as I say, not as I do". You are aware of that.'

'Don't try gaslighting me, Dr Black,' I seethe as I unstrap my sandals and kick them halfway across the room. 'It won't work on me. I'm not fifteen. Which is how you seem to prefer them these days.'

The glass pauses at his lips and his eyes swell with panic. 'What do you think you know this time?'

'I don't *think* anything. I have proof,' I scream in triumph. I'm doing it at last. I'm putting my foot down with him. As I've been telling myself to do for weeks, ever since I learned about the girl . . .

Her name angrily spills out of my mouth. 'Gabriella.'

'Who?' he asks in wide-eyed innocence. He feigns ignorance and takes another gulp of his wine, but he doesn't fool me. That must have got him in the gonads.

'How could you? With your own son's girlfriend,' I sneer, and shake my head in disgust.

'You're mistaken. That is something I would never do.' He puffs out his chest, acting all offended.

'Mike, save your breath.' I heave a sigh. 'I have photographic evidence of the two of you getting cosy in your car, as well as a video of you and her checking into a budget hotel that you wouldn't normally be seen dead in and leaving an hour later.'

'Shit,' he blurts out without thinking.

One thing my husband is not is stupid. He knows when to fight and when to quit. 'Shit,' I repeat, rolling my eyes.

He stumbles over to the island then, yanks out a chair made of plush velvet and falls into it. 'Madeline, I can explain—'

'Are you the reason she dumped our son?' I interrupt sharply.

'Tonight, was the first I heard of it. I was as shocked as you were.'

'But not as shocked as our son,' I jeer sarcastically, wishing I could lash out at him the way Joe did me. But I experience a tug on my heart when I notice how crushed he appears. I've committed to always loving this man no matter what. That doesn't mean he is more important than my son. Nobody is. And when I stipulate, 'You must finish it with her. Tonight, or tomorrow, but as soon as possible,' I'm thinking about Joe.

'Of course. Consider it done.'

Without having seen the evidence, his quick compliance with my ultimatum indicates that I have him exactly where I want him.

'I still find it hard to believe you would risk everything for a fling with a flat-chested fifteen-year-old. Shit, Mike, you could have gone to prison for having sex with an underage girl, and still could if you screw up how you end things with her. We can only hope that Gabriella doesn't turn into a little bitch who wants revenge on her sugar daddy.'

Hope unexpectedly dawns on his face as he exclaims, 'Perhaps she'll get back together with Joe and we can forget that it ever happened.'

Behind us, the deliberate and savage clearing of a throat . . .

We both turn to face our enraged, red-faced son, who is glaring at us from the doorway with a face full of disgust. Shoulders stiff with fury, he seems close to imploding with hatred.

'What? After your dick has been inside her!' Joe's voice pulsates with anger as he yells this. His eyes then narrow to mere slits as they zoom in on his father. 'No fucking way.'

CHAPTER 7: ZOE

As an incurable romantic, I've always dreamed of finding "the one" and up until recently, when early menopause wrecked my chances, I had hopes of one day settling down, getting married and raising a family. Even so, whenever I arrive home, alone, like tonight, after being dropped off by Maddie, I'm always secretly relieved. Because life as a singleton means I can rip off my bra, shrug off whatever I'm wearing in exchange for my PJs, and drink as much alcohol as I choose. When I close the door to my terraced limestone property on Burghley Lane, all pretence at moderation vanishes.

My little house, hugged on all sides by its neighbours, is situated practically on the street, allowing passers-by to see inside. Which is why there are blackout blinds at the windows. The front door opens straight into the living room which features a forest-themed photo wall. The matching bookcases on either side of the unsightly gas fire are stacked with romance novels and chick lit. Two velvet-buttoned sofas face each other across a shaggy rug, while a lava lamp regurgitates red and purple bubbles.

I like to think the room reflects my fun-loving personality, but Maddie claims it resembles a young person's bedsit because it's kitted out in cheap tacky Ikea furniture.

As opposed to her, I don't like minimalism or black and chrome, hence why my home is crammed with ornaments and mementoes. "Tat", Maddie laughingly calls it, and I can tell by the way her eyes sweep the room, she yearns to de-clutter not only me but my house too.

Kicking off my heels, I enter the cramped galley kitchen which never sees the sun. It looks out onto the tiniest courtyard where there is room for one deckchair and a tomato plant. One of my favourite smells is that of homegrown tomatoes. I avoid spending too much time in the kitchen as the "beige everything" offends my tastes. Since I don't own my home, I can't rip out the existing units as I'd like. Apple green tea towels, an orange kettle, and herbs in pots at the window spice things up. As do the motivational quotes on the walls, that preach "Be kind", "Never miss a chance to dance" and "Believe in yourself". The word "hypocrite" is never far from my mind when I see them.

I open the fridge, devoid of any real food — just cheese, pickles and condiments — and wrestle out an opened box of white wine. I fill a glass to the top and take it back into the living room with me. As I sink onto the ochre sofa and stare at the forest green one opposite, I can't shrug off the feeling that something is missing . . .

Chris, of course. He's been gone over a year now, but I still miss his presence. My kind, compassionate, Scottish-born mental health nurse boyfriend, who knew all about stress and anxiety, cowardly left a note on the coffee table one morning explaining that he didn't want to be with me anymore. He then proceeded to block me on his phone and social media accounts and go no-contact. I haven't heard from him since.

"Men rarely leave women without lining up another one to go to," Maddie had warned me darkly. She's as furious with Chris now as she was then and talks about "karma" and "success being the best revenge", but I didn't care about any of that and still don't. I could never wish Chris any harm since I loved him so much. Besides, at the time all I wanted to do was quietly die since I was unable to tell Maddie the real reason Chris left me. We had just returned from a trip to Portugal, and due to my fear of flying, I got absolutely trashed on the plane, causing a scene and hurling insults at my boyfriend for daring to move seats. "He'd felt disrespected," he'd said and things were never the same between us after that. Never mind that he used to get pissed out of his head at times and even got charged with assault once for getting into a drunken brawl. "Double-standards Chris" is how I refer to him now. It doesn't ease the hurt though.

A warm, content feeling washes over me as I curl my hand around the purple stem of the glass and put it to my lips. This is the moment I think about and long for from the moment I get up in the morning till I walk in the door at night. Wine is my substitute for a husband and a family. As are dates with men I've lowered my standards for. Secret pissheads like me. The occasional online hook-up. Married men pretending to be single. You name it, I've dated them all. I sleep with very few of them though. My body count has risen only by two since Chris left. Even then, I don't know why I bother. It's not as if any of these men bring me happiness. Let alone to orgasm. Even the good guys that come along — the ones that promise to call you later — never do.

I've only been in three long-term relationships, and Chris was the longest of them all, lasting three years. I've never gotten over him. He was my last chance at having a baby, but ironically, I'd told him he needed to get sober and quit smoking weed before we tried for a child. I wasn't much of a drinker back then. Sometimes I love and hate him in equal amounts, but mostly I just love him. I'll never forget the look on his, and the cabin crew's, faces when I called him out for being an "arsehole" at 42,000 feet. But in the end, it turned out I was right. Because, the arsehole had left me, hadn't he? The last I heard, Chris was shacked up with some new bird and had been sober for three months. I wish the same could be said of me.

Nobody would ever suspect I'm an alcoholic from looking at my sleek bobbed hair, flawless-looking skin from wearing wonder-glow cosmetics, and well-groomed appearance. Or that I frequently experience blackouts, which lead to anxiety, panic attacks, guilt and self-hatred. Maddie would have me whisked into rehab if she knew any of this. She would be devastated that I hadn't told her. But I'm such a mess, how can I?

When there's a knock at the door, I shoot forwards and slosh wine down my dress, leaving a wet spot on my left boob, as if I'd been breastfeeding. *Chance would be a fine thing.* By the second knock, louder this time, I'm on my feet, eyes on stalks, going into full panic mode. Who could it be at this time of the night? My eyes slide automatically to the shiny peacock wall clock that Maddie detests. It's gone midnight. I stealthily peer through an inch of blind to see a shadow of a man on the pavement outside.

CHAPTER 8: MADELINE

'You have to go and find him,' I yell at Mike after we've raced through the endlessly long and slippery black-and-white tiled entrance hall to find the double entrance doors swinging open. At first, we were both too stunned to pursue Joe, but once we realised that he had stormed out of the room *and the house* and wasn't coming back, we were spurred into action. I reached the black glossy doors first, and as we fell into a pile outside, one after the other, Joe was nowhere to be seen. He had already disappeared up the path, through the gate, and into the darkened street.

'He could be anywhere,' Mike protests, his guilt-ridden gaze fixed on the pavement that leads into town.

'This is all your fault,' I seethe, adding for good measure, 'Joe was right when he threw that parting shot at you. You can't keep it in your pants.'

'That's hardly helpful,' Mike complains while scratching his head as if trying to come up with a plan. He's always been very solution-orientated, has my husband. But this time *he's* the problem.

'Oh God!' I cry out, tightly closing my eyes because I can't believe what has just happened. That Joe overheard his father's confession. 'What are we going to do?'

When Mike cluelessly scrunches up his face and shrugs his shoulders, I glare at him before marching back inside, to the kitchen, where I help myself to a glass of water from the specially installed filtered-water tap. The Black family do not drink everyday tap water. As I knock it back in one go and wipe droplets of water from my mouth, Mike comes back inside.

'I've shut the doors but left them unlocked. For when he comes back,' he says quietly.

'*If* he comes back,' I fume.

Mike gulps nervously while slipping off his jacket. 'Where do you think he would have gone?'

'Not to Gabriella's that's for sure. Unless . . .'

'Unless what?'

'He was really angry.'

'Understandable, don't you think?'

'But I've never seen him quite like that before. You don't think he'd . . . hurt her, do you?'

'Of course not.' Mike puffs out his chest, offended. 'He's been brought up to be better than that, to hit a girl.'

'Has he though, Mike?' I grind out. 'And what about me? I'm a girl. Woman. And it didn't stop him from lashing out at me.'

Mike lets out a deep breath and his glossy black head falls onto his chest. When he looks up again, his eyes are filled with ruthless determination. 'I'll go around there now.'

'Where?' I ask wide-eyed.

'To Gabriella's.'

'What? No. You can't.' I grab a handful of Mike's shirt to prevent him from leaving. 'What if Joe *is* there and you and him get in a fight?'

'I promise you that won't happen.'

'What if he hits you?'

'Then I'll take it on the chin. It's no more than I deserve.'

'That's the first decent thing you've said tonight.' I'm deliberately sarcastic.

'Madeline, everything will be fine,' Mike asserts, placing a hand on my cheek. 'I swear.'

I'm torn between wanting to shrug him off and accepting any shred of comfort I can get. I'm so used to leaning on him. 'Do you promise?' As I ask this, tears start to form in my eyes.

'I may not be the best husband in the world, but you and Joe are the only people that truly matter to me. You do believe me, don't you?'

I nod tearfully and step into his embrace, mumbling, 'Yes.'

Whilst it feels reassuring to have my husband's arms around me, another more worrying thought has me springing out of them.

'Her parents will be there. They'll want to know what Joe's father is doing turning up at their house in the middle of the night.'

'It's all right. I've already considered that. They left this morning to spend a long weekend at their cottage in Norfolk.'

'How do you know that?' I demand, folding my arms defensively.

'You don't want to know,' Mike cautions, his gaze once more hitting the floor. In my opinion, his head doesn't deserve to come up again. Ever.

'Shit, Mike. You were there earlier today, weren't you?'

'I'm so sorry, Madeline.' Mike's eyes sparkle with unshed tears as he continues, 'I think I need help. Some kind of counselling. I can't seem to stop myself. It's like an addiction.'

When I hear his voice break, my heart starts to ache. 'Okay, Mike. We'll get you some help. First things first though.'

'Joe?'

'Of course, Joe. Who else?' I'm rattled that he would even consider I'd put him first when the situation we're in is of his own making. 'Ring me as soon as you've spoken to Gabriella. But if Joe's not there, don't let on to her that he knows about you and her. I'll stay here in case Joe comes back.'

'Right.' Mike checks absentmindedly in his pocket for his phone and then gazes around the room as if bewildered. His earlier resolve now forgotten.

Once more, I feel compassion for the man I've known since I was a young woman myself. How did we get here, I wonder? "Because boys will be boys", as my mother used to say. Another proverb of hers was that "all grown men are boys underneath and need mothering". But the only boy who matters to me right now is Joe.

Mike jumps in alarm as I bark, 'Well, go on then. You won't find our son by standing there doing nothing.'

'Yes, of course, I'm leaving now.' He approaches me and kisses me on the forehead. It's a worn-out married custom that irritates me no end. Even though time is of the essence, he continues to procrastinate . . . looking at me with puppy dog eyes, as if he were deserving of a hero's badge. One thing my husband is not is anybody's hero — least of all mine.

I step back from him, wrinkling my nose at the smell of alcohol that seeps from the pores of his skin. As my blazing eyes turn into mere slits, I growl menacingly, 'Don't fucking come back without him.'

CHAPTER 9: ZOE

A visibly upset and furious Joe stands on my doorstep, then rushes past me before I even get the chance to invite him inside. Knowing my godson as I do, I don't press him to explain what's wrong right away. Like his mum, he'll talk when he's ready. And not before. Instead, I watch him storm into the kitchen to open one of the cold beers that I keep in the fridge just for him. He wrings off the top as if it were someone's neck before placing the bottle to his lips and taking a long drink. I lift my eyebrows in an enquiring manner when his angry eyes eventually land on me.

'I hate him,' Joe roars.

'What's your dad done this time?' I heave a sigh, gesturing for Joe to sit down, while I retake my seat on the ochre sofa.

As he hurls himself at the sofa across from me, I curl my legs under me in a more comfortable position since I have a feeling this may end up being a long night. He has the aura of a rebellious, hormonal teenager about him. Not the man I glimpsed in the restaurant earlier. Poor Joe. He's neither one nor the other. It must be difficult raising a son. Maddie has certainly got her work cut out. However, she always maintained her boy was as close to perfect as possible up until recently. And why wouldn't I believe her? She knows I would never criticise her parenting style. But now that I think about it, she stopped proudly boasting about Joe's achievements a while back, which leads me to suspect once more that not all is as it seems in the Black household. And that the model son has now become the troubled son.

'I don't want to talk about it. *Him*,' Joe snarls, clenching his jaw.

'What *do* you want to talk about?' I study him over the top of my glass as I take a sip of my drink. But he just shrugs, so I try again. 'How about Gabriella? Do you want to talk about what went wrong?'

The look of absolute horror that flashes across Joe's face, accompanied by an exaggerated roll of the eyes, tells me he doesn't, so I quickly change the subject. 'I stupidly thought it was Chris knocking at the door just now.'

'You must have been disappointed when you realised it was me.' Joe scowls jealously.

Gutted more like. Heartbroken all over again, I'd go as far as to say. When am I ever going to get it through this thick head of mine that he is never coming back? Instead, I respond with, 'Of course not. I'm always pleased to see my godson,' which seems to appease him.

'Sorry to rock up so late.'

His shoulders go down a notch as he releases some of his pent-up frustration. I'm relieved because I'm not sure what to do with an enraged sixteen-year-old. It's so far out of my comfort zone. I'm used to friendly Joe. Smart Joe. Kind Joe. Boy Joe. The kid I helped raise. Held. Bottle-fed. Rocked to sleep. Babysat. Dried his tears. And bum. Told off. Praised. Loved. Introduced to marijuana. Oops.

'What about you?' Joe asks, hunching forward to prop his chin up with his hands.

'What about me?'

'You always want to know about us. How me, Mum and Dad are, but nobody ever asks about you.'

'That's not true, Joe,' I stammer, thinking once again that this is far too adult a conversation for someone his age to be having. 'Your mother asks how I am all the time.'

'But does she actually listen?' Joe snaps. 'She never does with me.'

'Oh, so that's what this is all about.' I celebrate too soon, thinking I've got to the bottom of the problem. 'You've had another of your rows.'

'This has absolutely nothing to do with Madeline and everything to do with you . . . Zoe.' His alert, all-over-the-place eyes fasten on mine as he says this and I don't imagine it when his gaze then travels to my mouth.

I shudder at what I can only describe as an adult male's admiring glance being directed at me and I start to feel increasingly uncomfortable around him, much like I did earlier in the restaurant. It's also unusual for him to call me by my first name. Normally he addresses me as "Aunty Zoe".

'I can't see why it should have anything to do with me.' I flap a hand dismissively at him and clumsily climb to my feet, adding, 'I'm going to get a top-up. Do you want another beer?'

'Sit down,' he orders, imitating Mike's domineering manner, and gets up from the sofa to firmly remove the glass from my hand. 'I'll get it.'

I open my mouth to argue, then change my mind, so as not to antagonise him. 'Thanks, Joe,' I say meekly.

As I listen to the sounds of the fridge opening and wine glugging into my glass, I have a sudden, burning desire to be alone. I want to grieve all over again that it wasn't Chris at the door. It's nearly midnight and I don't want to be responsible for a teenager's volatile moods. Nor do I want one throwing a six-foot tantrum in my tiny house. I start to worry whether Joe's taken something given how irregular his mood seems to be. It would crush Maddie's heart if her son started using drugs. I don't see any harm in occasionally relaxing with a joint, but class A drugs are something else entirely. Even though I'm aware that he hangs around with a group of boys that his parents would disapprove of, I keep it to myself.

While Joe is in the kitchen, I'm tempted to secretly text Maddie, to let her know he's safe. *She'd come and get him then.* She's bound to be worried about Joe. When isn't she worried about Joe? But if he catches me doing that, he'll feel he can no longer trust me and then he'll have no one at all to talk to.

'Do your parents know where you are?' I call out, worried that Maddie will hold it against me if I don't let her know where he is.

'I'm not a child,' Joe grumbles, slouching back into the room.

'I know you're not.' I stumble on my words, thinking it's almost impossible to know what to say to him without getting my head bitten off. Maddie is the same. She's been that way for about a year now.

'Here,' Joe says, handing me my glass and holding my gaze.

When our hands accidentally collide, his touch stirs up the wrong kind of feelings in me like panic and unease. But I mustn't let Joe know this as he's an unpredictable, somewhat disturbed young man. I wonder why it has taken me until now to realise it.

'Thanks.' I nod dismissively, tearing my eyes away from his. I'm relieved when he's no longer towering over me and has retaken his seat opposite. But when he undoes his laces and removes his trainers as if he were staying the night, I'm mildly alarmed.

'You didn't text Mum when I was in the kitchen, did you?' His suspicious eyes jump to my mobile phone, which is on the coffee table in front of us. 'To let her know where I am?'

'No, of course not.' I act offended. 'I'd never do that.'

'Good.' He nods approvingly, in a way that reminds me once again of his father. I am not sure why, but just hearing the word "good" used in such a menacing way, has the power to make me feel afraid. Just as I'm beginning to believe his being here couldn't get much worse, I watch horrified as he deliberately moves the phone out of my reach.

Tightly, he says, 'Let's keep it that way.'

CHAPTER 10: MADELINE

'Why isn't she picking up? Answering my calls? It's so unlike Zoe.' I'm talking to air, because I'm alone in the kitchen, staring at my mobile phone and wanting to hurl it at the wall. *Where is my friend when I need her?* is all I can think. Zoe would understand what I'm going through and how very concerned I am about Joe. Mike, on the other hand, only acts as though he's worried. Since he obviously loves his only son, it's not that he's heartless, but because he's a man, he won't worry till concrete proof that our boy is in danger of never returning home is put in front of him.

Assuming Zoe must have gone to bed and is soundly sleeping, possibly with earplugs in, I slam the phone down on the gleaming kitchen island and bite down on my lip. She's been there for me for the majority of my life, ever since we were eight years old with pigtails. I've never felt the need for another close friend and I've always seen us as sisters rather than friends. Honestly, I have no idea what I would do without her. Or my son.

This is all Mike's fault, I fume inwardly, unable to shake off the fear that Joe might never return, not after finding out that his father has been screwing his girlfriend. Whatever you want to call it — an omen, a gut instinct, a mother's intuition — the sensation that tonight marks the beginning of something profoundly dark for our family won't go away.

As I mull over that thought, a sob escapes my throat, and I can feel the kitchen's white brick walls pushing in on me until there's no air left to breathe. I ask myself what sort of family we have become — with mother and son both in therapy and my sex-addicted husband soon to join us. "The fucked-up Blacks" is what our neighbours and friends would call us if they knew.

The truth is I only went into therapy because of Joe. Not for dealing with my husband's infidelities, as I implied to Mike since he deserved to be punished regardless of how little I cared. Although Joe's diagnosis of antisocial personality disorder and the therapist's description of him as a "pathological liar" would be enough to make any parent insane with worry, my motivation for seeking counselling went even deeper than that.

Mike lived in perpetual denial that there was anything wrong with our son and believed that he was simply going through a phase that all boys go through. *As all boys go through, for fuck's sake*, I'd wanted to scream when he came out with that statement, which implied Joe would grow out of it, but I recognised arguing wouldn't accomplish anything as Mike only ever changed his mind when he wanted to and wasn't amenable to persuading. Only his superiors at the hospital had the power to influence my husband, and even then, he believed he was smarter than them.

However, I have been aware that something was wrong with Joe since he was six years old. He appeared to be missing a part of his brain and heart since he had neither empathy nor sympathy and had a stronger propensity for cruelty and violence. It began with him slowly and methodically pulling the legs off spiders with a delighted look on his face. Then, he moved on to small mammals, demanding a hamster as a pet only to starve it to death on purpose. Since I didn't find Joe's diary until after the poor thing had died, I wasn't able to help it. He'd diarised the unfortunate animal's demise, using language like, "Today it's wobbly on its feet and can hardly walk which is so funny," and, "It looks as though Mum had anesthetised it," or, "Even Dad couldn't bring it back to life now. Lol."

I've never told Mike about the hamster. I couldn't bring myself to as I felt so ashamed. He was deliberately blind to his son's flawed character anyway. Instead, I tried harder, to be a better parent, role model, better everything, yet still I failed. Occasionally, I would see glimpses of goodness in Joe. For instance, his connection to Zoe. He had always acted like the ideal godson in her presence, and she loved him like her own, which is partly why I've never confided in her. But "our boy Joe" as we referred to him, was skilled at pretending. He was even more skilled than Mike.

It wasn't even Joe's physical assault on me that drove me to seek out counselling. It was the knowledge that he was responsible for another boy's death. Joe went to the same private school in Stamford as Rupert Forbes, who was a quiet, studious boy with fire-engine red hair. He wasn't popular or unpopular, liked or disliked, but for some unfortunate reason he caught my son's attention. I didn't learn about this until after Rupert hanged himself, at which point I, along with all the other mums and dads, grieved his loss. The children in Rupert's class were offered help and support, grief counselling if needed, but Joe appeared indifferent. Callously so. His behaviour disturbed me but Mike convinced me that it was just his way of processing loss at a young age, so I didn't intervene.

A broken-hearted Mrs Forbes then showed up at my door a few weeks later accusing me of being a terrible parent. "Raising a monster" she called it. Knowing that she was grieving for her son, I tried to make allowances for her and even invited her in, thinking it might help her to talk about Rupert's suicide, but she spat in my face, actually spat with a full mouthful of phlegm, before storming away, but not before screaming, 'My boy is dead because of your son. It's all there. In his diary. Make sure you read it.'

Along with a sense of profound discomfort, I was left with the torn, sobbed-over pages of teenage writing that, once I read them, would never leave me. His words crushed me, and I sobbed until I resembled Mrs Forbes in a shattered snotty mess. Rupert's young, brilliant mind was soon revealed to be muddled with self-hatred and low self-esteem. He was convinced that everyone hated him, but in reality, it was just Joe who was guilty of that. Self-loathing and self-disgust screamed from the page, as did my son's name. "Joe this" and "Joe that" populated the pages.

Once Joe had made up his mind to cruelly torture, harass and bully the poor boy, he was unrelenting in his pursuit of him. He constantly humiliated Rupert by making fun of him, goading him, tormenting him about his appearance, and calling him a "ginger freak". Up until that day, I had never wished to be childless. It hadn't stopped there. Joe had somehow managed to get hold of Rupert's phone number and sent him hundreds of text messages suggesting he kill himself since he was a loser and everyone hated him. *Your life isn't worth living anyway*, he'd texted, adding a disturbing suicide-by-hanging GIF.

Again, I didn't mention any of this to Mike in the hope that it would go away by itself, but of course, it didn't. When the police showed up to interview Joe, I pretended it was the first I'd heard about it. I was forced to watch in horror as Joe outperformed even me, effortlessly transforming into a sympathetic, understanding person who insisted it wasn't him who had sent those texts. His phone had been stolen at that time and he could prove it, he said. He also claimed that Rupert had named Joe, who had only ever been kind and pleasant to the rather reclusive youngster, out of fear of naming the real bully, who Joe then went on to name because he said he wanted to be as helpful as he could. The parents knew better, of course, as did I, but all of their threats to take us to court and sue us vanished once they were met with Mike's indignant, outraged counterclaims that he would hire the best lawyer in the country to sue them for slander instead.

41

Joe's demeanour quickly reverted to what I now know is "normal" for him once he realised that he was out of the woods, and I even overheard him laughingly refer to Rupert as a loser. I didn't know who he was talking to on his phone at the time, Gabriella, I suspect, but as soon as he'd said it, he knew what a mistake he'd made and turned to see whether me or his dad had overheard. That's when our eyes had met. He guessed then that I knew the real truth, but rather than making him scared, it seemed to make him braver. That glance between mother and son had guaranteed his protection. I was his mum and I would never betray him. I could tell that he viewed me as weak for this, whereas I saw him as dead inside. Nevertheless, I continued to love him with all of my heart since I didn't know how to stop doing that, but I grieved for him in equal amounts.

Threads of anxiety pull at my insides when I hear the front doors opening. Is it Joe or Mike returning? Dare I hope for both?

'It's me,' Mike calls out from the hallway, sounding defeated.

'Is Joe with you?' I demand scratchily.

'No. Sorry.' Mike appears in the doorway, his mouth drawn in a thin line. His eyes, dark as midnight, are a piercing reminder of my son's.

Anger surges inside me as I lock my burning gaze on his. 'I thought I told you not to come back without him.'

CHAPTER 11: ZOE

I wake up face down in a pillow, terrified because it feels as though I can't breathe, and I have no idea where I am. Swivelling my head to the side I gulp in air before opening my eyes. My heart twists when I find myself in darkness but I'm able to make out a familiar white bedside table next to me with a table lamp and a pink alarm clock on it displaying 2 a.m. This reassures me that I'm at home. In my own bed. My mind is racing — my heart pounding — as I switch on the lamp. My eyes feel like crusty slits. My mouth tastes of vomit. A wave of nausea washes over me when I see that my bra and knickers, as well as the light-blue wrap dress I wore to my birthday meal, have been discarded on the floor next to the bed. My heart rate increases when I even slightly move, so I remain as still as I can. My first thought is, *What's wrong with me? Am I about to have a heart attack?*

What the hell happened? Did I get so drunk that I blacked out? I can barely recall anything about last night other than Joe picking up my phone. After that, there's nothing except a distant memory of his voice in the background. No. Strike that. I do remember stumbling upstairs to bed after being sick. I must have been drunker than I imagined. But hold on, I also recall feeling a hand in the middle of my back as I tripped up the stairs. Someone had guided me into the bedroom. Joe!

Panicking, I flip on my side, conscious of how fast my heart is beating inside my chest, and I'm shocked to find a body lying next to me. When I reach out a trembling hand to pull away the bedspread from their face, I'm horrified to find Joe laying there, on his back. He has his hands casually folded behind his head and is grinning manically. Something tells me he's been patiently waiting for me to open my eyes.

'Hello, sleepy head,' he murmurs as if it was perfectly natural and normal for us to wake up in the same bed.

'Joe. What the hell?' I cover up my nakedness with the bedspread, exposing more of him than I've seen in a very long time. My mind is numb with fear. Does his being here mean what I think it means? It's not possible, and yet—

'What are you doing in here? Get out!' I yell, kicking at him under the duvet with my feet. 'Get out of my bed.'

Joe chuckles and sits up in bed without attempting to get out of it. 'That's not what you were saying a couple of hours ago.'

Acid curdles my stomach when I hear this. 'I mean it,' I snarl.

'Okay, okay.' Still smiling like a cocky little shit, he does at least get out of bed and begins pulling on pants, then jeans.

I avert my eyes, not wanting to see my godson naked. All the while my mind is racing with terrifying possibilities. Joe stayed over, but was it just because he didn't want to go home? He would have slept in the spare room though, which he thinks of as his, if that were the case. I can only think of one reason why I'd wake up to discover him in my bed and it's a revolting one. *Please God don't let this be true. Not with Joe. I couldn't have . . .*

'You don't need to look so scared, Zoe. I'm not under-age, you know. I am legal.'

'Tell me we didn't, please,' I beg, trying and failing to hold back tears.

'You don't remember any of it?' Joe laughs before placing his hand over his heart and feigning anguish. 'It hurts to hear you say that.'

'Stop it, Joe. It's not funny. Tell me the truth. Did we or didn't we have sex?'

He nods. 'Affirmative.'

'Oh, God. Seriously?'

'Don't beat yourself up over it. I won't tell anyone if you don't.'

'That's not the point. I am your . . .'

'Godmother? I know. The coolest, hottest kind.'

'That's enough, Joe,' I warn, watching him slip a T-shirt over his tight, adolescent muscles. Nothing about this feels right to me. No matter how much alcohol I consumed I would never have slept with Joe. I think of him as a son and always have done. It repulses me to imagine him touching me in a sexual way. And vice versa. I've had blackouts before but even at my drunkest, I've never "accidentally and without my knowledge" had sex with someone. Then I recall that Joe had been acting strangely all night, his mood kept shifting, and I had suspected him of taking drugs. On that thought my muscles stiffen involuntarily and my body runs cold.

Bile rises in my throat as I ask, 'Did you put something in my drink?'

He scans my face before answering matter-of-factly. 'You needed to chill out. Both of us did. You were stressed about hitting forty and Gabriella had just broken up with me. It's no big deal.' He shrugs, as if to prove this, before adding, 'It was just a drunken one-night stand'

'Shit, Joe. How could you? What was in my drink? Tell me right now.'

I want to leap out of bed and hit him. Shake him. Find the drugs and confiscate them. But I'm naked, so I do nothing.

'Calm down, Aunty Zoe.' He rolls his eyes, mocking me. 'It was only one roofie.'

'A roofie?'

Mirroring his father's arrogant tone, he states, 'Rohypnol is the technical term for it, I believe.'

I feel my jaw drop open. 'The date rape drug?'

45

His words are like a weight around my heart and I take my eyes off him for just a second because my head is spinning. I realise my mistake when he stealthily creeps over to the bed and sits down on the edge of it. When he sees me visibly flinch, he turns into nice Joe. Kind Joe. Boy Joe.

'You won't tell Mum about the drugs, will you?' he pleads.

'Joe. You realise what you've done, don't you?'

'What *we've* done,' he insists, but there is a spark of truth in his eyes that wasn't there before. This suggests to me that he *does* know and that this is all an act.

'Joe, you *raped* me.' The words are dragged out of the darkest, saddest part of my soul as my eyes bore into him.

He lurches to his feet. No longer nice Joe, his dark eyes flash with anger as he scoffs, 'I don't have to rape anyone. I can get whatever girl I want.'

'That's exactly what you did though. The drugs in my system will prove it.'

'Prove it? What do you mean by that?' His eyes suddenly swirl with panic. 'You don't plan on telling anyone, do you?'

'You had sex with me while I was drugged and unconscious, which means you've committed a crime.'

'You wouldn't . . . I mean, think about what it would do to Mum. She's your best friend.'

'You're not a child any longer which means you have to take responsibility for your actions.'

'I'll tell everyone we've been having sex for years and that you seduced me when I was still a little kid,' he rages, while tearing at his hair and stomping around the room. 'I'll say it was you who introduced me to drugs just like you did weed as a way of getting me to have sex with you. What will your precious Maddie think then, when she finds out you're nothing more than a pervy paedo?'

A flame of anger rears up inside me and my voice pulsates with rage as I scream, 'Get out of my house, you fucking sick freak. Get out.'

CHAPTER 12: MADELINE

It's 2.30 a.m. and we've moved into the living room and are sitting on the large U-shaped white leather sofa drinking tea. Green for me. Earl Grey for Mike. We both felt uneasy remaining in the kitchen where Joe learnt of his father's fling with his girlfriend in the worst way imaginable. I might add right after she had spectacularly dumped the poor boy. Mike has changed into lounge pants and a tight figure-hugging T-shirt while I'm still wearing my long black dress but my makeup has been washed away by my tears.

Mike has asked for a moment's calm to give us time to reflect and decide on a course of action. This is why we take silent sips of our tea, inhale deeply, and make regular eye contact. To face the challenges ahead, he says we must unite. Meanwhile, the black Fornasetti wall clock ticks away the minutes and I worry that its unrelenting hands are taking my son further away from me. The monochrome New York prints on the walls serve as a painful reminder of the last trip our family took when we were truly happy. At the time, Joe would have been around fifteen.

Deciding that I've had enough of this so-called "calm", I set my cup down on the curved glass coffee table in front of me, spin the rings on my left hand and ask, 'So, what did Gabriella say?'

Mike sighs. 'It's not good.'

'None of this is good!' I explode, as calmness exits the room, much like Joe had.

'She said she hadn't seen Joe and didn't particularly want to.'

I shake my head and mutter, 'Charming.'

'She was only interested in seeing me. In fact, she claims to be in love with me,' Mike goes on, taking a big shuddering breath.

I can't help but snort at this, because, despite his wide-eyed amazement, Mike exudes a smugness that he either cannot or doesn't want to hide. As usual, his ego is more important to him than anything else. Including me or his son.

'In love? With *you*?' I gasp incredulously, wanting to tear him down a peg or two. It works because Mike is immediately defensive. I can tell this by the way he braces himself as if he's about to be thumped in the chest. *It could happen.*

'There's no need to be insulting, Madeline,' he complains.

'There's every need,' I groan loudly and get to my feet so I can move around the room. I can't remain still any longer. Tremors of anxiety cause my hands to tremble. *Where are you, Joe?*

'She said she broke things off with Joe because she felt like she was cheating on me by continuing to see him.'

'Good God, she really is just a child,' I mutter, glaring at the gold band on my wedding finger and wanting to rip it off. Toss it in his face. How could he do this to us? Put us in a position where we are at risk of losing everything. Reputation. Respect. Wealth. His freedom if he were to go to prison for sleeping with an underage girl. But most importantly, our son.

When I next glance at Mike I see that his eyes have dropped away from mine as if he is mulling over what I have just said.

'Yes, I see that now,' he admits, nodding along while stroking his chin in a thoughtful gesture. 'I once thought her mature for her age but I see now that she was just trying to impress me and that it was all an act.'

My next words come out strained. 'God. What are we going to do, Mike?'

'She said she'd be heartbroken if I ended things with her and that she wouldn't want to live.' Mike clears his throat, obviously rattled, before adding, 'She reckons her parents would probably guess that something more than breaking up with Joe was upsetting her and that they were likely to wrangle the details of the affair out of her.'

'She's blackmailing you then!' I exclaim. Shocked, I stop pacing and come to a stop, my bare feet sinking into the ice-white velvet-pile carpet.

'It looks that way,' Mike acknowledges ruefully while burying his head in his hands.

'The little bitch,' I seethe, virtually baring my teeth.

'We must keep in mind that she is still a child.'

'A child you fucked,' I hiss as I revert to stomping up and down the room, murder in my eyes and heart. 'And a dangerous one.'

'Agreed,' Mike murmurs, maintaining his serious demeanour. 'And while I'm aware that we will eventually have to resolve this, I am unable to walk away from Gabriella just yet. I could get arrested or, as you quite rightly pointed out, possibly go to prison if her parents find out that I've been sleeping with their daughter.'

'It's a shame you didn't think of that before!' My eyes shoot accusingly in his direction, but when I see how defeated he looks, with a crumpled face and shattered eyes, my heart softens. He has always had this effect on me.

'I'm so sorry, Madeline. I don't know how many times I can keep saying it, but—'

'Save your apologies,' I interject sharply. 'Just promise me that if, and when, you do see her again, you'll keep it in your pants this time.'

'There's no need to be vulgar,' he mutters sheepishly.

'Interesting word choice,' I snap again, unable to resist one last dig at my cheating husband, before refocusing on the situation and my missing son.

'You will continue to see her *for now*. Keep her sweet *for now*. But first, we must concentrate on finding Joe. After . . .'

I hesitate, wondering what "after" is going to look like for our family. 'After Joe returns, we'll come up with a plan. Hopefully, Gabriella will get bored of you like she did Joe and move on to someone else and nobody will be any the wiser that you and she were ever an item.'

'Whatever you say, whatever needs doing, you can count on me. I swear.' Mike gives me a melting stare that is intended to restore my faith in him. I heave a sigh because I have no choice. But when I see him pull out his phone, panic clutches at my heart.

'Who are you calling?' I whisper.

'The police. To report our son as missing.' Mike's words are stilted and sharp.

'Do you think they'll take us seriously? He's only been gone a couple of hours.'

'They'll have to. He's only sixteen,' Mike states simply.

It's on the tip of my tongue to bark out "a year older than the girl you slept with" but I decide that we have both been punished enough for one night and instead say, 'Promise me one thing.'

'Anything.'

'When speaking to them, please avoid using your "you don't know who I am" voice. We need them on our side from the very beginning. To help us find Joe. And if Gabriella's parents *do* find out about you and her and they report it to the police, we'll need them to believe that we're squeaky clean and that you, a respected doctor, would never do something like that.'

Mike is aghast. 'You mean you'd want me to lie? To perjure myself?'

'Mike, don't be an idiot. This is more important than your pride. After what has happened, you're not in a position to adopt a moral viewpoint.' I cross my arms defensively and jut out my jaw. 'And yes, I bloody well would expect you to lie about sleeping with an underage girl if it meant saving our family. It wouldn't be the first time. And I dare say it won't be the last either.'

CHAPTER 13: ZOE

After yelling at Joe to get out of the house he angrily bolted down the stairs, cursing as he collided with walls. Right before he left the room, I noticed a glimmer of recognition and hurt in his eyes, which made me think that he was coming down from whatever drugs he had taken and might be feeling remorseful. Part of me wanted to reach out to him then and reassure him that everything would be okay, that we could get through this. I still loved him and would find him some support, but he stormed out of the house at that precise moment, ignoring all my calls to "get back here", and raced straight out into the street instead, leaving the front door wide open.

I was so desperate to go to the loo that I climbed out of the bed where Joe had had sex with me while I was unconscious and went to the toilet. I moved slowly and occasionally stumbled since the pill Joe had slipped into my drink was probably to blame for my cloudy brain and racing heart. When I felt sperm dripping down my inner thigh like a death knell, any lingering doubts about what had actually transpired were put to rest. Then I threw up into the toilet bowl. Feeling dead inside, I shut the door against the stink of last night's swordfish and wine and made my way along the landing to the spare room. Joe's room.

It has a single bed in it with a stars and stripes duvet, some discarded toys and games, an ancient PlayStation, and a small wall-mounted TV. On the chunky pine chest of drawers, there are framed pictures of Joe, Maddie, Mike and me. Put there to make Joe feel at home. One had captured us all screaming on a rollercoaster ride at Alton Towers. Then there was one of Joe as a newborn, with startled eyes, perilously balanced in my arms. Joe wearing his first school uniform with pride. His mum and dad on their wedding day, posing as if they were famous. Me as a bridesmaid, *and never the bride*, looking small and inconsequential next to them.

I grabbed the duvet from the bed and wrapped it around my nakedness as my head continued to spin and throb, and tears streamed down my face. I then went downstairs to lock the front door. I considered going after Joe. Although I was not his biological mother, I was unable to switch off my feelings for him. But, feeling light-headed, I eventually collapsed on the couch while high and hungover, dozed off and eventually woke up a couple of hours later.

It's now 5 a.m. and I am on my third mug of sweet milky tea, *for the shock*. I still can't decide what to do. Should I contact the police? Or call Maddie? To let her know what has happened. But would she even believe me? I know how incredibly loyal and protective she is over her family. But then again, isn't she constantly telling me that I'm part of her family too? I'd like to bet though that she would take Joe's side over mine because after all, blood is thicker than water. I'm horrified every time I try to imagine what took place in my bedroom, while I was out of it. What had he done to me? My body? Had he crawled all over it with his hands and mouth while I was defenceless? I had been raped by a sixteen-year-old boy in my own home, where I was supposed to be safe. By my godson no less.

I stare at the green sofa where Joe was sitting last night — guarding my phone with one hand while gazing moodily at me. He must have slipped the drugs into my drink when he was alone in the kitchen. I pick up my empty glass off the coffee table and sniff it. But it just smells of wine. Acid churns in my stomach at the thought of drinking again. My boss Angela, who has been sober for six years, claims that alcohol is nothing but poison. I'm beginning to think she's right. I wouldn't be where I am now if it weren't for the awful stuff.

Every time I close my eyes, memories of waking up to see Joe in bed next to me . . . grinning spitefully, come back to me. I recall his threats, which though likely uttered in the heat of the moment, need to be taken seriously: "I'll tell everyone we've been having sex for years and that you seduced me when I was still a little kid" followed by an even crueller attack he knew would hurt me the most: "What will your precious Maddie think of you when she finds out you're nothing more than a pervy paedo?"

Who would the police believe in this instance? Joe or me? A bright, exceptionally good-looking (as he'd pointed out, he could have any girl he wanted), privately educated sixteen-year-old and the son of my oldest and dearest friend or a dumped, average-looking, depressed forty-year-old alcoholic who lived alone. The shame of people finding out I'd been drugged and sexually assaulted by a schoolboy is enough to put me off reporting it. The thought of my younger female colleagues in the salon looking at me pitifully with their Lancôme made-up eyes makes me want to cringe.

I jerk forward and grab my phone when I catch a glimpse of it hidden under one of the gold cushions on the sofa across from me. But who should I call? Maddie is my go-to for everything but I can't tell her about this, can I? For all I know, Joe has beaten me to it already and is at home right now telling his parents that I have been sexually abusing him for years. Might I expect a furious call from my best friend at any moment, or that the police will knock on my door and arrest me? Will she send Mike around to have words with me? I don't know why, but I'm more terrified by the prospect of him pounding on my door than I would be if the police turned up.

I remind myself that I don't deserve any of this. All I've ever done is love and cherish Joe as if he were my own. What could have happened to make him target me? Drug me? Rape me? He has hurt his parents as well as me by doing this and the damage is irreparable. Was that deliberate, I wonder? Did Joe purposefully set out to harm his parents? An act of revenge, perhaps? If so, he's got exactly what he wanted because it means even if I choose not to report the incident to the police and Joe remains silent, I can no longer have any contact with the Blacks, who are the only family I've known since my mother passed away when I was eighteen.

Maddie has always been there for me and I can't imagine life without her. Except I will have to. Because, if I'm being completely honest with myself, and despite my earlier desire to help Joe, I will never be able to bring myself to be around him again, no matter how much I may have loved Joe when he was a boy. Fear creeps into my heart when I remember the dark, menacing way he spoke to me last night before I blacked out.

Needing to hear a familiar voice, and not caring if it's an angry or defensive one, I bring up Chris's number on my phone, and press dial. But it goes straight through to voicemail. I don't hang up even though I have no intention of leaving a message — in case he plays it back to his girlfriend — I mean what would I say anyway? 'Come home please. I've been raped by my godson. Yes, Joe. And yes, I was drunk, so of course, once again it must all be my fault.' Instead, I wait to hear his much-loved Scottish accent . . .

'You've reached the voicemail of Chris Walker. Sorry I'm not around to take your call. Unless you're my ex, feel free to leave a message and I'll call you right back.'

CHAPTER 14: MADELINE

The police are like ants, swarming over all three floors of the house colonising it. They pose their questions quietly and calmly, but the sheer number of them causes my head to bounce on my shoulders. It's tomorrow already. 7 a.m. to be precise. The day I didn't want to have to face without Joe. Daylight had surprised me, bringing with it the shock that my son had stayed out all night. I imagine him alone and terrified but in reality, he's just as likely to be angry, driven with rage, and a desire to punish. Like his father, Joe will seek revenge. I'm certain of it. It's in his blood.

I worry for Gabriella because I know Joe can be violent towards women — my bruised face from last year is proof of that — but I'm not as concerned about her as I should be because of the way she treated my son. The phrase "little bitch" is never far from my mind when I think of her clinging on to my husband and blackmailing him. Even though I know in my heart she isn't to blame, I now see her through entirely different eyes.

This is all Mike's fault; I think for the hundredth time even though I am aware that churning the same negative thoughts over and over in my head is not helpful. I observe my husband smiling and nodding in agreement to whatever the investigating detective is saying. Even though I was the one who pleaded with him to behave himself, it still disgusts me that he can act as if our world hadn't collapsed around us. He's in full host mode but keeps throwing questioning looks my way, as if to say, "Look at me, aren't I doing well?" I swear his ego will be the death of him. Mike has showered, and, somewhat irrationally, I hate him for this. In a tight-fitting black shirt and pair of pressed trousers, he appears as shiny, attractive and trim as ever.

I, however, look like a vampire who hasn't consumed human blood in a while. I hardly recognised myself when I accidentally caught a glimpse of my reflection in the wall mirror. My long black hair, dulled with stress, hung lifelessly about my shoulders and my orange eyes had no fire in them. Fear crouched over me like a towering bully cutting in front of me in a queue. The house is full of people but I only wish for Zoe to be at my side, holding onto my hand and not letting go for even a second. But she still isn't answering my calls. Should I be concerned about her too?

I keep my phone with me at all times. It's either in my hand, on my lap or the coffee table in front of me. Every time it pings, I jolt in alarm and my terrified gaze finds Mike, whose eyes are always waiting for me. One minute I'm hoping it's an irate Joe demanding that I pick him up from wherever he crashed last night, or Zoe wanting to know what's wrong and offering to come over right away. But the only thing to light up my screen is spam: a two-for-one offer from Domino's Pizza. Like I could eat anything!

Suddenly, Mike is at my side whispering into my hair, 'We should tell them what happened.'

'Are you mad?' I hiss, as venomously as I can while keeping my voice low so the detective and the uniformed police officers won't overhear.

'I don't mean about Gabriella.' He sounds startled. 'But we could tell them that we argued. They would understand and think it was quite normal behaviour for a teenage boy to run away in those circumstances.'

56

'There's nothing normal about Joe,' I cut in, causing a crack in his confident demeanour. 'Besides,' I huff, 'telling them about the argument won't help them find our son.'

'But what if he is so furious with us that he never returns home,' Mike persists.

I raise an indignant eyebrow at that and he immediately changes tack. 'Furious with *me* then,' he concedes.

'Exactly and the police won't look for him if they know that. They'll say he's just another troubled adolescent out to teach his parents a lesson.'

I see real concern in Mike's eyes then and this frightens me more than anything. If he is worried then we really do have a serious situation on our hands. 'Have they spoken to Gabriella; do you know?'

Mike shakes his head, avoiding my gaze. 'No. She's not answering their calls so they're sending a police officer over there now to talk to her.'

I watch Mike gulp nervously, before continuing, 'Not that it will do them any good.'

'Oh my God,' I gasp. 'You've heard from her, haven't you? She's texted you.'

Mike shoots me a warning glance that reminds me to keep my voice down. I don't need telling twice. 'What did she say?' I whisper.

'That she's worried about Joe.'

I roll my eyes. 'That'll be a first.'

'She's promised she won't mention anything about me and her . . .' Mike gazes down at his shiny shoes, unable to look at me.

Irritation surges inside my chest. 'Fucking.' I finish his sentence for him.

'She's popular at school—'

My hands scrunch into fists as I glower at my husband. 'I bet she is.'

'What I was going to say is that she's promised to rally the troops and ring round all their friends,' he snipes.

'Help us you mean?' I can hear the disbelief in my own voice.

'Exactly. And if anyone can. Gabriella can.'

'That's something, I suppose.' When I imagine a distraught Joe pounding the streets, tears sting my eyes and my vision blurs. To be betrayed by your girlfriend is one thing but to be betrayed by your father is something else. And what of his mother? Haven't I let him down most of all, for not exposing him sooner? For not getting him the help that he so desperately needed. For protecting him from himself.

Mike places a reassuring hand on my shoulder but when he notices the investigator staring curiously at us, he turns and slinks away silently. I use this opportunity to take another quick look at my phone. Still no texts or missed calls from Joe or Zoe. Then, I recall Gabriella's promise to ring round their friends and every hair on my body stands on end as I realise that Joe, unlike his ex-girlfriend, is not well liked and doesn't have any friends of his own. The closest thing to a friend he's got is Zoe.

CHAPTER 15: ZOE

There are fifteen missed calls from Maddie on my phone and countless texts that repeatedly ask, *Are you okay?* and *Ring me please*. As I read them a second and a third time, I can hear the anxiety in my friend's voice. As there is no menace to her tone, I think it's safe to assume that Joe hasn't carried out his threat to expose me as a paedophile and that our secret — *his secret* — is safe for the time being. But something is obviously up, otherwise, she wouldn't have tried ringing me so many times. It's still only 7 a.m. If this isn't about Joe then what else could be wrong?

As it dawns on me once more that our friendship must come to an end, a shudder tears through me and I pull the duvet around me for comfort. The window blinds are closed, but shards of stark white light peep through them, casting a warm glow on my cheek — a sign that summer has finally arrived. Even though I've been looking forward to warmer days for weeks, now that they're finally here, I wish everything would return to being depressingly grey and cold. I no longer desire to bare my arms and legs, wear flimsy wrap dresses, and sip chilled Pinot Grigio. Instead, I want to hibernate in my small house with a blanket over my head, not showering, brushing my teeth, or answering the door, let alone my phone — which I push back under the gold cushion so it's out of sight.

As I gaze unseeing at the walls of the living room which are crammed to the brim with flamboyant nick-nacks and mementoes, I'm haunted by horrific images of Joe. Flashbacks to when his face was scrunched up in a vicious sneer while he threatened me. And before that, of him guarding my phone and smirking as he patiently watched me finish my drugged drink. The smell of his skin on my bed sheets. His breath on my face. A stray black hair on the pillow beside me. The damp patch in the middle of the bed. Semen dripping down my thigh.

Up until last night, we'd always been such good friends. We had fun together all the time. He even claimed I was the only person to see him for who he really was, not what his parents wanted him to be and continuously pointed out how different I was from his mother, but in a good way. Why would he deliberately hurt someone he professed to love and respect? The fact that he'd planned to assault me, makes it a thousand times worse.

But if the Joe I met last night is the *real* Joe, that is a truly terrifying prospect. Because how could he have kept that brutal part of himself hidden for so long? In the past, I had put him right about so many things, telling him to respect his parents and to quit acting like a spoiled brat. Even though he wouldn't have taken this from his mother, he accepted it from me. I always had the impression that because I loved him for himself, flaws, and all, this somehow meant more to him than his mother's all-consuming and overly protective love. Joe once told me he didn't feel he had to be perfect all the time while he was with me. But he had fooled us all.

I can't begin to imagine what this will do to Maddie if she finds out. It would cripple her to know that her son is a rapist. But what of me? Without my best friend, how will I survive such a traumatic event? Alone!

I stiffen in fear and slide farther down the sofa when a shadow pauses outside my window as if someone were attempting to peer inside. My first thought is that Joe has returned, either to apologise or torment me further. It might be my silence he's after this time. But when the man's silhouette moves away from the window and is replaced by a loud knock at the door, my stomach cartwheels. I stare at the door in fear, a scream gathering inside me as I half expect to see the door handle rise and fall. My phone then starts to ring. It's loud and insistent. The individual at the door cannot fail to hear it, so I fumble for the phone and manage to abruptly end Maddie's call. But by now, the man at the door knows I'm at home even if I'm pretending not to be. I hold my breath and start to count down from one hundred, desperate for them to go away and leave me alone.

When the letter box opens and I glimpse a pair of inquisitive eyes staring back at me, I let out a piercing scream. The metal flap then snaps shut and I see the man speeding past the window. Realising I must have frightened him off, I leap off the sofa with the phone glued to my hand and, taking two steps at a time, bolt upstairs to my bedroom. I reach the window in time to observe the man getting into the passenger seat of a saloon car parked on the street. He is flanked by another man. I don't recognise either of them but the dark suits scream plain clothes policemen to me. This suggests that I was mistaken earlier and that Joe must have followed through on his threat to report me for grooming him for sex while he was still underage. I sit on the edge of the bed for a moment because my heart is thumping so loudly it feels as if it's about to explode. When it eventually subsides, I check my voicemails and listen to Maddie's last message.

'Zoe. I don't know what is going on with you or why you're not returning my calls or responding to my messages but this is really urgent, so please call me back as soon as you get this voicemail.'

I bite down on my lip as I detect real fear in Maddie's voice. She sounds insane with worry. But doesn't seem angry with me, which is a good sign. So far so good . . .

'It's Joe,' she sobs down the phone and that's when I pick up the murmuring of official-sounding voices in the

61

background. Mike's voice is louder than anyone else's and I can picture him dutifully playing host. 'He didn't come home last night,' Maddie stammers. 'The police are here now. Mike's talking to them as we speak. They've sent someone over to your house to see if you've heard from Joe since you haven't returned our calls.'

The phone drops from my hand and white stars flash across my forehead.

Joe did not go home last night.

Joe is missing.

A sickening sense of guilt consumes me and my stomach jerks into action as I fight back the renewed urge to vomit. Somehow, I manage to punch out a reasonable-sounding response to Maddie: *So sorry to hear this but I'm sure he'll be home soon. Wish I could be there for you but I have a virus and can't stop being sick.*

As soon as the text has been sent, I stumble into the bathroom and throw up in the toilet. I wasn't lying when I said I had a virus. A sickness invaded my home last night when Joe did.

CHAPTER 16: MADELINE

It has been the longest day of my life and I find it strange how time is now measured by how long Joe has been gone . . . how many cups of tea have been made and handed out to the police with trembling fingers . . . how many times we've answered the same questions without ever getting anywhere. I can tell that Mike is just as rattled as I am and is in danger of losing his doctorly cool. Nothing is happening as fast as we'd like it to. Why are the police still here, sitting cross-legged on our cream corner sofa when they should be out on the streets searching for our boy?

Joe will have been missing for a full twenty-four hours in another thirty-two minutes. I don't need the police to warn me that things will only get worse for us the longer he remains gone. Most kids come home in a matter of hours, not days, especially in the case of runaways, who are typically apprehended by the police shortly after being rounded up among their friends. However, nobody — not even Gabriella — has been able to guess Joe's possible whereabouts. She reportedly told the cops that he had been hanging out with undesirables recently. People we don't know. Older boys in their twenties. Drug users whose names — Nate, Red and Baz — are unfamiliar to us. They never made it onto the guest list for Mike's popular "family and friends" garden parties but I'd gladly welcome them into our home now if it meant the safe return of my son.

I finally gave in and took a shower at the urging of a family liaison officer named Sharon, who has been assigned to us as if she were a volunteer pet sitter. I detested the thought that my freshly washed skin had never come into contact with my son. He had spent months, if not years, of his life in my arms, and I ferociously wanted him back there this very second. Despite being assured by everyone around me that Joe is alive and will return home soon, I am unable to suppress the horrifying thought that he is getting farther and farther away from me.

Sharon seems preoccupied with getting me to eat — as if that's going to happen when I don't know what's happened to my son — and urging Mike to stop pacing up and down for a minute or two to "relax". She means well but it's all I can do not to scream in her oily post-box red face. The one person who could bring us some comfort is noticeably absent. When I told Mike that Zoe must have contracted food poisoning after eating the swordfish at the restaurant and had been sick all night, preventing her from coming over, he barely listened. When I explained to the cops that this must be the reason why she hadn't answered the door when they called around to see her, Mike looked at me in bewilderment, as if to ask, "Why are we talking about Zoe?" Clearly, she doesn't know anything either, but our son can't have simply vanished. Stamford is a small town. It didn't hit me till an hour or so ago, when I finally agreed to nibble at a piece of plain toast *to keep my energy levels up*, that we'd all eaten the swordfish, so it must have been something else that caused Zoe to be so ill.

Someone enters the lounge and the ambience of the room changes. I feel the shift as if it were a hand wrapping itself around my throat, cutting off my airways. Everyone rises to their feet. I choose to ignore the marks left by so many pairs of shoes on the carpet, but when Mike's eyes catch mine from across the room and I recognise the dread in them, I am forced to get up and follow everyone else's gaze. Their eyes drag me in the direction of Gabriella.

It's surprising how similar to Joe she is. Same dark hair and eyes. They could easily be brother and sister so it felt almost unnatural, from my perspective, that they were ever a couple to begin with. Like me, she has long dark hair but that's where any similarities between us end. She is excessively thin without any discernible hips or bust. Her black, gothic, pencilled-in eyes are her most distinguishable feature. They sweep the room in a wide-eyed, innocent circle and I realise at that moment that I have never truly liked her. I've always regarded her as manipulative and fake, even before she had an affair with my husband and cruelly dumped my son. She has a panther-like quality, and I get the impression that when she grows up, she will be the kind of woman that men will constantly want to protect, but I also sense that she is dangerous. She will stop at nothing to get what she wants. She's only here now, pretending to help us, because it suits her. A self-labelled empath, she loves nothing more than being the centre of attention even when the focus should be on Joe. And *only* Joe.

But since I'm just as skilled at deception as she is, I welcome her into my arms and don't take "no" for an answer even though I can feel her awkwardly writhing to be free. As I do, I realise with a sickening thump in my chest that she smells of my husband. An earthy wooden fragrance.

'Gabriella. Thank you for coming. It means so much to me and Mike. And I know Joe would say the same if he were here.'

'I had to . . . I mean, I couldn't think about anything else once I heard. Is there any news?' she asks tearfully.

'Not as yet,' Mike says tightly, coming to kiss her lightly on both cheeks in a deliberately fatherly way, which is entirely for my benefit.

'I thought as much which is why we're holding a vigil for him.'

'A vigil?' I suck in my breath. I don't say what immediately springs to mind, like, *aren't vigils for dead people?*

'Everyone will be there. All our school friends and Joe's teachers too,' Gabriella gushes enthusiastically. She even breaks into a smile as she continues, 'There will be hundreds of candles lit in Joe's honour on the school playing field and it will be held tomorrow at midnight, to mark his being missing for forty-eight hours.'

I can't imagine going another twenty-four hours without my son. And I'm about to tell her that I don't believe the vigil is a good idea at all because it might imply that Joe is dead and is never going to return home, when Mike pulls her into a grateful hug.

'What a wonderful tribute to our son. You can count on us being there. Can't she, Madeline?'

As he beams eagerly at me, I also notice the lead investigator — I believe his name is DCI Saunders — staring at me with interest, as though he were evaluating me. He'll be thinking that holding a vigil is a brilliant idea because it will raise awareness of Joe's disappearance and undoubtedly lead to an influx of sightings. So, I grit my teeth and play along by nodding icily. 'Of course.'

CHAPTER 17: ZOE

DCI Saunders sits across from me on the sofa that Joe had occupied just over twenty-four hours ago with a guarded expression. He has nothing new to share with me since Maddie has been updating me via text all day and night. Since Joe left his parents' home in the early hours of Saturday morning, nobody except me has seen or heard from him. The detective has a lean physique and tired, wintry-blue eyes. He has dark hair that is flecked with white, along with a fashion-able, well-groomed grey beard. He appears to be in his early fifties, and I would say that he's had a hard life. Divorced and with kids, most likely that he hardly sees anymore due to the long hours he works, I imagine that a much younger and more demanding girlfriend is on the scene. A rebound, I'll bet, that he's realised too late isn't going to work out but doesn't have the energy to do anything about it. He'll wait for her to finish with him rather than hurt her feelings.

'Are you sure I can't get you a cup of coffee?' I ask for what must be the third time, even though it's far too late — or early, depending on how you look at it at this ungodly hour — to be drinking caffeine. In my panic, though, at finding myself being questioned over Joe's disappearance, I cling to formality. At this rate, I'll be starting a conversation about the weather next. As if he anticipates this happening, he leans forward in his seat and examines me with what I can only describe as Jesus-like eyes. They're so crinkly and, well . . . divine, I can't help but wonder if Maddie felt the same when she met him for the first time. Or would she have looked through him as she does most men?

'So would you say the meal out was a pleasant one?'

'Yes,' I stutter. 'It was my birthday. A special one.' He doesn't ask me how old I am and I feel a pang of regret that he finds me so uninteresting. I imagine Maddie had a bigger impact on him. Of course, I instantly feel conflicted about developing a crush on a stranger when I was drugged and raped less than twenty-four hours ago. 'And we were all looking forward to it. It's not often the four of us get together these days.'

'Why is that?' he asks, eyes suddenly sparking with interest.

I murmur, 'Busy lives, I guess.'

'And how did Joe appear that night?'

I look at my shaking hands in my lap before answering. 'Oh just Joe, you know.' I'm aware of how flippant I sound.

'No. Tell me.'

'Things were a little tense, that's all.' I shrug, feeling as naked as I did earlier when he knocked on the door and I answered it wearing nothing but the duvet from the spare room. Joe's room. After Maddie's calls and texts, I knew there was no point in ignoring the police any longer. It would only arouse their suspicion. Am I a suspect in his disappearance, I wonder? Is that what this visit is about? Do they know something? But how could they? I mean only Joe and I know what happened. And he's missing.

'Am I right in thinking Joe had broken up with his girl-friend?' Saunders asks.

'Actually, it was the other way around. She dumped him just before the meal out.' I pull at a loose thread of wool on my oversized jumper. I'd slipped it and the jeans I'm wearing on in a hurry while he waited for me to get changed. Too late

I realise it's one of Chris's sweaters and it still smells of him even though he's been gone over a year. Fag papers, tobacco and anti-dandruff shampoo. This makes me want to howl.

'He said he didn't want to talk about it.' I tightly close my eyes as my mind takes me back to yesterday and the horrified look on Joe's face when I asked him if he wanted to talk about Gabriella.

'When did he say this?'

'During the meal,' I lie, reminding myself to get my story straight. I haven't forgotten the fierce way Mike looked at his son in the restaurant when Joe admitted that their relationship had ended. I had not imagined it. But I won't let on. No matter what Joe's done, I'm on my best friend's side.

No one can know that Joe was here. At my house. Not even Maddie. Or that I might have been the last person to see him before he disappeared. What if Joe never returns home? It's a possibility. Knife crime is on the increase among young men and Joe had boasted of hanging out with a group of older boys that were known drug dealers. Could he have been stabbed and left for dead? He could easily have antagonised someone in the dark mood he was in. He had been looking for trouble. Had he stumbled across it?

I can't tell a single person what occurred until we find out what happened to Joe, where he's been, and who he's been with. Selfishly, it's already occurred to me that if Joe doesn't make it home, tonight or any other night, I'll get to keep Maddie in my life. It's not that I wish Joe any harm. Not in the sense that I want him dead, even though I'll never forgive him for what he did to me; but I can't add to Maddie's troubles given the current situation by reporting what her son had done to me. In addition, with Joe missing, it would be my word against his, and who would believe me? Not Maddie and Mike. Probably not the detective either.

'What do you think has happened to Joe?' I avoid making eye contact with him in case he sees right through me.

'Boys will be boys. I'm sure he'll be back when he's good and ready and not before.'

I smile warily at him then because, at times like this, inane reassurances are unexpectedly comforting. But I can't stop myself from catastrophising. 'What if he doesn't?'

DCI Saunders ignores my question and gets to his feet, absentmindedly scanning the room, as if searching for clues. I tense up then, shifting in my seat and biting my lip. Had Joe left any evidence behind? Drugs perhaps? The glasses from the previous night have still not been washed up. They will be covered in Joe's DNA. *Oh God, listen to me, like I know what I'm talking about when it comes to crime scenes and investigations.* I even question whether the policeman can smell nonconsensual sex on me. Is that possible?

'What was Mike and Joe's relationship like?' DCI Saunders asks quietly.

'They are a close family.' I stick to what I know Maddie would want me to say. If I were to reveal that Joe and his father frequently quarrelled, as they had the night Joe disappeared, it would do the Blacks absolutely no good. Mike was strict and had high expectations, but unlike Maddie, he didn't appear to notice that his son was having problems. In many ways, Joe took after his father. They were both prone to angry outbursts.

I remember there was a time last year when Maddie's face was covered in bruises and I began to suspect that Mike might be hitting her, but when I insisted on knowing the truth she'd laughed the accusation off, claiming she could take care of herself and no man was going to lay a hand on her. I hadn't believed her at the time, but it occurs to me now, since I've witnessed Joe's brutality first-hand, that she was telling the truth. Because it was a boy, not a man, she was protecting . . . Joe. I come to the realisation that I don't know the Blacks as well as I previously believed.

CHAPTER 18: MADELINE

The sprawling Gothic building is lit up behind us, and orange light streams through its arched windows to cast flickering shadows across the Wimbledon-worthy striped lawns. These beams of light remind me of the searchlights used in prisons to hunt down escaped convicts. However, my own troubled runaway is nowhere to be seen among the faces present. The school has 400 sixth-form students aged between sixteen and eighteen at the St Martin's campus, and it appears that the majority of them have shown up for the midnight vigil. I don't fool myself that they are here to honour Joe, as Mike does. We have Gabriella to thank for the high turnout.

When we first enrolled Joe at the private co-ed school, we were told that ninety per cent of its students could expect to go on to study for degrees at some of the best universities in the UK, like Cambridge and Oxford, but I think I knew even then when my son was just a junior, that he would not be one of them. Since joining the sixth form last term, he had been studying A-level biology and maths, at Mike's urging, but he was struggling. It's not that Joe isn't bright — he's actually quite brilliant — his issue is that he gets bored easily. That's when he becomes a "disruptive" influence in class, according to his head teacher. Of course, Mike is set on him becoming a doctor, like father like son, but Joe hates the idea.

We have had many animated conversations about Joe's future, some with and some without our son present, but Joe would only ever jokingly admit to wanting to be a racing driver. Mike would then respond with a long list of reasons why he wasn't willing to spend £30,000 a year on Joe's education for him to become a playboy. The school's motto is "It's not about who you are, it's what you can become", yet I worry that what my son had become, or was becoming, would not have led to a Nobel Prize for him like some of the school's notable alumni. Many had gone on to achieve greatness as actors, journalists, award-winning playwrights, Olympian athletes and members of parliament. It got to the point where if my son avoided prison, or an early death, I would consider myself fortunate.

Everyone, including Mike and I, is dressed in black, and it doesn't escape me that it feels as if we are already mourning our son. Even though I expected to feel that way, it still surprised me to see so many fake-sad faces among the crowd that break into smiles whenever they think they're not being observed. Although I am aware of how despised Joe was — and for good reason — I still feel a nagging animosity towards his classmates. I know I shouldn't blame them. After all, they're still only children. But it's the parents that get me. I can't bring myself to glance their way without wishing it was their child who had gone missing instead of mine. I reassure myself that I'm not a bad person and that it's okay for me to have such dark thoughts because, undoubtedly, they are in turn thanking God it's my child and not theirs that we are praying for the safe return of.

I observe Gabriella sporting much more black eyeliner than usual while sheathed in a barely-there, low-cut black dress. As Mike guides me across the grass, he places a hand on my elbow as if I were a fragile old lady. And tonight, I suppose that's what I am. I am aware of how bony my face looks. The thick long plait I've braided down my back and tightly pulled back from my face doesn't help. I am, of course, wearing no makeup. I mean, when one's son has been missing for two days, who can think about lipstick and blusher? Except Mike, who gently reminded me that we must keep up appearances. It was expected of us, he'd informed me. In response, I merely shrugged. Exhausted from the lack of sleep, I didn't even have the energy to roll my eyes. I experienced a new wave of bereavement when I realised Zoe wouldn't be joining us because she was still unwell. She is missing from our family tonight, just as Joe is. Mike and I are strangers without their presence and it appears as though we no longer know what to say to each other or even how to act.

Mike and I stop at the edge of a group of teenagers who are all busily admiring Gabriella. They nod obediently as she skilfully manages their expectations for tonight's vigil. I can see why she's already in charge of the school's debating team, even though she's only fifteen. *Only fifteen* — there's that ugly word again. *Nearly sixteen*, I remind myself for no other reason than it makes me feel better about my husband having had sex with an underage schoolgirl. She's undoubtedly clever and I suppose one has to admire her for that, but she is also cold and brutal. Look at how ruthlessly she dumped my son and is now blatantly blackmailing my husband. As soon as Mike nervously announces our presence by coughing into his palm, Gabriella forgets about everyone else and dazzles us with her dark, unreadable eyes and undivided attention.

'Mr and Mrs Black.' She exudes enthusiasm while yet managing to convey sympathy. 'I'm thrilled that you're here. The vigil is trending on social media, and as you can see, we're packed out.' Gabriella draws a big encompassing circle with one blue-veined white, taut arm, before boasting, 'We couldn't have hoped for a better response which means we are going to do Joe proud tonight. Just you wait and see.'

Mike and I both nod along, as the fascinated teenagers had done, but we're saved from having to praise her efforts as the head teacher is about to join us. I smile inwardly when I see Gabriella's irritated frown, but it is gone in a second. It doesn't hang around long enough to catch Mike's attention because let's not forget it's him she's trying to impress. Not me.

'Mike. Madeline.' The head teacher's wobbly chin is almost resting on his chest when he says this. He is dressed in his customary three-piece pure wool suit with a vivid paisley waistcoat underneath. He belongs to the small group of men who still wear cufflinks, like my husband.

'Good evening, sir.' Mike nods back energetically and his shoes come together in a squeaky salute, reminding me that as an Old Stamfordian himself, Mike has a lifelong relationship with the school and still plays a part in supporting its community. I wonder if he gave that a thought when he ended up in bed with one of its senior year students.

'I wouldn't call it good, Mike.' The head admonishes gently before turning to me. He knows I'm not such an easy win as my husband.

He lets out a long-suffering sigh. 'The school isn't the same without Joe.'

His attempt to empathise is way off the mark, so I respond with justified vitriol, 'Yet you were on the verge of expelling him for good.'

'Now, now, Maddie,' Mike tuts. 'It would never have come to that. You know that.' He seals his disapproval with a grimace, signalling to me that the topic is off limits at least for this evening. I have to bite my lip to keep from saying anything more even though I know he is right.

Gabriella slinks off to rejoin her friends while Mike and the head teacher continue to converse in hushed not-for-the-women voices, but not before staring at me as if I'm intruding. I then observe DCI Saunders mingling with the crowd. He warned us earlier that there would be a police presence at the vigil tonight to distribute flyers and speak with those they hadn't already interviewed as part of their investigation. He catches my glance and throws me a flimsy smile before approaching. So far, Mike has done most of the talking where this man is concerned while I have slouched on the sofa and gazed hopelessly at my phone. However, tonight it seems that he is set on speaking to me personally, which immediately makes me uneasy.

The crowd around him fades away as I watch him come closer and closer, never taking his piercing blue eyes from mine. The same can be said of the whispered conversations that, up until a few moments ago, had filled my ears with talk of "Joe this", "Joe that" and the dreadful pauses that came after statements like, "It's already been forty-eight hours", which imply that it's too long a time for a teenager to still be missing and that my son won't ever return. I get the sense that Saunders knows something as he comes to stand in front of me and fixes his worn-out gaze on mine. A flash of panic cuts through me and it's all I can do not to faint.

CHAPTER 19: ZOE

While Maddie and Mike are praying for Joe's safe return, I've been eradicating every last trace of him. *Good riddance.* I've stripped the sheets from the bed and put them in a ninety degree wash cycle even though a small voice whispered in my head that they wouldn't ever be used again. When I finally got around to washing and putting away the wine glasses though, a bubble of panic rose inside my chest, but I managed to beat it back down.

After that, I took a lengthy shower in which I subjected my body to waves of ice-cold and then excruciatingly hot water. I am fully aware that by doing these things, I have eliminated all evidence that I was ever attacked, but I feel so much better now that I've made the decision not to report Joe's crime to the police. I had my chance when Saunders was here last night, but I just couldn't go through with it. I have too much to lose. As soon as I knew what I was going to do, the overwhelming anxiety I had been experiencing shifted to something else . . . determination. I wasn't going to allow Joe's actions to ruin my life. I was stronger than that.

So, I'm sitting here in my PJs and glaring at the sofa that will forever remind me of Joe. It, along with the bedsheets, is going to have to go, I decide, because I can't erase the image of him slouching there smirking at me. The look on his face had been predatory. *Did he know what he was going to do even before he set foot through the door?*

It's gone midnight, which means the vigil will now be underway. I refrain from glancing at my phone after stumbling across posts discussing it on social media. I don't want to witness images of Maddie, stick-thin and dressed all in black, sobbing over her son. It would kill me to know that I am partly to blame for her pale face and shattered eyes. I don't believe myself to be in any way responsible for the attack when I talk about blame — that's entirely Joe's fault — but I am withholding crucial information that might aid in locating her son. Only I knew what state of mind he was in when he took off. Apparently, I was the last person to see him. Maddie would never forgive me if she knew this. That ought to be the least of my concerns considering what her son had done to me. But it wasn't. We have a long history. Without her, I am alone in the world. *Joe, how could you do this to the people who loved you most?*

Only now is the gravity of Joe's disappearance beginning to dawn on me. Is it possible that he could have hurt himself in some way as punishment for what he did to me? In his drug-induced state did he think suicide was his only option? It was either that or risk being accused of rape. Even though I'm not at fault, if that were the case, I would be devastated.

I imagine Maddie must be as worn out from the lack of sleep as I am. We have both spent the last forty-eight hours worrying about Joe but in quite different ways. Hasn't that always been the case though? No matter how much I now despise him, I loved him for sixteen long years. And, just as with Chris, who also abused my love and trust, I have a hard time letting go of the men in my life. Deep down, I loved Joe even more than I did his mother, who had been everything to me before he came along. But Maddie became completely absorbed in family life after getting married and having a child and our relationship changed as a result. Although understandable, she had less time for our friendship, which at the time had stung.

It was our shared affection for Joe that reignited our closeness. I was just as enamoured of her son, who had Mike's wonky grin, as she was and that proved impossible for any mother to resist. In terms of how I felt about my godson, only Chris came close. But when he first moved in with me, Joe did not appreciate having his nose pushed out. To say he was possessive over me would be an understatement. Knowing what a spoilt brat he could be, Maddie and I would laugh at his tantrums. Chris, however, asserted that we were harming the "overindulged" child by wrapping him in cotton wool. Maddie and I had both taken offence over that.

Chris wasn't overly keen on Joe staying over at our house, finding it a little weird, I think. It was about this time that Joe started acting differently. Was I to blame? Did he feel rejected and is that why he set out to punish me? To teach me a lesson for choosing Chris over him. Had I unintentionally played with Joe's affections? He wasn't a toy to be picked up and put down. At the time, it had felt as if I had two rivals battling for my attention and I shamelessly revelled in it, glad of the adoration for once. Something Maddie was undoubtedly bombarded with all the time and had grown used to given her stop-and-stare looks.

Joe has benefited from his parents' exquisite looks and is easily the most handsome boy at his school. Hadn't he brutally reminded me of this before rushing down the stairs and out onto the street, saying he could have "any girl he wanted"? A fact that was also alluded to when he was accused of assaulting his female teacher. Naturally, I had sided with Maddie when the "absurd" accusation was made. When she first told me this, I got the impression that she did not want to appear vulnerable, but her desire to have her feelings understood without being judged got the better of her. Now that I'm aware of what Joe is capable of, I believe the teacher was telling the truth even though the claim was swiftly disproved and attributed to misunderstandings amid disparate accounts of what happened.

Like Joe, Maddie was the one to turn heads when we were younger. In comparison to her, I was the plain, quiet, shy one. However, the saying, "the quiet ones often turn out to be the worst" had shown to be accurate in my case since, if I am being completely honest, I have far more skeletons in the closet than my best friend could ever guess at. Not only have I kept the real reason Chris broke up with me from her, but I've also hidden my humiliating addiction to alcohol and the fact that I'm going through early menopause. And then there is the rape . . . and the knowledge of her precious son's final movements.

Although Maddie is a mother and wife first, and a friend second, Joe, worryingly, is not the only barrier to our friendship. If I told Maddie about my other, even darker, and more disturbing secret, that I had previously betrayed her in the worst way imaginable, it would destroy her.

CHAPTER 20: MADELINE

The same teacher who accused Joe of sexual assault is standing next to me, as if in solidarity. *Never* is what I say to that. Her sensual perfume lingers in the air around us as we gaze down at the candle holders in our hands, which cast a hazy, far-reaching, shimmering arc of light in the midnight sky. Mine trembles in my hand and hot wax spills onto my fingers, burning them. Hundreds of flames have been lit for Joe and while I know I should be praying for his safe return, all I can focus on are the degrading accusations made against my son by his too-attractive English teacher. As if he were a sexual predator! I consider how effortlessly beautiful she is as I study her soft yellow curls and busty hourglass figure and feel my mouth curl into a grimace. I don't like to think of her hands on my boy's flesh.

She could never persuade me of his guilt no matter what she said. I'm convinced that he still had — *has* — the innocence of a young boy. I recognise my son's shortcomings, at least inwardly, if not outwardly. But if it *did* happen, she, the seductress, obviously encouraged it because he wouldn't have cornered a grown woman in an empty classroom and placed his hands on her without her permission. She may have panicked later, fearing Joe might report the incident himself, and, realising she could lose her job if he did, she then blamed him in an effort to absolve herself of responsibility. I know my son and I am well aware that he is capable of bullying and animal cruelty, due to his antisocial personality disorder, but never sexual assault. I one hundred per cent refuse to accept this. Like his father, he enjoys the company of women and is, as a rule, very respectful of them. You only have to look at his relationship with Zoe to know this. However, a niggle pricks at my skin when I consider that Joe has proven he is capable of physically injuring a woman. I'm living proof of that.

A crushing sadness washes over me when I recall what DCI Saunders told me a few moments ago, while Mike was still speaking with the head teacher, that they've found CCTV footage of Joe staggering around on Stamford Bridge at 2.07 a.m. on the day he disappeared. This was two hours after he'd left the house. Where had my boy been in the hours in between? And who with? He had been drunk or high, was the detective's verdict even though I argued that was impossible because Joe rarely drank . . . except for the odd glass of wine or beer at home and he never used drugs. As I watched Saunders's silver eyebrows draw together in doubt, his eyes said that I needed to wise up.

As I feel Mike's arm curl around my disappearing waistline, I lean against him for a moment, before tipping my chin up to watch his face going through several different emotions.

His voice is thick with anguish as he utters, 'I miss him, Madeline. I miss him so much.'

I feel a flicker of unease in my chest when he takes a tissue out of his pocket and dabs at his watery eyes. There's a knot of fear in my belly as I study his broken demeanour.

'We mustn't give up, Mike,' I whisper.

'I know. I'm trying not to,' he snivels, worry flickering in his eyes.

'The police have CCTV footage of Joe taken around 2 a.m.'

'Seriously?'

I nod through my tears. 'DCI Saunders said that as soon as the vigil is over, we're to go to the police station to view the video for ourselves.' Seeing my husband's face clouded with worry I get the impression he is feeling lost, alone, and deeply ashamed of the things that he has done, which caused our son to run away. Who knows where . . .

'If he was okay then, two hours after he left the house . . .' He gulps nervously, before continuing, 'There's a chance he could still be . . .' He lets the unspoken word "alive" hang in the air, like an invisible fog.

I'm reminded of the old Mike then. The protective, sometimes controlling, alpha-male husband and father. Provider. Leader. He doesn't have to be any of these things, of course, but patriarchy seems to demand it of him. How difficult it must be for him to continuously feel the need to prove himself when we already love him for who he is. As I study his frozen smile, which is no more than a bold attempt to persuade me that he is okay, it awakens the protective lioness in me. He may be a liar, a cheat, and the reason we are at this pointless vigil praying for our son's return, but he's still my man. I've loved him since I was sixteen. And he's Joe's dad.

A priority for me has always been my family. Loyalty is everything. Because of this, I surround myself with people I trust. Joe. Mike. And Zoe. If she needed one of my organs, I would gladly donate it to her. That is how important she is to me and I know she shares my sentiments. Zoe is the only person I can rely on to never hurt or betray me. Not Mike. Never him. That's why it's such a blessing to have her in my life. She might not be able to be present with us right now in person, but we will be in her thoughts as always. And it will break her heart not to be here with us sharing our sorrow and suffering. I take comfort from the knowledge that she is with us in spirit, praying, no . . . pleading for Joe's safe return because she loves him as much as I do. Unlike the majority of those present here tonight, who couldn't give a fuck about my son.

My attention then shifts to the head teacher, whose jowly, sagging chin is even lower on his chest, to Miss Crowther, whose alluring eyes are fixed on the moon, and finally to Gabriella, who appears more preoccupied with her phone than any attempt to establish a spiritual connection with Joe. I couldn't have imagined spending time with these people a few nights ago. On that thought, a switch in my brain flips as I swing from grieving to flight mode, which causes my anxiety to increase by another couple of notches.

As though reading my mind, Mike grabs my free hand. His breath is visible in the cold night air as he asks, 'Do you want to go now? To the police station to view the CCTV footage?'

'What about Gabriella? Won't she be offended if we leave before the vigil is over? We can't afford to upset her.'

Mike's mouth twists in annoyance as he mutters, 'Leave her to me.'

I want to say, *That's what I'm afraid of*, but I don't. Instead, I lean into him as we navigate the crowd, which somehow separates like a wave of uncertainty as we walk into it. All the while I can feel Gabriella's velvety black eyes boring into my shoulders, burning the skin off my back.

CHAPTER 21: ZOE

Unexpectedly, I find myself pacing the streets, instead of being shut inside my tiny house which used to be my "safe place" until Joe violated it. The pavements are slick and black, the air damp from residual summer rain. The clouds have now cleared and, behind me, the moon is attempting to guide me along but it's not needed as I could find my way blindfolded around Stamford, even in the dead of night. Like Maddie, I grew up here. As did Joe. Mike too. We call it home. But just now, it seems hostile. I feel my heart still with fear every time I see a man walking home alone from the pub. Is that how it's going to be from now on? Every waking moment spent anticipating another attack.

If it weren't for Chris, I wouldn't even be outside. Who would have imagined that after receiving a missed call from me, he would ring me back, albeit a full forty-eight hours later? I hadn't personally answered the call, which I'm now kicking myself for as I was avoiding looking at my phone at the time, not wanting to see posts or pictures from Joe's vigil. If Maddie knew I was going to meet Chris when I had pretended to be too ill to join her and Mike on the school grounds, she would be furious.

I've always felt it was my duty to please my best friend, maybe out of fear of losing her to a more interesting person. *Maybe also out of guilt.* She could have been friends with anyone, but she chose me. It occurs to me too late, as I make my way across the old sheep market, minutes before I'm due to see Chris again, that I've never felt deserving of her friendship. I ought to be appreciative of the love and attention she lavishes on me, but instead, it occasionally makes me feel suffocated and I have to ask myself, *why me?* I had anticipated that our friendship would end once she married Mike, the charming and handsome young doctor, but rather than lose her I ended up becoming part of her family. *A dark toxic family that never leaves my mind.*

I push Maddie out of my thoughts and concentrate on my last-minute meeting with Chris and the message he'd left me. "It's me. I've received several missed calls from you, so I'm guessing something's up. I'm out tonight. Want to catch up afterwards? Say around twelve thirty." I'd blushed on hearing it, remembering that I'd called him not once, but seven or eight times, never once leaving a message but simply wanting to hear his recorded voice. "You've reached the voicemail of Chris Walker."

Maddie would have insisted that I stay at home. That I was a fool for pursuing him and that nothing good would come of it. *She's back in my head once more.* But I long to see him again. I've somehow managed to persuade myself that this could be the chance I've been hoping for and that we might get back together. The rebound can't have worked out, I muse, crossing the street once more to avoid a bunch of young men, *like Joe*, standing outside the Stamford Post smoking. Perhaps Chris realises he's made a mistake and now wants to apologise. Imagine how unimpressed the new girlfriend would be if she learned that her partner was meeting up with his ex. I suddenly find myself grinning — something I haven't done in days. Serve her right for stealing him off me in the first place. Except I don't know for sure that she did.

Then, right on cue, Nice Zoe gives herself a hard time for benefiting at the expense of someone else's misery. 'You're too good for your own good,' Maddie used to say. If she knew what I was guilty of, she wouldn't think so. She doesn't know the real me. Like Joe, I've hidden the less pleasant aspects of my personality to fit in. Has it taken the assault on my body and the betrayal of Joe to make me face up to this fact? They say that self-reflection and healing from trauma is good for the soul but the journey it takes you on is hell . . .

There he is. Chris. Seated at a table outside the Golden Fleece. Just as he said he would be. Like the lads I just bumped into, he is also smoking. What's more, he has a pint in his hand. That means the rumours I had heard from our mutual acquaintances about him giving up smoking and becoming sober were untrue. My mind screeches to a halt when a mental picture of his girlfriend's pregnancy belly hijacks my brain. *I don't want to know about the baby. Yet, I do. Badly.*

'Hi,' I say quietly, sliding onto the bench across from him. We are the only ones outside. Everybody else has gone home, the pub has already closed. When he remains silent, I press my lips together in mild irritation, determined not to be the first to speak again. He's not looking his best. He appears to have lost a ton of weight. A couple of stones he couldn't afford to drop in the first place.

'You wanted to speak to me,' he blusters at last, his hands fidgeting by his sides and his fingers clenching into fists.

A beat of silence, awkward and tense, tiptoes between us, buttoning our lips. And after an incredibly long pause, *too uncomfortable for a fixer like me to sustain*, I eventually blurt out the first thing that leaps into my brain.

'You're still mad at me.'

'What is it you want, Zoe?' he slurs.

'I thought you'd given up drinking,' I point out weakly.

It was the wrong thing to say. Now that I notice the challenge in his eyes and the tight-lipped look on his face, dread swirls in my stomach. His eyes are the coldest I've ever seen them.

'The messages you left me before, after I moved out, you said you wanted closure. Is that still the case?'

I stare at my hands, which are firmly clasped together, and my eyes then travel to his dirty-brown beer. Around the rim of his glass, there are frothy traces. At that moment, I know I will never touch a drop of alcohol again. It destroys lives like mine and Chris's and leads people like Joe to commit terrible crimes. On that thought, a burning disappointment settles in my chest, weighing me down until I feel soldered to the seat.

'I've apologised a million times for my drunken behaviour on the plane that day. . . when I disrespected you. However, if you'll allow me to finish,' I add, sensing he's about to launch his own attack. 'You used to be a heavy drinker, Chris, and said and did some terrible things as well. But I forgave you.' I hesitate because my eyes are stinging with tears and I don't want him to see me cry. Not ever again.

He puffs out his chest, clearly offended. 'You think that's why I left you?'

'If that wasn't the case, then why?' I ask, stunned.

He leers drunkenly. 'You really want to know?'

I blink and nod simultaneously, briefly feeling trapped in a dead end. Chris's startling revelation has blown my mind to a million pieces.

He turns to face me and snaps, 'I know what you did, Zoe,' without further explanation.

CHAPTER 22: MADELINE

Mike is still holding my hand as we walk through the glossy, blue-painted door of Stamford Police Station, an impressive Victorian manor-style structure on North Street. Since it has been in his palm for such a long time, I can barely feel it anymore. As if he were the owner of a house that was up for sale and was proudly showing us around it, DCI Saunders ushers us inside where there is a desk with a uniformed police officer behind it, shielded by toughened glass. Given the town's low crime rate, I'm surprised by this. Described as one of the nicest and safest places to live in the UK, high property costs mean most criminals can't afford to live here.

'This way, Mr and Mrs Black.' Saunders motions for us to follow him down a narrow, brightly lit corridor that has numerous doors going off it. Mike and I exchange a cautious glance before following his instructions.

The fear inside me builds with each step I take. The sense of impending doom is making it hard for me to breathe. Suppose it isn't Joe? They could have made a mistake. The teenager captured on their surveillance video might not be my son at all. Because there isn't enough room for us to walk side by side, Mike has had to let go of my hand, and I feel the loss of it more than I can say. In contrast to me, he seems composed. He will have had words with himself, bracing himself for what's to come. Mike won't want to come across as emotional, or, in his own words, "weak", in front of an authoritative figure like Saunders.

'Through here.' Saunders invites us into a windowless interview room which has a small table in the middle and four plastic chairs around it. My eyes are instantly glued to the screen mounted on the wall. Switched on, it displays a paused grainy still of what appears to be part of a gloomy pavement. Mike looks at me again and I start to shiver uncontrollably.

'Sit down, please,' Saunders suggests, less formally this time, as if he senses how difficult this is for us. I don't know why, but it feels as if I'm about to identify my son's dead body rather than simply look at security footage of him. I swear Mike feels the same. As a result, the tension in the room feels like a sharpened knife slowly being dragged across my throat.

I happen to notice Saunders's eyes for the first time as I settle into the chair he's pulled out for me, and they catch me completely off guard. Only the disappearance of a son could make a woman forget to pay attention to those crinkly arctic blue eyes. Being under his gaze is like getting some type of electric shock.

Mike, who like the detective has elected to remain standing, nods respectfully as Saunders continues, 'As I stated earlier to Mrs Black, the tape we uncovered of Joe was captured from a security camera from a business in Wharf Road. We had to zoom in and enhance the film because the town bridge is some distance away. The footage isn't great but it does what we need it to.'

Without further ado, and much to my alarm, since I'm not yet ready for this — I'll never be ready for this — the detective points a remote control at the screen and hits play. I chew at a fingernail as I wait, time seeming to stand still, as I watch footage of the town bridge appear on screen. White lines down the middle of the road then emerge. As does a dark stone wall. The video is jerky and grainy at first, and nothing else is visible until a passing car is caught on camera driving over the bridge. Its shape and colour is indistinguishable from the hundreds of other 4 x 4 diesel-guzzling vehicles that crawl around the town searching for parking spaces.

Panic flutters in my chest when a small dot appears on the left side of the screen. I know it's Joe, or at least the boy the police think is Joe, because someone has inserted a red circle — almost like a lasso — around his body to draw attention to his movements. As the image is blown up pixel by pixel, and the shadowy figure staggers drunkenly beneath the light of a streetlight, exposing some of his hooded face, I recognise him immediately.

My hand flutters to my mouth as I whimper, 'Joe,' and I hear Mike gasp next to me. We're both aware that we might be observing our son's last movements before he vanished and that this could be the last time we ever see him. The police have no idea what happened to him after the film was taken. Who knows if we'll ever find out? I'm told that hundreds of teenagers go missing every year and are never heard of again. I know if Joe doesn't want to be found then he won't be. He is just as obstinate as his father. Like most mothers, I'm sure, I would rather believe he ran away from home than speculate about the terrible things that might have happened to him.

I scoot forward in my seat for a better view of Joe as he stumbles and bumps into the wall. Blood rushes in my ears and adrenaline fires through my veins when I consider how easily he could have fallen into the river. And my boy can't swim! Head down, Joe is hunched over and has his hands buried in his pockets. He appears to be kicking a stone or some other object out of frustration. Then, on the opposite side of the street from my son, another person is seen walking across the bridge. They are going in opposite directions and do not exchange glances as they pass each other. My pulse races as I realise Joe is travelling towards home rather than away from it, and like a doomed spaceship, my heart soars and then plummets. Who or what happened to him in the half-mile between him and home?

A sob lodges in my throat as Joe disappears from view after moving out of frame, but then, my God. Then . . . the man on the opposite side of the road stops in his tracks and slowly revolves his head 180 degrees to stare after Joe. Mike and the detective are back to discussing the case by this point, so they aren't paying any attention to the stranger, who isn't a stranger at all because I identified him just as easily as I did my son when I saw his eerie, white-eyed-on-film face twitching in astonishment.

Mike and Saunders turn to look at me as if I've lost my mind, *and perhaps I have*, as I cry out, 'Him! He's the one who has our son!'

CHAPTER 23: ZOE

When he's like this, loud and argumentative — intentionally so — I remember all the things about Chris I never used to like. His bad side if you like. We all have one, *don't I know it*, but with him, alcohol used to turn him into a real bore. It jolts me back to the times when he'd pick fights with just about anyone who got him started on his "beloved Scotland" or the "independence referendum". But I can tell this is something far more serious when I dare to meet his gaze and his chin jerks upwards in a defiant motion. My body runs cold and I sit up straight. When he told me he knew what I had done, I felt like I had been punched. My breath comes out in little gasps, even now, as I try to figure out which of my sins he might have exposed. There's no point giving myself away if I don't have to. For all I know he might be referring to one of my lesser offences.

I attempt a jokey laugh, but it falls flat. 'What am I meant to have done?'

He fixes me with a steely glare. 'Don't act like you don't know.'

'Chris, I really don't.' I sigh while continuing to play a part because I feel on the verge of being consumed by panic.

There's no way we're ever going to reconcile now. *Not if he really does know* . . .

'I always used to think that out of the two of us, you were the much nicer person. The stereotypical girl next door and the girlfriend everyone loved. Mum and all three of my sisters thought I was mad to leave you, but that's not who you really are, is it? Nice Zoe doesn't exist.'

'That's not true, Chris!' I protest. 'I always try to be a good person. And I don't know how you can say that to me after three happy years together.'

'Happy until they weren't,' he grumbles.

'Every couple goes through hard times,' I point out, wondering why we are suddenly going down the "couples" route.

'When I found out what you had done, I couldn't believe it at first. I thought I was losing my mind. I mean this was lovely Zoe I was talking about. Everyone's so-called best friend—'

I flinch at his words because they are true. Chris. Maddie. Mike. I've been a terrible friend to them all. Even Joe, who I introduced to weed. My muscles stiffen involuntarily as I realise that Chris really does know what I'm guilty of and that there's no point in me denying it. This means I have lost him for good. The second he found out, he was no longer mine. How much he knows or how he made the discovery I may never know but either way, it's over.

'How could you do that, Zoe?' His voice crackles with rage.

'Who told you?' I demand, feeling spooked.

'*You* did.'

'What do you mean?' I bark louder than I intended, and quickly cast my eyes around the square to make sure nobody else is nearby.

'I had my suspicions so I watched you when you were around other people. And I didn't like what I saw. I couldn't believe it at first—'

I stop listening because shame has crushed and enveloped me. I regret coming tonight. Maddie is in my head again, pointing a finger and remonstrating, 'I told you it wouldn't end well.' I miss her. I really do and I want to help her in her hour of need but I am unable to do so. Because of her bastard son.

'You made a fool of me and everyone else, Zoe, but worst of all I had to witness you carrying on as usual as if nothing had happened. You did it so convincingly I stopped feeling anything for you after that.'

'Chris, I'm so sorry.' Tears run down my face as I say this. I can feel my pulse pounding in my head. Even the sound of my own voice is jarring. 'Can you ever forgive me?'

'It's not me you should be asking.' Chris sneers as he downs the rest of his drink and wipes his mouth on his sleeve.

My nerves spike at the thought of him walking away. Leaving. I wanted so much to tell him about what had happened to me. I'd been violated. Was it so wrong of me to hope for some sympathy and understanding?

'You won't tell anyone about this, will you, Chris? I mean it would . . .'

'There she is,' Chris snarls, clambering to his feet. 'The real Zoe who doesn't care about anyone other than herself.'

'That's not true!' I stand up too and square my shoulders, mirroring Chris, but I also hug my waist for comfort. Standing next to him I feel small in every way. 'I care about lots of people,' I tell him, but I don't mention who because that would be unwise, so I say instead, 'you most of all.'

'No.' He thrusts out a forceful palm, keeping me away from him. 'You don't get to say that to me. Not to my face. Not after what you did.'

'Chris,' I gulp, hardly able to breathe, as my brain is paralysed. 'Please stop. There's something you have to know . . .'

'Two more minutes.' His words come out strained as he checks his watch. 'And then, I'm going home to Vicky.'

Vicky. Her name is Vicky. And they're still together. I feel a prickle of jealousy at the back of my neck and force the unwelcome emotion away. What an idiot I was to believe that he would choose me. No one picks me. Only Joe. On that thought, I feel myself shuddering violently. I consider holding off telling Chris about the assault at this point, but I'm in too deep and I desperately need to tell *someone*. For my own sanity if nothing else, so it might as well be Chris, who I'm unlikely to ever see again anyway.

'Joe put something in my drink, and then . . .' I feel my heart break simply looking into Chris's unforgiving eyes. Does he feel nothing for me? Can that be true when I am still so much in love with him? Even now when it's clear he hates me. And for good reason.

'I woke up to find he'd had sex with me without my consent.' The words come tumbling out of my mouth so fast that I trip over them.

His face crumples and the anger seeps out of him. 'Shit, Zoe.'

I watch his face go through a slew of emotions and while I'm not up for a barrage of questions, I would kill for some kindness.

When he cautiously approaches me and, seemingly making up his mind that it would be appropriate to comfort me, puts his arms around me, I sob into the reassuring shoulder that I used to think of as mine. The fact that he's here for me despite knowing what I have done, reinforces what I've always known about Chris. He's a good man. A keeper.

'Vicky is a lucky woman.' I force a laugh while patting him on the back, giving him permission to let me go. Forever, it would seem.

'I'm sorry for what happened to you, Zoe, really, I am. No one deserves that.'

His eyes remain kind but there is gravel in his voice and a determined set to his jaw. I know he's angry on my behalf. And that he also believes me but can't allow himself to get involved. It's more than I deserve and beyond anything I could have ever hoped for.

'Joe was always a little creep. I never could stand him,' he grunts out stiffly, before continuing in the same vein, 'but then again, with a father like Mike, it's hardly surprising. The cunt once told me when he was drunk that he fancied teenage girls. Fucking paedo. And to think—'

As I take in what he is saying, tears drip off my nose. Everything is moving and spinning around me and I'm finding it difficult to keep my emotions under control. Black dots fill my vision. Feeling dizzy, I extend a hand out to the pub table in an attempt to prevent myself from collapsing to the ground.

CHAPTER 24: MADELINE

'He must have followed Joe and attacked him,' I mumble, pointing at the screen, which has now run out of tape and is fuzzy with white noise, appearing ghostlike. 'Or kidnapped him.' I can feel my eyes bulge as I say this.

'Who, Madeline, *who*?' Mike is desperate to know and is wringing his hands. DCI Saunders, meanwhile, is looking on with startled eyes.

'Rupert's father, of course.'

'Who is Rupert?' Saunders asks, perplexed.

'You mean Forbes?' Mike interrupts, his frow burrowing.

'Yes. Didn't you recognise him in the film?' Panic sharpens my voice, raising it a couple of octaves. *How could they not have seen what I saw?*

'I barely know the man.' Doubt enters Mike's voice as he continues incredulously, 'But it couldn't have been him, could it? That would be too much of a coincidence.' Mike suddenly loses his footing and stumbles backwards, arms windmilling as if to prevent himself from falling.

'Exactly. That's how I know he's done something to our boy,' I plead with the detective this time, understanding that my husband needs a few minutes to gather himself.

'Who exactly are we discussing, Mrs Black?'

'The father of the boy who hanged himself last year,' Mike announces coldly, demonstrating that he's once again in control, but he collapses into a chair anyway and agitatedly runs a hand over his stubble.

'You mean the father of the boy Joe *told* to hang himself,' I correct my husband. Right now, I'm so angry with my son for possibly bringing about his own abduction, *or worse*, that I fold my hands into fists and clasp them to my chest, willing myself to stay strong. It's time to act, not crumble.

'You mustn't say such things!' Mike explodes.

'Why not? They're true,' I hiss. At the back of my mind, I'm wondering why we're wasting time on petty arguing, but it feels good nonetheless to let off steam. Now that I've vocalised my true feelings on the subject, I realise they have been gnawing away at me for months and that I'd pushed them aside.

Mike, avoiding my gaze, addresses only the detective. 'There is no evidence to support my wife's accusation. Nothing was proven and the case against Joe was dropped.'

'Shall we start at the beginning?' Saunders fishes a note-pad and a chewed pen out of his trouser pocket and sets them down on the table.

'We don't have time for that,' I argue, thumping a fist on the table, causing his notebook to bounce. 'You need to send someone over to the Forbes's house *now* and find out what that man has done to my son.'

'And you need to calm down, Madeline,' Mike warns in his infuriating doctor's voice.

'You'll be telling me next that I need to smile more,' I bite back.

'I don't think arguing is helping,' Saunders points out, causing a twinge of shame to appear in Mike's eyes which I'm sure is mirrored in my own.

Mike nods in agreement, and, as if to prove this, he picks up my hand and gives it an apologetic squeeze, which causes me to immediately choke back tears. 'Yes, of course. You're quite right.'

'Mrs Black?' Saunders prompts, armed with his pen which he has retrieved from the table.

'After Rupert died, his mother came to see me.' I bow my head in disgrace at this point, but go on I must. 'She brought her son's diary with her and left it for me to read. In it, Rupert described how one of the boys in his class was tormenting and bullying him. This boy—' I shut my eyes to block out the excruciatingly painful images of all the pages of schoolboy writing that I had seen — 'kept urging Rupert to commit suicide. He even sent him a GIF of a gruesome hanging.'

'And you believe that this boy was your son?' Saunders's hypnotic eyes are wide with disbelief as he says this.

'I know it was. I overheard him discussing it with someone afterwards on the phone, mocking the poor boy.'

'Clearly, my wife misheard what was said,' Mike cuts in. 'My son would never do something like that.'

'But *my* son would.' I glare at Mike, thinking that even though we have just decided to call a truce we are back to square one and fighting again. How unreliable we all are, I can't help but think. Each and every one of us.

'Let's assume you're right for the time being.' Saunders is looking at me, not Mike, when he says this and I want to jump out of my chair and fling my arms around his neck in appreciation. 'But what leads you to believe that . . .' He pauses to consult his notebook. 'Rupert's father had anything to do with your son's disappearance?'

'Revenge,' I gasp, thinking it was obvious. 'I saw the way he stopped and stared after Joe on camera. He obviously couldn't believe his luck when he stumbled across the boy responsible for his own son's death, when, as you say, Joe looks like he was either drunk or high on drugs. Vulnerable and alone.' *All alone.*

'I see what you're saying.' Saunders stands up, appearing suddenly anxious, and slips his notebook back into his pocket, patting it as if to protect it. 'I'm just going to nip out of the room for a bit to update the team, and then I'll be back to take a proper statement.'

Nothing can prevent me from shooting daggers at my husband after that. Looking stunned, he coughs nervously into his hand. Mike obviously doesn't like the direction the conversation had taken. He would say anything to prevent his son from getting into any kind of legal trouble because doing so would discredit our precious family name. I imagine he expected the detective to share his stance on the situation and the fact that he hadn't, has wounded his male pride. And yes, I know I am still being petty but it helps me take my mind off other things. Like kidnap. Beatings. Torture. Stabbings. Suffocation. Death.

'Oh, just one more thing.' Saunders pauses, Colombo-like, with his hand on the door handle. 'Did you mention the other matter to your wife?'

'I haven't as yet, I'm afraid.' Mike's eyes shiftily hit the floor.

'What other matter?' I ask warily, my body rigid with fear.

CHAPTER 25: ZOE

As I make my way back over the town bridge towards home, I sniff tearfully and wipe my nose with my sleeve. Thank goodness the streets are no longer littered with lone guys. After falling to the ground in the square, Chris had helped me to my feet and seemed genuinely worried that I might have hurt myself, but I pushed him away. His concern was never going to be enough for me. When he was furious with me, the pain was lessened. I could cope with that version of the man I loved, but not Vicky's version. Chris, being the nice guy he is, offered to call me a taxi or even to walk me home, but I declined. That would have been agonising after all the times we'd returned home together, hand in hand and loved-up after a night out. In the end, I wrenched myself away from him and left, ignoring all his pleas for me to "come back" just as Joe had ignored mine.

I must have caught my chin on the pavement when I fell because it's scraped and stinging. More bruising to match the ones on my inner thighs which I discovered in the shower earlier tonight. Joe's watermark. And what of Mike? Was Chris telling the truth when he said that he had a predilection for underage girls? Oh God, poor Maddie on top of everything else. Imagine knowing that about your husband.

I'll definitely be seeing him with different eyes from now on. Like his son, he's not the person I thought he was.

And what about me? Do I deserve any of what has happened to me? Even though I lied to Chris and deceived him in the worst way possible, wasn't losing him punishment enough? Surely, no one would wish sexual assault on anyone. Even Maddie, were she to find out what her so-called best friend had done! I stole something from her that I can never give back and I have to live with that every day of my life. It's not as if I don't regret it. I do. But at the same time, I can't guarantee that I won't do it again.

Taking my phone out of the pocket of my tight white jeans, worn especially for Chris because I know I look good in them, I groan when I see that Maddie hasn't left any new messages. I would have thought the vigil would have been over by now. She had promised to keep me posted, so I start to worry that something new and unexpected has happened. Could Joe have returned home? And if so, will he keep his mouth shut as I plan on doing? Of course, it would be best for me overall if he never showed his face again . . . but because I love his mother, I can't wish for that.

I'm incapable of texting while walking like the younger generation do, so I come to a halt and punch out a message: *Hope everything is okay. Let me know how it went when you get the chance. Sorry once again for not being there. Got a doctor's appointment at last for tomorrow morning.* The last bit was untrue. Actually, everything I said was a lie. Another thing I'd always vowed never to do where my closest friend was concerned.

As I stand there sighing, waiting for a message that may or may not arrive in the next few minutes, I slump against the stone wall and gaze down at the river. In some strange way, the sounds of the fast-flowing water as it bubbles and crashes over rocks is calming. When a disturbing image of someone falling into the water, hands flailing wildly, enters my thoughts, I pause, trying to recall where the memory came from. Then I remember witnessing a construction worker jumping off the bridge a few years ago and assume that's what prompted it. It was a hot summer's day, I remember, and he had intended to just cool off in the water but ended up breaking his neck in three places. I can only imagine how his family must have felt when they found out. As far as I know, the man is still alive. But even so . . . why would anyone jump off a bridge into a river?

I jump in fright and almost drop my phone when I hear the authoritative wail of a siren behind me. I whirl around just in time to see two police cars speeding by. My shoulders immediately slump as I consider what Maddie is going through. She must be at her wit's end every time she sees a police officer or hears a siren. The one time in her life when she genuinely needs me, rather than the other way around, when I could perhaps make up for what I have done to her in the past, and I can't bring myself to be anywhere near her.

Thank God I don't have to go to work tomorrow since it's Monday. Hairdressing salons don't open on a Monday in this neck of the woods. That gives me an additional twenty-four hours to sort myself out. I'm going to need it. The trouble is, once Maddie finds out I've gone back to work, and she will find out because she and Mike know everybody in this small town, she'll insist on seeing me. I'll feel compelled to go to their house and set up "Joe camp" and keep her company while we wait for him to come home. I'm just not able to do as she wishes. It would be impossible. I would only end up spilling the beans about Joe. I know I would. It's useless, I decide; I'll just have to come up with another plan that involves skipping work. Maybe I will go and see a doctor after all and get him or her to sign me off on sick leave for a couple of weeks until all of this blows over.

I also resolve that there will be no more damsel-in-distress calls made to Chris. It's not fair on him or his girlfriend to continue to entangle him in the mess I've made of my life and, if I owe him anything, it's giving him a chance of a decent new life. One he would never have had with me. Tonight, when I get home, I'll dispose of all his belongings, the same ones I'd sworn blind to Maddie that I'd gotten rid of ages ago. I won't even re-read the birthday and Valentine cards he had sent me or stroke the jumper one last time that he accidentally left behind and which I'd taken to wearing because it was the next best thing to his not being there. The only silver lining in all of this, *if you can call it that*, is that I haven't craved a drop of alcohol since I was attacked. I feel nauseous just thinking about it.

I reflect on what Chris accused me of as I continue walking, no longer dragging my feet but eager to be at home, sealed away from the world, even if my house will always bear Joe's imprint from now on. Neither of us discussed the betrayal of what I did in any detail and that's just as well, because I fear it was much worse than he could ever have imagined.

A sickening sense of guilt consumes me, because in reality I don't want to think back on my past transgressions any more than he did, for fear it will arouse a longing in me. I'm an addict. Whether it's sex, cigarettes, or alcohol. I can't be trusted.

CHAPTER 26: MADELINE

We were dropped off by a uniformed police officer an hour ago. Even though it was almost two in the morning by then, our neighbour's curtains were twitching as the police car pulled onto our drive. On the journey here, we had accidentally tagged on behind Saunders's flashing and wailing police car in a game of cat and mouse as his team headed for the Forbes's house. He had refused to tell us where that was and we lost them when we took a left turn immediately after the town bridge, bound for home.

Because Zoe had been on and off my mind all night, I imagined I caught sight of her, or someone who looked like her, on the town bridge as we passed over it. She was facing away from us and gazing down at the water, but not in a way that made me fear she would jump. I know it couldn't really have been her. She was presumably curled up in bed at home and still terribly ill. *I must text her back when I get the chance.* Since I knew I would be accused of seeing things, I didn't mention it to Mike. Besides, he wouldn't have been interested. Zoe was my friend not his, although he'd always been very accepting of her. At least outwardly.

Even if it meant waiting in a car outside while the police searched the Forbes's house, I'd wanted to go along with

Saunders and his team. I needed desperately to see the guilt on that man's face when he was marched away in handcuffs, but Saunders was having none of it. Mike, of course, thought that was wise. But it wasn't all about Forbes. My primary goal was to be near my son. I wanted to be there when he was released whether he was being kept as a prisoner or, God forbid, worse, in the Forbes's home.

Our family liaison officer, Sharon, is in the kitchen, making sandwiches we won't eat and loading the dishwasher as quietly as possible so as not to disturb us. It would appear that her role is to be invisible. Except, of course, when she is needed. Which isn't very often. I long to have my house back to normal, free of strangers, but I fear that is what Mike and I are becoming to each other more and more. We have retreated to the living room, to silently bite our nails and watch the clock while we wait for news from Saunders.

I can tell my husband is dying for a drink by the way he keeps tapping his foot on the floor. He doesn't realise he is doing it, and I don't call him out on it since he won't want to admit to feeling overwhelmed with anxiety. Although Mike is a surgeon and accustomed to handling extreme situations, no amount of medical training could have prepared him for this. When he finally fixes his weary gaze on me, I glance away, trying to keep my eyes open. Exhaustion is never far away but I mustn't go to sleep. That, in my opinion, would be a betrayal of my son, who might be suffering much worse treatment than sleep deprivation at the hands of his abductor.

'Where is Saunders? How much longer is he going to make us wait?' I grind out through clenched teeth, twirling the rings on my fingers.

'All in good time, Madeline.' Mike feigns a composure I know he's not feeling, before adding, 'We must be patient a while longer.'

Even though I know he doesn't mean to belittle me, I demand with a tight voice, 'Why didn't you tell me about the appeal sooner?'

He hesitates before saying, 'Detective Saunders mentioned it to me yesterday. Said he wanted to sound me out before bringing it up with you. I was waiting for the right moment, hoping the appeal might not be necessary . . . if Joe were found.'

'That's not your decision to make, Mike. I'm not a child.'

He doesn't exactly roll his eyes, but he seems to be insinuating as much as he furrows his brow, so I have to control my rage as I declare, 'I want to be told everything. We're in this together. Even if it doesn't feel like it.'

'Fair enough,' he concedes while looking down at his clasped hands. 'They're talking about doing it first thing tomorrow, on . . .' His pause is longer this time. 'The bridge where Joe was last seen and then broadcasting it on the local evening news. They're also going to release the CCTV footage.'

I let out an agonising groan. When my head snaps up again, Mike's expression has changed. In a split second, he has transformed from an authoritative doctor figure to a little boy. He reminds me so much of my son at that moment that I want to reach over and cup his face in my hands. But I don't. Instead, I insist, 'How can we go public with this and appear on TV, knowing what we know?'

'For Joe's sake, Madeline, we must.'

I whisper, 'But we're the reason he ran away in the first place.'

Mike takes in a very deep breath, and I can see his Adam's apple bouncing up and down as he gulps at the air. 'We both know you're being kind when you say that, as I am solely to blame.'

'But what if you're not?' I ponder aloud.

'What do you mean?'

'Suppose Gabriella had something to do with it?'

'How?'

'She could have deliberately set out to seduce you before making plans to get rid of Joe.'

'She's fifteen,' he scoffs sarcastically.

'Don't remind me.' My words come out stilted and sharp.

'I am aware of what you are doing, Madeline.' Mike sighs sympathetically, while nodding along, again as if he were talking to a child. 'It's understandable.' He has always fancied himself as a man who understands women but he couldn't be any further off the mark.

'What is?' The words are dragged out of me as I outstare him.

'You're looking for someone else to blame for our son's disappearance, and—' he staggers guiltily to his feet as if he's about to admit an even bigger sin than betraying our son and me — 'for how he turned out.'

I respond, wide-eyed, as this is the first time Mike has ever acknowledged that there is something wrong with Joe. 'Even so, she's a manipulative bitch.' *It takes one to know one*, I think, before cautiously suggesting, 'I believe she got inside Joe's head and forced him to do things he wouldn't have otherwise done.'

'Like what?'

'He hasn't been the same since they were an item and he never had a problem at school before they started dating.' I conveniently forget for the moment that when Joe was younger, he used to cruelly torture animals. Is Mike right when he claims I want to place the responsibility elsewhere?

'There's something wrong with her,' I persist doggedly, even though I am aware that I have applied this very same phrase to my son on more than one occasion. 'I was watching her tonight, the way she interacted with kids her own age, and I'm starting to think she encouraged Joe to bully that boy and that she was the one he spoke to on the phone that day when I overheard him mocking Rupert. It was as if he were reporting in to her after being assigned some kind of sick teenage dare.'

Mike pinches his nose in frustration. 'Where is your evidence for this conspiracy theory?' He'd like to tell me to "get a grip" but doesn't quite dare.

Hackles raised, I stab a finger at him, aiming for his chest. 'The only data-driven evidence, Dr Mike, as you like to call it, is that our son is missing.'

Mike turns to glare at me and is about to retaliate, when—

The doorbell.

Sharon rushes to answer it, her fluttering bird-like steps echoing down the hall.

Mike and I look at each other when we hear Saunders's voice. They are talking in hushed tones. The kind the police use to convey bad news.

CHAPTER 27: ZOE

As I arrive home, to the crime scene, the darkness of that night begins to engulf me once more. Even though I try to close the front door on what's left of the night, Joe's face continues to haunt me. Not knowing exactly what he did is somehow worse than if I'd been awake during the assault. Instead, my imagination keeps replaying the attack, leaving me helpless and stuck. It's the worst blackout I've ever experienced. And there have been lots of them. All previously down to drink. But even when I dredge the remotest corners of my mind, my memories remain out of reach. All I can recall is waking up to Joe's grinning face on the pillow next to mine. That in itself is truly terrifying. I'll never forget his smug, celebratory expression. It was as if he'd passed a test. Or a dare!

Feeling bruised and dejected, I slip off my denim jacket and let it fall to the floor before going into the kitchen to switch on the kettle. More sweet, milky tea, for the ongoing shock. When I open the fridge door to retrieve the milk, I realise I'm out. It's not entirely unexpected. Shopping has been the last thing on my mind. Noticing the crumpled box of wine on the bottom shelf, I feel a chill travel down my spine. Bile starts to rise in my stomach as I imagine drinking it. Instead, I make a black coffee and bring it into the living room, pausing to look around . . . as if seeing it for the first time. Maddie was right when she cuttingly remarked that it resembled a rundown bedsit. I've never actually grown up, I realise despondently, as I have always thought of myself as young with no responsibilities. *Until now, that is.* Is that why I can sometimes be childishly dismissive of other people's feelings? Either way, it's something I intend to fix.

Sinking onto the sofa, I kick off my sandals and tuck my legs under me before listening to Chris's voicemail. On the way home, he'd tried to call me numerous times, but I had ignored him. As far as I am concerned, we have nothing more to say to each other.

'It's only me. I was worried about you when you rushed off like that. Look, I'm sorry, okay, for giving you such a hard time over something that doesn't matter anymore.'

'Except it does, Chris, doesn't it?' I have a bitter conversation with myself. 'Because it destroyed our relationship and I wasn't even aware that you'd guessed my dirty little secret.' Being the fool I was at the time, I thought I had outwitted him. And everybody else.

'Let me know that you got home safe. That's all I'm asking.'

I have no intention of calling him back. Now that he has seen me for who I am — or *was* — back then, I can no longer bear to be near him or even to hear his voice. He was the one person who thought I was perfect. He used to refer to me as *his lovely Zoe*. A sob lodges in my throat and I chase it away by gulping down scorching coffee.

For the first time in my life, I realise that men are not the friends and protectors I've always considered them to be. They are, in fact, the enemy. You can't rely on any of them. They're not to be trusted. Look at Joe. And, if Chris is to be believed, Mike too. As for Chris, he might not have abandoned me because I drunkenly called him an "arsehole", as I had long suspected him of doing, but he is still a coward for keeping quiet about his real reason for leaving. Only to use this information to hurt me a year later after I had just been assaulted and raped. Somehow, it feels as though I lost him all over again tonight. My heart is hardened by this knowledge. But the most important thing I've discovered over the past few days is that I'm tougher than I thought. Girly, giggly Zoe is gone forever.

I close my eyes for just a few seconds, and before I know it, my head is slumped on my chest and coffee is dripping from my mug onto the carpet. Then a loud, persistent beeping jerks me awake. After I've unravelled my limbs, I unlock my phone and check my text messages. It's almost 4 a.m. It can only be Maddie at this hour.

Still no news of Joe. It was him on the CCTV footage though. It was hard to watch but we somehow got through it. The police might have a lead, but they're being very evasive about it. Hope you're feeling better. Don't forget your doctor's appointment in the morning.

Two thoughts simultaneously race through my confused mind. First: what lead? And why would they be evasive about it with Madeline, who had every right to know? For fuck's sake! It was her son who had vanished. Could they have found out that Joe was here, with me, on the night he disappeared? Is that what they're keeping from her? For now . . .

Even though I haven't committed any crime, *aside from not telling the truth*, I'm paralysed with fear at the thought of the police pounding on my door and demanding I go down to the station with them. Tears of frustration stream down my face. The nightmare refuses to end. I realise I'm upset with Maddie even though I have no right to be. Her compassion for me is equivalent to me seeking comfort while lying down on a bed of nails. After everything I've done to her, she even remembers to remind me of my fake doctor's appointment. Admittedly, Maddie knows nothing of my secret. Until Chris worked it out, I assumed nobody did. But I'm too much of a coward to want to find out *how*. My chest is now so tight I can hardly breathe. The shock at all that has happened is freezing my brain.

Without a doubt, Maddie is a better person than me. She's been generous and considerate her entire life. She does, though, sometimes strike me as having a coldness about her, and a predilection for snobbery. With outsiders or those she perceives as inferior, she can be standoffish. But I always attributed this to her preference for being around people she knew, loved and trusted. Poor Maddie has no idea she is surrounded by liars and frauds. Rapists. Drunks. Druggies. Cheats. Even paedophiles.

She, like me, is not one for making new friends. Mike is the sociable, more outgoing one of the two, and to this day, he still enjoys being the centre of attention. Something Maddie despises. I used to wonder which of his parents Joe would take after the most because it could have gone either way. I doubt I will ever find out now because even if he were to return home, I will never be in the same room with him again.

Whether he's dead or alive no longer matters to me. He's out of my life for good.

CHAPTER 28: MADELINE

'Mike,' I whimper, instinctively reaching out for his hand. 'What happens if Joe never comes back? What if he's—?'

'Don't say it. Just don't.' Mike shakes his head, swivelling his panicked gaze in DCI Saunders's direction, before adding, 'Oh God, I need a drink.'

'You can't,' I protest. 'Not if we're going to be filmed in the morning.'

Mike lets out a sigh of acceptance he obviously doesn't feel. 'It's morning already. It's gone 4 a.m.'

While he seems surprised that time is slipping away from us, all I can think about is how long Joe has been gone. That is why I can't stop looking at my phone. So I can count every second of every minute.

'I don't want to do the appeal,' I whisper, not wanting Saunders or Sharon to overhear. In a corner of the living room, they are engaged in their own private discussion while Mike and I remain seated next to each other on the sofa. I can't stand their whispering. Everyone seems to be hiding something from me. It's as if I'm the only one not in on the secret.

'We have to, Madeline, especially now—'

'Now that they've let Forbes go, you mean?' My eyes narrow as I say this. The thought of that man walking free is never far from my mind.

'You heard what Saunders said,' Mike counters. 'He arrived home ten minutes after that film was taken. Alone. This was evidenced on Forbes's house Ring camera.'

'They didn't even search his house?' I object, knowing that I'm fighting a losing battle. Nobody, not even Mike is on my side in this.

'To obtain a search warrant they need evidence or a strong suspicion at least. He's not our man, Madeline, face it.'

'I'm not convinced,' I grind out.

'Not so long ago you were convinced that Gabriella was involved in Joe's disappearance,' Mike reminds me, causing me to flinch. *Is he defending her? Protecting her?* I can only think of one reason why he would do that.

Deciding to keep my thoughts on that matter to myself, I look over to Saunders and Sharon and wonder what they are talking about. She is like a little mouse and begins every sentence with "sorry". I find this aggravating rather than appealing. Because what exactly has she got to be sorry about? She hasn't lost a son, has she? Apologetic Sharon is what Zoe and I would have called her. Having lived in our house for the last couple of days, she must be thinking it's no wonder our son ran away with me and Mike for parents. Always arguing. Years ago, we mistakenly called it "passion" but, of course, it wasn't. It was, and still is, just mutual resentment.

Like the unassuming creature she is, Sharon creeps stealthily up on me, startling me with yet another apology. 'Sorry to intrude. I was just wondering if I could get you anything. More tea perhaps?'

More fucking tea! I want to scream. Everybody seems to believe drinking it takes the pain away — it's so British of us — but of course, it doesn't. Nothing can. When we remain silent, she pulls a face as if she knows she has walked in on something she shouldn't have. Another row.

'I'll leave you to it then,' she chirps in an odd raptor-like way while wringing her hands. She appears uneasy as a result of my staring. I think I must be losing the plot when my exhausted brain takes an unexpected turn and I find myself thinking along the lines of, *She must have to keep out of the sun with that bright red hair and white skin.*

'Is there any more news?' Mike asks her bluntly.

My ears prick up at this, but I quickly lose interest when she shakes her head and unclasps her hands to steeple them in prayer. Mike and I are both transfixed by her twisty, lived-in face.

'No. I'm really sorry.' For once, she actually sounds it, which causes me to warm to her for the first time.

Mike rudely dismisses her with a sweep of his hand then and she rejoins Saunders, who is wrapping up a conversation on his phone and appears to be getting ready to leave. Mike might as well have physically shoved the woman away. Unfortunately, because of the way my husband is built, he is most polite and hospitable among those he admires and wants to impress. Sharon is not on that list. This doesn't imply he would be unkind to her, but since she's not important "in his eyes", nor beautiful and young, she doesn't really register with him. The young doctor I fell in love with all those years ago was ambitious and only hung around with the smartest, most successful and most attractive people because he believed that's what he deserved. And I went along with all of his superficial wishes because I was his wife and, for a while, I idolised him. Just as Joe had done Gabriella until she ended things with him so she could be with Mike. Did she really think she stood a chance of becoming Mike's official girlfriend? Was he meant to divorce me, his wife of eighteen years, so he could be with her? Clearly, the girl is not insane. On the contrary, she's incredibly clever. But she's also delusional. And let's not forget, young and naive.

I try not to let emotions cloud my vision, but I'm certain she had something to do with Rupert's suicide and that Joe was not acting alone. She might even be responsible for my son's disappearance, although I can't for the life of me imagine how. Nor can I talk to Mike about this because he doesn't see her the same way I do. His penis is involved and he finds her obsession with him validating. Middle-aged men's egos make them easy prey. Regardless of what he says, I have a feeling that my suspicions about her are right, so I decide to act.

I know that all of my focus should be on Joe, and it is, it really is, but what if the person in our midst — Gabriella — knows more than she's letting on? Put me in a room alone with her for ten minutes and I think I could wrestle the truth out of her. But since I'm unable to do that, I go with my second-best choice . . . It's time to hire the private investigator again to look into Gabriella's actions. He might even help us to find Joe! Mike would be furious if he found out, but he need never know. Unless he intends to see Gabriella behind my back, of course. I wouldn't put it past the man sitting next to me holding my hand. Or am I being paranoid?

But, and there's always a but, isn't there . . . if it feels as if everybody is out to get me, plotting against me, perhaps it's because they are.

CHAPTER 29: ZOE

I haven't slept a wink all night and it's now daylight. Even though the double bed where *it* happened looks very inviting with its freshly laundered duck-egg bird-print bedspread, I still can't bring myself to fall into it. I gave in to my feminine side when I redecorated this room after Chris left me, and it's meant to be my sanctuary, with its soft pinks and baby blues. It's a bedroom deserving of *Lovely Zoe*. Not Boozy Zoe. Or Liar Zoe.

On that depressing thought, my shoulders sag. There are dark rings under my eyes. My body is bruised, and no amount of concealer will cover the cut to my jaw, caused by last night's fall. As I stand in front of the tall swivel mirror and scrutinise my naked body, I feel like clawing at my flesh, because I no longer recognise myself.

Today is Monday and that means I'm meant to be back at work tomorrow but feeling as I do, I know I'm not capable of returning just yet. The black cloud hanging over me makes living an unremarkable, routine life impossible. That includes having daytime conversations with clients about various types of hair shades and nighttime chats with emotionally unavailable and narcissistic men on Tinder. Before texting my boss, Angela, to let her know I wouldn't be coming in tomorrow and not to expect me for the rest of the week, I thought about telling her I was dealing with mental health concerns. It might actually be liberating to explain what I was going through to someone else, although this hadn't been the case when I was honest with Chris about what had happened to me. Then I thought that she would have likely heard about Joe going missing by now and would assume that my anxiety was connected to my godson.

Everything is about Joe. He's always there, looming over me, no matter which way I turn. I feel him even now. His hands on the back of my neck, lingering there, as he did up the clasp of the necklace that Maddie presented me with on my birthday night out, which seems like an eternity ago.

In the end, I spun Angela the same story I did Maddie, claiming to have a virus. I was too cowardly to go down the mental health route in case it sparked rumours at the salon. Instead of getting some shut eye last night when I got back from seeing Chris, I spent hours on the internet on my tablet finding out how to order an STI test online, which was a change from swiping men's profiles on Tinder. Who knew that you could get one delivered to your house the next day for free? Although I'm menopausal, I'm still taking the contraceptive pill to help reduce the severity of my bleeding, so that's one less worry. Thank God. Imagine getting pregnant at my age by a sixteen-year-old! But I will still need to book a doctor's appointment, if I can get one, that is, because if I'm off work any longer than a week, I'll need a certificate.

When I notice the edge of a yellow plastic box poking out from under the bed, I shrug on my absurdly short, silky dressing gown and kneel on the carpet to investigate. I stopped adding to what I call "my baby box" when Chris moved out and haven't given it a thought since. Once he'd gone, scarpered, skedaddled, call it what you like, my chances of having a baby were nil. Although I've always wanted children, I secretly had doubts that I would be able to conceive given that Chris and I engaged in a lot of unprotected sex without ever experiencing a pregnancy scare. Neither he nor Maddie knew about the box. It was another of my secrets that I kept from her since I knew she would make fun of me for it. 'Tick tock, old girl,' she'd have teased, referring to my biological clock. But when I got closer to forty, she stopped making remarks like that. Like a trained sniffer dog, she could detect my impending menopause.

And she was right. It had snuck up on me like the birthday cake I didn't want, screaming "Surprise". The night sweats, day sweats, itchiness, irritability, migraines and cognitive fog that came with the onset of menopause had got its foot stuck in the door just as Chris exited it for good . . . as if to reinforce the fact that I was done as a woman. My services were no longer required, thank you very much. Would you like some vaginal dryness to go with your blood-stained attire? There were days when I was too afraid to leave the house for fear that the severe bleeding would seep through my clothes as it did that time when I boarded a train to Peterborough and ended up having to buy and then change into a whole new outfit while out shopping after having an accident.

Sliding open the lid of the box, I pull out a handful of baby bodysuits. Some have animal prints on them. Giraffes and foxes. According to the labels, everything is sized newborn to three months. Despite never having come into contact with a baby's skin, they have a baby's fragrance — soap, milk and talcum powder — how is that even possible? There's a mint-coloured soft brush and comb set in there too, and a fleecy romper suit with elephant ears on the hood.

As I let the material slide through my fingers, I hold it to my face and inhale. Tears prick at my eyes as I grieve the loss of the baby that I will never have. And the man I have lost. Not to mention the godson who betrayed me and the friend I have deceived, and who least deserves it because she loves me as a sister. As for the lying, immoral Black men . . .

Filled with a sudden rage, as if to prove that Nice Zoe no longer exists, I get up off the floor and storm into the spare room, *Joe's room*, where I smash every single bloody photo of the Blacks onto the floor. The glass splinters everywhere until I'm standing in a circle of it, blood trickling from my toes.

CHAPTER 30: MADELINE

At either end of the town bridge, there are barriers and police cars to prevent members of the public from accessing it. Although it's still early, a crowd of inquisitive bystanders has gathered and are being kept back by a row of uniformed police officers. While the TV crew pauses to conduct a technology check, I envy these everyday people, who aren't being forced to live out their worst nightmare on film. There's an elderly man with a paper folded under his arm and a beagle at the end of a lead. Two female runners are catching their breath and swigging from water bottles. When I cast a quick glance to the other end of the bridge, I see Gabriella standing with a group of her girlfriends. Although they are all wearing school uniforms, her skirt is the shortest. Even worse, her laughter is the loudest.

My heart is thundering in my chest and my palms are slick with sweat as I whirl around to confront Mike. 'Did you know she was going to be here?'

He murmurs distractedly, 'It's the least of our worries,' while fumbling with the small, almost invisible microphone that is fixed to his jacket.

We have made sure we look the part because we are being put on display for the rest of the world to judge. This wasn't pre-arranged, but Mike smiled at me in admiration when he saw me wearing kitten heels and a simple but elegant sleeveless dress. He had put on a smart jacket, tie and chinos and smelt of his usual aftershave. I didn't like to admit how nice it felt to be properly clean, with washed and straightened hair, because it felt disloyal to my son. Who knows when he last had the opportunity to wash? For all I know, he could be living in squalor on the streets.

'Two minutes and then we're good to go,' one of the film crew shouts vaguely in our direction and Mike's head snaps up.

'How do I look?' he asks nervously.

'Like the handsome doctor you are,' I reply graciously while adjusting his tie, but I'm just thinking of the cameras and onlookers as I do this. Ironically, we've been persuaded that our job is to convince everyone that we are perfect parents who are completely devastated by the disappearance of our son . . . *because that's what gets the best results.* Neither Mike nor I have to fake the second part of that well-intentioned but profoundly hurtful advice, but pretending to have the perfect marriage is something I've been doing for the last eighteen years, so I consider myself an expert.

As we get ready for the camera to start rolling, Mike's terror is apparent, and I understand at that precise moment — as only a woman can — that if our son isn't returned to us, there won't be any more alpha male. I will be left to take care of not only him but also the household and everything else because my strong leader of a husband will retreat into himself and never be the same again. Suddenly, the sense of equality and independence I've always desired in my home no longer appeals. I had hoped that he would remain resilient and be able to support me in the worst-case scenario of our son not making it home, but now I realise how mistaken I was. Women are typically child-bearers and carers for a reason. This is because we are often significantly stronger than the men in our lives. I've always known this in my heart. Men are tough out of a desire to impress each other, not us, whereas we have a deeper, more inward strength. In the absence of a civilised society, I believe women would band together and kill the men who pose a danger to our children. Rapists. Murderers. *Paedophiles.*

I unintentionally shoot Mike a critical look as I think this, but he's preoccupied with reading the prompts he's scrawled in black pen on the palm of his hand. I don't mention that the words are already etched into my brain as I watch his mouth silently move. I've always been able to remember every word I've ever read, which is why I'm unable to get Rupert's anguished charges of bullying out of my head.

'We're good to go if you are, Mr and Mrs Black?' The lead reporter wants to know. He has floppy Hugh Grant hair, is around thirty and happens to be wearing a jacket similar to Mike's but with no tie. He is the only crew member I have seen so far who is professionally dressed. The remainder of them appear to be college students, not much older than our son, with an average age of early twenty I'd say. Joe would have referred to them as "nerds" due to their messy curls, unfashionable attire, and fascination with technology. 'You can tell they're not from the BBC,' Mike had complained prudishly when we were first introduced. Yet they have all been exceptionally kind and sympathetic, which is all that matters. Besides, they're not the ones on camera. We are.

'Counting down from three.' A young woman holds up a clapperboard that has our son's name on it, along with the daunting words: *Missing Stamford teenager.* 'Three, two, one . . . action.'

Everyone falls silent as the recording commences but a look of confusion flashes across Mike's face and he stalls. White-faced and helpless, he's frozen to the spot like a rabbit trapped in a car's headlights. As I watch his desperate eyes flicker from the words on his hand to the camera, his fingers claw at the tie around his neck as if he can't breathe. He darts me an apologetic look as his eyes fill with tears. 'I'm truly sorry. I can't . . .'

While my husband's shoulders slump and he wipes his tears on the back of his sleeve, I come to his rescue, as if all

123

along I knew I would have to. This may not be a live recording but we've been warned the TV crew is on a tight schedule so there's no room for delays.

'Our son, Joe, hasn't been seen since shortly after midnight on Friday which means he has been missing for more than seventy-two hours.' I speak clearly into the microphone, my eyes landing on Gabriella in the distance whose hyena-like laughter ceased the second she heard my voice. 'We want him to know how much we love him, how much we care for him, how much we miss him, and how badly we want him to return home. So, if you are aware of Joe's whereabouts . . .' I pause to gulp in a mouthful of air and to glare accusingly at my son's ex-girlfriend, before continuing, 'Please contact the police. And, Joe—' my voice breaks a little — 'if you are listening, please get in touch with us, sweetheart. You're not in any trouble and neither of us is mad at you for taking off as you did, are we, Mike?'

I turn to face Mike and notice that he is still seemingly in a trance-like state, gazing dazedly ahead but not appearing to see anything, so I prod him with a sharp elbow.

'No, of course not. Never,' he stammers and resumes his snivelling.

Then I fix my previously shaky gaze firmly on the camera and I'm thinking only of my son as I stare into it.

'And Joe, love, if you are . . . unable to reach out or come home, for whatever reason, please don't give up. You mean more to us than anything and have always been a perfect son.' I catch myself out in a lie, remembering that I had screamed words at Mike I never imagined I would utter as we were leaving the house earlier when he was rushing me out of the door. 'He's almost an adult and a little cunt. Do you honestly believe that anyone will be out searching for him after doing some stupid appeal.'

I pause to exhale deeply and am about to remind the public that our boy is only sixteen and has never run away before when I sense a shift in the atmosphere. The lead reporter is no longer gazing in my direction or nodding encouragingly at me, instead, his focus is on DCI Saunders, who had been keeping a respectful distance up until this point. My mind goes blank as he starts to head directly for us with a set jaw and a purposeful stride. *What now?* My heart is already pounding, and I can hear my quick, shallow breaths. Panic is beginning to set in.

He pauses momentarily, looking unusually flustered, to bark instructions at a colleague and when I notice their shocked expression, I realise that something terrible has happened. Saunders seems to be taking an eternity to get to us, and as I bite down on my lip, I can taste the tang of blood in my mouth. The world appears to be moving slowly, and a high-pitched screaming sound pierces my brain.

All eyes are back on us as the detective stops in front of us, with deadened eyes, and announces, with a cough of apology, 'I'm afraid there's been a development.'

CHAPTER 31: ZOE

The flimsy bit of paper, which bears the doctor's unreadable signature makes no apologies for its "Mental health" claim. I've never missed a day of work due to illness before and I've always been really proud of that fact. Even after Chris left, I never took a "mental health day" like so many of my co-workers did when they were faced with difficulties, but I'm starting to see that self-care has never been high on my agenda and that perhaps it should have been. I've resolved to put myself first more often as a result. So, I went shopping to stock up on nutritious food following my doctor's appointment — which I managed to bag after a long wait on the phone this morning, beating off others in the queue — but I kept a low profile in case Maddie or any of her acquaintances saw me out and about. Stamford has always been a small, friendly town where everyone knows each other, but lately, it's begun to feel more like a prison. There's nowhere to hide.

Now that I'm back home, I'm sitting on the sofa with a tray in my lap, about to tuck into a plate of steamed fish, broccoli, carrots and new potatoes — to be washed down with a tall glass of chilled orange juice — when I hear something on the radio that makes me drop my knife and fork on the carpet. The room around me instantly falls away. Everything slows. Then, as if I hadn't heard correctly, I scramble to my feet, green and orange vegetables scattering everywhere, and rush into the kitchen to turn up the volume on the radio.

'*Police searching for a missing teenager have just released news that the body of a young male has been found. Reporting from the Lincolnshire town of Stamford, where the sixteen-year-old went missing from in the early hours of Saturday morning, reporter Jon England, who is at the scene, has this to say . . .*'

'Oh, my God! Joe!' I stumble unsteadily back into the living room and, after frantically searching for the remote control, manage to switch on the TV, where I am confronted with a man in a smart jacket speaking into a microphone. His name, Jon England, is captioned at the bottom of the screen, but *Breaking News* is headlined at the top in a bold red banner.

'Police were called at around 7 a.m. this morning when a local resident discovered human remains in the water.'

The reporter is standing on the edge of Stamford Meadows, and when I realise this, my palm flutters to cover my mouth as I gasp in fear. Behind him, there is a vast green space, and beyond that, lies a tantalising glimpse of the River Welland. Near the water's edge, a sizable tent has been set up, and police activity is visible. Due to the police presence, flocks of family-friendly geese and ducks have been forced to temporarily relocate, and they are protesting by quacking, honking and flapping their wings. I find it incomprehensible that the pink ice cream van is still operating in its normal location, alongside the footpath that leads to the fish and chip shop. A police helicopter whirls overhead, forcing the reporter's heartthrob hair to fall across his eyes, as crowds of excited kids and curious spectators lick their ice creams and bite the tips off their crumbly flakes.

Feeling repulsed, I turn my attention back to the reporter who is determined to give us all the grim facts. 'The body was found close to Stamford Meadows which you can see behind me, where police activity is ongoing. An under-water search team and specialist officers were called to the scene earlier today and have sadly already confirmed that they have recovered a body. No formal identification has yet been carried out and we are unable to say whether this is Joe Black at this time. This process is still ongoing due to the length of time the body was in the water. In such cases, we are told, bodies can sometimes be unrecognisable.

'Joe's parents, who took part in a televised appeal to find their son just this morning, have been informed of developments. The police say their thoughts are with them at this most difficult time and they're asking everyone to respect the family's privacy.'

A shudder rips through me and every hair on my body stands on end when he goes on to say, 'The police have tried to track the missing teen's phone in an effort to learn about his last known whereabouts, but to no avail and we can now confirm that no phone was found on the recovered body. Its last recorded location was traced to the home of his parents, and it is believed to be switched off.'

His phone. Why hadn't I thought of that? Everyone knows teenagers are obsessed with their mobile phones, and Joe is no exception. However, I didn't see him with it when he came by late that night. He obviously had other things on his mind . . . Me, for instance. I resist letting my thoughts wander back to the assault. The leering grin. The black hair on the pillow. Semen dripping down my thigh. Instead, I push those disturbing images away. Then, with a sickening thump in the chest, I realise that the police would have traced Joe here, to my house . . . if the phone had been in his pocket and switched on at the time. He must have deliberately turned it off after leaving his house knowing that his mum would try ringing him when she realised he'd left. This knowledge knocks the wind out of me because it screams of premeditation on Joe's part. I feel as if I'm becoming increasingly involved, as if I were the criminal, when all I'm doing is protecting myself and Maddie from the awful truth. I owe her that.

Head spinning from this latest revelation, I turn off the TV. I don't want to hear another thing. I wish it were as easy to switch off my thoughts. My brain is scrambled. Why hadn't Joe turned his phone back on after leaving mine that night? Assuming he had it on him, that is. Is it because he really is dead? Is the young man's body they fished from the river actually my godson's? If that is the case, I can only imagine how Maddie is feeling right now. She'll be so upset she'll be tearing her hair out. It's no good. I'll have to give her a call. If I didn't under such grave circumstances, she would be suspicious. And who could blame her? I mean, I *am* supposed to be her best friend, even though I really am the worst. She just doesn't know it. But it's not like I ever intended to—

The black hair on the pillow next to mine . . . and Joe pulling on his jeans afterwards. Could his phone have fallen out of his pocket without him knowing? On that thought, I race upstairs taking the steps two at a time before bursting into the bedroom. Once inside, I throw myself down on my knees next to the side of the bed that Joe had slept in and grapple around under it. When my hand closes around something glossy and hard my head swims with panic and I hardly dare to retrieve it. But when I do, I see that the screen is cracked and does not automatically light up, so it must either be locked or dead. *Like Joe?*

CHAPTER 32: MADELINE

Our high-end residential street is lined with news vans and reporters are knocking on neighbours' doors in the hope that someone will eventually talk to them if they try enough homes. They won't. They're not those sorts of people. And what would they say anyway? Aren't we the Blacks? The most perfect family on our tree-lined street. Don't we live in the most expensive, architecturally designed house in the row? Aren't our hanging baskets, filled to the brim with white trailing geraniums, the prettiest? Mike is a surgeon for God's sake, and I, a specialist nurse. Joe attended the top school in Stamford and was a rising star, according to his teachers, who, now that a body has been found, seem to have conveniently forgotten that he was actually close to getting expelled.

Now that everybody believes my son is dead, even though they don't directly come out and say so, they are out in their droves, teachers and classmates alike, praising Joe to the press and saying what a terrific student he was. Kind and helpful. A model pupil, in fact. In their desperate attempts to be captured on film and made famous for five minutes, they have conjured up the version of the boy I always wanted Joe to become, which means, right now, the Blacks can't do anything wrong. Including my husband, who rather than remain by my side has snuck out to see Gabriella.

He is so afraid that she will turn him in to the police that he is willing to give in to all of her demands. There has been a morbid flurry of excitement in the air since the police discovered the body in the water. And Gabriella, like everyone else, has decided it is Joe. Having a friend who has died seems to carry more prestige than one who is simply missing. Numerous classmates have emerged claiming to be Joe's closest friend when in reality nothing could be further from the truth. Joe had no friends, remember? For these young people, who crave only status, it is a circus. I start to question why any of us parents spend £30,000 a year to educate our celebrity-obsessed children, who couldn't give a fig about learning Latin.

Mike claims Gabriella is utterly distraught and has no one else to turn to, but him, which is why he's with her and not me. She says she is afraid of breaking down again in front of her parents in case she should let something slip about her relationship with Mike. As I've said all along, she is a manipulative little bitch. It surprises me that I am still rigid with righteous anger — towards Gabriella and every other pupil at that school, teachers included, who had previously snubbed my son. But no matter what everyone else thinks, I won't accept that Joe is dead or that the body they pulled from the water is his until they let me see it for myself. For now, anger is keeping both of us alive.

There is no Zoe, either, to comfort me. While she sounded compassionate and said all the right things when she called to express her shock at the news, there was an awkwardness — no, a distance — between us that I have never felt before. I didn't ask her to come over to the house to support me, and neither did she offer. I do have some pride. After everything I've done for her, her attitude is astonishing. I'm beginning to doubt her excuses. No one can be that ill without being hospitalised. I should know. I am a nurse. So, what actually is going on with her?

Sharon can be heard moving about downstairs in her ugly brown leather shoes that are now at home in my contemporary, designer kitchen. DCI Saunders left a short while ago, a few minutes before Mike as it happens, promising to return as soon as he had any new information for us. Mike and I just stood there looking at him with wide eyes since we knew what that meant. He was talking about positively identifying the body.

When Sharon offered to make yet more tea, I ignored her and went upstairs to run a bath. I could think of nothing else to do but that. The only other choice was to sob uncontrollably while rolling around on the floor. Somewhat bizarrely, I think I thought I would feel closer to my son if I was immersed in water. Now that I'm in it, I know it was the right choice. The lavender-scented water is soothing. The large white freestanding clawfoot bath takes time to fill but it's worth it when you do. Just like every other room in this house, the ensuite bathroom is everyone's dream. Cool white marble sinks, bachelor-black fine oak cabinetry and mood lighting make it a luxurious and tranquil space.

I close my eyes and think about Sharon downstairs as I recline against the rolltop bath, where my twitching toes poke out of the soapy water at the other end. I now understand how neglectful I have been in not asking her if she has children. Her presence here seems to irritate Mike more than it does me as I'm learning to appreciate the things she quietly does for us, and it brings me comfort when I see her eyes widen in concern whenever Mike yells at me or speaks to me in a patronising manner.

Mike can bully her in a way he can't Saunders. Despite his gentle demeanour, the detective's personality type is made up of blue and green which means he focuses on logic and detail. He's not a yellow (visionary) like Mike or a red (emotional) like me. Not that any of it matters. But it's useful to know. I'm a bit of an expert on the subject since it fascinates me.

When Saunders pulled us to one side during the film recording, to tell us they'd found a body, but couldn't allow us to identify it until more tests were carried out, I found myself pleading, 'Do you think it is Joe?'

His expressive eyes had caught my attention at the time, and I had a sneaking suspicion that he intended to withhold something, but he must have sensed my desire for the truth — and nothing but the truth — because that is what he gave us.

'I think it's extremely likely,' he confirmed, with gravel in his tone.

Mike instinctively reached out for my hand on hearing this, but I snatched it away and refused to look at him, even though he whimpered my name. Saunders noticed, of course. He must think me a cold, heartless bitch for not consoling my husband, and perhaps that is what I am.

CHAPTER 33: ZOE

Since I didn't know what to do with Joe's phone, I slipped it into my bedside drawer and tried to forget about it, but I kept going back to it and holding it in my hand. Just looking at it. I dared not try to switch it on or charge it in case the police were still tracking it, otherwise, it could lead them straight here. But I'm interested to learn what secrets it conceals. Messages from Gabriella. Information about the source of the Rohypnol. Hundreds of missed calls from Maddie. Blunt texts from Mike telling him to return home. *Now, or else.* The odd funny meme from me.

Even though he's just sixteen, he's in serious trouble. There was the alleged assault on the teacher earlier this year that admittedly came to nothing and the last I heard he was on the verge of being expelled from school for his disruptive behaviour. He must have fallen into a spiral of loathing for women, especially after Gabriella abruptly broke up with him. *I wonder if he hurt her too and that's why she called things off.* As of right now, if you can believe what everyone's saying, he is presumed dead. They still haven't identified the body though, which leads me to suspect that whatever is left of him, *if it is Joe*, isn't pretty. Poor Maddie.

In my head, I alternate between hating Joe and remembering him as a boy and realising that I can't entirely suppress my feelings for him. If that's how I feel about him, I can only imagine how Maddie must be feeling as his mother. Knowing that it's extremely unlikely my friend will be out and about this afternoon, I've decided to get some fresh air. Being confined to my small house is making me stir-crazy. Even if I were to bump into Angela or any of the girls from the salon, I can just make out I'm picking up a prescription. One glance at my sunken cheekbones and hooded eyes should be enough to convince anyone that my illness is genuine.

I try not to look across at the police tent, which still hasn't been taken down, as I pass through Stamford Meadows. Even though the body has been removed from the river, a few sick, twisted individuals are snapping pictures of the scene. One man even has two small children with him. What the hell? It's a gorgeous day, but I can't bring myself to enjoy the brilliant yellow sun and flawless blue sky. Not when so many important people in my life are absent. Chris. Maddie. Mike. Joe too. Up ahead, I spy a group of young men who I recognise. They are the ones Joe used to hang out with. One of them visited my house once looking for Joe. I believe his name is Baz. It worries me that they know where I live.

I can't decide if I'm incredibly brave or incredibly stupid approaching them. They are known for being thugs but also have access to drugs and who knows what else. However, I won't let their watchful, suspicious eyes and ready-for-a-fight shoulders stop me. Even if I am only five feet and four inches tall.

'It's Baz, isn't it?' I enquire in a friendly manner, trying to hide my anxiety.

'What of it?'

I can't lie. I actually wince when he blows a mouthful of cigarette smoke in my direction. In addition to being a threatening gesture, the stench makes me feel sick to my stomach. Then I remember that I haven't touched my vape pod in days, and that I haven't had any cravings to do so.

'You came to my house once, looking for Joe.'

When I mention my godson's name, their demeanour immediately changes. The other two lads suddenly appear way more interested, while Baz relaxes and stops looking down his nose at me.

'I remember you now. You're his aunt or something, aren't you?'

'His godmother actually,' I correct him even though it isn't strictly necessary, but I don't want people to assume Joe and I are related. *Not now. Not ever.*

Baz shuffles awkwardly while looking down at his trainers. 'Sorry for your loss.'

'We still don't know if it *is* him.' I sigh, thinking that everyone is so quick to think the worst.

At that, Baz throws me a wary side glance, as if he believes I'm in denial.

'He was alright, Joe. For a posh kid, that is,' he observes.

'Thanks. I don't suppose you saw him after he was reported missing. His parents have been so worried.'

'Nah. We already told the police that.'

'Oh, I see.'

'We last saw him about a week ago.'

I hesitate and consider whether it would be wise of me to ask the following question, but decide I'm going to anyway. 'I don't suppose you sold him anything, did you?'

Baz frowns and quickly glances at the other two boys, as though to caution them not to say anything. 'What do you mean by *anything*?'

'He was acting strangely the last time I saw him,' I venture, worrying if I am saying too much. But if the police somehow find out what I have just said, I can make out that this occurred weeks ago. Besides, I seriously doubt that these youngsters would volunteer information to the police.

The third boy sniggers. 'That's Joe for you.'

Baz looks offended. 'We wouldn't have "sold" him something that might have harmed him, if that's what you're getting at.'

'No, I'm sure you wouldn't. But, well . . . I know he sometimes smoked weed and I wondered if—'

'He took anything stronger?' Baz completes my sentence for me, burrowing his frow as though deeply contemplating something. 'It's possible,' he concedes, 'but not from us. He was still just a kid.'

When I realise I've reached a dead end, I desperately search for something else to say and am about to come out with something lame, when—

'I know Joe used to do odd jobs for you around the house sometimes, building flatpack furniture or putting up shelves, so if you need any help at all, just let us know and we'll come over and take care of it for you.'

'That's very kind of you,' I exclaim, genuinely surprised. 'But I'm not sure I can afford to pay you.'

'We wouldn't want paying for it,' Baz insists, tugging at his baseball cap and squinting at the sun. 'It would be our way of honouring Joe.'

'I may take you up on that offer.' I laugh, while at the same time, I find myself blinking away tears. I'm moved by the compassion of the lads who I formerly considered "undesirables". As I walk away from them, I think to myself that you never really know people. That thought leads me back to Gabriella and I decide right then and there that I must meet with her to learn the truth about what really transpired between her and Joe.

CHAPTER 34: MADELINE

As soon as I heard the doorbell, I knew it was bad news. It sounded more insistent than usual, DCI Saunders had pressed his finger against the buzzer for a longer period. I then overheard him and Sharon speaking in low voices in the hall. Everything in this house echoes, even the smallest sound. A cough. A dropped pen. A swear word muttered under one's breath. Then came the official-sounding footsteps on the tiled floor.

I was lying on the bed at the time, my eyes fixed on the ceiling, thinking about my husband. It was almost five o'clock in the afternoon and he still hadn't returned. He had been gone for hours. He couldn't still be "comforting" Gabriella, surely? Now I was going to have to deal with Saunders alone. *Where the fuck are you, Mike?*

I had wrapped myself in my white bathrobe after taking my bath as I couldn't be bothered to get dressed again. It was too much effort. My long black hair is fanned out on the pillow around me and the scent of the lavender water is still on my skin. I wait for my name to be called before getting up from the bed, dragging my slippered feet downstairs.

As Saunders watches me trudge down the steps, I acknowledge him with a brief nod. 'Detective Saunders.'

'I understand Mike isn't here.' His voice sounds different somehow. More urgent with threads of apprehension wound through it. Or is it just me?

'That's correct.' I gulp nervously, not liking the fact that he won't look me in the eye. But as I turn to look at Sharon, I see that she is acting exactly the same way.

'Joe?' I gasp and put a palm to my heart.

'I think we ought to do this sitting down,' Sharon asserts, taking control of the situation and my elbow, as she leads me through to the living room and seats me on the large white sofa, which seems to envelop me in the only hug I'm going to get, given my husband's absence.

'Is it him? The body?' I ask shakily, as Sharon and Saunders take a seat across from me.

Saunders reluctantly acknowledges, 'We believe so, yes.'

'What do you mean, you believe so?' I explode. 'It's either him or it isn't!'

'I think perhaps we should wait for Mike before I say anything else.' Saunders slaps his thigh as if coming to a sudden decision.

'And I think perhaps that you should continue,' I manage coldly between clenched teeth. Don't ask me why I am so angry. I just bloody well am.

Saunders holds my steely glare for a few seconds before nodding slowly in agreement. His hypnotic eyes, so soft and sympathetic, will be my downfall if I continue staring into them, so I fix my gaze instead on Sharon's ugly brown shoes.

'The pathologist has determined that the body went into the water about three days ago which ties in with when Joe went missing.'

'That doesn't necessarily mean it *is* Joe. It could be anyone,' I argue.

'According to an examination of the pelvis and rib bones, the body was that of a young male, between the ages of sixteen and seventeen.'

'Oh, God,' I moan, my body curling forward in grief as I cover my face with my hands. 'Not Joe. Please. Not my boy.' Sharon settles down next to me and I lean into her as she wraps a soothing arm around me.

'I'm so sorry, Mrs . . .' Saunders hesitates before uttering my name for the first time, 'Madeline, but I'm afraid your son drowned.'

His words make my heart flip over, and in an instant, I'm out of Sharon's arms and pacing up and down the room while tearing at my hair. 'No. I don't believe it. I can't. My son isn't dead. I don't feel it in here.' I hurt myself by striking my chest too hard with a clenched fist.

'We checked his dental records and they were also a match,' Saunders explains in a voice that is intended to persuade me otherwise.

I turn to scowl at the detective, and when I declare, 'You'd better take me to see him then,' he recoils and bends his head. I go on, unstoppable in my rage. 'Until I see my son's body for myself, I refuse to believe it.'

As I observe them exchanging pitying glances, I have a gut feeling that he hasn't finished telling me everything. 'What?' I bark. 'I have a right to be able to identify my son's body, don't I?'

As Sharon says, 'In these circumstances, we don't advise it,' her lips are pursed in pity.

'Why not?' I demand angrily.

'He had been in the water for three whole days, which means—' Sharon steals another furtive look at Saunders as if asking for permission to continue — 'there is very little left to identify, and what is left isn't recognisable due to the bloating.'

'You're telling me that I wouldn't know my own son?' I bristle, rejecting what she is saying, but at the same time, an image of my son's bloated body floating face down in the water sears into my brain like daggers. 'What mother wouldn't know her son?' I swivel my ferocious gaze back on Sharon as if she were to blame for everything, yet Saunders was the one who ripped out my heart with his comments. Not her. That doesn't stop me from attacking her though.

'You think I'm a bad parent, don't you? And that's why my son ran away?' I stab a finger near her face and I'm about to unfairly lash out at her for judging me when I notice that they are both now staring at the door instead of me. As I follow their gaze, my attention shifts to Mike, who must have just entered the room.

Tears sting my eyes, blurring my vision as I take in his astonished expression. He has slouched his shoulders and is staring fearfully into the room. Realising that he must have heard everything causes my heart to halt. As I stumble unsteadily towards him, fresh anger surges inside me, forcing my hands into fists and my mouth into a snarl.

'You.' The disgusted sound in my throat does not match how angry I feel. 'This is all your fault. *You* did this.' I charge towards him like an enraged bull, screaming, crying and shaking all at once. 'Where the fuck were you? How could you leave me alone to deal with this?'

I'm in his face, tearing at his skin with my nails and drawing blood. I then slap him in the face since I'm still not satisfied. Not once. But three times, no, four. Saunders has edged closer, as if about to intervene, but Mike dismisses him with a curt headshake. Remaining stubbornly mute with his jaw flexed, as if encouraging me to hit him harder, Mike does not try to stop me, nor yet hold up a hand to defend himself. He takes it on the chin as if he deserves it. And he does. He bloody well does. Because my world has come crashing down and it's all his fault.

Suddenly I'm in his tight grasp — unable to move with my arms fixed to my sides — and he's whispering in my ear, hoarsely repeating the same words over and over again. 'I know. I know. I know.'

And then somehow, we end up on the floor together, kneeling. I'm not sure if he pulled me down or if it was the other way around, or if we just scraped the ground together as we fell, but I find myself being crushed in his arms and crying into his shoulder.

Mike's voice is thick with anguish and I can feel his tears on my cheek as he buries his face in my hair. 'Our son is dead, Madeline. Joe's gone.'

His words are like a weight around my heart.

CHAPTER 35: ZOE

Rutland Terrace, with its handsome display of regal archi-tecture is one of the most iconic streets in Stamford. The Grade II listed, four-storey townhouses offer far-reach-ing views across undulating meadows as well as the town's famous roofline. I feel out of place in my fashionably ripped denim shorts, flip-flops, and white T-shirt. Maybe a chiffon dress and kitten heels would have been more appropriate. Since I've only been to Gabriella's parents' house once, when Maddie and I dropped Joe off one day in Maddie's car, I hope I can remember which one it is. It would be an under-statement to say that I was astonished to learn that his always-in-black, anorexic-looking, self-styled gothic girlfriend came from such opulent surroundings. Her family must be even wealthier than the Blacks.

When I take my phone out of my cheap, faux-leather cross-body bag to see if there have been any further develop-ments regarding Joe, I'm not sure whether to feel concerned or relieved when I see there are no updates. It's getting on for five o'clock as I try to figure out which house Gabriella lives in. Honestly, I have no idea where the day has gone. Everything in my life right now, including daylight hours apparently, is a blur. At that moment, I see a man hurriedly leaving a residence with a stone-blue door and wrought-iron fencing. It stands out from its neighbours as it has a full-length balcony that spans the whole of the first floor and elegant black window shutters. I'm about to cross the street and head towards it after deciding that this is definitely the right house when something stops me. Is that Mike? If so, he is acting strangely, pulling at the buttons on his shirt and agitatedly running a hand through his ruffled hair in an attempt to tame it. Why would he be at Gabriella's and not at home with Maddie?

Even though I know it can't be him, I hide anyway — ducking out of sight behind a neighbour's front wall. If it *is* my best friend's husband and he does see me, he's bound to tell Maddie and she would then realise that I have been lying about being ill all along. The consequences of that fallout don't bear thinking about. Peering through the neighbour's sculptured box hedge, I watch the man getting into a gleaming black Porsche parked further down the street and then I know for sure it is Mike.

I'd know that car anywhere. Similar to how I would recognise the hunch of Mike's masculine shoulders amid a group of other men. It saddens me that he looks so distressed and worn out, but I suppose that's natural given what he and Maddie are going through. Once more, guilt consumes me for avoiding my friends when they need my support. I wish I could reach out to Mike and help him, but that's just not possible at the moment, thanks to his son who looks just like him. As I watch Mike driving away, I can't get over how wrong it feels that he's visiting Gabriella when the whole of Stamford is speculating about his son being dead. I know she was Joe's girlfriend but they broke up before he went missing . . . If people sometimes think Maddie is aloof, then Gabriella is something else entirely.

As I walk up the path to her house, admiring its pretty courtyard garden and beautiful arched sash windows, I feel a tremor of anxiety run through me. Will Gabriella continue to treat me with the same contempt she displayed when we first met? I could tell that she took an instant dislike to me and the feeling was mutual. At the time, I'd put this down to jealousy on her part, due to my close relationship with Joe. But looking back, I'm not sure if it went deeper than that. She might have known or guessed that his interest in me went beyond the fact that I was his favourite self-styled aunt.

The old-fashioned call to arms of the cast-iron butler-style doorbell on the wall is drowned out by loud, seductive laughter as I pull on it.

'You just can't stay away, can you?' A flirtatious female voice can be heard coming from behind the broad front door.

I'm not sure who is more shocked as it swings open to reveal Gabriella wearing a knotted, bandeau-style bikini. Clearly, I'm not who she was expecting to see on her doorstep.

This prompts me to ask, 'Was that Mike I just saw leaving?'

She folds her arms and glares at me as if to say, What do you want, bitch? before asking, 'Who?'

'Mike Black. Joe's dad.'

'Who wants to know?' Her tongue catches in the corner of her mouth as she speaks, and her cheek swells. It appears to be an "up yours" gesture.

'I'm Joe's godmother. We met once before.'

She rolls her eyes and shrugs as if it doesn't matter to her who I am. The attitude of these overprivileged, entitled, privately educated school kids infuriates me, so I move closer to her and invade her personal space. She then retreats and begins fiddling with her bikini bottoms.

I enquire coldly, 'Can I come in?'

I watch her eyes flicker nervously up the street as if she is hoping Mike will return. She then throws me another "see if I care" shrug before walking away and leaving the door invitingly ajar, so I decide to follow her.

The beautiful Olde English geometric tiled floor and abundance of natural light seems to beckon me inside. There are a plethora of original features. High ceilings. French doors. A staircase with a spindle bannister. Ceiling roses and picture rails. Stone steps lead down to what I imagine is a wine cellar. Even though I'm in awe of the sheer elegance of this house, I'm aware that something is going on here that I don't yet understand.

'Are your parents in?' I try not to stare at her impossibly pert bum cheeks as we pass through a pale green and gold library with floor-to-ceiling bookcases. There is a sheen to her skin that suggests she might have been sunbathing when I rang the doorbell but her skin is as white as milk. What else would have made her break into such a sweat?

'They're never in. Always working,' she quips over her pointy shoulder, just as we arrive in the back courtyard garden, which is enclosed by a high wall of vibrant climbing roses. The scent of apples, violets, clover and lemons associated with these flowers is overwhelming.

My eyes are drawn to two tall, ice-filled glasses of unfinished drinks on the patio table. As she settles into one of two matching rattan sun loungers that are parked very close together, she sees me eying the drinks and frowns, claiming, 'Mum doesn't care about me drinking underage.'

I lift one eyebrow. 'Oh, what else doesn't she care about?' I'm deliberately sarcastic for two reasons. First of all, I genuinely don't like her. And two, I'm feeling territorial about the Blacks. I can't help wondering if Maddie disliked her. If that were the case, she never said so, but she wouldn't have admitted that while she was still Joe's girlfriend.

The term "little bitch" springs to mind and anger churns inside me as I realise that Gabriella smells of rum, cigarettes and . . . Mike's aftershave.

CHAPTER 36: MADELINE

'It's not that I want to sleep with other people, but it's hard to approach my wife for sex when she flinches at my very touch.'

'Maybe if you tried harder to seduce me the way I want to be seduced, I wouldn't flinch every time you came near me,' I snarl, determined to wound him as much as he's wounded me.

His voice is cloaked in shock. 'Oh, we're back on that subject again, are we? On what a terrible lover I am?'

'If the glove fits, Mike.' Spittle sprays from my mouth as I scream this. We are nose to nose in combat, but when Mike notices I am visibly trembling, he reins himself back. As soon as there is a distance between us, I slip on my brand-new dress but my fingers are shaking too much to do the zip up. Normally, my husband would step in to assist, but all it takes is one stern warning glance from me to deter him from doing so.

He murmurs softly, not meeting my gaze, 'I can't believe you hired that private investigator again, to spy on me.'

'Actually, he was employed to keep an eye on Gabriella.'

'What on earth for?' Mike argues while fastening his tie and turning to stare at his reflection in the mirrored dressing-room wardrobes.

'Don't give me "what on earth for?"!' I glower ferociously at him. 'Blackmail, to start with. Not to mention the fact that she was screwing both my son and my husband. One of whom is now dead.'

'The decision to go around there was a mistake. I see that now.'

'Mike, you were gone for three hours on the second most important day of my life. The first being the day our son was born and the second the day we lost him.'

'I found it difficult to refuse her. Besides, we agreed that I should keep her sweet for a while because she was threatening to tell her parents about us having sex.'

'You bastard, that didn't give you permission to screw her all over again! You swore on Joe's life that you were only there for a short time before heading down to the river to reflect on all that had happened. You said you needed time to think!'

'I know. I know.' Mike tears at his hair before sinking onto the bed.

I stifle a groan. 'How could you, Mike? How could you?'

'What you've got to realise, Madeline, is that this happened several weeks ago and I wasn't in a good place at the time.'

'You weren't in a good place?' I rage indignantly.

'All right, that was a poor choice of words,' he stutters. 'But you have to concede that Joe's death has affected us equally and that we're both in need of comfort.'

Heat travels up my neck when I hear him say this, *how fucking dare he*, but I resolve not to retaliate. Instead, I grind out through clenched teeth, 'It's not a competition to see whose heart is broken the most.'

Mike bristles with frustration. 'I know that, Madeline, and I've told you it won't happen again. I have given you my word this time that I'm done with her.'

'That's what you said last time,' I point out petulantly while slipping on my most comfortable pair of heels. They're going to be necessary as I'll be on my feet all day.

Then, I turn my attention back to my lying, cheating scumbag of a husband and pick at the scab once more by yelling, 'You having sex with Gabriella one more time might have happened weeks ago, on the day our son died, I might add, but I only found out about it this morning.'

'Talk about poor timing. Didn't it occur to this knob-head investigator of yours what today meant to us?' Mike stomps all over my argument.

'It's not his job to take care of me, Mike. It's yours,' I snip, attaching a pair of ladybird earrings that Joe bought for me when he was six.

'I find it inconceivable that we're fighting over a girl who means nothing to me on the day of our son's funeral,' Mike says with a sudden catch in his voice.

Even though my heart is still thundering in my chest and my breathing is rapid and uneven, I can feel my heart warming to him . . . as a human being, that is, not as a husband. After all, he has lost a son too. I look across at him and see that the lines around his face have deepened.

'I can still be a good husband to you, Madeline,' he begs. 'Please don't write me off just yet.'

'We'll see,' I tut, sliding a chunky bracelet over my wrist. Again, Joe gave this to me one Christmas before he started going off the rails.

When I notice that Mike is sobbing into his hands, dismay lodges in my chest. I move to sit next to him on the bed but I don't touch him since he isn't to be trusted. Once more, he has spun me a web of lies and what I discovered has scalded me. He has permanently destroyed any illusions about our marriage, and I can't stop my mouth from twisting into an unpleasant scowl. I decide then and there that I will file for divorce once all this is over. But this is not the appropriate time to share that news with my husband.

A beat of silence hangs between us and Mike is the first to break it, suddenly exclaiming, 'Even though they're calling it death by suicide, I'll never believe it.'

'Me neither,' I reply, feeling like I'm gasping for air and drowning. Just as my son had done. I felt alive for the first time in weeks when I discovered that Mike had lied to me about the Gabriella situation, but the sudden surge of emotion has left me feeling light-headed, making my heart race.

Our shared belief that whatever happened to Joe wasn't suicide is the one thing we are united on. It's the only thing we have left. We both agree that Joe had too high an opinion of himself to risk his life.

The coroner determined during the inquest that Joe had intentionally drowned himself as a result of depression and mental anxiety. A distraught Gabriella had attended the court that day, and the coroner made a point of avoiding placing any blame on her by not implying that their break-up had likely been the tipping point. That had me so enraged I wanted to punch him. That rage is still present.

'He was alive when he went into the water,' I respond numbly. 'There were drugs in his system. I think we both know what that means.'

'The obvious solution is that he accidentally fell in, but I take it you suspect foul play?' Mike furrows his brow while nodding in agreement. I let him put his hand over mine and wrap his fingers around it since he's on my side. Then, I raise my eyes to meet his so he can see for himself how the pain of losing my only son has reached into the core of my being.

'Somebody wanted to hurt our boy, Mike.' I blink away tears, referring to the idea that first blossomed in my mind the day Joe went missing.

'Who?' He racks his brain. 'Why would anyone want to hurt him?'

'We both know he wasn't liked and that he could be a cunt at times.'

In a rare show of solidarity, Mike squeezes my hand despite blinking in surprise at my unfeminine choice of words. *Fuck him, I say.* When I cast my mind back to the night my son didn't come home, tears sting at my eyes, blurring my vision. I keep replaying in my head the image of his bloated, unrecognisable body lying face down in the water.

As I grind out, 'Joe's death was no accident,' rage fuels my voice. 'Someone pushed him into the water that night and I won't rest until I find out who it was, so I can do the same to them.'

CHAPTER 37: ZOE

I look around the church as it fills with mourners who have all been instructed to wear something blue (for a boy), but Mike and Maddie are nowhere to be found. I imagine they are in a shiny black hearse following the flower-laden coffin as it takes them on a tour of Joe's short life, starting with the house on Water Street where he lived for sixteen years. His lived experiences will revolve around the schools he went to and the parks he used to play in. There certainly won't be any references to the drug dealers he used to hang out with or the allegations of bullying or sexual assault at today's service. Mike will ensure those accusations are buried alongside his son. I'm relieved I'm not sitting in the back of the hearse between them, having to listen to Maddie crying and Mike clicking his tongue in annoyance. The only other person who was close to Joe is also present in church.

Gabriella. When we came across each other in the lengthy queue of schoolchildren and teachers waiting to be admitted into the church, we gave each other the side-eye, but neither of us acknowledged the other. We're now officially enemies. On the day of my visit to her house, I hadn't been able to wring anything out of her. She was shrewd, that one, and she masterfully sidestepped all of my questions about Mike and

Joe. 'Why do you care?' she enquired lazily, until I gave in and stopped talking. She had a certain all-knowing quality that was off-putting. If she is this clever and manipulative at fifteen, imagine what she'd be like as a grown woman. Her eyes were mysterious black pools. One minute she was scathing. The next she was laughing. When I pressed her for the truth about what Mike was doing there and afterwards, about her break-up with Joe, she gave off the sense that she was indestructible. It's difficult for me to acknowledge as an adult that I was intimidated by a child, but that's how I felt at the time.

My cheeks burn, even now, when I think back on how she looked at me when she caught me glancing at her youthful, perfect body . . . imagining Joe's and then Mike's hands on it. 'Do you like what you see?' she'd asked.

'That's disgusting. Why would you say that?' I demanded, feeling queasy inside, and wishing that I'd never set foot in her fancy house.

'Oh, I heard you were the adventurous type.' She'd chuckled and stretched seductively as if trying to tempt me into making a pass at her. I had never before come across a teenage Lolita and found myself pitying Joe for being associated with her. Not so Mike, who was a grown man and must have known what he was getting himself into. The knob.

'Gabriella, what do you know?' I'd begged her because I believed she knew something about Joe.

He might have confided in her about his attraction for me, but she just stared at me and said, 'You know, for his godmother, you don't seem that bothered Joe is dead,' with a teasing smirk.

My parting remark was, 'That's a terrible thing to say,' as I stormed out in tears, her obscene laughter following me to the gate. But as soon as I was out of that affluent, yet suffocating house, I found myself asking myself the same thing. Was Joe's passing really such a loss? And will his parents be the only ones who truly miss him?

Since finding out about Joe's death two weeks ago, when I received a terse, perfunctory call from Mike confirming that it *was* Joe's body that had been pulled out of the River Welland, I haven't communicated with Maddie in person, except to send flowers and a heartfelt sympathy card and to send and receive the odd impersonal text message. Mike continued by saying that his son's remains had been positively identified and that everyone could now stop speculating about what had happened. I was at a loss for words and could only express how deeply sorry I was and how tragic Joe's untimely death was. Mike appeared to soften a little at that, but when I enquired about Maddie, he coughed down the phone before saying that she was too distraught to talk to anyone. Even me, it appeared. Although my heart was torn in half for Maddie, this suited me perfectly.

As I pull my attention away from Gabriella, who is surrounded by a group of school friends who are all dressed in uniform, I see a change in the crowd's attitude as they crane their necks and cast glances behind them towards the back of the church. Before I see Maddie and Mike, I catch a glimpse of the steel coffin with the gleaming monarch-blue finish and my heart lunges in my chest. Joe! The congregation stands, and our gazes shift away from the coffin and towards the cherubic choir boy in a blue and white robe who has emerged at the front of the church to sing "*Ave Maria*". He has an angelic voice and many people are already in tears as Joe's coffin is carried forward by six very young, very tall rugby-playing schoolboys.

The location of All Saints Church is ideal for a lavish spectacle like this. Mike would never have allowed his son to be buried without planning an extravagant memorial service, even though it wasn't something Joe would necessarily have wanted. News crews wait outside the oldest church in Stamford which dates back to the fifteenth century, to film the coffin being transported to the cemetery on Radcliffe Road, which will serve as Joe's ultimate resting place. Even the tree-lined, stone-walled cemetery is in a prime location! The mahogany pews, worn smooth with time, are full inside the church. Those standing cast eerie black shadows on the stone walls behind them. Everywhere is a sea of blue. The majority of those present, have, like me, chosen to wear a small blue ribbon, but some have gone all out and are donning all-blue attire as if it were a football match.

The casket stops directly beside me, and I glance up fearfully to see Maddie staring down at me, which sends me into a panic. I give her a timid smile, but she acts as if she doesn't recognise me. A wave of relief washes over me as the coffin passes by, with Mike and Maddie plodding depressingly after it, but not before I take in the smell of Mike's unmistakable aftershave. I'm familiar with Louis Vuitton's Imagination because, at Maddie's suggestion, I always give Mike a bottle for Christmas. Acid curdles my stomach when I recall that it was the same odour that clung to Gabriella's body that day.

I have an overwhelming urge to get up and walk out then. But if I did that, I'd never be forgiven. I hadn't wanted to come. Taking part in a service celebrating Joe's life felt wrong on every level. How am I supposed to mourn him when I hate him? And how am I ever going to face his parents again knowing what I know about their son? I had considered using my continued illness as an excuse to get out of attending today, but Maddie was insistent that I come, even though she agreed I could sit at the back as I didn't want them to catch my virus. The fact that I used the same lie to avoid going to the internment and wake did not sit well with the Blacks.

I observe Maddie's movements as she follows the coffin carrying her son and notice that she is wearing a midnight-blue fascinator with bow detailing. It must have been purchased especially for Joe's funeral. This, together with her royal blue flared, nipped-in-at-the-waist crepe dress makes her look like a celebrity in a magazine. As Mike leads his wife to their seats at the front of the church, he places his hand where it usually rests: on the small of her back. I have to avert my eyes from the sight of it resting there because it stirs up memories in me that I'd prefer to forget. I look around for Gabriella then, and for once, she is caught off guard judging by the look of envy on her face. I'm surprised Maddie can't feel the jealousy coming off the girl's eyes as they bore into her back.

I then get the feeling like someone is also secretly watching me and I turn in my seat and inspect the people closest to me. That's when I notice Chris. He's seated two rows to my right. He was never a fan of the Blacks so I suspect he is here out of respect for me rather than them. He thought they were shallow and materialistic, but he did acknowledge that Maddie was "okay when she was okay if you know what I mean". I never pressed him for an explanation of what he meant by that as he could never understand what I saw in them. Thankfully, he hasn't brought *his* Vicky with him. That would have been too cruel. He greets me with the same faraway smile I had used to greet my best friend only minutes earlier, and I immediately grasp how hurtful it is. I respond in the same manner, quickly averting my eyes before he does. It's over, I remind myself once more. It was over a long time ago. The instant I betrayed him and everyone else, we were done.

Now that Joe's dead, I could rekindle my friendship with the Blacks without having to come clean about what had happened. But I'm unable to. It's not as if I haven't kept secrets from my best friend before, but I'm afraid I wouldn't be able to keep Joe's attack a secret from her indefinitely. And what bereaved mother wants to hear that about their son? This doesn't stop me wishing I could explain *why* I'm having to distance myself though, and that it's for her own good. My behaviour must be making Maddie suspicious, but she mustn't ever find out the full story.

Out of nowhere, I find myself entranced by Maddie's intense gaze. Even though she is inconsolable with grief, she still has the energy to look for me, her former best friend, among the congregation. Her cognac-coloured eyes appear out of focus as if she'd been administered a sedative to get her through today, yet there is still a deep burning question in her gaze. It's awful to see the expression of betrayal and confusion on her face. I don't blame her for looking at me this way. Who could?

CHAPTER 38: MADELINE

Now that Joe is dead, I'm free to love him in a way I could not when he was alive. Finally, he is perfect. The son I always wanted. These are not the thoughts I anticipated having on the day of my son's funeral, but no one imagines having to bury their only child at sixteen. Nobody deserves to die at that age. Whatever crimes Joe may or may not have committed, he was my son and I loved him. It's not that I was blind to his shortcomings — chance would be a fine thing — but Mike has accused me of being one of those insane parents who would visit their serial-killer child in jail and claim to still love them no matter what, although privately I believe that's what all mothers would do for their sons. He can talk, though. He's the one who wouldn't acknowledge our son had severe behavioural problems and refuses to listen even now when I tell him Gabriella isn't who he thinks she is. I suspect her of being a manipulative bitch who brought out the worst in Joe. Making him do the things he did. Like mercilessly bullying another pupil. Lashing out at me and God knows what else.

Zoe also loved Joe once, but she appears to have suddenly changed her mind. Not only about Joe, but also Mike and me. It's as if she's unable to stand being around us any longer even though we have done nothing wrong. On the contrary, we have been the best of friends to her, and in return, she has repaid us by abandoning us when we needed her the most. This is something that can no longer be overlooked or forgiven. It has gone on for too long. I don't listen to the excuses Zoe makes anymore, like the supposed virus she claims has left her fatigued and wiped out. Whatever she is experiencing, it is not a physical illness. She could be having a nervous breakdown for all I know but is too embarrassed to talk about it. I wouldn't be the least bit surprised. I've anticipated it this last year or so, what with Chris leaving her and her ongoing struggle with alcoholism, which she thinks I don't know about. I'm a nurse, though. I'm not fooled by her.

With so much on my mind, it's hardly surprising that I don't pay full attention to the songs and prayers that form part of the service. But my ears do prick up whenever I hear my son's name. People are taking turns standing up and expressing what an exceptional human being Joe was, and everywhere I turn, there is a whirl of different faces. Their lies cut through me like shards of glass. *In reality, nobody liked my son.* Mike must have arranged this spectacle in secret because I knew nothing about it.

Then, it's my husband's turn to stand at the pulpit, so he can recite a eulogy for our son that he has been rehearsing for days. I don't know how he can bring himself to be up there in front of all these strangers. I vastly underestimated him when I presumed that he would withdraw into himself in the event of our son dying. He has rallied, and apart from the Gabriella incident, has been supportive. His resilience will be severely tested though when he reads out the mostly made up material about our son — Joe's prowess at competitive sports (he hated physical activity) or his desire to follow in his father's footsteps and become a doctor (nothing could be further than the truth). Mike's hands are shaking as they settle around the microphone and his eyes sparkle with unshed tears, but he ends up doing a fantastic job. He occasionally looks for my face in the crowd but even though he sees me I know he won't find me anywhere. Inside, I am missing too. Like my son.

I gasp in horror when Gabriella ascends the podium to join my tearful husband. No matter how many women Mike has slept with, I don't have any jealous or possessive feelings towards them. But if I had to choose one person that he was not allowed to get his hands on, it would have been her. My son's girlfriend. Did he do it on purpose? To show he could?

Since Joe's body was discovered, Gabriella, who I've noticed is quite the actress, has been portraying the mourning girlfriend. She asserts that her level of heartbreak exceeds even our own. Normally, I take everything she says in my stride, but when I see her place her hand on my husband's arm and pat it warmly, I pay closer attention. She has misread Mike though, as he doesn't require rescuing and seems embarrassed by this gesture. He doesn't appreciate receiving assistance from a member of the opposite sex or having the limelight stolen from him. On cue, he glances apologetically in my direction. But my eyes are fixed on Gabriella and they continue to widen in disbelief as she slyly slips a comforting hand into Mike's palm, all the while staring up at him with Bambi-sized eyes.

Mike's guilty expression tells me everything, and when he snaps his hand away and steps back from her, I realise he was telling the truth when he claimed to no longer being romantically interested in her. Once Mike had gained the competitive advantage over his son and demonstrated his virility and sexual prowess, he probably tired of her at the precise moment she tired of Joe. Gabriella, though, appears deeply mortified and is left practically foaming at the mouth. Whilst I applaud my husband for his public rejection of this girl, I can't help thinking that it doesn't bode well for us. She has all the power and he could end up in jail if he doesn't play nice. How long am I going to allow this slip of a girl to continue blackmailing us before something inside me snaps? There's no telling what I might do then.

What does she want from my family? First Joe. Now Mike. And what lies and false promises had my husband made to this girl to lead her to believe that she was more than a passing fling? *An illegal fling.* Also, how involved was she in Rupert's suicide? Did she orchestrate the bullying campaign by pressuring Joe to mistreat the poor boy till he reached breaking point? What did she say or do to him? Is Gabriella to blame for Joe's disappearance? Did she see him as a barrier standing between her and Mike? Had Joe visited her that night after learning that his father was sleeping with her, and did she do something to him . . . Lure him to the water's edge perhaps and push him in as punishment for interfering with her plans? *Where was she when my son was killed?* My head hurts from all these unanswered questions but there is just one thing I am certain of. Gabriella is the main suspect at this time. Not only that, but she is also a threat to my family's existence. We are like puppets in her hands.

PART TWO

CHAPTER 39: ZOE

Three months later

My client, who was booked in at 3 p.m. for highlights and a trim, had to cancel due to illness, and because I was at a loose end, my boss, Angela asked me to do her a favour. I'm always happy to help out where I can, particularly as Angela is such a good boss, so I said I was happy to do so. A long-standing client of hers, and a good tipper too by all accounts, believes she may have dropped her purse outside the salon while she was putting it back in her handbag and wants to find out what happened to it after that. So, I've been assigned the mind-numbingly boring chore of going through our CCTV footage to see if I can find out.

'Here's that cup of tea I promised you.' Angela squirms guiltily as she sets the china cup and saucer down on the desk in her office. Despite having the best technology money can buy, she despises it even more than I do. The green tea is served exactly how I like it — without milk or sugar. I haven't been able to stomach dairy for weeks.

'How long do you want me to spend on this?' I ask hesitantly because the salon is extremely busy and I could be more valuable elsewhere. Even though I'm a senior hair stylist, or designer as we're called here, I don't mind doing junior jobs like sweeping floors and washing clients' hair. I'm not like some hairdressers who can be extremely stuck-up about such things. I've always been one to just get stuck in. This is why Angela treats me as her unofficial number two, which is rewarding in itself.

'Mrs Norman has been coming here since day one, and she is always so generous and kind that I would really like to be able to help her.' Angela's freckly face looks concerned as she adds, 'I know the purse will be long gone by now, but it might ease her mind knowing whether or not she lost it here. Reading between the lines, I think she's worried about her memory, she is getting older.'

'Oh, bless her.' I pull a sympathetic face, thinking how sad that is. 'Don't worry, I'm on it.'

Angela smiles warmly, tosses her head of crisp copper curls, and blows me a kiss on her way out, saying, 'I owe you one.'

Once I'm by myself in her office, which is as immaculate as Angela is, I open the shiny top-of-the-range laptop and launch the CCTV business app. Only then do I realise Angela never provided me with a date. It's possible that Mrs Norman could have misplaced her purse last week or last month. I get up from the chair and I'm about to go and ask Angela for it, but when I see her through the glass window seating another of her "favourite" clients at her workstation, I decide not to interrupt. Another customer is at the till making a payment so I can't check the booking system to find out when Mrs Norman's last appointment was, so I return to my seat at the clutter-free white desk and type in "last 120 days", as I believe the hard drive gets erased after that. When we first purchased the system, Angela and I spent two agonising days struggling to set it up. "Days we'll never get back". We'd laughed manically at the time.

Since I stopped drinking, Angela and I have discovered we have more in common than before, and I'm beginning to think — or rather, hope — that we might end up becoming closer friends. When I contemplate this, I suddenly experience a feeling of shame so powerful that it quickly transports me back to the day of Joe's funeral, when Maddie's penetrating gaze revealed to me what she would not: that I had betrayed her. I let her down. She has no idea how much.

I find myself looking around the room instead of completing the task at hand as I take in the white stone walls and rustic wooden beamed ceilings. The building is old, listed even, like so much of Stamford is. Angela, an expert in advanced aesthetics is not only naturally beautiful but loaded. And like so many wealthy people, she insists on having the best of everything. Not that I blame her. The salon is amazing. When you first walk in it feels as if you have entered an award-winning interior-designed home. Floral arrangements provide drama while the smoky glass clusters of hanging pendant lights add elegance. Every customer is offered a glass of Prosecco on arrival.

I don't miss alcohol at all. The best thing I've ever done was to give it up. I still vape occasionally, but nowhere near as much as before. I feel so much better for it. The blackouts, hangovers, headaches and anxiety are all gone. Even my menopausal symptoms seem like a thing of the past, at least for the time being. I'm not complaining. As an antidote for what happened to me three months ago, I remind myself that I have a lot to be thankful for and I turn my attention back to the screen in front of me.

Because the software includes features for fast-forwarding and searching for specific events such as timestamps and facial recognition, I find the footage of Mrs Norman almost immediately. It was shot three days ago. The poor woman was right. She did drop her purse. Right outside our door. I speed through the film in an effort to discover what happened to it. Bingo. It took all of ten minutes for a passerby to pick it up. I'm guessing by the eager look in the man's eyes when he opens the purse and takes out a handful of notes, that he has no intention of handing it to the police. I'm not sure why this shocks me so much. It may be because I still want to believe the best in everyone. Even if my life experience has shown me that this isn't always the case and that despite our best efforts, we all let each other down.

Look at Joe, and Mike, Gabriella. Me. Maddie is the only one among us to display any decency and loyalty at all. Since the day of the funeral, I haven't really seen her, not close up anyway. Although we now go out of our way to avoid each other, I have caught glimpses of her occasionally, but from a distance. It's so sad when I think about it. A part of me has been missing since we stopped talking. I wonder if it's the same for her.

Others had gathered to hug the Blacks as they left the church on the day of Joe's funeral, but I snuck out of the door. I didn't want to come face to face with either Maddie or Mike. Especially Mike, who I'm positive is having an affair with Gabriella, a schoolgirl of all things, who used to be his son's girlfriend. I wouldn't be able to spend five minutes in his company before I lost it over this. The lying, cheating bastard! God knows what will happen to him if Maddie finds out.

To take my mind off Mike Black, I furiously scroll through the CCTV footage, clicking through blurry images of cars, pedestrians and a dog walking by itself who stops to pee up against the salon door (Angela would be furious if she knew), until it somehow fast forwards itself to the end of the film and pauses on a 120-day-old, grainy, yet familiar image. Wait a second. It couldn't possibly be him, could it?

Joe.

CHAPTER 40: MADELINE

It seems ironic that she asked to meet at The Mad Turk in St Paul's Street as it's the last place I would have chosen, given that I haven't been back there since the night of Zoe's fortieth birthday, which turned out to be the last night of my son's life. But if she had asked to meet stark naked at Joe's gravestone I still would have come. I need answers that only she can give.

Rather than take the car, I decided to walk to the restaurant. It provided me with the ten minutes I needed to manage my mounting anxiety before seeing her for the first time in three months. Since Joe's funeral, actually. Now that autumn has arrived, the trees' dark green colouration is giving way to a crisp, copper hue. There is also a chill in the air. I feel it around my ears and neck, like a toddler's fluttering fingers.

When a suited man walks past me, I notice that his eyes are drawn to me and I know I'm not imagining it when his cheekbone lifts into an appreciative smile. If Zoe had been with me, she would have prodded me and sniggered, 'You've still got it, Maddie!' I don't want *it*, though. I never have. All my life, men have openly stared at me, followed me, tried to talk to me at the most inappropriate times . . . making comments about my appearance. Because of this, I learned at a very young age, around thirteen I'd say, that if I wasn't polite and didn't smile in those circumstances, their admiration would soon turn to resentment or even hatred, placing me in real danger. They behaved as if they were entitled to my attention and took offence when it wasn't given. Is it any wonder that I dislike men? Being married to Mike for eighteen years hasn't helped to change my opinion.

This area of town is so lovely. It's full of Georgian grandeur in the form of listed townhouses, cobbled streets and quaint shops. I half expect Mary Poppins to emerge from one of the glossy, polished doors that are painted in a range of Farrow and Ball colours and have stone steps leading up to them. Joking aside, I'm upset with myself because all the weight I lost after Joe died has crept back on and my cheeks have allowed themselves to become plumper again. I no longer resemble a gaunt, grey skeleton, which is obviously why the man noticed me in the first place. I even have new life in my amber eyes, which Joe always said were like gold coins. I continue to resist any outward sign of recovery though and cling to grief instead as it makes me feel more connected to my son.

One of the waiters recognises me as soon as I open the restaurant door, appearing surprised yet delighted to see me. Being a regular sometimes has its drawbacks. Especially when you wish to remain invisible.

'Mrs Black. Welcome. It's been a while. How are you?'

'Fine, thank you,' I gasp breathlessly as if I had just completed a marathon rather than a quick stroll through town. I imagine most bereaved mothers dread being asked how they are.

'And the good doctor and your son? Are we expecting them too?'

As I answer, 'No. Just me,' I make a conscious effort to smile and not appear shocked. 'I'm meeting someone here.' Coming across anyone who hasn't heard of Joe's death is an unexpected gift. 'Oh, I see her over there.' I gracefully withdraw from him, having made my excuses.

I take a deep breath and tell myself that "I can do this" as a shudder rips through my body, then I walk over. Even when I stop to stand right beside her, she still doesn't look up. She's too busy examining her phone and frowning. Anyone would think she was dining alone and not expecting anyone to join her.

A second deep breath, a quick check to see if I have my handbag with me — grief has a habit of making one forgetful — yes, it's strung over one shoulder and I'm suddenly announcing in a too-loud voice, 'Gabriella.'

Startled, her head snaps up and she drops her phone with a clatter on the table, before shooting a pair of dark narrowed eyes at me.

'What are you doing here?'

I smile brightly. 'Mike couldn't make lunch today.' I slide onto the seat opposite her. 'So, I thought I'd come instead. We wouldn't want to disappoint you.'

Ignoring me, Gabriella irritably retrieves her phone, her eyes darting all over the screen. 'He never texted me to let me know.' Her shoulders sink in defeat as she comes out with this.

'He's got a lot on his mind.' I'm deliberately mysterious. It feels good to be in control around her for a change. She has been dangling my husband on a piece of string for months. It's time to stop now.

She snorts, furious at being stood up. 'Like what?' I watch her eye the door as if she's about to make a bolt for it, but I'm too quick for her, and when I smarmily add, 'Like a new woman,' she looks visibly shocked.

'What do you mean?' she stutters and squirms uncomfortably.

I chuckle at that, thinking that my laughter sounds strange to my ears. 'I mean . . . that he and I are planning on renewing our wedding vows.' I pause deliberately and pretend to be interested in my surroundings before turning back to her. 'When I say *we*, I really mean *he* since it was all his idea and he's planning everything himself. That's why he's mega busy right now.'

'Congratulations,' she mutters unconvincingly while staring dejectedly into her glass of water.

Naturally, it's all lies. And I almost feel sorry for her, *almost*, since I would never agree to marry Mike a second time under any circumstances. Despite being heavily made-up, with black, gothic, smoky eyes and a vampirish white complexion, she looks younger than her age. It occurs to me that she probably has a miserable home life. Her career-minded parents are never there for her. It's no wonder she's troubled and desperate for attention from older men. She probably has daddy issues.

'Thank you, but I should be congratulating you.'

She scrunches up her face and asks warily, 'What for?'

'For becoming a woman, of course.'

'I don't know what you mean.' She shrugs dismissively, but her eyes betray her as there is real fear in them. She must think I'm ready to confront her about sleeping with my husband. But I'm not about to do that. Not today. Instead, I exclaim enthusiastically, 'Happy sixteenth birthday!'

CHAPTER 41: ZOE

I try to keep my fine blonde hair out of my face as my stomach spasms painfully and I vomit into the white, shining toilet bowl that has bluish gel all over it and smells like fresh flowers. Just as I start to feel better, I retch once again, bringing up the last of my lunch of a bacon, lettuce and tomato sandwich. Thankfully I made it to the staff cloakroom just in time before throwing up. Imagine if I had done that in Angela's office! All over her expensive flagstone floor. I wouldn't have been very popular then.

My eyes are watering as I turn around, intending to turn on the tap so I can wash my hands and mouth in the basin, but I hesitate when I notice that Angela is standing in the doorway, watching me. She must have heard me being sick because I left the door open in my haste to get here. How embarrassing. A frown somehow creeps onto her Botoxed face as she continues to watch me. Then she harrumphs as if to say, "I told you so" before asking, 'When were you going to tell me, Zoe?'

'Tell you what?' My frown matches her own.

She gestures to my stomach. 'How long gone are you?'

'What? Are you trying to say . . . ? Oh, God no!' I burst out laughing, anticipating that when I correct her, she will feel embarrassed about making such an absurd suggestion. I had assumed that by now she would have realised that I was in early menopause and that I had zero chance of becoming pregnant. She is, after all, older than I am. I'd say by four or five years. So, she should know all about it.

'I know how this must look but you couldn't be more wrong,' I assure her.

'No, Zoe, I don't think so,' she contradicts me. 'Did you think I'd be mad at you when I found out, because you'd be going off on maternity leave knowing how much I depend on you?'

She appears so serious that I'm stumped for a second. 'No, of course not,' I reply shakily since this is a lot to take in after seeing Joe on the video. 'I would never think that. But, Angela, I'm not pregnant. I can't be.'

'Why not? You're a woman, aren't you? And you've wanted a baby for a long time.'

'You don't understand. I'm going through early meno- pause so there's no chance of—'

Angela interjects, 'You do realise that you can still get pregnant throughout menopause, don't you?'

My mouth drops open when I hear this because I liter- ally didn't know that. I just figured you couldn't, that's all. Duh.

'All I'm saying is that you should get yourself tested.' Angela sniffs, sounding offended, before stomping off.

I consider calling her back to find out why she appears so upset with me when I haven't done anything wrong. And even if I were pregnant, which I most definitely am not — I know my own body — why would she be so put out? Because it's clear that she is. She claimed that she wouldn't be mad at me if I left to have a baby, but was she telling the truth? But then I remember that, like me, Angela is childless and, even though we've never discussed the reason for this, could it be that she is unable to conceive and is jealous at the possibility of my being so? Her being older also reduces her chances of having a baby. And I had drawn a similar conclusion about myself, given my age and circumstances. Still, I can't help but think to myself, "Could Angela be right?" as I wash my hands under the tap and splash water on my mouth. But I immediately reject her idea . . . for various reasons but mainly because Angela is unaware of the stress that I'm under and the effect it can have on your body. I was left both physically and emotionally abused after Joe sexually assaulted me and have only now begun to recover from it.

The second I saw his face on the tape, everything came flooding back. Waking up in bed not knowing where I was or what had happened to me. Being drugged. Joe's mocking smile. A black hair on the pillow. Semen on my thigh. The bruising afterwards. The disturbing memory of that night is the only reason I was sick just now. But the real horror wasn't when I zoomed in on his hooded face and was forced to gaze into those dark, menacing eyes for one last time . . . but that somebody had followed Joe that night. They were only a shadow in the framed image I saw, so I couldn't identify them, but I could tell from the way Joe spun around to glare at them that he was being approached by someone he knew. It took everything I had to keep from passing out at that point as my heart felt like it would explode from my chest. Along with the look of recognition, there was shock too and possibly even alarm on his face. The spiteful curl of his lip implied that this individual was not a friend, but rather an enemy.

The video I viewed in Angela's office was not the same as the one the police released to the media that was broadcast on all of the local news channels because it was shot in Bath Row rather than on the town bridge. This time, Joe had been captured on the footpath going into Stamford Meadows, where his body was discovered, indicating that it must have been taken moments before he died. This meant that contrary to what Maddie originally assumed, Joe had not been heading in the direction of home when he was seen crossing the bridge. He must have looped back on himself to cut through Stamford Meadows, so he might even have been planning to return to my house as it was only a short walk away. But for what? To apologise? I'll never know, but regardless of what his intentions had been, somebody had intercepted him that night. Could this have been Joe's killer?

If I'm being honest, I still find it hard to accept what I saw. Unexpectedly coming across new evidence like that was such a shock. I wonder why the police didn't request access to the salon's video footage, but I presume they focused exclusively on the area where Joe was last seen. Also, the salon is a good distance away from that part of the river and positioned at an angle to it, so they might have assumed it was outside of the reach of an average security camera, but they hadn't considered that some business owners, like Angela, were prepared to spend a fortune on their security systems, even if they didn't know how to use them properly.

That's how I know she won't figure out I have erased all the footage. I did this while closely monitoring the door in case she came back in and caught me. I didn't have any excuses prepared. I still don't. I may have been crazy to delete the videos so hastily, but I cannot let anyone, especially the police, find out about this. Nobody must ever know that Joe was so close to my house that night, otherwise, they might assume he was on his way to visit me or work out — as I had — that he had already been to mine and was on his way back again, and I could become a suspect myself.

CHAPTER 42: MADELINE

When I first asked Mike to arrange this lunch date with Gabriella, he was less than enthusiastic about it, until I explained that I would be the one showing up, not him. He became even more agitated then and demanded to know what I was up to. It was quite simple really. It was a significant moment for us because Gabriella would be sixteen and no longer regarded as a minor. The fact that they'd had sex when she was fifteen, however, might still get him arrested, as he quite rightly pointed out. And that's where I come in because I am determined to prove to Gabriella how unwise that would be. And the only way I can do that is by befriending her.

I intend to make her reliant on me, so I can investigate her involvement in Joe's disappearance while also protecting my soon-to-be-divorced husband's reputation. Am I as bad as he is for deliberately setting out to manipulate a child? Possibly. However, she has asked for it. Time and time again by expressing her intent to expose Mike if he doesn't do as she says. Although he keeps her sweet from time to time he has grown increasingly irritated by her childish antics, and she must have sensed his diminishing interest because he rarely sees her and when he does, there is no sex involved, regardless of her desperate efforts to entice him. I am aware of all of this since I was the one who installed hidden cameras and microphones in my husband's car, on his phone and even inside his clothing. I couldn't have done this without the expert advice of the private investigator though, who guided me on what digital spyware I'd need. He wasn't able to install it himself as it's against the law for him to do so, but a little thing like that isn't going to stop a wronged wife. Mike has no idea about any of this, but I'm adamant that I won't leave this marriage with anything less than I deserve. I'm referring to the house and our savings when I say this. If a fifteen-year-old schoolgirl can blackmail my husband, then so can I, regardless of whether these practices are legal or not.

I slyly watch Gabriella and wonder if killing Joe was always part of her calculating plan to destroy my family. Is it possible for a young girl to be that wicked, or is it only in my evil head? Mike would think me insane if I shared my thoughts, so I don't. She and Joe, in my opinion, had some type of pact. In it together. Until they weren't. While she played the role of head girl at school and everyone's friend, Joe alone was accused of the bullying that resulted in a young man's suicide. She forced him to do it, I'd wager my life on it.

'Shall we order some lunch?' I suggest, picking up a menu.

'Not hungry,' she mumbles and shrugs one shoulder.

'A meze between the two of us then?'

'Could I have a glass of wine?' she enquires hopefully.

I raise an eyebrow and glance at the waiters who are waiting for a sign that we are ready to order before suggesting, 'They won't serve you at your age, but I can get one for you that you can sip while they're not looking.'

She grins for the first time, and as her face lights up, I can see how pretty she is beneath the makeup. I wonder if she would listen to an older woman's advice about how some men prefer natural women. Then I chastise myself for being old-fashioned. Why is it important for women to care what men think? When I signal for the waiter to come over, I order the wine and a mixed meze for two. I've had it many times before and it's delicious.

We don't talk again until the glass of white wine arrives, which I sneakily slide towards her. She swallows a large mouthful of it, but no one notices because there aren't many diners and the waiters' attention is elsewhere.

'How's school?' I ask, for something to say.

'I'm in the sixth form now,' she boasts, and I catch a glimpse of her severely thin chest bone as she leans forward in her seat.

'I had forgotten it was a brand new term already.' I'm wistful, thinking of Joe, who would have been in his second term of sixth form had he lived. 'Does it feel different without him being there?' As I ask this, tears start to form in my eyes. I can't help it.

'Sometimes,' she concedes, not giving much away, but that's Gabriella for you.

'And what about you?' I try to sound more enthusiastic than I actually am.

She scowls. 'What about me?'

We pause our conversation as the waiter places a platter of hummus, baba ghanoush, falafel, olives and pitta bread on the table in front of us.

'Joe's favourite,' Gabriella comments and my appetite immediately vanishes. How can I eat my son's most loved dishes when he's no longer around to enjoy them?

'Are you seeing anyone new?' My voice comes out stilted and sharp, which isn't what I intended, causing her to raise a pencilled eyebrow as she tucks into the food, despite having claimed not to be hungry.

'A boyfriend, you mean?' She is scathing. 'It's barely been three months since we lost Joe.'

'As if I needed any reminder.' I sigh, thinking, *That didn't stop you screwing his father*, before quickly adding, 'He wouldn't want you to be alone and miserable.'

'How do you know?' she demands, her hand, full of pitta bread, pausing halfway to her mouth.

I shrug and take a sip of my water while she resumes eating. I proceed with my plan, gulping nervously as I speak.

176

'Joe would have made a wonderful husband one day, just like Mike.' I lie easily, then lower my voice to add, 'He can, of course, be a charmer and a lady's man when he wants to be, like most men can. I have to keep a close eye on my husband.'

Gabriella is now gazing at me suspiciously, as though she is having trouble believing what she is hearing. 'You think Mike is capable of cheating in a relationship? Even with a woman he loves?'

She has no idea that I know about her and Mike and means to trick me into confiding in her for her own questionable agenda, but she isn't nearly as subtle as she thinks she is since I noticed straightaway that she used the word "relationship" referencing her and Mike, rather than asking if he would cheat on his wife of eighteen years. The one thing Gabriella cannot stand is not being put first. A man who so much as looks at another woman is not the man for her. And judging by what she said just now, she truly believed my husband was in love with her. What must the arsehole have said to her to make her think that? It doesn't enter her head to consider that Mike was cheating on me when she was having sex with him. I'm just the old, dried-up, pre-menopausal wife who doesn't even like sex, so I don't count.

'It has been known,' I state truthfully, and since this is the first time that I've been honest with her, I am able to persuade her of this with ease.

While I watch her gulp down her wine, she bravely fights back tears, but then her face abruptly hardens, and she slams the wine glass down on the table, spilling some of her drink. 'Then he doesn't deserve you, Madeline,' she murmurs as she fixes her intense, seductive eyes on me, 'because you are very beautiful and it's wasted on him.'

It's inevitable that she should turn her attention to me, and that's what I was counting on. Gabriella has to be admired and desired by at least one of us Blacks. She is totally fixated on my family. And I intend to use that to my advantage. Her mistake is thinking that only children play games.

CHAPTER 43: ZOE

I left work early in the end as I was still feeling queasy and unsettled. Angela raised her head and gave me a comforting grin as I was about to walk out of the salon door as if to imply that she might have been mistaken after all. I nodded and gave her a "thumbs up" that I wasn't feeling. Despite my earlier objections, I went straight to Boots chemists in the High Street and stood in line behind a woman who wanted cream for her haemorrhoids. When it was my time to be served, I was unable to tamp down the nervousness in my voice as I handed over the pack of digital pregnancy test kits I'd grabbed from the shelves. The pharmacist did not wish me luck as I was leaving, and I imagined this was because she intuitively sensed I wasn't thrilled about having to take a test.

It wasn't a smart idea to walk home down Bath Row, where Joe's last walk had begun and ended, as his teenage ghost followed me everywhere. Mocking me. Poking me. Taunting me. I jumped each time I heard someone's footsteps on the pavement behind me, expecting to be grabbed. Although this was the quickest way home, I was spooked, and five minutes later I was virtually running as I turned the corner into my quiet little street.

So now I am currently seated on the toilet with my pink, lace-trim knickers around my ankles, staring at all three of the pregnancy kits that I have neatly arranged in a row on the ugly, porcelain tiled bathroom floor. Each one screams "Pregnant 3+ weeks". Aside from the shock I felt on seeing this I was also confused until I read the packaging again and realised that it could only accurately predict weeks 1-2, and 2-3. After that, it was anybody's guess. Except it wasn't. Because I knew exactly how many months, weeks, days and hours I was pregnant. I had my last sexual encounter — involuntarily, I should add — three months ago on my birthday.

This means that I am carrying Joe's child, and I am knee-deep in quicksand. For the love of Christ, how could I have gotten pregnant by a sixteen-year-old schoolboy? One who drugged me, attacked me sexually, and then oh-so-conveniently drowned while returning home. Jesus. How much misfortune can a girl endure? To think that all those times Chris and I had unprotected sex and not once did it result in a pregnancy scare. And, let's be honest, I wasn't that reliable about taking the pill, either back then or now. It wasn't deliberate. I was just scatty and disorganised. In addition, I had believed wrongly that I couldn't become pregnant while going through early menopause. It appears that Angela was correct all along.

Despite the difficulties and concerns that come with being a single parent, I would be over the moon if I were having someone else's baby instead of Joe's. I could find a way to make it work. Is bearing the child of a dead rapist my atonement for what I did to Maddie and Chris? If that's the case, it's a heavy load. Even I can't believe I deserve this. As I try to sweep to the back of my mind those final images of Joe, taken just before he died, I realise nothing can erase the memory of how startled and terrified he appeared when the shadowy figure approached him. Although he'd acted in a belligerent Joe-like manner to save face, it was as if he knew his life was in danger.

Enough of him. What about me? What am I going to do? It's not too late to have an abortion. I've already checked the NHS app. I have a legal right to a termination up until the twenty-fourth week of pregnancy. Even though I have done some unforgivable things in the past and injured people I love, I want desperately to be a good person, like Chris once thought me. Kind. Compassionate. Loyal. And I adore babies. Memories of Joe's newborn gurgles coming from his cot roar unexpectedly in my ears, and I cover them with my hands to block them out.

'You don't get a say in this, Joe,' I rage in disgust, shivering with fear and adrenalin. Then, I get up from the toilet, pull up my big-girl pants and wash my hands, before turning to face the pregnancy test kits once more. I resist the urge to boot them across the room even though they refuse to take back their "pregnant" claim.

'You did this to me, you little fucker.' I stare at my numbed expression in the bathroom mirror. The knot of fear in my stomach won't go away. I need to gather my thoughts.

I've been secretly rejoicing all these months that I'd skipped the heavy periods I had come to dread and all of my menopausal symptoms appeared to have gone away. The hot flushes, itchiness, headaches and brain fog were a thing of the past. But it turns out being pregnant was the only reason for the temporary reprieve. I never in a million years would have thought that pregnancy could be a cure for perimenopause. Who knew?

'Zoe, what are you going to do?' My mouth is as dry as sand as I stare back at my watery eyes in the mirror, which are swollen from crying. My world has come crashing down. I close my eyes. My mind has gone blank and I am unable to think clearly. When I open them, I feel my heart twist. The answer is in my "baby box" under my bed. It's in the mental pictures I have saved in my memory of meeting Joe for the first time after he was born and experiencing a love that I never anticipated feeling. An unselfish, nurturing emotion different to any other. Not the same as the feelings you have for a man.

Why am I hiding from the truth when I think I already know what I intend to do? I am fully aware that this is my only chance to have a child of my own, and if I can allow myself to temporarily forget that Joe is the father, then my heart instinctively knows what it wants. I'll keep it. Love it. Cherish it. Joe is no longer a threat to me because he is dead. There is no danger of his being involved in the child's upbringing. Nobody need ever know that the baby is his. I'll make something up. Say the father was a one-night stand who is now out of the picture. Most of the people I know wouldn't have a problem believing that, since I'm single and prolific on Tinder. Only one person would see through the lie — Maddie — as she knows me better than anyone else.

She must never know that I'm carrying her dead son's child. The notion is too unspeakable to even consider. Because I no longer have any evidence that Joe assaulted me, she would not only accuse me of having groomed and taken advantage of her son for sex, but she would also be possessive around the child. As a grieving mother, she wouldn't be able to help herself when it came to her grandchild. I can conceal my pregnancy for the time being, perhaps even for a few more months, but when my baby belly begins to show, everyone will know.

I feel a twinge of guilt when I consider that Maddie has only recently lost her child, whereas I am ready to begin a new life with one of my own. But that's hardly my fault. The blame lies closer to home in her case.

CHAPTER 44: MADELINE

Two months later

Gabriella is hunched over a laptop, her dark hair hanging down in curtains obscuring her face. She chews on a nibbled pen while holding it to her wafer-thin, maroon-coloured mouth. She is a bunch of nerves at all times, just like I am. Along with having slept with my husband, it is another thing we have in common. I don't think I've ever seen her shoulders drop into a relaxed position. She is sitting at a small desk close to the sliding glass doors that open onto a balcony area with a view of the river. We both avoid looking out of the window since it is a sad reminder of our loss.

I've agreed to return to work gradually, so I'm easing myself in by signing off paperwork at home. As I stare at the laptop in front of me, which captures my returning-to-normal reflection, I find it difficult to focus on post-surgery pain medication and my gaze keeps drifting back to Gabriella. She appeared extremely grateful when I had the desk moved down from Joe's room for her to use. Since she's been coming here, her school grades, which had been declining for a spell after Joe died, have improved.

She visits our home most days after school to complete her homework, and, if Mike isn't around, to dine with me. It's one way of keeping an eye on her, even if Mike despises having her here.

'She's always here,' he grumbles but, to be fair, he never says it in front of her. He is aware that I am up to something more than just safeguarding his reputation, but he is unable to discern what it is.

Gabriella no longer wants anything to do with Mike, which is fine by him. And me, naturally. Every time he walks into a room, she makes a face as if it were her house and not his. *Half his*, I remind myself as I drum my fingernails on the handmade elephant-grey desk that Mike had shipped in all the way from Malaysia. The study is on the first floor of the house and it resembles a chic Manhattan loft space with its edgy, masculine aesthetic. A softly illuminated glass-encased stairway leads up to the matching bathroom.

Gabriella has taken to going without makeup due to my influence, which is not insignificant, and the transformation has turned her into a genuinely lovely-looking girl. If only she would gain some weight. She is stick thin. Although I have no room to talk. I'm fortunate in that I've always been naturally slim and don't need to work at it.

In the past two months, Gabriella and I have come a long way. She still doesn't entirely trust me, but I'm working on it. When we're alone, I've shocked even myself at how much I enjoy the female company — maybe I should have had a daughter rather than a son — but I can't afford to let my guard down with her.

She even dresses like me now, in timeless elegant clothing, which is, I believe, one of the biggest compliments a female can pay another female, but with Gabriella, it's not as straightforward as that. She is now just as fixated on me as she was on Joe originally, and then Mike. She seems to want to develop a romantic relationship with me, but of course, I won't be pursuing that path. However, I do drop hints and signals that it might be possible in the future. Just enough to keep her interested.

'Have you heard anything from the solicitor?' she asks with affected brightness because we both recognise what a delicate issue it is.

'No,' I sigh, gracefully arranging myself at the desk as she saunters over, catlike, to my end of the room. 'Not since our visit last week.'

'How long do divorces usually take?' Her tone is half reproving.

Irritation courses through me and I answer snippily. 'As long as they take. Besides, it depends on a variety of factors.'

'Like what?' She counters.

I'm not going to make this easy for her. 'Like whether adultery has occurred.'

As she struggles with her demons, I watch her press a hand to her temple and sigh guiltily. In response I plaster on a smile and say, 'You're such a good friend to ask.'

Her fiercely intense gaze comes back to rest on me. 'I'd like to be more.'

I pat the seat next to me and nod thoughtfully, saying, 'I know you would.' She dutifully takes a seat, and I murmur, 'But all in good time. You are aware that when it comes to extramarital affairs, I have strong values.'

At that, her head snaps upward. 'But that didn't stop him—'

I lightly touch her hand and then lay one finger on her lip to gently hush her. I even let her stroke the ring finger of my left hand, but when she lifts it to her mouth, as if to kiss it, I find it is too much, so I gently retract my hand, nodding to the door to let her know it isn't safe.

'Mike's home,' I remind her.

'When isn't he?' she grumbles.

She still hasn't and won't ever admit to sleeping with Mike out of fear of losing me. That doesn't stop me from asking the private eye to continue tracking both my husband and her. Just in case. You can never be sure.

184

'You know, I couldn't have done it without you, Gabriella.'

'Done what?' she queries, perplexed.

'Gone to see the solicitor and commence divorce proceedings.'

'That's what friends are for.'

Our other just-as-fake friends and acquaintances are moved and express sentiments like "Oh, how lovely. That's so nice to hear" and "Joe would have loved that" when they hear of my developing bond with Gabriella. Even the girl's notoriously absent parents are happy with this outcome since they believe I will have a positive impact on their daughter. *Hmm, I'm not so sure about that.* My husband is the only one who objects to the fact that the mother of his deceased son and the dead boy's former ex-girlfriend, who is also a former lover of his, have become inseparable.

'Talking of friends . . .' Midway through her speech, Gabriella pauses, as though debating whether to continue.

'Yes?' I prompt, brow furrowing.

'I heard some news the other day about your other friend.' As she says this, jealousy crawls onto her face, like a spider that doesn't belong there.

I'm wide-eyed. 'What other friend?'

'Joe's godmother.'

'Zoe?' I suck in my breath.

'Yeah. Her.' Looking like she wants to slit someone's throat, Gabriella rolls her eyes overdramatically.

As I let memories of my ex-best friend, and her cruel, neglectful treatment of me after Joe died, resurface, the walls around me are swaying and drifting like a lost ocean liner at sea. Oddly, I haven't thought of Zoe in a while, not since Gabriella became my new pet project.

'What about her?' I demand, a heavy feeling settling on my chest.

Gabriella's eyes gleam. 'She's having a baby.'

CHAPTER 45: ZOE

Already five months along, my limbs feel leaden and use-less as I lie on the hospital couch mentally preparing for my mid-pregnancy scan. Since my morning sickness subsided, I am compensating for it by eating like a truck driver. Sadly, Angela wasn't able to come with me today, but she has been by my side every step of the way. When I eventually found the courage to ask her whether she would be my birthing partner, tears came to her eyes, but it turned out she was thrilled about the idea. As soon as she said this, I felt a surge of relief as I was terrified of doing this alone. For the past two months, she has unquestionably been my rock. Honestly, I'm not sure what I would have done without her. She has embraced my pregnancy as if it were her own, which reminds me of how I took on the role of surrogate mother when Maddie became pregnant.

Merry, *short for Meredith*, which is a fantastic name for a sonographer tasked with scanning new life and delivering happiness to families, stands next to me in front of a screen with a large circular keyboard that resembles a spaceship. She is in her fifties and has a pair of sombre black glasses hanging from a chain around her neck. Her warm chestnut eyes peek out at me from behind a blunt dark fringe. I nervously peel back my dress, exposing my bump, as she dons blue nylon gloves and squeezes ultrasound gel over her hands. Every time I see my belly, it seems to have grown. That is, at least, how it appears to me because I can no longer see my sparkly, indigo-blue painted toenails when I look down.

'Ready, Zoe?' Merry asks kindly.

I nod before pulling a face as the gel gets to work. 'It's much colder than I was expecting.' I laugh.

She smiles brightly. 'You're twenty weeks, I understand?'

'Yes.' I nod in agreement as I crane my neck to look at the screen, only there's nothing to see yet.

'Is this your second scan?'

'Yes.'

'So, you know to expect some light pressure on your stomach as I pass the probe over it.'

My head bobs again, like one of those nodding dog car toys. All I can think about is getting a photo of my baby to take home with me. It will feel real then. I can't wait to show it to Angela.

'Somebody wants to say hi.' Merry gestures to the screen while beaming.

'Oh, my gosh, it's grown so much,' I gasp when I see the alien-looking creature with its giant head and lizard-like spine writhing around inside me. The eyes appear to be turned in my direction as if they were staring directly at me and something happens to me at that precise moment for which I've been praying in secret. I sense a connection for the first time and my eyes start to well up. Merry notices and seems to understand because the silky blue of her glove lightly touches my hand. Even she stands marooned for a moment, not moving, until she suddenly gives a guffaw of laughter. 'I think you've got a fighter on your hands.'

'I see what you mean!' I exclaim wide-eyed when I realise the baby has raised its tiny little fist and appears to be shaking it at us in annoyance. My heart fills with both sadness and resolve as I try not to think of Joe's propensity for anger and hope that my baby hasn't inherited it.

'Would you like to know if it's a boy or a girl?' she asks, smiling.

I've been debating whether or not I want to be informed of my baby's sex for weeks, but now that I'm here, I make up my mind that I do. 'Oh, go on then.' I pretend at a casualness I don't feel.

She runs the probe over and around my tummy for the next few minutes, all the while keeping her eyes fixed on the screen. As I wait, sweat blooms on my skin dampening the small of my back.

'I knew it!' she trills, which startles me.

'What?'

'He's a little thug all right.'

'It's a boy, then?' I start in surprise, open-mouthed, but I can't lie — a flicker of disappointment passes through me, if only for a split second. I remember that I used to refer to Joe as my secret son and now I have one of my own. Truthfully though, I had settled on a daughter in my head since I imagined she wouldn't remind me of her father as much. Now that I know I'm expecting a boy, I wonder if he'll resemble Joe and, if so, will my son unintentionally reveal the secret of his parenthood to those who knew him?

Merry's laughing eyes meet mine. 'Any names yet?'

'Pesky blinder,' I chuckle as I tell myself everything will work out in the end. It must. The baby's health and well-being are what matter most, as demonstrated by Merry, who is now describing in great detail how "Baby Archer" is growing and developing nicely. As I struggle to process the fact that I'm having a boy, giggly, girly Zoe, who is still inside me someplace, drifts off like a rebellious teenager. My mind is on other things. Angela will be over the moon. She said all along it was a boy.

'I have three top boy names,' I announce too brightly, still processing my baby's gender. I was certain I was having a girl. Since I now know I am expecting a boy, it feels as though I am having to mourn the loss of a daughter whom I had named Poppy in my head.

'What are they?' Merry gently enquires, which makes me wonder how she can seem so enthusiastic about my baby when she must encounter dozens of expectant women every day, all of whom have, essentially, the same stories to share.

I bite my lip as if sharing a secret. 'Arthur after my dad, which is still a credible name after making a bit of a comeback. Then, Zak and Thomas.'

After a brief pause, Merry confides, 'Arthur Zak has got my vote.'

With a twitch of a smile, I agree, 'Arthur Zak it is then.' And I laugh and put a protective hand over my bump when my baby, *my son — Arthur —* gives a sharp kick of approval.

CHAPTER 46: MADELINE

'Where are you going?' Gabriella sulkily demands having followed me from the study into my bedroom.

My silence speaks volumes as I pull on my coat and put on a pair of leather gloves. Now that Gabriella is seated rigidly upright on the bed, I can feel her cold, accusing glare on me. 'Well?' she persists icily.

I mutter softly under my breath, 'I told you,' as I tuck my keys and purse into my handbag. 'I'm going to look at a house.'

She braces her shoulders, fully alert. 'For you? For after the divorce?'

'Yes.' I am an expert liar because I will never part with the home where my son was raised. My husband is unaware of my intentions to divorce him, but when he finds out, he will battle valiantly to protect what he sees as his. But I have enough information on him to convince him otherwise. *Gabriella* for one thing. He can go fuck himself if he thinks he's getting his hands on the house.

Because I can tell by looking at Gabriella's narrowed eyes and scornful expression that she isn't persuaded, I sigh and say, 'Believe it or not, I'm trying to protect you. Don't you think it would look strange if word got out that you had been going house hunting with me?'

'Strange to who?' Gabriella scoffs.

'Your parents, for one thing. You're meant to be here doing your homework not looking at houses with a soon-to-be-divorced woman.'

Gabriella folds her arms, nods pathetically and smiles in defeat, but she is not fooled. I can see the doubt behind her eyes.

'Will you let me move in with you once you have your own place?'

'You're only sixteen,' I point out kindly.

'That's old enough to do a lot of things,' she suggests sordidly, while raising a provocative eyebrow.

Shocked by this, I consider how damaged she must be to come out with something like that. And when I tell her, 'You're worth more than that,' I'm doing so out of kindness.

'Am I though?' She gets up from the bed and walks over to where I am standing. That's when I notice the purple smudges under her eyes and that she appears groggy with sleep.

'You don't use drugs, do you, Gabriella?'

'No. Why would you ask me that?' She scowls at me as if she were angry with me, but I can also see that she is being evasive.

'Neither Mike nor I will tolerate drug use in this house,' I warn.

'Who cares what he thinks?' she grumbles.

'He is still my husband.'

She doesn't say anything but shrugs her shoulders as if to imply, "Is he?"

In the silence that follows I check my makeup in the mirror and smooth down my hair. To lighten the atmosphere I ask, 'How do I look?'

'Beautiful as always.' She takes a deep breath and exhales slowly as her eyes fill with sorrow. 'You're going to see *her*, aren't you?'

'Who? I'm not sure what you mean?' Now it's my turn to look away. *The girl is cleverer than I gave her credit for. I must watch out for that.*

'You know who. *Zoe.*' Gabriella lets out a puff of exasperation as she sinks back down on the bed. My bed. Correction, Mike and mine's bed.

'That's nonsense,' I say cuttingly. *But she's spot on.* Because that's exactly where I'm headed. Wild horses wouldn't stop me. 'I have told you where I'm going even though it is none of your business. I don't have to answer to anyone. Not Mike. Not you. I am an adult, and you are a child.'

She gives me a weird look as if she's trying to determine whether I'm telling the truth. 'I might be a child in your eyes, but I don't see myself that way . . . not since I was thirteen,' she admits tellingly, before continuing, 'besides, I thought *I* was your friend. Not her.'

As if what she is saying is insignificant, I frown at her and shake my head. My intention is not to be cruel, but if I were to reflect on my relationship with Gabriella, I'd have to acknowledge that it hasn't turned out the way I wanted. She won't confess to anything that might connect her to Rupert Forbes's suicide or Joe's death, no matter how hard I attempt to pressure her. And given that I'm divorcing Mike, I also wonder how much more time I should invest in saving his arse. Maybe I'm as over Gabriella as I am over him? Knowing Zoe is pregnant has brought about a sudden change in me that I wouldn't admit to anyone else, but if you had asked me if this was possible two hours ago, I wouldn't have believed it. I once shared my son with her. Will she allow me to do the same with her child?

'I thought you two weren't friends anymore.' As she says this, Gabriella looks like she's on the verge of crying.

'We aren't,' I snarl irritably, but I then decide being upfront might work to my advantage. 'I'm just curious, that's all. About the baby, I mean.'

When she learns this, her face falls. 'See. I knew it,' Gabriella accuses jealously. 'You *are* going to see her.'

'If you'd like, we can have dinner together later,' I offer, looking around the room to make sure I haven't forgotten anything. But as my gaze returns to Gabriella, I find myself holding my breath because I am startled by the murderous intent in her eyes.

'She's going to ruin everything, just like Joe tried to do.'

'What do you mean by that, Gabriella?' I ask, startled.

'Nothing.' She lowers her dark eyes and sulks moodily.

She is just as shocked as I was a few seconds ago when I storm over to the bed and drag her from it. 'Did you hurt Joe?' I demand.

'No. I would never do that,' she sniffs tearfully and rubs the spot on her arm where I had gripped it.

As she squirms under my enraged glare, I realise that she seems scared of me. Suddenly, I understand how she must perceive me. A liar, a bully and a manipulator. This is exactly what I accused Mike of when I found out he had been having sex with an underage girl. My initial reaction to this is, *What the fuck have I turned into?* and I'm about to apologise profusely to Gabriella when she completely destroys me by coldly stating—

'You do know Zoe has another best friend now.'

CHAPTER 47: ZOE

When I walk straight into Chris as I'm leaving the hospital, I'm not sure which one of us is more shocked. Him or me. Although we pause to chat, it feels awkward. Not only because he has his girlfriend Vicky with him, but because they've just had their baby and are about to return home with it. A little girl by all accounts, if the pink baby carrier Chris is swinging in one hand is anything to go by. What an emotional day this is turning out to be.

Chris is more flustered than I've ever seen him. 'Hello.'

I look at the girlfriend, who is also eyeing me up and down and say, 'Hi, Chris. How are you?'

'As you can see, no longer pregnant.' He chuckles uneasily.

'A little girl,' I coo. 'What did you call her?'

'Vicky. I mean, not the baby. We didn't call her that.' He sighs as if he is aware that he is not making sense but is helpless to do anything about it. 'This is Vicky.' He points to the female next to him.

Territorially adding, 'His girlfriend,' Vicky nods her head in recognition. 'And this is?' She stares interrogatively at Chris and I get the sensation that she wears the trousers in their relationship, which I find interesting.

'Zoe,' Chris explains lamely, his eyes darting between me and her.

'It's a pleasure to meet you, Vicky,' I lie.

'Same,' she agrees, but I sense she is also lying.

'It's been forever,' Chris casually remarks.

I realise then that he is afraid I'll land him in trouble by revealing that we met up a few months ago. Vicky obviously has no idea. I was right about her wearing the trousers.

'It has indeed.' I let him off the hook.

'How have you been?' he asks, a little more at ease.

'Oh, you know . . .' I am deliberately vague.

But not vague enough, because Vicky's sharp eyes immediately lock onto my belly. 'You're pregnant!' she exclaims, sounding friendlier than she did just now. 'How long?'

'I've just had my five-month scan,' I reply while turning away from Chris, who I can already tell, without looking at him, is dumbfounded by this news. He does a double take when he notices my protruding belly.

Vicky, who is nothing like I had envisioned, still has a noticeable baby bump, and she appears exhausted, bloated and washed-up after giving birth. I remind myself that I can expect to feel the same in four months. Whoopee.

'Willow is two days, three hours and—' she pauses to check her watch — 'forty-six minutes old.'

Chris grins idiotically at that, and then gazes admiringly at her as if she had just uttered something remarkable.

Vicky isn't smarter, funnier, or prettier than me; the opposite is true, and I smugly interpret this to mean that he has downgraded. This may not be very nice of me, but when you're the dumpee, you feel entitled.

'Chris was amazing during the birth. He never once left my side, not even to go to the toilet. Did you, Daddy Bear?'

At that, Chris proudly shakes his head, *somebody give Daddy Bear a pat on the back*, and they laugh together as though they find themselves cute. I'm no longer surprised they named their daughter after a tree!

I finally comprehend what he sees in her when I observe the way she looks at him, as though she is as in awe of him as he is of her. I was wrong before about her wearing the trousers. That's just a front, put on for me. Because she is easier than I am, she allows him to lead her in ways I would not. I may have been a people-pleaser in the past, but never when in long-term relationships. She is also softer than me, even though I appear more outwardly feminine than her. I am, or *was*, giggly, girly Zoe, remember? Knowing this changes how I perceive Chris as if he is now inferior to me. He always claimed to seek equality in a partner while we were together, but like many men, he had reverted to type and chose a caregiver. Someone who would put him first, mother him, and take care of his every need. He goes down in my opinion as a result. I deserve better than that. These are words I've never told myself before, much less believed.

I've changed a lot since finding out I was pregnant, but I have a feeling that having a child will transform me into a whole different person. Already, I feel more self-assured, less frightened, and prepared to fight like a lioness if necessary. I will stop at nothing to protect my unborn child, and I can now understand how difficult it must have been for Maddie and why she convinced herself that Joe was innocent of the sexual assault charge against the teacher and the accusation of bullying, choosing instead to place the blame on behavioural issues that, although I didn't say so at the time, I felt were largely made up. Even Joe ridiculed the diagnoses the medical experts gave him. I often wonder if he would have developed into a dangerous psychopath destined for prison if he had lived. Then I remind myself that his attack on me was, in itself, a crime deserving of a custodial sentence.

'Do you know what you're having?' Vicky asks.

I find myself biting on my lip then, irritated. It's not as if I actually know her. Chris might have already linked my pregnancy to the attack, which worries me as well. I regret telling him now. Then it occurs to me that he was never that perceptive when it came to me. Everything revolved around him. His work. His self-respect. His independence. His trust.

Finally spluttering, 'A boy,' I place both hands on my belly bump as if I were introducing him. Is it my imagination or do I observe something like regret flicker at the back of Chris's eyes?

'Have you decided on a name yet?' This is from Vicky again. Prying Vicky is what Maddie and I would have called her.

I'm tempted to do some prying of my own and ask her what she did with the real Chris — the beer-drinking, weed-smoking, former boyfriend of mine — but I resist the urge and say something much worse instead.

'Chris,' I announce, straight-faced. That stalls them for sure. They can't tell if I'm joking or not so their faces are frozen in uncertainty. 'Gotcha!' I burst out laughing, thinking, *Since when did I become so hilarious?*

CHAPTER 48: MADELINE

As I stroll along Bath Row and enter Stamford Meadows for the first time since Joe died, I can feel the emotion building inside me, rising up through my stomach and into my throat until I find myself back in the murky past. For months I have avoided coming here. Even now, I still can't bring myself to glance in the direction of the river. At the thought of its muddy, dark waters, I quake all over as I can't help but think of my son's bloated body lying face down in it. There are more direct paths to Burghley Lane from my house, so I didn't have to come this way, but I did since I felt it signified a change that was needed. Time to move on, as people say . . . even when their advice isn't solicited. However, I see Zoe's pregnancy as a sign that she needs me as much as I need her. Together, we'll work it out.

Once I am out of the town meadows and I've entered Wothorpe Road, my heart finally stops hammering. Then, as I turn down Church Street, I feel spots of rain on my eyelashes. I squint up at the sun which is still bright in the wintry-blue sky and it burns warmly through my eyelids. As the raindrops turn into a sudden shower, I increase my pace, not wanting to get soaked. Even though my thoughts are on Zoe and the baby — whether or not she will be home when I call around and if I should have thought about ringing her first — I keep going back to what Gabriella had said about Zoe. 'She's going to ruin everything, just like Joe tried to do.'

What did she mean by that? What exactly did Joe try to do? Did he get in the way of something Gabriella wanted? Mike, for instance? I realise too late that I could have handled the situation better. I should have adopted a more diplomatic stance and persuaded Gabriella to open up rather than reacting aggressively and accusing her, which simply led to her sulky silence. I'm now cursing myself for it. If I'm ever going to learn the truth about what happened to my son, then I need the girl to trust me. Her telling me that Zoe has another best friend was taken with a pinch of salt. She said it solely to hurt me. I don't believe for a second that it's true.

I fix a smile on my face in an effort to disguise my anxiety before knocking on Zoe's forest-green door. The blinds are down, as usual, making it impossible to discern whether she is home or not. When I think I hear a distant 'Just coming' from behind the door I'm astonished to discover that I'm paralysed with something resembling panic. So, I forcibly remind myself that this was . . . *is* my best friend, who I loved . . . *love* as a sister. Suddenly, Zoe appears in front of me looking as traumatised as I feel. My eyes go straight to her distended stomach.

'It is true, then,' I state matter-of-factly, even though that's the last thing I'm feeling right now.

'What are you doing here, Maddie?' Zoe asks, wide-eyed, while attempting to conceal her pregnancy belly by wrapping her longline cardigan around it.

She's a pale, ghostly version of herself and is clearly distressed. My turning up out of the blue like this has obviously shocked her. *Good.* She deserves a rocket up her arse for how she treated me.

'What do I want?' I reply curtly, unable to keep the promise I made to myself not to let anger stand in the way of rebuilding our friendship. 'How about some answers?'

'Answers?' Zoe blinks at me blearily before nervously glancing up and down the street as if hoping someone might rescue her.

'Like what did I ever do to you to make you hate me so much.'

'I don't hate you, Maddie. I never could,' she protests, blushing.

Even while knowing that helps relieve some of the righteous anger that I was holding on to, I am not done yet. 'Nevertheless, you behaved as if you never wanted to see me again. When I needed you the most, you couldn't be bothered to pick up the phone and call me. You weren't there for me when my son died. Do you have any idea how hurtful that was? I lost my son, *Zoe. Our boy Joe is dead.*' As I watch Zoe's face crumple, I break down into tears myself.

'I know and I'm so sorry,' Zoe chokes out, blinking back tears.

'Are you though? Your actions don't reflect that.'

'Maddie, I'm not a child,' Zoe replies, her voice going hard. 'So don't talk to me like one.'

I instantly realise that the Zoe I am speaking with is not the same as the Zoe I previously knew. She has undergone the same changes as I did when I became pregnant. Even her body language conveys confidence. I also recognise that she no longer looks up to me and that she has set some boundaries. Deciding that I can respect that and live with that, I also get the impression that she is more my equal now than she has ever been. It's odd because I never noticed the disparity in our relationship before.

'I loved you as a sister, as my own flesh and blood, and look at how you repaid me.'

'It wasn't about *you.*'

'Then what was it about?'

'I was going through a difficult time.' As she says this, Zoe's hands flutter to her stomach.

I sigh in frustration as I struggle to take my eyes off her abdomen. 'I can see that.' And then, lowering my voice an octave, I implore, 'You should have told me about the baby. I would have helped you.'

At that, Zoe's head bounces up and her eyes sparkle with what appears to be hatred, which surprises me because she just said that she couldn't possibly hate me. *If not me, then who?*

'Your son had just died. The last thing you needed was me crying on your shoulder,' she points out rationally.

I offer her a reassuring smile, thinking that we are getting somewhere at last. 'If only we'd spoken about this before. I would have understood.'

Although Zoe nods in agreement, she doesn't say anything.

'So, are you going to let me in or keep me at the door like a stranger?'

I can tell that Zoe doesn't really want me here as she opens the door and motions for me to follow her inside. She might not have any intention of continuing our friendship, but by reluctantly admitting me into her home, she has unknowingly invited me back into her and her baby's life. Because I'm here to stay, whether she likes it or not.

CHAPTER 49: ZOE

It's shaping up to be a truly incredible day, and not in a good way. W*hat the hell*? I mean, who would have thought that when I woke up this morning — when I was still unaware that I was carrying an "Arthur" — I would run into both Chris *and* Maddie? And now, instead of spending hours daydreaming about my son, which is how I had anticipated spending my afternoon, I am being forced to confront my past. Maddie has no idea how traumatising it is for me to be sitting across from her on the ochre sofa while she is on the forest green one. It reminds me too much of the night of the attack when it had been her son staring back at me. Just as I was back then, I am like a rabbit caught in the headlights, while she remains comfortable in her own skin and surroundings. Or at least appears to be. She has unwittingly brought Joe to life again in a way I could never have predicted by mirroring her son's actions, so I avoid looking directly at her or making any eye contact.

After a stunned silence, Maddie puts her head on one side and smiles. 'You must come to dinner one night. Mike would love to see you.'

I offer her a reassuring smile but it is fake and she must realise this. 'How *is* Mike?' I ask out of politeness, remembering back to the day Joe died and how Mike had been with Gabriella rather than his wife, who had reeked of his aftershave.

'Oh, you know . . . Mike.' Maddie curls her lip and laughs bitterly.

This isn't the first time I've thought so, but there's something exceedingly privileged about the Blacks. They exude confidence and take what they want from others as if it were a given right. *I should know.* Mike and Joe might have been born into that entitled environment but Maddie had not. On her most vulnerable days, it shows. I now understand that over the years I had clung to this more relatable and grounded part of her. The familiar, sweary, sarcastic Maddie, who would threaten any man who made a disparaging remark about her best friend (me) in a bar or side with me when I fell out with Chris, regardless of who was in the wrong. Despite her faults, she embodied what a loyal friend should be. Whereas I . . .

I wriggle in my seat and nervously pluck at imaginary loose hairs on my cardigan when I realise Maddie is talking and that her accusing stare is on me as if she is wondering what is going through my head.

'I hear you made a new friend,' she enquires casually, *too casually.*

'What?' I ask, perplexed.

Tightly, she replies, 'It's okay,' in a voice that tells me it's *anything but okay.* 'I made a new friend too. Gabriella . . . she's practically moved in.'

Mouth wide open, I exclaim, 'Gabriella!'

Oh no. This isn't good. Doesn't Maddie know? Hasn't she guessed what Mike has been up to? It's not my place to tell Maddie this as we're no longer friends. Even if I were to mention it, I'd only end up saying something I might regret. There is one subject I do want to tackle Maddie on, however . . .

I struggle to find the correct words as I ask, 'How did you find out? About my pregnancy, I mean.'

Maddie blinks at me as if she doesn't know what to say, and then she starts to twirl the rings on her fingers, which indicates to me that she is either apprehensive or reluctant to share something. She acts as though she wants to shield me from everything that might harm me.

Finally, with a certain amount of coolness, Maddie admits, 'Your new best friend.'

I search her expression for clues. 'My new best friend?'

'Angela, of course.' Maddie's face puckers into a frown. 'Or should I say, Boss Angela?'

I'm not sure how she found out about my growing friendship with Angela, but knowing Maddie, she could just be making an educated assumption. A stab in the dark! In either case, I can tell it has rattled her. 'Angela. *My* Angela. She told you I was pregnant?'

'I shouldn't have said anything.' Maddie looks suddenly horrified, as if aware she's made a blunder. 'I'm sorry, Zoe. I wouldn't have brought it up if I had known it was meant to be a secret.'

'It's not,' I cut in, except it bloody well is. I'm furious with my so-called new best friend and birthing partner for blabbing to Maddie *of all people* about the baby when I expressly told her I didn't want her to, claiming we'd had a falling out.

Deciding I will deal with her later because right now I have Maddie to face, I say, 'It's fine. Really, Maddie. And . . .' I pause, dejectedly thinking that what I'm about to say is actually true because it seems I can't trust anyone. 'She's not my best friend.'

'Well, I for one am fucking delighted to hear it.' Maddie laughs dirtily and before I can fight her off, she's out of her seat and wrapping her arms around my ribcage in a crushing embrace. Just as quickly, she's lowering herself back onto the sofa again.

She obviously wants to pick up where we left off as if nothing had happened but I'm not sure how realistic that is, even though I would like it to be . . . more so now, knowing Angela is not the confidante I thought she was. What if I'm wrong, though, about Maddie? She seems prepared to

204

overlook the terrible way I treated her after Joe died, and it's not as if he can come between us anymore. Our secret died with him. Maddie has cleverly persuaded herself that my past behaviour was solely the result of my pregnancy because, like a true friend, I didn't want her worrying about me when she was grieving her son. But I am perfectly aware of Maddie's propensity to view things her way, particularly when it comes to her son.

While Maddie is distracted, scrutinising the room, her expression, as always, disapproving of my house and tastes, I wonder if it's prudent to have her around once the baby is born. Wouldn't she eventually recognise her son in mine and make the connection if she had the opportunity to watch Arthur grow up? But then, I remind myself, we both live in the same small town so she might just as easily learn of any resemblance this way. Of course, I could be overreacting. It's impossible to predict who the baby will look like — me or Joe — when he might not look like either of us. He might, however, be the spitting image of his father, as Joe was Mike. Even so, it doesn't necessarily follow that Maddie will notice or draw any conclusions. What are the chances of finding a likeness if nobody is looking for one?

As I sit there, listening to Maddie chatter about this and that while painfully avoiding discussing *Joe* for fear of upsetting me, because as she says, 'We can't have that with you being pregnant', I feel myself being drawn back in. Like a fly trapped in a spider's web. Yet Maddie only has my best interests at heart. She's always looked out for me. Hasn't she?

CHAPTER 50: MADELINE

There's a dusting of frost on the garden this morning and the ever-watchful river also has a silvery gunmetal sheen to it. Mike asks me almost daily if I would like to sell up and move somewhere else. Anywhere but here, where the river that took my son is ever visible. My response is always the same: no. Joe grew up in this house. He never lived anywhere else so, naturally, his presence is everywhere. All I have left of him now are memories. The living room was where he took his first baby steps. In the kitchen, he said "Mama" for the first time. Sometimes I see and hear young Joe. Boy Joe. Other times, I keep an ear out for the heavier footsteps of teenage Joe thundering down the stairs. When I pause outside his bedroom at night, as I frequently do without ever going inside, I imagine I can hear him talking on the phone to Gabriella, and I can also make out the green gaming blur of his Xbox coming from beneath his door.

Sipping black coffee, I look out through the bi-folding doors that open onto our garden as I ponder whether Zoe is at work. No one is on the salon balcony today. But then again, Zoe had professed to quitting not only cigarettes but alcohol too, since learning of her pregnancy, so I doubt she has any reason to be out on the balcony anymore. Especially on a cold day like this. If Zoe is telling the truth, and I have no reason to doubt her, then I am extremely proud of her. The baby must come first, obviously.

Zoe's pregnancy has injected new life into me. Now I have a reason to get out of bed in the mornings. Nothing has been able to fill the void Joe's passing has left. Not Mike. Not work. And certainly not Gabriella. But a new baby! That's something else entirely. The fact that Zoe is back in my life also means a lot, and I want to do everything I can to support her and her baby. They will now be my main focus. That's why I'm hoping she'll allow me to play as big a role in her child's life as she did my son's. Maybe I can be to it what Zoe was to Joe — a second mother. She did, after all, love him just as much as I did, and I'm sure I'll feel the same about her child, male or female. When I asked her if she knew the sex of her baby, she refused to say, and I pretended not to be offended, but of course I was. I have to constantly remind myself that it will take a while to rebuild our friendship, even though I naturally want to pick up exactly where we left off because I'm impatient like that. I've never been good at waiting.

Mike sweeps into the room, sticky and hot from his workout at the gym. As he kisses the top of my head in greeting, and his mouth brushes momentarily against my hair, I realise I no longer feel his touch. It's like I truly am composed of ice around him.

'Are you okay?' he asks with concerned eyes.

'Fine.' I turn to face him and nod obligingly before continuing to stare out the window.

He asks me this question twenty-plus times a day. He doesn't appear to be aware just how annoying it is. I start to wonder if he has been reading self-help books on "How to support a grieving parent" because he seems to think he is being caring and considerate. But what about his own grief? He seems to have buried it, along with our son. *New Mike*, as I have labelled my husband, is finally putting others before himself. He claims that this is a result of the counselling he is receiving. He says it has enabled him to mature and develop into the kind of man he wants to be. But sadly, it's all happening too late for us. Without Joe, there is no Mike and me. I just can't see a future for us anymore. I haven't brought up the subject of divorce with him yet. When he is working so hard to be the perfect husband, I can't bring myself to do it. I care about him too much to want to hurt him. I take him at his word when he says he loves me, but love isn't always enough.

'You seem better. Different,' Mike observes, arching one eyebrow.

When he says this, I do pay him attention and even offer him a warm-for-me smile. '*I feel* different.'

'That's great news, Madeline,' he enthuses, sounding as excited as any schoolboy. 'I must be doing something right at last.'

The rage I felt months ago after learning that he had been sleeping with Gabriella bubbles to the surface. He believes he is responsible for the transformation he sees in me. How egotistical can you get?

I cut him down to size by saying, 'I went to see Zoe yesterday.'

'And?' He fixes me with a curious gaze.

The corners of my mouth twitch and I find myself smiling once more as I tell him, 'She's having a baby.'

His eyes widen. 'Zoe? Really?'

'Really. And we're friends again. Isn't that wonderful news?'

'Oh, yes, simply wonderful,' Mike says unconvincingly. 'I thought you'd be happy for me.'

'I am, Madeline. Of course, I am. I just don't want you to take a backward step in your recovery.'

His comment instantly sets my teeth on edge. 'I'm not a drug addict.'

Mike appears to be about to say something, but then he seems to change his mind and backs down from the challenge — again, this is not like him. 'How long gone is she?' he mutters, eyes averted.

I have to admit that I find this question strange, yet I still respond. 'Five months more or less.'

He nods then, attempting to appear interested, but his eyes betray him, prompting me to ask, 'What is it, Mike? What's wrong?'

'I had hoped that one day *I* might become your best friend.'

Just as I'm about to treat him to one of my famously sarcastic Maddie laughs, I realise he's being completely serious. Had Mike felt resentful towards Zoe all these years? Was he happy when she left our lives so that he could have me all to himself? How could I not have known this about my husband? Had my focus on my son, first, and Zoe, second, blinded me to his needs and harmed him and me in ways I never anticipated?

'You can tell me all about it once I've had a shower.' Mike excuses himself and leaves the room looking like he is about to cry.

Although I feel sympathy for my husband, I find his behaviour unfathomable. I have never been friends with a man in my entire life because they have always demanded something from me in return. Mike is no different to the rest of them in that he sees women as sexual objects or possessions, making platonic relationships impossible. Because of this, Zoe has always been important to me, even more so than my husband. Mike is unaware of the extent to which I have had to use manipulation, first as a child and later as an adult, just to fit in with other women. He won't have realised how much they despise me for being considered beautiful — enough to want to steal my man from me — and some even succeeded, albeit briefly, revelling in the fact they could because they saw me as competition.

Zoe, who is attractive enough in her own way, is the only exception. We had grown up together, so she didn't perceive me as a threat. No one can match that kind of friendship, least of all Mike. No other woman either. Even if my identification of Angela as the "new best friend" was based on an educated guess, it was still wrong of me to lie to Zoe about her being the one who informed me of the pregnancy, but I am not going to let Angela interfere with our friendship. Or allow her to get her hands on Zoe's baby. If anyone is going to be Zoe's birthing partner it is going to be me.

CHAPTER 51: ZOE

We are in Angela's office. The scene of my crime two months ago when I deleted the images of Joe taken before he died and the CCTV evidence. Because of me, there is no longer any proof that he was being pursued that night or any reason to think his death wasn't an accident. Since I have convinced myself that it is best if everyone reaches the same conclusion, I have to continue living my life as if that night never happened. Given that I am carrying Joe's child within the walls of my womb, this is difficult.

It's Friday and Angela has purchased doughnuts for everyone. A selection of glazed, melt-in-the-mouth pink, brown and nude treats from Krispy Kreme. My stomach is doing cartwheels from the overpowering aroma of sugar, sprinkles and icing. But even though I'm starving, I won't be indulging since I'm trying to maintain a healthy, balanced diet for Arthur's sake. The speed at how quickly I transitioned from calling the bump "my baby" to "my son, Arthur" has taken me by surprise.

'As you are pregnant, you get first dibs.' Angela chuckles and tosses her mane of fiery red locks out of the way as she opens one of the boxes.

'Oh, not for me, I'm trying to be good,' I explain, chewing on a fingernail as I wonder how I should approach the subject of confidentiality with her.

'Well, that just leaves more for the rest of us,' Angela says distractedly, slipping off her beautiful Holland Cooper tartan trench coat and hanging it on a coat hook. 'Would you mind taking them through to the girls?' She gestures towards the doughnuts, while sitting down at her desk and opening her laptop. 'I've just got one or two things to do first.'

'Of course,' I reply as I pick up the box of doughnuts and walk towards the door. But before I get there, I tell myself to quit being such a coward and grow a pair. And it works. Because I find myself returning to the desk. Angela eventually frowns and looks up, 'What is it?'

'I'm sorry, Angela, but I need to speak to you about something.'

'Okay.' She shuts her laptop and motions for me to sit down.

I shake my head, preferring to stand. 'It'll only take a minute.'

She is watching me with interest, which indicates that she has already guessed something is up.

'You're my boss, so this is hard for me, but . . .' I finish lamely, unable to go on. My silence must speak volumes because her eyes never leave me.

'Whatever is it, Zoe? It's not the baby, is it?' She looks suddenly anxious, grabbing the desk like she's about to leap to her feet and call an ambulance.

'Oh, no, nothing like that.' I bat the suggestion away with my hand.

'Then what is it?' Angela pulls a disgruntled face.

'Maddie came to see me yesterday.' Irritation surges in my chest and I ignore the look of bewilderment that appears on Angela's face as I continue.

'Madeline? That's nice of her, considering.'

Her comment throws me. 'Considering what?'

'Considering that she lost her son and you're now . . .' Angela's hand flutters to my very obviously pregnant stomach.

'She said that you told her I was pregnant,' I announce curtly while congratulating myself on having the courage to say what is on my mind.

'Did she?' Angela blinks in confusion. 'I genuinely don't recall when I last spoke to Maddie, let alone told her you were pregnant.'

'So, you have seen her then?' I ask interrogatively.

'Now that I think of it, I did see her in Waitrose, about a week ago.' Angela grins indulgently as she experiences a light-bulb moment. For a successful businesswoman, her memory is abysmal. 'I was looking for truffle salt and Madeline was after artichokes.'

'Did you tell her I was pregnant or not?' I interject rudely.

Angela clambers to her feet and sticks out her chin in defiance. 'Like I said, I can't remember. Why is it so important?'

'Because I told . . . *asked you* not to say a word about the baby to her.'

Angela flinches at my tone. 'I may have mentioned it to her but I can't be certain either way. What is the big deal anyway, Zoe? It's not as if you can hide it any longer. It's quite obvious that you're pregnant.'

'What matters is that I specifically asked you not to mention it to Maddie since we had a falling out and it is none of her business anyway.' I'm conscious that my voice has risen to an unacceptable level when Angela's gaze darts to the door to see if any of our salon co-workers have overheard. They haven't, but she still puts a finger to her lips to shush me.

'Well, I think that was quite harsh of you in the circumstances, especially after all that woman has been through. You've said yourself that she was a wonderful friend to you and yet you're prepared to cut her out of your life and choose not to tell her about the baby all because of some silly disagreement. I didn't have you down as a petty and cruel person.'

'Petty and cruel?' I wail in outrage, yet I find myself blinking away angry tears. 'You don't know what happened or why I—'

'And I don't have to, Zoe; everyone can see that you have been thinking only of yourself the entire time and have never given a thought to poor Madeline Black. I have experienced the pain of losing a child, so I know exactly what it's like.' Angela slams her fist on the table in a rare display of passion but she quickly regains her calm, collected demeanour, and lowers herself back into her chair. 'Now, if you don't mind, I have work to do.'

Dismissed, I drag my eyes away from Angela's cold, unfriendly stare, place the doughnuts back on the desk since I'm obstinately resolved to leave them behind, and walk towards the door with my head and shoulders erect. Angela might have been brutal in her criticism of me but it is clearly no more than I deserve in the eyes of everyone who knows me. It serves as a stark reminder that not everyone sees the Blacks as I do. A danger that needs to be kept at a distance.

CHAPTER 52: MADELINE

As Zoe turned her nose up at my suggestion to have lunch at The Mad Turk, which would have brought back all kinds of memories of the good times had between the four of us, we are meeting at her request at the Orbis restaurant in Stamford. It's a Saturday and Christmas is only a few weeks away. I can't tell you how much it pains me to see the town centre's festive lighting and decorations. When I passed the pine-scented Christmas tree, all I could think of was Joe and how his two-year-old eyes had once glowed when he saw it. His eyes had reflected the bright red, blue and green baubles when I looked into his adorable little face. I'll always remember that. Mike may have been too busy to accompany us to the official switching on of the town lights but Zoe was not. She loved Christmas and we went together every year after that, feasting on mince pies and mulled wine from the outdoor market. We insisted on Joe coming along too, even when he was older and no longer interested.

My phone pings in my bag just as I'm about to enter the restaurant. I fish it out and groan irritably when I see that Gabriella has sent me another of her angry and demanding text messages. It shrieks: *When are you going to tell him?* I type: *After Christmas*, while secretly thinking, *or the New Year*. Mike has been so nice to me lately it's becoming increasingly difficult to raise the subject of divorce with him. If he knew what I was planning, he would undoubtedly suggest that I postpone making any life-changing decisions for a period following Joe's passing, claiming it was too soon. I don't disagree but I had let myself become engrossed in Gabriella's desire to "Teach Mike a lesson" and things quickly got out of control. I no longer remember the precise moment I decided to get a divorce from my husband, but I'm certain it was when I discovered he had slept with Gabriella on the day our son died.

Mike hasn't changed at all, in Gabriella's opinion. She is convinced that he's already moved on to someone new, but I am confident that isn't the case. I receive regular updates from the private eye on what Mike and Gabriella are up to and it doesn't make for very interesting reading. While both continue to be what I can only describe as obsessed with me, I can only think of Zoe and her baby. I try to hide my feelings from them both but for very different reasons. While Gabriella is furious, Mike just appears wounded, as if he can sense my growing indifference to him. Gabriella's jealousy and resentment have developed a life of their own and are now stalking me everywhere.

But more on that later. Right now, I have to focus on my lunch date with Zoe. With that in mind, I cling more tightly to the JoJo Maman Bébé bag that contains the gift I can't wait to show her.

As I enter the restaurant, I see that Zoe is already there and is seated at a table in the rear. I wave and make my way through a battlefield of buggies crammed with sleeping babies to reach her. She doesn't stand up to hug me like she used to, but I take it in my stride. We have a different, more reserved friendship now, but I'm optimistic that things will improve over time. With no son to raise and worry over, I have plenty of that.

'Hi. How are things?' I ask brightly as I slide into the seat opposite her.

'All good.'

When Zoe says this, she throws me a ghost of a welcoming smile but doesn't meet my eye, and I immediately sense that something is wrong. Her face is etched with anxiety and she looks like she is about to cry.

'Zoe, what's wrong?' I come straight to the point.

'Angela,' she replies flatly, rolling her water around a solitary ice cube.

'Boss Angela?' I enquire, attempting to keep my voice from sounding irritated. Mentioning her new friend the second I sit down is not what I was hoping for. 'What about her?'

'We had a terrible argument yesterday and spent the whole day at work not talking.'

'How awful, poor you.' I reach out and reassuringly squeeze Zoe's arm before removing my hand again since I don't want her to feel uncomfortable about being touched. I feel like a bitch when I probe, 'What was the row about?' because I already know the answer.

Obviously, Angela got into trouble for supposedly revealing Zoe's secret when in fact she hadn't. When I finally got around to questioning Gabriella about where she had gotten her information from, she admitted that her mother, who was a regular client at the salon, was the source. Mrs Ellis had personally observed Zoe's growing belly and had told her daughter about it, thinking she might be interested. After all, it's a small town where everyone knows everyone else. Then, just last week, I ran into Angela in Waitrose and we exchanged a few niceties but didn't talk for very long. Our chance encounter provided me with the perfect excuse to fabricate the lie I had told Zoe. Whenever I think about Angela, I feel a prickle of jealousy at the back of my neck and have to force the unwelcome emotion away.

Zoe frowns. 'She wasn't meant to tell anyone about the pregnancy. It was supposed to be a secret.'

She neglects to disclose the fact that it was only intended to be kept a secret from me; nonetheless, I won't hold that against her because she had a good reason. At the time of

Joe's death, I believed Zoe was cruelly and deliberately avoiding me but the opposite was true. She was aware that after losing Joe, I wouldn't have been able to handle news about the baby at that time, and that's why she stayed away.

'It no longer matters, does it?' I remind Zoe, but what I really want to say is "Angela no longer matters". Every second I think and sound more like Gabriella, I realise with a sinking feeling. I'm so consumed with jealousy over my best friend's friend that it feels like we are all still in school. 'Is that why you looked so frightened when I turned up at your door?'

Zoe's face pales and a sliver of panic swirls in her eyes. 'I was surprised, that's all.'

'I should have contacted you sooner instead of sulking and refusing to speak to you.' I have to pause while I talk to fend off tears. 'I should have been the better person.'

Loyalty lights up Zoe's eyes even more than the baubles on the Christmas tree that I passed on my way here, as she vehemently objects. 'You've always been the better person.'

'No.' I shake my head and admit with a pang of guilt, 'I should have rung, got in touch, found out what was wrong.'

'Well,' Zoe hesitates, 'you have now and that's all that matters.'

Her vacant expression gives me the impression that she is still holding something back from me, and isn't fully convinced that our friendship will survive, so I try once more to persuade her. 'Angela may have let you down, in such a way that you can never forgive her.' I think I've done a clever job of planting this suggestion in Zoe's head, which I then follow through with, 'But *I* never will. And I hope you know that.'

At the same time as she says, 'I do,' Zoe shifts uncomfortably in her seat. I can't help but worry when she puts her hand to her stomach and grimaces in discomfort.

'Are you alright? Is it the baby?'

I'm surprised when Zoe chuckles. 'He's been moving about all morning.'

Feeling the familiar sting of loss, I exclaim, 'So it's a boy then?'

CHAPTER 53: ZOE

I watch Maddie tuck into her plate of bang bang cauliflower as I fiddle with my pan-fried seabass and kick myself all over again for inadvertently revealing the gender of my unborn child. I knew that my having a boy would upset her so I'd resolved to keep it under wraps for as long as I could. But I had royally screwed up. I keep expecting her to bring up this topic again, but she hasn't done so as yet. Maddie excels at maintaining a quiet dignity, well beyond anyone I've ever met.

Maddie has her back to the window, so she hasn't seen her, but Gabriella has walked past the restaurant window at least three times, glaring in at us. There's no mistaking her dark, vengeful eyes that look as if they intend to hurt someone. Thinking that it's none of my business, I don't say anything to Maddie. She will undoubtedly find out that the girl is stalking her at some point. I still can't get over the audacity of her befriending the wife of the man she was having an affair with. It's terrible to think that she was also Joe's girlfriend. I'll never forgive Mike for what he has done.

'Before I forget,' Maddie announces unexpectedly, reaching down to take hold of a plastic bag and setting it on the table in front of me. 'I bought you something for the baby.'

I sigh, since I don't want to feel obligated to the Black family. Despite this, I put on a fake smile of appreciation. 'You didn't have to do that.'

Maddie flashes me a toothy grin. 'I know, but I wanted to.' Then, pointing to the logo on the bag she boasts, 'It's from JoJo Maman Bébé.'

'So, I see,' I observe quietly, determined not to be impressed. Although I am aware of the expensive designer store, I have never been inside as it is out of my price range. Not Maddie's though, evidently. Buying me expensive gifts is nothing new. She has always done this but given the current situation and the fact that she is not aware of how closely linked she is to my unborn child, it feels strange. However, because I can't actually tell her this, I pretend to be happy as I take the cot mobile out of the bag.

'It's from the Hundred Acre Wood collection,' Maddie tells me with pride. She points to the soft toy and says, 'Look. It has Winnie the Pooh, Piglet, Eeyore and Tigger hanging toys.'

When I lift it up, it produces one or two very familiar musical notes. They have me questioning where I've heard it before.

Maddie announces, 'Brahms' "Lullaby",' before I can, beating me to it. Her hands are cupped together as if she is about to applaud.

I nod. 'Yes, I thought I recognised it.'

'Joe had one just like it. Do you remember?'

I respond, 'I do indeed,' gulping hard as I do so.

'It only comes in one colour, I'm afraid,' Maddie apologises, sensing my annoyance at the reminder of Joe.

Conscious of how ungrateful I must seem, I express an appreciation I do not feel, 'Thank you, Maddie. It's lovely,' before stuffing the unwanted cot mobile back in the bag. 'Even if it is beige,' I add to cheer her up.

This makes us both chuckle because Maddie knows how much I adore colour, which is evident in my home. Even though I admire her elegance and flair, I couldn't live in her house. I wouldn't be able to breathe in its stark black-and-white minimalistic surroundings.

The dead-eyed fish on my plate is making me feel queasy so I shovel sticky rice into my mouth instead. After barely finishing four mouthfuls of food, Maddie has already pushed her plate to the side. When they bring over the dessert menu I know she will perk up. The next time I hear Maddie speak, my head snaps up.

'So, are you going to tell me who the father is?' She gives me the benefit of her golden gaze as she stares curiously at me.

I am deliberately vague. 'No one important.'

'You obviously don't want to say, and I can't say I blame you if it was a one-night stand, but answer me one thing, Zoe . . .' She pauses for dramatic effect while I feel as if I am perched on the edge of a cliff and about to plunge to my death. 'Is it Chris's?'

'No!' I snarl, annoyed at her for presuming I'd had a one-night stand and relieved that she hasn't accused me of having a sexual relationship with her son. 'It absolutely isn't. Besides, you know he has a girlfriend?'

She shrugs. 'Since when did that stop men?'

She has a point, *Mike being one of them*, but I don't say so. Instead, I watch her take a sip of her lime cordial and soda before pursing her lips. 'I assume you *do* know who the father is.'

I slam my knife and fork down, glad of the excuse not to have to eat the remainder of my meal and fix my wintry-blue gaze on her. Inhaling deeply, *how bloody dare she?* I explode, 'Of course I know who the father is, but as he is not going to be a part of my child's life, that is something I am not going to share with anyone! Not even you, Maddie, and if you cannot accept that then there is no point in us being friends.'

I'm ready to walk out and she knows it so I'm taken aback when she raises her glass in celebration and exclaims, 'Good for you,' as I was expecting a lecture.

'Maddie, do you mean that?' I implore, wanting it to be true.

221

She nods emphatically. 'Just because we're friends doesn't mean we have to tell each other everything.'

I burst out laughing at that. 'Oh my God, will the real Madeline Black please stand up?' The joke is on Maddie but she reluctantly joins in. Her obsession with knowing everything about everyone is commonly known.

Maddie's eyes start to unexpectedly shine with tears as she murmurs, 'I guess we've both changed in the last five months.'

'We've had to,' I reflect thoughtfully.

'I have one more question and then I'll shut up.'

When I hear this my shoulders sag. 'Go on then.'

'We are proper friends again, aren't we? You're not just pretending or trying to be nice because of what happened to Joe?'

I'm so moved by Maddie's vulnerability that I almost cry. We've already been through so much without one another that I start to think it really is time for us to mend our relationship, since like her, I have no one else. The Angelas and Gabriellas of this world aren't to be trusted. Maddie and I have a long history together and there's nobody I trust more. So, I lift my glass and say, 'Toast,' just as we did on the night of my birthday celebrations all those months ago.

'To my best friend who I love as a sister,' Maddie responds.

CHAPTER 54: MADELINE

When I get home, Gabriella is nowhere to be found, but Mike is in the kitchen cooking, of all things, which instantly makes me suspicious. I eye up the black oval glass dining table which has been set for two. He's used our finest dinnerware and glasses and I'm astonished that he knew where to find them or that they even existed. Dressed in a pink checked shirt and dark jeans, smelling of aftershave and his hair wet from the shower, he looks very handsome. Like the perfect husband, he greets me by coming over to kiss me on the top of the head as he always does.

'Who are you expecting?' I try to make a joke, but since I'm not really in the mood, it backfires and he rolls cynical eyes at me, while playfully grinning, reminding me of the Mike I originally met and fell in love with. I frown as I follow his movements around the kitchen. One minute he's chopping up piles of jewel-coloured vegetables, the next he's filling a jug with chilled, filtered water and setting it on the table. He periodically hums along as opera arias play in the background and the wall-mounted glass floating fireplace is ablaze with the colours of the rainbow.

'I've already eaten. I had a late lunch with Zoe,' I tell him this so he won't have expectations of us enjoying a romantic supper together. *If he thinks he's on a promise he's got another thing coming! No way.*

He is facing away from me, and although I think he squares his shoulders at the sound of Zoe's name, I may have imagined it.

'Dinner won't be ready for a while. Take a seat and I'll join you in a minute.'

Reluctantly, I do as I'm told, all the while wondering what is going on. 'No Rotary Club dinner and drinks with the boys tonight then?'

'Not tonight, no. I thought I would spend some time with my beautiful wife instead.'

'That's not like you,' I snip, drumming my fingernails on the glossy surface of the table. When he doesn't respond, I ask, 'Have you seen Gabriella?'

'She popped in around six or so, but when she saw it was just me, she popped back out again.'

'Sounds about right,' I comment darkly. Then, thinking I have him all figured out, I exclaim, 'Is that what this is all about? You're trying to win me over in the hope that I'll finally ditch her and give her her marching orders as you've been wanting me to do for months.'

Mike visibly recoils at my tone but recovers quickly, saying, 'Fortunately, Gabriella is not on my mind at all these days. Now, can I get you anything, some olives and bread perhaps?'

I nod silently, suddenly feeling ravenous. I was too anxious at lunchtime to eat properly. Zoe was the same.

'There you go, dig in.' Mike sets a wooden platter of black and green pitted olives and buttered sourdough on the table in front of me and takes a seat opposite. Lights from the fire shine onto his black hair until it is illuminated like Blackpool pier.

I can see him watching me as one of the greasy, salty olives slides down my throat. 'What?' I bark.

'Can't a man look at his wife without being accused of anything?' he chuckles.

'Hmm.' I pull a face, letting him know that he doesn't fool me, not even for a moment. 'So, what is it you want to talk to me about?'

'Why don't you tell me about your day first?' he suggests while nibbling on some bread. 'Isn't that what couples are meant to do?'

'Is that what we are?' I scoff, rolling my eyes.

'Eighteen years is a long time, Madeline,' he says softly.

I'm immediately on my guard. Does he know about the divorce? Is that what this is about? Had Gabriella taunted him with this information in my absence, in an attempt to cause trouble between us? But surely, he would just come out and say so if that were the case? Mike is not one to play games as a rule, except when there's another woman involved. But I know for a fact he isn't seeing anyone so it can't be that.

'Zoe is having a boy,' I blurt out brokenly as if it were the most important topic in the world, and for me, I suppose it is.

'How do you feel about that?' he asks gently.

'Oh, you know, delighted for her, but also devastated. I realise that's selfish of me, but—'

'It's not selfish at all, it's perfectly understandable.' Mike reaches out a hand to caress my cheek, which is burning with shame.

'I suppose as a doctor you think Zoe is a little old to be having a baby?'

'No, not at all. Actually, that's what I wanted to talk to you about.'

'Zoe?' My face stretches in surprise.

Mike replies hesitantly, which is uncharacteristic of him, 'Not exactly.'

'What then?'

'I figured if you wanted to, we could try for another.'

I ask, baffled, 'Another what?' But when he smirks at me as if he had just scored a goal, the realisation strikes . . . 'Oh my God, you're talking about us having a baby, aren't you?'

'If Zoe can get pregnant at forty, maybe you can, too.'

225

'Mike, for fuck's sake, are you crazy?' I bat away his hand and spring to my feet, wailing, 'This is the last thing I was expecting.'

Eyes lowered for once instead of blazing with certainty, Mike muses, 'I've seen how Zoe's pregnancy has positively impacted you, and I thought if you were to get pregnant, it might help us come to terms with what happened . . .'

'Are you suggesting that we simply replace Joe and get on with our lives as if he never existed? As if I never gave birth to him?'

'No, Madeline, of course not. He was my son too.'

'Don't you remember, Mike, that we tried to have another child for years after Joe? But nothing happened. I was unable to get pregnant again.'

'We could go down the fertility route this time if you wanted to.'

'Why now? When you rejected that option for years?'

For a moment, Mike doesn't move and then he's on his feet bellowing, 'Because I wasn't in danger of losing you then.'

The force of his yelling sends me staggering backwards, and a sob lodges in my throat, catching me unawares as I watch Mike's body heaving with pent-up grief. Wave upon wave of it pours out of him in anguished howls. Eventually, he hangs his head, unable to meet my gaze. Then, with a gut-wrenching groan, his words are dragged out of the darkest, saddest part of him as he implores, 'I don't want to lose you as well as my son, Madeline. Every day it seems like you are getting farther away from me and I need you. I need you so much. Without you I'm nothing.'

CHAPTER 55: ZOE

Since our argument, Angela has maintained a chilly demeanour towards me and hasn't apologised for what she said. She
plainly believes that she is not at fault, just as I do. We are
professional at work, but I feel like I have to tread on eggshells
around her and our relationship has certainly reverted to that
of boss and employee. I'm seriously considering switching
jobs, and I intend to begin my hunt while I'm on maternity
leave in a few months' time. But for the time being, I need
this job more than ever because, at five months pregnant,
who in their right mind would hire me?

Being on my feet all day doesn't help. I'm always worn
out. My back aches constantly, I have terrible heartburn and
I have to wee all the time. To her credit, Angela has identified
ways of working that will help me, but cutting hair while
seated is simply not practical. She won't let me bleach or
colour customers' hair because she fears the chemicals may
harm my unborn child and she has also allowed me to reduce
my hours to thirty-five a week, so from an employee's perspective I can't complain. But it's evident that I'm no longer
her number two. That accolade is now held by Pug-owning
Stacey and when she and Angela are in the office having a
coffee and a natter, I hear them laughing together, exactly

like Angela and I used to. Every time that occurs, self-pitying tears well up in my eyes.

Stacey, like Angela, is childless, but she makes up for it by lavishing all of her maternal love on her dog, Prince. Angela even allows her to bring him into the salon on occasion, claiming it's because he is well-behaved and the customers adore him. At times, I want to point out how unfair it is that one of my co-workers is permitted to bring her dog to work but I won't be allowed to do the same with my baby, because of all the chemicals and potential disruption to customers. But then I remind myself how childish I am being because no one in their right mind would want to bring a newborn to work. Since Angela and I are no longer close and rarely speak on a personal level, I'm unable to ask her about the child she claimed to have lost, but that hasn't prevented me from quizzing my co-workers.

As Angela is highly respected and well liked, not everyone was willing to gossip. But with Book Club Scarlett, who blabbed everything, I struck gold. Angela had a little boy, aged around seven or eight years old, who drowned when the nanny's car spun out of control and slammed into the river. The nanny survived but was unable to save the boy. Upon learning this, I immediately felt terrible for my former friend and regretted talking about her behind her back. The fact that both Angela and Maddie's sons had tragically perished in the river made it clear why Angela was on Maddie's side rather than mine. My heart breaks for both of them, and I wonder if Maddie is aware of what happened to Angela's little boy. Since she has never brought it up, I don't believe that she is. I would expect Maddie to be a lot more sympathetic towards Angela if that were the case. Instead, Maddie seems to despise the woman.

Calling out, 'Good night, everyone,' I move towards the salon door. It's a Friday so everyone else is working late, but they all smile at me as I leave as if they don't harbour any resentment, which is nice of them. This is likely due to the fact that at least some of them will have babies at some point. When I glance over at the reception desk where Angela and Stacey have their heads together chatting about price increases, neither of them looks up or even acknowledges me. I won't lie; I find this upsetting, but I console myself by remembering that Maddie is coming over tonight. She has been extremely elusive and difficult to pin down the past week or so. Normally, she returns my calls and messages right away, but ever since we had lunch together last week, she has appeared preoccupied. I hope everything is okay. I might broach the subject with her tonight depending on how she seems.

Even though I know it must be a harrowing prospect for Maddie, she has volunteered to help me redecorate the spare bedroom, which we always referred to as "Joe's room". As far as I know, she has never once gotten her hands dirty decorating her own house, instead choosing to hire interior designers, painters and decorators, so the fact that she is willing to give up her time to physically help is massive. I would have been more than happy to get stuck in by myself but Maddie had insisted. *And she's not easy to say no to.*

She even offered to buy all the paint but I couldn't let her do that. Money is tight, I'll give her that, but I'm not a charity case. After having Arthur, I'll have to return to work full-time once my maternity benefits run out and he'll have to go to a creche, which is something I don't like thinking about. When I imagined myself as a mother, I pictured getting married first and then staying home with the kids while my husband went off to work. Despite the challenges that come with being a single mother, at least Arthur won't grow up in a household where bickering is the norm, as it was in my relationship with Chris and others before him. I'm glad I have Maddie in my life though. Because I certainly can't rely on anyone else.

All of the paint for "Project Arthur" was delivered to the house yesterday and it has been stashed in my small outside courtyard for the time being because, according to Maddie, I'm not allowed to carry it upstairs in my condition.

However, there are a few smaller items I intend to pick up on the way home. Brushes, white spirit and a new paint roller as these are things I *can* carry.

While passing through the High Street on my way to Harrison and Dunn's hardware store, I happen to glance in the JoJo Maman Bébé window and notice a Winnie-the-Pooh and Friends cot mobile on display which is almost identical to the one Maddie bought me. But this one is decorated in vibrant cartoon colours: a Pooh in yellow and red. A Tigger with orange stripes. A bright blue Eeyore. *Definitely not beige!*

Knowing that Maddie may have lied to me over something so trivial as colour options is unsettling. Does she intend to impose her tastes on me and my baby knowing how I feel about boring beige? If that's the case it feels domineering and overbearing. Or am I overthinking this? Isn't it more likely that when she made her purchase, the shop simply didn't have any other colour in stock? Maddie may have been speaking the truth when she said they only had it in beige. I sigh and tighten my coat about me before deciding that there is only one way to find out, so I grab the door handle and go into the shop.

CHAPTER 56: MADELINE

Tall white flowers. Black glossy surfaces. An abundance of glass. I like to think that my home's interior reflects who I am. Cool and composed. Elegant and timeless. Others might see me as cold and harsh. Or not very welcoming. And let's not forget that I'm a neat freak too. Everywhere is spotless. Mike may tease me about having OCD, but I know he appreciates the tranquil atmosphere of our home, at least when Gabriella isn't around that is. She continues to be a painful reminder of Mike's adultery and betrayal for both of us, but, in my opinion, it's necessary to have her around. Gabriella is like rain on your wedding day or having a black cat cross your path.

I'm still not sure what to do with her now that Mike and I have decided to try for another baby. When she finds out, she's going to flip. I haven't adjusted to the idea myself yet. If you had asked me two or three months ago if there was any possibility of Mike and I giving our marriage another shot, I would have said there was zero chance of that happening. I believed he had squeezed every last drop out of me as a woman and that I was done. But what if we had a child to raise? A chance to be the perfect parents the second time around? Do it better? That was a very different matter. On our exotic vacations, we had looked for fresh starts in every part of the world, but we never found one, or each other. But a child. Perhaps another boy. Joe's brother . . . that was a chance I couldn't walk away from.

Before I even step inside the living room, I already know what I will see — my husband relaxing on the sofa, arms raised above his head, a glass of red wine next to him. He has removed his tie, unbuttoned his shirt and is watching an episode of a US medical drama. When he sees me, he tilts his head a little and smiles.

'Are you off?'

'Yes, I won't be late.'

As I bend to kiss him on his sculptured cheekbone, he gently pulls me in for more of a hug. Involuntarily, I feel myself freeze. He senses my unwillingness too and releases me quickly, his pleasure melting away with his smile. I shoot him a warning look. 'Don't wait up,' which is morse code for "We won't be having sex when I get home". Just because we have decided to pursue fertility treatment doesn't mean I'm going to start sleeping with him. That's what artificial insemination is for.

'Are you taking the car?'

I shake my head. 'No, walking.'

He frowns. 'Be careful.'

'I'm always careful.' I sigh and wish I could be a little warmer, happier, easier and more approachable. Like Zoe.

I leave then, and as soon as I close the shining black double entrance doors behind me, I am greeted by a familiar voice. It seems to pounce on me from out of the shadows.

'Why are you dressed like that?'

I can't see Gabriella even though I am standing under the powerful exterior light, which came on as soon as I stepped outside, but I am aware that she is lurking in our front garden somewhere, hiding.

Needled, I ask, 'Where are you?'

Then, she emerges from behind a large bronze metal garden structure and I'm struck by how much she resembles me.

Under the porchlight, her black, glossy hair, and dark, pick-me-girl eyes both gleam. Her transition into, well, myself, is completed by her youthful glow and serum-plumped cheeks. She's decked out in an ivory cowl-neck knitted dress with a soft-white cape over the top and brown suede knee-high boots. She hasn't stolen the outfit from my wardrobe but she may as well have done. I could argue that I have done a good job in turning her into a mirror image of myself, but meeting one's own creation in the flesh is disconcerting. Her appearance makes me think of Mary Shelley's *Frankenstein*. I worry whether I might also have created a monster. Or, as in the book's narrative, is the true monster the beast's creator (i.e. me)?

'Well?' She gives me a disdainful look, as if disgusted with how I look.

As I cast a quick glance down at my striped top, dungarees and trainers, I decide she's right and that this isn't me at all. Feeling self-conscious, I stammer, 'I've offered to help Zoe paint the baby's bedroom.'

'You?' she scoffs.

'Why not me?' I retaliate, looking along the rain-slicked street, realising that if I don't go back inside for my umbrella, I'm going to get wet.

'You look like a lesbian,' she sneers.

I lift my chin and take a deep breath. 'And you'd know all about that.' As soon as the words are out of my mouth I regret them, so I add more kindly, 'What are you doing out here anyway? Why didn't you come inside?'

Her jaw drops open. 'You have to ask?'

'Evidently.' I shrug.

'Because of him,' she hisses, throwing me a hard stare. 'You two are all loved up again. I saw you cuddling through the window. It's disgusting considering everything he has done.'

'Oh, you don't know the half of it,' I warn, my voice tense. She has no idea how close she is to triggering me. Mike's role in our son's disappearance the night he died is something I will never entirely forgive.

Gabriella becomes less of a woman and more of an impressionable teenage girl when her bottom lip droops childishly and her eyes fill with angry tears. 'You're meant to be divorcing him,' she says and she actually stomps her foot.

Observing how distraught she is, I push my resentful feelings for her aside as I try to gently explain in a way that someone her age might understand, 'That's sometimes how it is with married couples.'

When I notice that she is gawping at me as if I were speaking a foreign language, I try again, almost jovially this time. 'One minute you hate each other and are yelling all kinds of terrible things and the next—'

She abruptly cuts me off by yelling, 'You're thinking about having a baby together!'

CHAPTER 57: ZOE

When I hear the knock on the door, I'm upstairs. That will be Maddie. She's right on time, as usual, so I yell, 'Doors open. Come in,' thinking nothing of it. When I hear it opening, letting the hum of the street in, I call out, 'I'm up here. In the spare bedroom.' The room has been cleared and there are no further reminders of Joe. The TV, old toys, PlayStation and the stars and stripes duvet have all gone. For a small fee, my landlord removed the bed, the chest of drawers and even the shelves from the wall for me.

Unlike my room, which overlooks the street, this one faces the back of the house. In daylight hours it has a view of Stamford High School's campus. I like the thought that Arthur will be able to watch the comings and goings of older boys and girls from his window, assuming we stay here long term. And why not? There was a time, after Joe assaulted me, when I hated living here, but practically speaking, it's in a great location and is within walking distance to town, work and schools. Besides, I have grown to like my little house again.

Shouting, 'Do you want to start by bringing up the paint tins from the courtyard and I'll make us a cup of tea in a bit?' I hear an answering grunt and the back door click open, so I focus on the stack of boxes in the corner that need to be moved before we can start slapping paint on the walls. A hot air balloon mural is going on one of the walls, although I suspect it will be a nightmare to stick on, and a silver LED name sign is going to be mounted on another. To see Arthur's name in lights will be amazing. But I feel the corner of my mouth tug downward as soon as I glimpse the JoJo Maman Bébé bag. When the shop employee told me they had been selling the cot mobile in a variety of colours for months, it confirmed my hunch that Maddie had lied to me. I've told myself to let it go. It's not important enough to stir up conflict. But I'm still bothered by it.

The sound of metal clanging against metal tells me that Maddie is making her way up the stairs with the paint tins. As she's not used to physical work she's probably struggling. 'You've only got yourself to blame since you told me I'm not allowed to carry them,' I chuckle.

'Quite right too,' a man's voice says.

'Chris!'

I can't even express how astonished I am to see my ex standing in the doorway, holding four paint tins sheepishly in his hands and smiling. As his eyes sweep the room, and me, my face puckers into a frown. 'What are you doing here? I thought you were Maddie.'

He jokes, 'And there's me thinking you get all of your visitors to do manual labour the second they walk through the door.' Then, gesturing to the paint tins, he asks, 'Where do you want these?'

'Oh, over there,' I say, giving him a weak, unconvincing smile.

'Blue for a boy,' he comments, setting the tins on the floor.

'How are Maple and Vicky doing?' I enquire awkwardly.

He corrects me, 'It's Willow,' but frowns as though he's ashamed of his daughter's name. It wouldn't have been his choice, I realise with sudden clarity. I can tell he's not happy with his situation but he won't let on.

I smooth a hand over my hair and risk a quick look in his direction, only to find him staring at me. 'Chris, why are you here?'

'I felt I had to come and see you again once you told me about the baby.'

He keeps looking at my stomach, which makes me feel extremely self-conscious. Gulping nervously, I ask again, 'But why?'

'I'm not sure, Zoe,' he grimaces as if he really is unsure.

I see the beginnings of a receding hairline as he agitatedly runs a hand through his hair. Knowing how vain he is, I try not to let him see that I've noticed. *Once a people-pleaser always a people-pleaser.*

'I guess I always thought we'd have a little boy together someday. It was a bit of a shock to see you at the hospital, all excited about the baby and knowing you'd moved on.'

'Moved on? Moved on from what?' I ask, bewildered.

'Me, of course.' He gives a soft chuckle as if hoping to deflect my attention away from his ego. He isn't successful. Gesturing to my baby bump again, he goes on to say what is really on his mind, 'I mean you've obviously met someone. Is it anyone I know?'

I'm relieved that he hasn't considered Joe as a potential father to my child, but I'm furious that he thinks my life is any of his business.

Guardedly I tell him, 'I *was* seeing someone, the baby's dad, but it didn't work out.'

'Oh right.' He seems pleased with my response.

He coughs to clear his throat and is the first to look away after our eyes unintentionally lock. Red cheeks. Even redder hair. Ghostly white skin. Hands bunched in his too-big jeans. He's unable to disguise his jealousy. Not from me. It's amusing yet depressing at the same time. Six months ago, I would have quite literally sawn my arm off for this man.

'So, you're going to raise the baby by yourself?'

He makes it sound like I have options, which further annoys me. To deliberately wound him, I say, 'I won't be alone. I'll be with my son.'

He's always wanted a mini version of himself to kick around a football in the park with and to hurl dangerously high into the air. That's why his eyes are expressing the regret I had hoped to see after he left me but never did. Don't all men aspire to be gods and create people in their own likeness?

'Zoe, just let me know if there's anything I can do for you,' he implores, reaching out for my hand in a sudden, desperate move that makes me shudder as if it were a snake about to bite me. 'And I'll be there for you.'

'Is that what you promised Vicky when you were still with me?' I snip.

'I never cheated on you,' he responds angrily.

'If you say so, but I bet you were already talking to her, getting to know her.'

When he gulps and looks away, I know I'm right. And to think that all this time he has blamed me for our failed relationship. How could he? He and Vicky might not have been sleeping together but they were emotionally involved and that counts just as much. If not more.

'I don't think we should see each other again, Chris.' These are words I never imagined saying to him.

'Are you worried you won't be able to resist me?' he jokes bitterly, with a self-satisfied gleam in his eye.

I raise my eyebrows and fold my arms before saying sarcastically, 'Hardly! You are no better or worse than I am, Chris, yet you made me feel awful for what I did to you. For *letting you down* as you called it. But when it suits you, like now, you'd treat Vicky the same way.'

I can't help but think that people are all the same. We're all lying, cheating scum.

He's on a roll now, refusing to listen to me and giving his fantasies full rein, as if I hadn't called him out on his behaviour. 'But I only want to see you so I can help you. I miss you, and care about you, Zoe, And you shouldn't have to go through this alone.'

'It's too late for that, Chris,' I inform him curtly. 'And I suggest you go back to *your* Vicky before Maddie gets here.' I want to add, *there's a good boy*, but of course I don't. As much as I'd told myself that I'd already let him go, I now realise that I hadn't fully done so in the year and a half he has been gone. However, in all honesty, I no longer have any feelings for the man I once loved with all my heart. He pales into insignificance to how I feel about my unborn child. My Arthur.

CHAPTER 58: MADELINE

As I shove Gabriella up against the house wall, growling, 'I told you to keep your voice down,' her lips open as if she is about to argue, but when I place a smothering hand over her mouth, her head snaps up and her eyes flicker from side to side in panic. The realisation that I'm just as much of a bully as my son was, for physically assaulting a schoolgirl, hits me like a brick to the back of my head. Since this is Gabriella, who is herself a master manipulator, I don't pause to reflect on what I have become. *She deserves it.* Millimetres separate our faces as I hiss menacingly at her, 'I mean it.'

When she reluctantly stays silent and there is no sign of my husband coming to the door to find out what all the commotion is about, I release my hand, but continue to wave a threatening finger in her face. 'I want you to tell me exactly how you found out about the baby. And no lying.'

'I have my ways and means.' With her shoulders arched in wrath, Gabriella sulkily brushes me off and moodily turns her back on me. She doesn't fool me though. I could see genuine terror in her eyes just now. She'd be wise to remember it.

'Have you been poking around in the study when I'm not there?' I accuse.

She whips around to face me, and I detect a flash of superiority in her gaze. 'Oh, Madeline,' she says over brightly, 'you really need to do better. I figured out your laptop's password in less than a minute. I mean, come on, JOE1302 — your dead son's name and his birthday!'

I bite my lip because I'm not sure whether to be angry or embarrassed.

'When I clicked on your Google search history, I found dozens of open tabs for private fertility clinics, which have nothing to do with the house hunting you claimed to have been doing.'

Although I can't think clearly because my brain is spinning so fast, I manage to grit my teeth and say, 'This is none of your business, Gabriella. It's personal. Between Mike and me.'

A flicker of disbelief crosses Gabriella's face as she mimics sarcastically, 'Mike and me! Do you have any idea how pathetic you sound? This is the same man you told me can't keep it in his pants and is constantly cheating on you. And how about your so-called best friend who dumped you when your only son died? Does she know that you intend to get pregnant too?'

As I confess, 'No, she knows nothing about this and I'm warning you—' I catch myself blushing.

'Warning me of what?' she challenges, scrunching up her face.

'You must not discuss this with her or anyone else,' I protest fiercely, before asking, 'do you understand?'

She curls her lip. 'Or what?'

Coldly, I answer, 'Or you and I will no longer be friends. I'll have nothing more to do with you.'

'You said I was like a daughter to you and that you would always be there for me,' she gasps, as though my words have left her in shreds.

I never intended to hurt her this deeply, and I feel my attitude towards her softening as I suggest, 'Look, why don't you come with me to Zoe's? It might be fun.'

Gabriella wrinkles her nose as if this were the worst idea ever and perhaps she is right. She hates Zoe, and I'm fairly certain Zoe feels the same way, although she's never directly come out and said so. I find myself genuinely moved when Gabriella's shoulders start to heave and she bursts into tears. *Once a mother always a mother*, I suppose. Wrapping a comforting arm around her, I respond, 'I should have told you I had paused the divorce for the time being and that Mike and I were going to try for another baby, but, well, it might never happen and I knew it would upset you. Believe it or not, that's the last thing I wanted.'

She then casts mournful doll-like eyes my way, and I brush a stray black hair from her face. Her body relaxes into mine when she notices the unshed tears twinkling in my eyes. I could crush the girl with one hand because she is so thin. It brings out the protector in me.

'Aren't you past your prime to have a child? At your age, isn't it risky?' she frets, hands clasped together in turmoil.

Out of the mouths of babes, I think, but don't say anything. She'll find out for herself one day what it's like to age and how to deal with the younger women who criticise you for it. They're much harsher than men.

'Not always. It can make things more difficult. And, Gabriella, things between Mike and I are not certain.' I sigh, feeling suddenly psychologically and physically drained. 'This could be our last chance and if I can't get pregnant and things don't work out for us, I'm going to need a friend.'

She stiffens in my arms then, like a small, dead animal, and enquires hesitantly, 'You mean Zoe?'

'No, I mean you, actually.' The lie catches in my throat as I consider that it's a real shame I can't trust her. Then, leaning in closer till our faces are practically touching and our matching heads of hair are intertwined, I add, 'Old friends don't get much attention from new mothers like Zoe, especially those without children.'

'I swear I won't let you down, Madeline,' she insists, twirling a strand of my hair between her thumb and forefinger in a very childlike manner. How easily she transforms from predatory female to vulnerable adolescent.

'I'm sure you won't.'

'Doesn't this mean you'll have to sleep with Mike to get pregnant?' she exclaims suddenly, pulling a disgusted face. 'How could you?'

I want to respond with an equally indignant, *"How could you?"* but I remind myself to wait it out. "Pick your battles", as Zoe would have said. On that note, I wonder why I haven't yet told Zoe about my plan to try and conceive. She is, after all, meant to be my closest friend and confidante. And I realise that the reason is I don't want to be seen as a loser or a failure (I sound just as competitive as Mike). I will only let her in on the secret if and when I get pregnant and that way, we'll be closer than ever as we raise our children together. Wouldn't it be wonderful if we both had boys?

The chatter inside my head grows louder. However, Gabriella is still droning on in my ear, demanding my attention as usual and voicing what she perceives as a more pleasant alternative. 'Or is it done by artificial semination? You wouldn't have to let him touch you then.'

I put a shushing finger to my mouth, implying that what I'm about to confide is top secret. 'You are a clever girl for working it out and you are quite right about the procedure. Sadly, I have to go though, as Zoe is expecting me. But since tomorrow is Saturday, why don't we do something special together, just the two of us? Whatever you like. You decide.'

In awe, she asks, 'Do you mean that?'

'Yes of course.' It takes everything I have not to flinch away from her skeletally thin frame as I offer her another hug. How could Mike go anywhere near a child's body like that? It's not right.

As if reading my thoughts, she whispers into my ear, 'I hate him.'

'I know you do.' I pat her reassuringly on her back, and I sigh regretfully, 'I do too sometimes.'

Tearfully, she asks, 'And if you have a baby? What will happen to me?'

One of those severe guilt attacks, which are happening more frequently, strikes again as I realise that I've gone too far with this. And for what purpose? In the months Gabriella and I have known each other, I've learned nothing new about the blackmailing of Rupert Forbes or the circumstances surrounding Joe's death. I'm starting to believe that I was mistaken before and that she is completely innocent of all the things I have secretly accused her of. If true, that would make me a terrible person for meddling with a damaged child's mind, and all of it would have been for nothing.

Looking up at the cauldron-black starless sky, I tell her firmly, 'Then you will be like an older sister to it.'

The way her feline pupils light up suggests that she finds this prospect appealing, but I know in my heart that, innocent or not, I will never in a million years allow her to be anywhere near my child. If I am to trust what the coroner, the police, and everyone else said, and I'm reluctantly coming around to that idea, my son committed suicide as a result of this little bitch's cold-blooded abandonment of him. She later threatened to have my husband arrested for having sex with her when she was underage. As I recall the wrongs she has done to my family, my heart, which was in danger of softening, hardens once more towards her.

CHAPTER 59: ZOE

There is so much tension in the room you could cut the atmosphere with a knife. I'm not sure what's up with Maddie, but I think she and Mike may have gotten into an argument before she left the house, because I can hardly get a word out of her. To be honest, I'm still struggling to get over my encounter with Chris. His visit has left me feeling unsettled. He had a bloody nerve showing up like that. Though I'm aware that my reaction to him would have been different if it had happened six months earlier, would I truly have taken him back after he left me for another woman? The answer is. . . probably, yes. I really was that stupid and gullible back then.

I'll be the first to admit that I'm disappointed in Chris for trying to cheat on Vicky with me because I honestly thought he was one of the good guys. It's a scary thought but what if there are no good guys? Perhaps there never was, and all along, we women were sold a fairytale. Knights in shining armour aren't supposed to just walk out on you without offering any closure. Chris owed me that regardless of what I had done wrong — and I acknowledge that I made some terrible mistakes. This says more about him than it does me though because despite my flaws I would never have done that to him. I cared and loved him too much to block or ghost him in the way he had me. I might have been addicted and unable to resist temptation, but I never intended to hurt him, or for him to discover how I had betrayed him but was unable to prevent it.

I take a few deep breaths to settle my anxiety and turn to face Maddie, wishing I could tell her about Chris's visit but knowing she will only get angry if I do. She likewise seems preoccupied. I thought it would be a fun experience to decorate with her but her mind certainly isn't on painting. She looks the part, otherwise, she isn't trying too hard. She continues to pout while glaring at the paintbrush in her hand and the paint splashes on her skin. Unlike me, she doesn't seem to have a clue about DIY. And from the multiple creases on her otherwise smooth forehead, I can tell she detests the midnight-blue hue we have painted on the walls.

'Want another cup of tea?' I enquire, stretching my back after being in the same position for so long.

She mumbles, 'I'm good,' and then, upon noticing my frown, adds, 'Is it the baby?'

I guffaw. 'If he isn't poking me with his feet, he is digging me with his elbows.'

But Maddie doesn't laugh back or even grin. Instead, she lets out a long exhale. I decide to cross-examine her because I can't take the silence any longer. 'What's up, Maddie? You've barely said a word all night.'

At that, she throws me a ghost of a smile and gets up from the floor where she has been pretending to do the cutting in around the skirting board. 'Sorry, Zoe. I have a lot on my mind, that's all.'

I narrow my eyes at her. 'Are you okay?'

'I'm fine,' she says breezily.

I don't believe her but since she won't tell me what's wrong, I decide not to press the issue. She'll tell me when she's ready or she might not, as seems to be the norm on both sides these days. Then, hoping it will make her feel better, I exclaim joyfully, 'You have to look at this—'

Maddie's face lights up as I approach the box with the LED name sign in it. 'Have you been shopping for the baby?' she gushes.

'And some.' I chuckle, pulling out the sign, but when she sees Arthur's name her face crumples.

'What? Don't you like it?'

Maddie hesitates before saying, 'It isn't that.'

'So, what is it then?' I don't understand why she suddenly has tears in her eyes.

'I thought . . .' She trails off, avoiding my gaze.

'Tell me,' I compel Maddie.

'This might sound silly but I was hoping you might name the baby after Joe,' Maddie suggests.

My spine goes ramrod straight in response to her arrogance, and I'm tempted to scream the house down. Then I remind myself that Maddie is innocently ignorant of the real identity of the father of my child and that, in those circumstances, her request is totally reasonable and, in certain circles, would even be welcomed. The Angelas of this world would think I owed it to poor Maddie. A woman who has already been through so much.

So, rather than jumping down her throat, I break the news gently. 'No, Maddie, I'm sorry but that's not possible.'

Maddie retaliates with more tears. 'Well, I don't see why not.'

'I'm calling him Arthur after my dad.'

Maddie gets on her high horse. 'You never even got along with your dad. You used to say he never had any time for you—'

I interrupt impatiently, 'The answer is no.'

Maddie's eyes disappear into slits as she glares at me. 'I practically shared my son with you for sixteen years. I would have thought that the least you could do in return would be to name your child after him.'

'I can see you're upset, Maddie,' I counter, 'and I understand why, but I have already decided on a name for my baby. Besides, think how upsetting it would be to hear Joe's name being said all the time.'

'I suppose,' Maddie concedes, drying her tears on her sleeve.

She seems incredibly helpless, lost, and vulnerable all of a sudden, which is not at all like my friend, so I nip into the bathroom, grab a handful of toilet paper, and return with it, kicking myself constantly. Why on earth had I not thought of this before? Naturally, Maddie would want me to give my baby her dead son's name. It makes perfect sense, and I would certainly be wishing for the same thing if I were in her shoes. I'm not, though. Thank God. My son is alive inside me, whereas hers . . .

'Don't cry, Maddie,' I plead, handing her the tissue while also stroking her hair. I feel so bad for her that I let her put one hand on my stomach to feel the baby move without trying to stop her. When she smiles up at me in a way that reminds me of Joe, I have to resist the urge to push her away.

CHAPTER 60: MADELINE

Six weeks later

I'm certain that something is wrong. While performing the scan, the nurse deliberately avoided my gaze and immediately went to fetch the doctor. In the past, Mike would have assured me that everything was fine as if I were one of his patients. Now, however, he doesn't, which only makes me more anxious. Instead, he holds onto my hand and searches my face as if I were the one with all the answers, but I am just as puzzled and worried as he is. That makes sense given that we've just undergone six weeks of rigorous testing, which included consultation after consultation, thyroid and ovarian blood tests and sperm and egg assessments. Once we were given the all-clear this eventually culminated in in vitro fertilisation. My mind and body are worn out from all of this, not to mention the agonising wait that followed when we finally learned that the IVF had been successful.

I swallow nervously before mumbling, 'Mike, what's going on?'

Mike stammers, 'I'm sure it's nothing. Try to stay calm, Madeline.'

Our ears prick up when we hear the soft tread of footsteps approaching and then the door clicks open and Dr Khan enters the room. Over the previous six weeks, we have gotten to know him quite well. He is about our age, with perfectly slicked-back hair that is flecked with grey and an expensive veneered smile. He doesn't wear a white coat like the majority of consultants do; instead dressing in a bespoke tailored Savile Row suit.

He greets us with the same charming smile we've grown accustomed to from him, but when he announces calmly, 'Madeline and Mike, I do apologise but I believe we may have encountered a problem,' blood rushes in my ears and every hair on my body stands on end.

'What is it, Malik?' Mike insists.

Since my husband insisted on picking a top London clinic with a proven history of medical expertise, we decided on the Valentine Clinic in Harley Street. It is housed in a regal, period building with a roof terrace and underground parking and it promised a discreet, luxurious five-star service. Due to the fact they are both doctors, Mike and Malik hit it off right away. The Khans have even been to our house for dinner.

'As you know, three fertilised embryos were replaced back in Madeline's womb, in the middle of the cavity of the uterus to be precise,' Dr Khan states simply as he pulls on a pair of blue medical gloves.

While I lay there motionless, ready to scream because they are using words like "embryo" to describe my precious unborn children, Mike nods wisely, totally engrossed in the medical terminology.

'But we learned that only two were successfully embedded when we carried out the hCG pregnancy test ten days later,' Dr Khan adds, continuing where the nurse left off with the ultrasound scan. His and Mike's eyes track the blurry black-and-white images on the screen, but I avert my gaze because I don't want to see. In case there's *nothing to see.*

Asking, 'I take it you've been continuing with the pro-gesterone pessaries?' Dr Khan chews on the inside of his bottom lip, frowning and pressing harder with the probe on my stomach.

'She has indeed,' Mike answers for me.

'Hmm,' Dr Khan pauses to stroke his chin as if deep in contemplation. 'It appears that the lining of the uterus has proven unreceptive to the embryos and that's why they are no longer visible on the ultrasound.'

'What does that mean?' I snap, reddening at the doctor's injured expression.

Fixing me with sympathetic eyes, he replies, 'It means you are no longer pregnant, Madeline. The embryos have not developed as expected.'

On hearing this, my muscles stiffen involuntarily and tears prickle my eyelids. When I glance over at Mike, I see disappointment flash across his face and I find myself closing my eyes so I don't have to witness his suffering, knowing this pregnancy means as much to him as it does me.

'I'm so sorry, sweetheart.' Mike moves closer to the bed and strokes away the tears that have landed on my cheeks. For once, I don't push him away. I want so much to be comforted. Yet I fear it's impossible as I have just lost another child. Two, even. Twins that might have been boys.

'Would you like a few minutes alone before we discuss the next steps?' Dr Khan winces as if he genuinely cares.

Mike nods. 'Yes.'

'No,' I bark, desperately wanting to get up from this bloody bed. Having my childless belly exposed in such a way fills me with shame.

Seeming to understand my predicament, Dr Khan thoughtfully removes the probe so I can pull my top down over my belly. After that, he moves a chair over to the other side of the bed and sits down opposite Mike.

Taking in my pinched expression, he points out reasonably, 'It's perfectly understandable for you to have a lot of questions and concerns. That's what I'm here for, to help address them.'

'You mentioned next steps, but what if there aren't any?' I demand, imagining that they can both hear the loud, continuous thump in my chest.

'We don't know that for certain, Madeline,' Mike interrupts convincingly, determined to make us think we still have a chance to have children.

I turn my fiery gaze on the doctor as if holding him personally responsible for my failure to conceive, and screech, 'But you said I had an abnormally low egg count and combined with Mike's low sperm count that meant our chances of getting pregnant in the first place were very slim.'

'Every woman's fertility is different and you cannot compare one to another.' Dr Khan sighs dejectedly, as if well versed in repeating this claim.

On that thought, I immediately think of Zoe who is still very much pregnant. For that reason alone, how can I not compare myself? The knot of anxiety in my chest refuses to loosen as Dr Khan continues speaking.

'Although age does have a significant impact on fertility and egg quality that doesn't mean we can't explore other options.'

Mike frowns sceptically and asks, 'Like what?'

Dr Khan cautiously suggests, 'Like surrogacy.'

CHAPTER 61: ZOE

I'm here at the antenatal clinic for my six-month check-up and for once I feel fantastic. All of my aches and pains have vanished, and the morning sickness and heartburn are nothing but distant memories. No more swollen ankles either. I'm currently in that radiant, glowing phase, which appears to affect not only my mood but those of others. Hence, I am greeted with happy smiles everywhere I go when people see my distended belly.

Men routinely get up from their seats to let me sit down, proving that the age of chivalry is still alive. Even elderly men with walking sticks feel compelled to do this, and it is useless to argue with them or point out that they need a chair more than I do — trust me, I've tried. Arthur will be a Pisces to my Gemini because I am due on March 15th, not that I had even the slightest interest in the zodiac previously. At work and at home, I have written his name and expected birth date on every calendar I can find. My son, Arthur, is all I think about. My fingers itch with longing to hold him.

All obstetrician and midwife appointments are held at Lakeside Health Care, which is close to my home. My boss, Angela, generously gave me the entire day off as paid leave in case I felt weakened after giving blood. Despite being consistently kind, considerate and interested in the baby, we have not resumed our former close friendship. Now that Maddie is back on the scene, it's just as well. She would only end up competing with Angela, and where my best friend is concerned there can only be one victor. Maddie is more possessive of me than she is her own husband. But it's Mike she should be keeping her eye on. The cheat.

However, Maddie has seemed happier and much more content lately, which makes her more pleasant to be around. As far as I know, she hasn't lied to me again, nor have I had to set strict boundaries with her regarding my pregnancy as I anticipated having to do because her occasionally domineering nature has remained in check. Thankfully, since she suggested that I name my child after Joe, there hasn't been any further friction between us; at times, she can be as scratchy as a stray cat.

I watch all the other pregnant women waiting to be seen as I patiently wait for my turn to be called. Like me, they rest their hands on their stomachs and occasionally look down at them as if keeping an eye on their "little one". A few of the women are already mothers and have toddlers with them. I stare at them in awe as they playfully slide across the surgery floor and create imaginative shapes out of Lego in the play area.

A deep, smoky voice cries, 'Zoe Archer,' and as I glance up, I recognise the same midwife from before. Lela will be delivering my baby in three months and I consider myself in good hands. She is a larger-than-life character in every sense of the word. Size and personality. She's funny too.

I get to my feet and follow Lela into an adjoining room and even though I know there won't be a vaginal exam today, I suspiciously eye the bed that has a roll of disposable blue paper folded over it. As a first-time mum, I occasionally experience fear over what to expect, but Lela always puts me at ease by reminding me that everything is a choice and nothing is mandatory. However, she did try to influence me when I said I wanted a home birth and strongly advised against it, claiming it wouldn't be wise in case any complications occurred. But she went on to say that she would support a home delivery if I were to have another child. Since I knew I wouldn't become pregnant again, I heeded her advice and we decided on a natural birth at the maternity hospital.

'Come on in, lovely, and take a seat.' Lela directs me to a chair in the corner as she gathers an assortment of medical items together.

I say, 'Thank you,' a little breathlessly, more out of excitement than anything else. She doesn't notice, which is a good thing, otherwise, I would have been put under interrogation.

'How is Mum?' She fixes me with jolly brown eyes.

'Fine. Great, in fact.'

'That's my girl,' she laughs boisterously, as is her way, before continuing, 'And baby Arthur?'

When I hear his name spoken, my hand instinctively flutters to my stomach. I'm tickled that Lela has remembered it, so with a twitch of a smile, I jest, 'He kicks so much I'm convinced David Beckham is his father.'

She exclaims, 'You're certainly pretty enough to catch someone like him,' which causes me to blush in embarrassment because I've never been good at accepting compliments. 'And where's your glamorous birthing partner today?' Lela asks less animatedly.

When I catch her wrinkling her nose, I begin to suspect that Lela may not have taken to Maddie on our first visit, even though she had been quiet and well-behaved throughout. But Lela likes everyone, so I must be mistaken. I'm reminded of Chris, then, who nicknamed my best friend "Maleficent" which I thought was cruel even if I did laugh at the time.

'She has her own hospital appointment to attend today.' It strikes me as I say this how odd it was that Maddie hadn't provided any explanation of why she was going to the hospital. I hope she's okay.

But as I glance up, I see Lela isn't listening to me rattling on about Maddie anyway and is instead indicating for me to roll up my sleeve.

'Bloods, young lady.'

Obediently, I roll up my sleeve so she can tap at the veins on my arm.

'Expect a slight scratch,' she warns before injecting me with the needle. I fix my gaze elsewhere at that point because I don't want to see my blood travelling up the syringe.

'Any concerns?' she wants to know.

'No, none at all, I'm glad to report.'

After labelling my blood sample, Lela turns to face me, giving me her undivided attention. 'That's what I like to hear,' she booms while clapping her hands enthusiastically. 'I will now measure your abdomen to see how many cream cakes you've been consuming.'

'None,' I chuckle.

Her eyes gleam with humour as she comes out with, 'You wouldn't lie to me, mother of Arthur, would you?'

'Uh huh.' Because Lela always has this effect on me, I respond childishly. On my most recent visit, she revealed that she was mother to five children and jokingly added, "And would you believe it they all have the same father," while appearing indignant. "Robbed of fun, I was." She roared with laughter after that and I joined in although I thought her joke might not have been entirely appropriate. Even so, I liked her.

Lela laughingly instructs, 'Right, unleash the tummy,' while lashing out with a tape measure as if it were a whip. When it circles my tummy, I recoil from its cold edges and I can feel my unborn child gently brushing against the wall of my womb as if he too were trying to get away from it.

As I am overcome with love for my baby, I remind myself once more that he is all mine and that I won't have to share him with anyone else, with the possible exception of Maddie. And when I have to register his birth after he is born, there will be pride in my voice when I instruct the clerk to list the father as unknown on my son's birth certificate. And that's how it must remain. Forever. Even Arthur can never know who his father was.

CHAPTER 62: MADELINE

I've come down to the river to be with Joe. And to escape Mike, who is driving me insane. He means to be kind and claims that he doesn't want me to suffer alone but his constant attention is making me feel claustrophobic. When did he become so needy?

On this chilly January day, as I walk down to meet the muddy, brown water I can see traces of my breath in front of me. I can't imagine what it must have been like for my son in the cold, unforgiving river. Was his death really a tragic accident or did he intend to kill himself, as the coroner claimed? I no longer give the darker possibilities, like murder, much consideration. I don't have the stamina or rage left to maintain those thoughts. I was slowly dying from it. Convincing myself that someone other than us, Joe's parents, was to blame for what happened had become a dangerous obsession for a while. But if it was an accident, Joe would have had no way of knowing when his face first skimmed the water that Stamford Meadows would be the last thing he would ever see. In the moment before he drowned, would he have remembered that I brought him here when he was young so we could have ice cream and feed the ducks?

Only this morning I asked Mike, 'What are we going to do now we can't have another baby?' and his response had been, 'Whatever you like,' which infuriated me. At least we've decided unanimously that we won't be putting ourselves through IVF again. Although it had cost thousands of pounds, the key factor was the damage to our mental health. Both Mike and I found the idea of surrogacy intolerable. I couldn't let someone else carry my baby for me. It would destroy me. We cannot blame each other for our infertility either, openly or secretly, because we are both at fault. While I have a low egg count, which is fairly normal for a woman my age, and an unreceptive uterus, Mike's sperm count is equally low. A fact I think he struggled to come to terms with for a while.

This makes me feel doubly privileged to have carried Joe to full term and given birth to him at all. Imagine if that hadn't been the case. Knowing my twin babies died inside me without my knowledge still hurts terribly. There was no pain or clutching at my stomach and no blood to indicate any loss. Life shouldn't be permitted to slip away so easily. I've since discovered that this is referred to as a "Missed" or "Silent" miscarriage. The mother is typically astounded when they learn of it during a routine scan, as was the case in my situation because there were no warning signs that anything was amiss. Dr Khan chose the term "undeveloped" rather than "died" as if to lessen the severity of my suffering.

They may have only been six-week-old embryos that were brought to life outside of my womb, but to me, they already seemed like little people and very real. I imagined them as black-haired, dark-eyed twin boys. My secret sons. Or a combination of a boy and girl, perhaps. In no scenario did I imagine two girls. I wanted . . . *needed* a son. Now we'll never find out what sex I was carrying. Dr Khan stated that they most likely failed at the four-week mark, so I must have been walking around with a big smile on my face for weeks without knowing. Thank God we had resolved to keep the news of the pregnancy to ourselves until the three-month mark, although I suspect Gabriella might already have guessed because I occasionally caught her intrusively staring at me, her eyes on my waist. She sometimes surprises me with how perceptive she is. Maybe by touching my stomach too much or by simply appearing smug, I gave myself away. With her big baby belly, Zoe is now the smug one.

My pregnancy hormones eventually started to drop three days after the ultrasound, at which point the physical miscarriage began. I'd like to say that I writhed in agony to make it seem more real, but in truth, the pain was no worse than a period. Feelings of shock, loss and denial continue to overwhelm me and Mike insists on me having plenty of peace and quiet so that I can "recover". This is why he won't currently allow Gabriella to visit, *and* so he can keep me all to himself. She is enraged by this and insists that he has no right to act this way, but I don't respond to her savage texts because, in reality, he is correct. I do value the silence.

I felt numb when Dr Khan initially told us about the failed pregnancies, but once I got home and over the next few days, I found myself being taken back to the time I lost Joe, when I stopped eating and drinking and rocked myself in a chair for hours at a time. I sobbed till my tears dried up. Screamed till my voice broke. And starved myself until I was so weak that I could hardly function. I didn't want to live if my children couldn't. A mother without any living offspring is no mother at all.

And what of me and Mike now? Without a child to unite us, we have nothing left, apart from shared memories. But a new sense of loss sets in when I picture life without Joe's father in it, who has the same dark good looks as his son. Why hadn't I considered this before? I can't imagine not having somebody to discuss Joe with. Countless memories of him will undoubtedly fill the empty years that lie ahead. Who else but Mike am I going to share them with? Together, we can reminisce over incidents like the time Joe built a sandcastle at the beach and a giant dog knocked it over or when he fell off his bike and angrily kicked it but wound up hurting his foot. Or the times Mike had carried Joe on his shoulders and when he insisted on hearing a second and third bedtime story before falling asleep.

Other than myself, Mike is the only person in the entire world who knew Joe as well as I did. Loved him as I did. Although Zoe may once have loved Joe, after her son is born, she will be preoccupied with him and it won't feel the same. That just leaves Mike.

When the ducks on the water begin to quack and paddle towards the water's edge as if anticipating being fed, I glance up and that's when I notice Mike. As if I had conjured him up, he's walking towards me carrying two Starbucks coffees, his coat collar pulled up against the chill. He is surrounded by a white cloud of breath and has a rolled-up blanket tucked up underneath one arm.

He sounds anxious when he greets me with, 'I saw your note on the table and thought I'd come and join you.'

I relieve him of his suffering by saying, 'I'm really glad you did.'

He beams at me then, seeming happy, and I ask, 'What's the blanket for?' as I take one of the coffees from him.

'Knowing you're a floor dweller, I thought we could sit on the river bank for a while and watch the world go by.'

'Nice.' I nod, thrusting my hands into my coat pockets to warm them.

'Here you go.' Mike pulls a pair of my gloves out of his pocket and hands them to me.

This makes me chuckle. 'You've thought of everything.'

I watch my husband thoughtfully as he spreads the blanket out on the ground. Even though he is attractive, wealthy and successful, I don't love him for any of those qualities. Couples in their eighties or nineties are known for saying it's the small things in life that count and Mike has been doing a lot of those lately. The coffee. The blanket. The gloves. Is it possible that he still loves me after all this time and everything we've been through together? The lack of sex. The affairs. Gabriella. Joe. IVF. The miscarriage.

Mike may not be perfect, far from it, but he's Joe's father and he cares about me, *about us*, and that is all that matters. So, perhaps we do stand a chance after all.

CHAPTER 63: ZOE

Two months later

Now that I'm eight months pregnant I feel like a whale. I experienced a brief period of being on top of the world, but it only lasted a matter of weeks. Since I'm now on maternity leave, my days are unstructured, and I have nothing much to do besides wait for Arthur to arrive. So, I spend my time "nesting" which entails a lot of spring cleaning and reorganisation. I have trouble falling asleep at night, so I find that I doze off frequently during the day. Getting comfy is challenging due to the size of my stomach.

The worst part of my pregnancy so far is that my backache has returned with a vengeance. Some days I cry from the pain and I don't know what to do with myself. Maddie keeps inviting me to stay at her house so she can take care of me, but I always decline. I can't stand to be near Mike given what I know about him. I would only end up saying something to the lying, cheating arsehole and that would undoubtedly cause friction between me and Maddie. And she doesn't deserve that because she has been a terrific friend to me. I'm sad I ever doubted her. The only thing I'm not so keen on is that she insists on keeping Gabriella around, which means I occasionally have to tolerate her presence. I'm not sure what Maddie sees in the girl, but I have to presume it's her tenuous link to Joe.

I must admit that when Maddie picked me up in her car to drive me to my pre-natal yoga session, I was bloody annoyed to discover Gabriella seated in the back of it. Maddie had come up with the idea for the classes, and before I could think of an excuse not to attend, she had registered us for six sessions. They reportedly provide a variety of benefits for expectant mothers, and Maddie, who is my birth partner, emphasises that light exercise is "Good for mum and baby". She certainly takes her duties seriously. Even though I was initially sceptical, the exercises do, at least temporarily, help soothe my aches and pains.

'Is Gabriella coming to baby yoga with us?' I'd asked incredulously in the car, craning my neck to stare at the girl's bored-to-death expression. Only to be laughingly told by Maddie that of course, she was up for it.

And now, here we are in our comfy leggings and baggy T-shirts, surrounded by lots of soft, squishy cushions, exercise balls and mats practising the butterfly pose. I can barely bring my toes together due to the amount of weight I've gained but Maddie and Gabriella don't have that issue. At least Maddie has dressed modestly and is wearing similar attire to mine. Gabriella on the other hand, is wearing a black bra top and the tiniest of shorts and is determined to surpass us all with her sexy yoga moves. I can tell that she is the most hated person in the room as I cast a quick peek around at the other expectant mothers.

When our forty-five minutes are up, we all pile into the changing rooms and I sit on a hard bench sipping water as I wait for one of the showers to come free. I'm covered in an unpleasant sheen of sweat and I'm eager to wash it off. Hungrily, I take several bites out of the protein bar that Maddie thoughtfully gave me before disappearing somewhere to take a work call, even though it's a Saturday. Gabriella had rudely jumped into a shower cubicle before any of us pregnant mums got the chance and this earned her many angry glances that she nonchalantly shrugged off.

Most of us avert our eyes and feel uneasy when Gabriella exits the shower cubicle and begins to wander about naked with only a towel covering her wet hair. I feel even more uncomfortable when she decides to sit down next to me. I've forgotten what it's like to be young and slim. Except Gabriella is a bit too thin for my liking. It's difficult not to notice.

'How did you like baby yoga?' I ask, for something to say.

She answers with her trademark one-shouldered school-girl shrug. 'Bit boring.'

'We won't expect to see you next week then,' I remark with a smug smile.

She answers matter-of-factly, 'If Maddie comes, I'll come too.'

I'm at a loss for words, so I don't say anything else and continue eating my not-so-tasty pregnancy snack.

Her eyes bore into mine as she asks, 'Have you seen anything of Mike lately?' and I feel my back arch.

I can't resist responding to her with a 'No. Have you?'

Another shrug and then, 'All the time at Maddie's house, but I never see *you* there. How come?'

'It's not so easy to get around these days,' I joke, gesturing to my belly but she responds by pulling a disbelieving face.

'That day when you came to my house, you said you wanted to know about my break-up with Joe.' She speaks conversationally, as if this had happened recently, rather than eight months ago.

'That was a long time ago,' I point out.

'Do you still want to know why I broke up with him?'

There's no shaking her off, I'll give her that. 'Why now, Gabriella, when you wouldn't discuss it back then?'

'You know why.'

It sounds like a threat because it is a threat, but as she continues to stare at me with her dark, menacing eyes, she manages to frighten me once more. She has an unsettling, occult-like presence about her.

'I'm afraid I don't.'

She hisses, 'Because Mike asked me to.'

'I don't believe you,' I snap. And I don't but as I roll that thought around in my head, I realise a change of tactic is called for, so I add for good measure, 'And quite frankly, I don't know why we're discussing it after all this time.'

'Because this is the first opportunity I've had to speak with you when Maddie isn't around and she mustn't find out about it either.'

'Find out about what? Besides, I don't keep secrets from my best friend, and *she is* my best friend, Gabriella, whether you like it or not.'

'You knew about Mike and me. You figured it out that day, didn't you?' she persists tenaciously.

'If you must know, yes I did.'

'You said you don't keep secrets from Maddie, but you clearly haven't told her about that, otherwise I'd know about it.'

My gaze hits the floor in shame as I reply, 'No, I haven't.'

'Why not?'

'Because they had just lost their son, and I didn't think—'

'You're not the friend you think you are, Zoe. I would have told her right away if it were me.'

'How can you say that when you were the one screwing both her husband and her son?'

'You'd know all about that wouldn't you, Zoe?'

Rattled, I snarl, 'What's that supposed to mean?'

'You were jealous when you found out about us. Admit it.'

I am scathing. 'Of you? That is absurd.' But I remember to lower my voice as people are looking over at us. I'm terrified of what she might come out with next. How much does she know?

'Joe told me you had a thing for him—'

Nothing can stop me from yelling, 'Joe lied,' at that point but it only makes the other pregnant women who are already staring at us with wide eyes pay us even more attention. One of them yanks her young child closer to her as if she's afraid they're about to witness a real fight. I'm sure Gabriella would win outright if that were to happen.

'So, Zoe, why are you blushing?'

I splutter, 'I'm not, I . . . it's not what you think.'

'It's been over between Mike and me for ages, but if you mention any of this to Maddie, I'll tell her you were shagging her son.'

Once again, I'm being blackmailed for sleeping with a child. Joe was the first one to do so, and now Gabriella, which is ironic given her history with Mike. She has no idea how much this conversation is triggering me and it takes everything I have to remain calm.

'I'm not sure why you are bringing this up now,' I exclaim when I really want to say, "when I'm almost healed". 'But I can assure you that I have no intention of saying anything to Maddie.'

Gabriella murmurs something along the lines of, 'Some friend!' as I rush into the shower cubicle that has just become available. 'I bet you also knew about Mike's other affairs but kept them from Maddie too.'

CHAPTER 64: MADELINE

G: WTF LSR Forbes finally did it.
J: NFW nailed it.
G: Awesome hanging GIF tipped him over the edge.
ROFL.
J: Cool idea of yours.
G: YGM like no one else.
J: GYPO IWSN.
G: GTG POS.

When I first came across Joe's phone hidden in Gabriella's pocket, I felt as if I had been knocked to the ground and my legs kicked out from under me. The moment I saw the shiny black case, I knew it was his, the chip in the screen's upper corner proved it. Although I hadn't intended to go through her things, my curiosity was aroused when her coat thumped against the door as I brushed against it in the cloakroom. Despite not knowing what this yet meant, I went in search of a charger and plugged it in right away. As I waited, time seemed to stand still as tangled strands of my hair fell forward on my face and I gnawed viciously on a fingernail.

A few minutes later, as the phone lit up, my heart hardened into a piece of stone. As I scrolled through endless messages, I twigged straight away that they were from Joe and Gabriella but I couldn't understand what the texting acronyms meant, so I Googled them . . . only to find out LSR stood for "Loser", ROFL was "Rolling around on the floor laughing", YGM equalled "You get me" and GYPO IWSN meant "Get your pants off I want sex now" and lastly GTG POS "Got to go, parent over shoulder".

My long-held belief that Gabriella had encouraged Joe to cruelly bully the Forbes boy has just been confirmed. The evidence is there in black-and-white. Unaware that anything is wrong, she waltzes into the kitchen unphased asking, 'Have you seen my coat as I am about to head off?' She trails off when she sees my expression and the smile freezes on her face as she realises the coat and Joe's phone are on the table in front of me.

I jab a finger at her as an angry heat rises on my neck and travels into my chest before flaring on my cheeks. 'This is Joe's phone,' I accuse. 'Where did you get it?'

Wild-eyed, she stutters, 'It's not how it looks, Madeline.'

'Where did you get it?' I repeat through clenched teeth.

Lowering her eyes, she mutters, 'Zoe's. I found it at Zoe's house.'

'Zoe's?' I echo incredulously. 'That can't be right.'

She protests earnestly, 'It is, Madeline. I went round there today and I found it in a drawer next to her bed.'

I shakily get to my feet to confront her. 'Did she tell you it was in there? Is that what you're saying?'

'Of course not,' she snorts with derision. 'There's no way she'd want me getting my hands on it, as it's evidence.'

'Then how?' I demand.

'I let myself in when she wasn't there using the spare key to her house that you keep in the kitchen drawer. For emergencies!'

I exclaim indignantly, 'You broke into her house?!'

She argues, 'You're missing the point,' as if annoyed with me for not keeping up. 'She's had Joe's phone all this time. I knew something was going on with her and Joe. I just knew it. That's why I finished—'

I cut in not letting her finish, 'Wait a minute, slow down. What do you mean?'

'I wasn't going to say anything but this changes everything.'

'What does?'

She steeples her palms together in an act of prayer. 'Don't you see? Joe must have been at her house the night he disappeared.'

'And he left his phone there . . . ?'

'Yes, which means Zoe's been lying the entire time. She was with Joe the night he died, but she never mentioned it. Not to you or the police.'

'But why would she keep quiet about something like that?'

Gabriella arches one eyebrow higher than the other and tilts her head to one side as if daring me to make the connection. When Zoe vanished from our lives all those months ago, I had silenced and suppressed my concerns but now they're back tormenting me as my jumbled mind winds its way to a possible conclusion. After Joe found out that his father had betrayed him in the worst way possible, it was only natural for him to go to his one friend, Zoe. But why hadn't she said anything? Unless, of course, she had something to hide? Because Joe's disappearance was under investigation by the police, she had risked going to prison for perjury. Why?

I feel myself bristling as I realise that the threat of prison has also been hanging over my family's heads for too long, because of Gabriella, whose smugness I'd like to pummel from her face. I force myself to bite back the remark that is on the tip of my tongue, "I'll fucking deal with Zoe later."

Instead, I advance on Gabriella. 'You're loving this, aren't you? You're only ever happy when you're making other people miserable? Families like mine.'

'No.' She springs away from me, feigning hurt. 'I care about you, Madeline. That's why I did what I did, so you'd know the truth about Zoe.'

'And what about the truth about you?' I ask sarcastically as I cross my arms tightly over my chest.

At that, her eyes guiltily flick up to mine for a second before dropping away again. Her face is flushed and there's a split second of hesitation before she replies, 'I don't know what you mean.'

'Oh, I think you do,' I snort, a bubble of snot exploding in one nostril as I try to rein in my anger which has been kept under control for far too long. 'You think I don't know about you and Mike.'

Gabriella gasps, 'Zoe told you? What a bitch.'

When I hear this, my chest tightens. So, Zoe was also aware of their affair but kept it from me. Can I endure any more betrayals in a single day? My so-called best friend has royally screwed me over. As Gabriella put it, "What a bitch". Every step I take feels like I'm pushing against the current and wading through water. When is it going to end?

'Actually, Zoe didn't tell me. I've known about you and Mike all along. He told me everything.' I decide it's not in my best interest to come clean about the private investigator, so I lie.

'Mike did?' Gabriella asks in amazement as her eyes swirl with panic and her blood red lips open in shock.

'Yes, my husband, Mike, who you've been blackmailing for months. Why else would someone like me befriend someone like you if not to prevent you from going to the police?'

I can tell Gabriella realises that our friendship is over when I see regret appear in her eyes and when her shoulders sag in defeat.

'I want you out of my house, right now!' I shout, my voice echoing around the vast black and chrome kitchen. The world outside is humming with cars, rain-slicked pavements, and midday gloom. Inside, I'm feeling unmoored from everything, adrift, as if I might float away. Like my son.

Gabriella's expression immediately changes upon hearing this, and I can see the tension in her body as her shoulders stiffen. Her eyes burn with rage as she cries back at me, 'And he still could go to prison, don't forget. He had sex with me when I was underage. And that's against the law.'

'As is encouraging a defenceless boy to commit suicide.'

As her suspicious black eyes sweep over me and evaluate me, I am once more reminded of a dangerous predator. 'It was your precious son who did that. Not me,' she gloats, jutting out her chin.

'Really? That's not what your texts to Joe imply.'

She opens her mouth to argue then but changes her mind when she sees me cradling the incriminating phone in my hand. It's game over and she knows it. 'You really need to do better, Gabriella,' I snap at her, remembering how she recently used the same words against me. 'And delete evidence like that, in future.'

She throws me an unrepentant smile before promising, 'I won't tell if you won't.'

'Then we have a deal.' I narrow my eyes at her but wince at how cold, unforgiving and distant I sound. *This is not who I want to be.*

I watch her wordlessly as she hesitantly approaches the table to take her coat as if fearful that I might spring out of my seat to throttle her. An*d I just might*, as I feel both angry and disappointed with her, for proving me right about the blackmailing. As she shrugs on her coat, her eyes linger on the phone, as if she might be thinking of making a sudden grab for it.

Her voice suddenly softens with concern and fear loosens my knees when she puts a hand on my arm and warns—

'Before I leave your life for good, think, Maddie,' she urges, her dark eyes fixed on mine and going nowhere, 'because whoever kept hold of that phone when everybody else was looking for it might have been Joe's killer.'

CHAPTER 65: ZOE

I had given in to my sudden craving for fresh fruit and dashed into town before everywhere closed. This is my second outing of the day and I tell myself the extra exercise will do me good. While I hand over my tenner and wait for my change, the same friendly market vendor I see most Fridays at the outdoor market packs a bag with oranges, apples and grapes for me. He chuckles and hands me my change while saying, 'That's a healthy baby you're growing in there thanks to my five-a-day.'

I reply with the usual inane remark, 'An apple a day keeps the doctor away,' as I always do, then move on. I've always felt at ease with small talk. In contrast to Maddie, who would rather have her eyeballs poked out.

I'm walking down the pedestrianised area of the High Street, absently peering into shop windows when I notice how everywhere is quiet and deserted. It's late in the day and the market traders will soon disperse, leaving behind a ghost town due to the thick veil of fog that has descended over its cobbled streets and quirky passageways. The sun is setting and visibility is poor. As I turn left at the church, and think about going home, the wind whistles behind me and strokes the back of my neck.

That's when I start to feel as though someone is watching me, and the sound of footsteps behind me increases my dread. When a figure emerges from the wintry dusk to stop in front of me, fear flutters at the back of my mind.

'You killed Joe, didn't you?' a voice cries.

My mouth suddenly feels dry with nerves. I still haven't recovered from my last spikey exchange with Gabriella, who is now glaring at me with barely concealed loathing. She appears sinister and even more menacing than usual due to the mist that is clinging to her shoulders.

'As usual, I have no idea what you're talking about, and I don't want to,' I say with a prickle of sarcasm as I brush past her, determined to continue on my way. She pursues me, of course. That's Gabriella for you. She is tenacious beyond belief.

'That's why you've kept his phone hidden all this time.'

As I abruptly come to a halt, I feel a sudden rush in my chest and any scars left over from my recent argument with her flare up again. The prospect of turning around to face her makes me feel physically sick. But I do turn around, to demand fiercely—

'What phone? What are you talking about?'

'Don't play the innocent with me, Zoe,' she responds mysteriously, curling her lip as if poised to attack. 'You know exactly what I'm talking about. I found it and now Maddie has it.'

'Found what?' I gasp, cowering in terror. The hatred I harbour for her spreads like cancer inside of me. But I'm compelled to react to the superior smile of triumph on her face, so I bark again, 'Found what?'

'After you left your house this morning to meet Maddie for coffee, *how very cosy for you both by the way*, I let myself into your house using her spare key. It's fascinating isn't it, how best friends do that, trust each other enough to share the key to all their secrets?'

The truth of her words make me shrink into myself, but I am still able to manage a resentful, 'Go on,' while asking myself, *How bloody dare she?*

'You and I both know Joe was too much of a coward to kill himself. Besides, he wouldn't have done anything without my say-so.'

'And did your say-so involve telling him to sexually assault women?' I could smash her head open right now, I'm so mad at her. But she's looking at me in confusion as if she has no idea what I'm talking about, so I go on the attack again. Anything to swipe the smug expression from her face.

'You had him wrapped around your little finger, didn't you?' I yell. 'He would've done anything you asked.'

'You can talk. You were the one he fancied and never stopped talking about. It was disgusting really. That's why I ended things with him.'

'You claimed the other day that Mike made you.'

'Yeah, well, I lied but I'm not the only one, am I? All I know is that when Joe and I started dating, he told me you were jealous as hell.'

'He was delusional. Can't you see that?' I feel apoplectic with rage.

'No!' She angrily shakes her head. 'You wanted him all to yourself but were afraid Madeline would find out which is why you came to my house that day to see if I knew anything about the two of you—'

'Gabriella.' I'm so sick of lying that I sigh heavily. It is suffocating me. Killing me. 'Don't you get it yet, you foolish girl? It was Mike I was seeing. Not Joe. We've been having an affair on and off for years.'

'You and Mike!' She steps back from me, stunned.

Looking up at the darkening sky, I cry, 'Yes! So, you see, you're not the only one with a secret.'

'What about the phone though? That doesn't explain why you had it.'

I shudder and take a long breath before admitting only part of the truth, 'Joe did come to see me that night, but he forgot to take his phone with him when he left. He was under the influence of drugs and had no idea what he was doing.'

273

'That doesn't make sense. If that were the case, why didn't you inform Maddie or the police when you knew they were looking for it? And him.'

'It's complicated,' I inform her coldly.

'Complicated how?'

She assumes the worst when I don't answer, saying, 'Oh my God, you were fucking both of them, weren't you? Father and son? I was right all along about you and Joe.'

'I did no such thing. Joe was my godson. I would never have . . .'

She cuts through my words. 'As if that would stop someone like you? For fuck's sake, you slept with your best friend's husband.'

'Gabriella,' I warn, moving towards her, wanting to silence her, 'keep your voice down, people will hear.'

'Oh, they'll hear all right. The whole town will, including Maddie.'

'You can't tell her,' I object. 'We had a deal, remember? And—' I play what I think is my trump card, *something that will shut her up for good* — 'don't forget I could still tell her about you and Mike.'

'She already knows,' Gabriella cries hysterically, now in floods of tears. 'So you've got nothing on me. And when I'm done, she won't want to be your friend anymore. In any case, you don't deserve her. You're not fit to wipe her boots.'

For the first time, Gabriella and I agree. I've always felt inferior to Maddie, and I believe this was a contributing factor as to why I was attracted to her husband. I had reasoned that if he picked someone like me, who was distinctly average, over her, then that would prove I was just as special as she was. But he never intended to leave Maddie for me, despite all the lies he told me. Mike Black was the reason for me losing everything. Chris. My self-worth. And even my sanity for a while. When I ultimately ended things with him, I wanted him to fight for me and show me that he cared. To prove that he was just as addicted to the sex as I was. But he simply moved on to Gabriella. Since then, I have detested her.

Why won't she shut up? For even a second? Childishly, I want to cover my ears with my hands to block out her insults, "bitch", "liar" and "worst friend ever", *all of which are true*, but instead, they act independently and reach out to push her until she is staggering backwards and flailing her arms. She looks at me in shock and horror as she falls, and then there is a sickening bone-splintering thump as her head hits the cobblestones. She stares up at me with glazed eyes as blood seeps out from behind her head, creating a horrible red halo around it. I think her eyes are still on me as I walk away.

CHAPTER 66: MADELINE

'I know what you did. I've worked it out with some help from Gabriella.' After waiting for Zoe to open her door for a full ten minutes, my tone is harsh and accusing. She obviously doesn't want to talk to me but I'm not having it. I'm not leaving either. If necessary, I would have stood on the front doorstep and waited all day. That's how furious I am with her.

'How is she?' Zoe asks, her hands flying to her mouth and her eyes instantly filling with panic. 'Have you heard from her?'

'Word gets out fucking fast in this town, I'll say that. She's in the hospital in a bloody coma, would you believe. I just got done talking to her parents on the phone. How did you find out about her accident so soon?'

'Angela, if you must know,' Zoe responds quickly, looking red in the face as if she were lying, but that doesn't make sense. She also seems relieved, almost like she's gotten away with something, which further baffles me.

'I might have known.' I can't resist the jibe at her friend. 'Now,' I insist, 'are you going to ask me what it is that I know?'

Zoe glances up and down the street and noticing a neighbour nearby who is about to dismount his bicycle, she cautiously invites me inside.

I bang the door behind me with a loud crash and observe that Zoe still has her back to me and is stuttering uncomfortably. 'What exactly am I supposed to have done?'

'What haven't you done?' I give a caustic bark. 'Before we start on how you knew about Mike's affair with Gabriella but chose not to tell me, let's talk about how you've been hiding Joe's phone all these months.'

Zoe instantly bursts into tears. 'Maddie, I'm so sorry. If I could go back and change everything I would.'

Zoe's outburst has me wondering what has got into her lately. It's not as if she has been through anything as traumatic as losing a son. Hence, why my voice crackles with rage as I shout, 'Sorry! My son died and I almost lost my husband too. And you're sorry?!'

Zoe collapses onto a brand new sofa that hasn't been properly unwrapped yet, her head resting in her hands. The old green sofa has gone, I notice, and the new one still has the tags on.

'What do you want me to say?' Her voice wobbles uncontrollably.

I throw myself onto the couch across from her and curtly suggest, 'Let's start with the phone, shall we? Gabriella seemed to believe that Joe was here on the night he disappeared. Is that correct?'

With tears streaming down her face, Zoe turns to look at me and whispers in a heartbroken voice, 'Yes.'

We both know that she has sealed her fate with those words. 'How come you didn't tell me?' I cry out angrily.

'I'm not sure, Maddie. He arrived just after midnight and was only here for ten minutes. He muttered something about arguing with his dad and left soon afterwards, saying he was going home. I didn't find the phone until several weeks later. It must have dropped out of his pocket and onto the floor behind the pipework when he went to the toilet. Joe had already passed away by then, so I thought telling you would only make things more difficult.'

'Difficult for who?' I demand, adding, 'Because it sounds to me as if you are making all this up off the top of your head.'

When Zoe avoids my gaze and refuses to answer, I realise with a sinking feeling that I am right and she is lying. Don't ask me how I know this. I just do. Haven't I known her forever? Gabriella was correct; Zoe does have something to hide. What could it be? *Think, Maddie, think.* A stark and hurtful reminder flashes through my mind then. Earlier today, Gabriella had urged me to 'Think, Maddie, because whoever kept hold of that phone when everybody else was looking for it might have been Joe's killer.'

But I dismiss that thought now just as I did then, with an impatient toss of my head. Zoe is not a killer. It's obvious to anyone she couldn't hurt a fly when you look at her now, her shoulders heaving with sorrow and her head bowed in shame. What possible motive could she have for hurting Joe anyway? Gabriella also hinted that she believed something was going on between Zoe and Joe. But what? Then, as if I had been kicked in the stomach, it dawns on me that Gabriella had begun to insinuate that this was why she had ended her relationship with Joe, but I had foolishly refused to let her finish.

My son had stayed over at Zoe's house for years. That is how much I trusted her with him. I now recall that she had flirted with Joe that evening at the restaurant for her birthday meal, telling him he could marry her when he was eighteen. Additionally, I observed the way she smiled up at him when he placed the necklace around her neck. Three months later, Zoe is miraculously pregnant, but she won't reveal who the father is to her best friend. I realise now that I was an idiot not to suspect anything before and that Gabriella was right all along. But, no, it's impossible. Inconceivable. Zoe would never have . . . However, I would have said the same thing about Mike and underage girls had I not learned the terrible truth.

I would have died defending Zoe, but nothing she says makes sense. Her actions simply don't add up. She first of all abandoned us when we, *I*, most needed her — when Joe vanished — and then she refused to name her child after him, even though it would have been a loving and natural thing to do. You could argue, as Zoe had done, that this was an unrealistic expectation on my part, and I have to admit she was right about how upsetting it would have been to hear Joe's name constantly spoken, but my anger and grief prevents me from taking a calmer, more balanced approach. Now, I have exposed her deceit once more. Every nerve ending in my body is affected by her lie. As if to prove this, Zoe hasn't moved a muscle during my agonising silence. Her eyes, which are puffy and wet, dart all over the place but never land on me. This tells me everything.

'You sounded almost convincing just now,' I remark in a lofty tone as if unaffected by her disloyal behaviour.

'What do you mean?' Zoe's eyes widen as she picks at imaginary threads on her clothing with shaking hands.

'Joe was filmed on the town bridge at 2.07 in the morning, almost two hours after he left our house. If he got to yours at midnight and spent only ten minutes with you, as you claim, then where was he for the remainder of those missing hours?'

Zoe lets out a puff of exasperation, before adding in a whiney voice, 'I don't know. He told me he was going home.'

I remark gloomily, feeling hollow inside, 'But he didn't make it home, did he, Zoe?'

I watch Zoe stagger to her feet, unable to sit still any longer. She claws at the skin on her neck and then holds both fists to her head, as if about to flay herself. It's unlike anything I've ever seen her do before.

My head snaps up as I point out dangerously, 'I can always tell when you're lying, Zoe, so I'm going to ask you one question and I want you to tell me the truth this time. Is that understood?'

She looks at me with wild deer-like eyes and nods. Based on something in her glance I would say that she has dreaded being asked this question for a very long time. Despite feeling as if I already know the answer, I proceed anyway.

My eyes dart to her stomach, as I ask, 'Is it Joe's baby?'

CHAPTER 67: ZOE

When I first heard the loud knocking on the door, I knew in my heart it was Maddie and I spent a stressful ten minutes hiding in Arthur's bedroom, praying she would go away. Since the heated exchange with Gabriella, I have been dreading this moment as I have no way of knowing what she may have told Maddie or even if she is okay. Though I wasn't acting rationally, it was so wrong of me to leave her unconscious and spread out on the ground like that. I had lashed out impulsively and now I'm regretting it. I tell myself that she will have pulled herself to her feet shortly afterwards and not suffered any real harm, despite the blood. Or maybe someone saw her and helped her. To make myself feel better, less guilty, I tell myself that it wasn't as if Gabriella hadn't asked for it. She was long overdue a slap in the face. Gabriella is the least of my troubles, though, compared to all the things I *could* go to prison for.

I did eventually let Maddie in and I was relieved to discover that Maddie knew nothing about my attack on Gabriella, or my affair with Mike since those would have been the first things she'd have used against me. But I *was* shocked to learn that Gabriella was in hospital. In a coma. I instantly regretted thinking that she was the least of my worries because, as of right now, she is on par with Mike and Joe. My other two guilty secrets.

As Maddie waits for my response to her question, I let my eyes close for a moment, before dragging them open to fix on her. There are no right words for what I'm going to say, but I can deliver them kindly. My voice is therefore soft and indistinct as I say, 'Yes, Joe is the father.'

Maddie flinches, putting a hand to her mouth as though to stifle a scream. When she suddenly jerks to her feet and paces the room while twirling the rings on her hand, I don't try to stop her. It takes her a few more minutes to stop and look at me. Her orange eyes glow from within as if they were on fire, burning my skin.

'Maddie, I . . .' I plead, but she fiercely shakes her head at me.

'Don't Maddie me,' she roars. 'How could you sleep with my son? He was sixteen. *Sixteen.*'

Slumping back on the sofa, head down with my elbows on my knees, I tell her, 'I know, but it wasn't like that.'

'You'll be telling me next you were in love.'

My head bounces up when I hear that. 'No. Never that.' I scowl.

'What then? Do tell. I'm dying to know,' Maddie barks sarcastically.

I hesitate to find the perfect words, a black cloud in the shape of Maddie is hanging over me, but her insistent voice pulls me back into the room.

'Well?' she wails.

'It wasn't consensual.' As I admit this, a sharp pain shoots through my chest and I start to sweat profusely. The terror of that night is never far away.

'What do you mean it wasn't consensual?' Maddie growls, freezing as she stares at me.

My mind flails around for the least hurtful thing to say but my heart opts for the truth. 'That night, when he came here, the night he went missing . . .' I clutch at my chest, desperate for air, thinking that I'm on the verge of having

281

a panic attack. 'He drugged my drink with Rohypnol. And after that, he had sex with me.' I can feel six-inch nails drilling into my forehead from the look of incredulity in Maddie's eyes. 'Say something please,' I implore, unable to bear her silence any longer.

'Oh, don't worry, I have plenty to say,' Maddie snarls and I feel myself shrink away from her. She wouldn't physically hurt me, would she?

'If you're trying to tell me that my sixteen-year-old son not only had access to a date rape drug, but he also used it on you so he could forcefully sleep with you, then you are insane.'

'I'm not insane, Maddie. I'm telling the truth. Whether you like it or not, that's what happened.'

Maddie jerks to her feet once more, and her towering presence fills me with anxiety. 'You are a fucking liar! That is what you are. And all you're doing now is attempting to hide the fact that you had sex with a boy who was less than half your age. He was your godson, for crying out loud.'

I rise to my feet then so that we are standing in front of each other, so close I could easily touch her, but I don't because that would be like setting a firework off in my front room. Instead, I repeat, 'Your son raped me.'

'I don't believe you and nor will anyone else.' Maddie chokes on her words as her anguished eyes fill with tears. When she's emotional, like this, she's less of a threat and I feel safe. She turns away from me then, to hide her tears, mumbling, 'My son would never do something like that.'

Deciding to challenge her, I point out reasonably, 'No? What about the English teacher who accused him of sexual assault? And your bruised face last year? Tell me these are not signs of abuse directed at women.'

She gets right up in my face. 'Don't you dare say such things about my son.'

Her hands are clenched into fists at her sides and the air crackles with electricity as our hands accidentally touch. I stand my ground and yell back at her, 'Are you never going to wake up to what your son was?'

'He wasn't a rapist. I know that much. And I would never believe it in a million years. As for you!' She jabs an angry finger at me and it almost grazes my chin. I do take a step back from her then. 'You are nothing but a whore for seducing my son and I will never forgive you for it. Never, do you hear?'

'I hear, Maddie, and I'd like you to leave now,' I tell her firmly.

'I'm sure you would. That would be convenient for you, wouldn't it? Just like it must have been when my son died the night after he impregnated you. Because, unlike you, he isn't here to defend himself. But I am—'

'You've always defended him even when you knew he was in the wrong. And it never helped Joe. He could have learned to take some responsibility for his behaviour if you hadn't protected him so much.'

Maddie glares at me at first, like she might actually hit me, but then her expression changes. I can practically picture her mind working as she puts two and two together and comes up with six.

She accuses viciously, 'I get it now, why you're making up this ridiculous accusation of rape. You're the reason my son died and you can't handle it. He committed suicide after you tricked him into having sex with you because he felt abused. He was so repulsed by you he felt he would rather die than be reminded of it.'

I scream, 'Get out!!' because enough is enough and I rush to the door to fling it open, furious. 'I realise now how foolish it was of me to expect any compassion at all from the woman whose son raped me.'

'Raped you,' Maddie laughs sarcastically. 'As if! Joe was a good-looking boy and he could have had any girl he wanted.'

'My God, you sound exactly like him,' I gasp. 'I would rather give birth to the child of a dead rapist than a living one.'

I want to take back these nasty comments as soon as I say them. How could I have said something so terrible? But

Maddie surprises me by walking towards the door without retaliating. I think I'm safe from any more insults and that our argument is over, but then she turns to stare at me.

'You killed my son,' she states matter-of-factly as if she could prove it. Her gaze then deliberately travels down to my stomach, where it remains for a second or two until I feel fearful for my unborn child. 'And I take my revenge cold.' As she says this, she smiles cuttingly, just once, before walking away.

CHAPTER 68: MADELINE

One month later

I'm seated at my high-gloss dressing table applying makeup. The white unit occupies the entire length of the dressing room and the giant mirror is illuminated with soft-white stage lights. Mike and I are going on a dinner date tonight; therefore, I'm applying more blusher and a bolder shade of lipstick than usual because he expects me to look nice, stunning in fact. I hope I've succeeded in winning his approval. I'm wearing a short black silk dress with plenty of leg on show and my hair is up in a messy chignon that exposes the skin on the back of my neck which Mike likes to kiss. Escaping tendrils of delicate curls soften the look. Poised at my ears are the elegant Kiki McDonough gold and diamond drop earrings that Mike presented me with after I miscarried the twins. No matter how inappropriate or even downright inconsiderate this was of him, I wasn't going to refuse the beautiful and exorbitantly expensive gift.

We plan on dropping in on an acquaintance's party first, before our dinner, to which I had somehow managed to wangle us an invitation. Mike is keen to go as he knows a lot of wealthy and influential people will be present. But I have my own agenda for wanting to be there.

The door frame brushing against the thick carpet alerts me to Mike's presence and I greet him with a smile as he comes into the room. His dark blue suit, teamed with a crisp, pale blue shirt, hugs his masculine shoulders perfectly. In the soft lighting, his jet-black hair gleams, and he smells incredible. I want to say it's his aftershave, but what my husband smells of most is money.

'You look very handsome, Mr B,' I say with admiration.

A grateful smile races across his lips. 'As do you, Mrs B.'

He approaches and kisses me very gently on the top of my head, while promising, 'I won't mess up your hairstyle.' However, as I anticipated, he changes his mind upon seeing my bare skin and instead puts his lips to the back of my neck, whispering, 'You are a very beautiful woman.'

I murmur, 'And you are the best husband in the world,' staring up at him through my eyelashes and tilting my ear to my shoulder in a manner reminiscent of Princess Diana.

'How did I earn that title?' he solicits playfully, leaning nonchalantly against my dressing table as if it were a trendy wine bar, where he was waiting to be served a whiskey sour.

'You know how,' I tease.

I turn in my seat and observe him when he doesn't say anything. The flicker of doubt in his eyes makes me feel fearful.

'You're not having second thoughts, are you?' I exclaim in panic.

'Not exactly,' he mumbles, becoming uneasy.

'Then what?'

Catching the panic in my eyes, he stands up straighter and adjusts his expression to reassure me that everything is fine. 'Madeline, there is nothing at all for you to be concerned about.'

'Are you certain? Because we can't back out now. We made a deal, remember?'

'No one said anything about backing out, but it is a big ask.'

'You feel like I am asking too much of you?' I reply sharply, reverting to the old Madeline of a month prior, before we came to an understanding.

His shoulders tense up at that, as though I've insulted his manliness. 'Of course not,' he responds tersely, 'you can always count on me, Madeline. I'm a man of my word.'

Instead of telling him what's really on my mind, like, "That hasn't always been the case," I offer him a trusting smile.

'Another five minutes?' he enquires, removing a stray black hair from his lapel.

'Make it ten. I'm almost there, I just have one more thing to do.' I glance back at my reflection, knowing full well that Mike is watching my every move. I've given him a compelling cause to never take his eyes off me again. Now that he knows exactly what I'm capable of, he knows to exercise caution. The same could be said of him. We're as bad as each other.

'I'll warm the car up for you.'

'Darling, that would be amazing. Thank you.'

'What time do we need to be at Angela's?' he asks, pausing at the door.

'Not until seven, so if you'd like, we can go out for a drink in town first.'

His face lights up. 'Fine by me.'

When I'm by myself, I put down my lipstick and stare at the stranger in the mirror, wondering what Mike thinks of me. A dangerous, heartless and cold woman? Or a bereaved mother driven by a thirst for revenge?

When I first told him about Zoe a month ago, he didn't seem as shocked as I did, but he did agree that Joe would never have raped her. I was astonished when he claimed, 'Zoe has always been a flighty one,' because even I don't view her that way. He had wanted to go to her house to warn her to keep her mouth shut about our son and threaten her with legal action, but after I pleaded with him not to, since stressful situations like that wouldn't be good for the baby — who was, after all, our grandchild — he changed his mind. In all honesty, the term "grandchild" had stunned him.

I believe he assumed I was just having a tough time grieving for my son when I burst through the door that day, sobbing and screaming, 'I wish Joe were here now so I could kill him all over again,' after finding out Joe had slept with Zoe. However, Mike appeared horrified when I eventually revealed my disturbing-to-my-own-ears plan. It took him a few weeks to come around to my way of thinking, but luckily, I was able to avoid using coercion to force him to agree to it. Mike is fully aware of how much I have on him and that I could potentially ruin him, his being a highly respected surgeon and all. But I didn't want to take that path if I didn't have to as I needed him to work with me on this. My plan could never succeed if he wasn't as committed to it as I was.

Remembering that I still have one more task to do, and a very important one at that, I fetch my laptop from the study and after opening it up, I click on my mobile banking app. The details of our joint bank account appear on the screen, and I swiftly transfer £30,000 into the account of a very close friend.

CHAPTER 69: ZOE

I'm on my way back from the doctor's and I regret not having booked a taxi. Even though it's only a short walk home, my feet — which are encased in ugly, beige comfort shoes — are already swollen, and my blood pressure is up as a result, which is why I went to the doctor in the first place. The days of feeling invincible and wearing heels are a thing of the past. I keep telling myself that it will all be worthwhile when Arthur gets here, but it's difficult to stay upbeat because depression has been eating away at me for the past month or so, ever since my fallout with Maddie.

These days, feelings of isolation and loneliness weigh heavily on me, and I find myself chatting to just about anybody who will give me the time of the day. Midwives. The busy Lakeside Health Care receptionists. Neighbours. Shop Assistants. Dog walkers (even though I'm scared of dogs). When they see me waddling towards them, they must let out a loud groan of frustration knowing I'm going to talk incessantly at them. I'm also anxious about the impending birth because I don't have a birthing companion anymore. How could I have gotten through two in one pregnancy? And what does that say about me? I've given up on punishing myself for being a bad person because there is sod all I can do about it. Besides, I have Arthur to think of. He's all that matters. He's my life now.

I walk past the salon with my head down, but once I'm almost past it, I take a crafty peek over one shoulder to glance inside. However, all I can make out are the blurred shapes of people moving about. None that I can identify. I never imagined that I would miss chatting to customers and being on my feet all day. Making endless cups of tea for clients and coming home smelling of bleach and nail polish. But I do. Massively. Just as I'm about to turn the corner onto the town bridge, wondering what the salon girls would think if they saw me now, without any makeup, with greasy unstraightened hair and chipped nails . . . I walk straight into Angela.

Who is more shocked or embarrassed, I'm not sure. She recovers faster than I do, though, plastering on a smile. She looks amazing as always in a dark-green knitted dress, an orangey-red wool jacket and impossibly slender black knee-length leather boots. Just thinking about toddling around in them makes my blood pressure go up another millimetre.

'Zoe! It's lovely to see you.'

Even though I don't believe her, I agree and say, 'You too.'

'You're looking well.'

'Am I?' I reply gloomily, trying not to notice how her eyes are frantically avoiding scrutinising my shoes, hair and nails. She is literally the last person I would have wanted to run into, other than Maddie. We both seem uncomfortable, so I go into people-pleasing mode.

I pretend to laugh as I crack a joke, 'It's been months since I've seen my toes and my legs swell up as soon as they see a pair of shoes. I can't tell you how much I envy you your slim ankles and high-heeled boots.' Gesturing to my enormous tummy, I add, 'Believe me, I'd swap those for this any day of the week.'

My attempt at humour backfires as she flinches at what I've said, and her smile disappears. She even seems distraught, and I'm at a loss as to why, until it dawns on me that she, like

Maddie, had lost a child. Whoa. Talk about being inconsiderate. What was I thinking? Book Club Scarlett told me that Angela had tried for another baby for years but was unable to conceive and here I am essentially declaring that I don't want mine, even though nothing could be further than the truth.

I clear my throat and murmur, 'I was so sorry to hear about your little boy, Angela.'

'Oh, that,' she replies evasively, glancing down at the pavement. 'Enough about me. What about you? When is the baby due? It can't be long now.'

I'm saddened that she doesn't feel like she can talk to me about her son and, so I tell her bluntly, 'He's due on Tuesday.'

She gasps in alarm, 'Oh my goodness, that's only three days away.'

Throwing her a weak, unconvincing smile, I admit, 'I've had the last nine months to prepare myself for Arthur's arrival and I still don't feel ready.'

She brushes off my concerns with a, 'You'll be fine,' as so many people do. Will I though? Truly? I have a bad feeling that refuses to go away.

'How is everyone?' I gesture vaguely in the direction of the salon.

'All good. You should pop in one day,' she suggests amiably.

'Yes, I really should. Perhaps when the baby's born.'

'It's ironic that I should run into you today since we were only talking about you last night.'

'We?'

'Me and Madeline.'

'Maddie?' I screw up my face in surprise.

'She came to the party but only stayed an hour.'

'Oh, what party was that?' I enquire disingenuously since I have no interest in parties. What I'm doing is stalling for time, so I can lure Angela back to her conversation with Maddie.

'It was my fiftieth,' she admits with a tiny grimace.

Stunned, I exclaim, 'Oh wow. I assumed you were closer to my age.'

'I wish,' she chuckles. 'I now know that I am not able to keep up with you younger women. The girls from the salon danced me off my feet last night, and I'm exhausted this morning, and . . .' She glances at her watch, adding, 'Late as a result.'

'So, everyone from the salon was there?' I ask, rattled.

'Yes, sorry,' Angela confesses, blushing the same colour as her jacket. 'I thought, with you being so—' her eyes dart to my belly — 'pregnant . . .'

When I tell her, 'Oh, yes, you're absolutely right, I'm much too pregnant for parties,' and laugh weakly, I am being kinder to her than she deserves.

Perhaps realising she has hurt my feelings and wanting to make amends, Angela's emerald gaze comes to softly rest on me and she takes a deep breath as if to bolster herself before exclaiming, 'Can I just say that I think it's a wonderful thing that you're doing for Madeline.'

When I hear this, my brow crumples and I lose the phoney smile. 'What do you mean?'

'Oh, sorry,' Angela stammers, 'shouldn't I have said anything? Me and my big mouth. I just thought that, well, everyone will find out soon enough.'

'Find out what?' My words come out stilted and sharp.

'About you being the Black's surrogate and bearing their child for them because they're unable to. I now understand why you kept the identity of the father a secret as it was Mike and Madeline's baby all along. You were obviously trying to protect them during those fraught early days of IVF. And to think you went through all of that to help them, because of what happened to Joe. I was moved to tears when Madeline told me. And I want you to know, Zoe,' she says gently, reaching out to take hold of my arm, 'I was wrong about you before when I called you petty and cruel.'

Upon hearing this, anger surges inside me turning my mouth into a snarl and my hands into fists. Thrusting her off, I make a disgusted sound in my throat that does nothing to match how furious I feel. Angela's jagged words have caused

292

my heart to flip over and a string of vengeful thoughts go off in my head when my mind wanders to Maddie.

It is several seconds before I can speak. And when I do, my voice is full of thunder. 'No, Angela, you *were* right about me before and just so we're clear, this is my baby—' I thrust an angry finger at my stomach — 'and the Blacks are the last people on earth I would trust with it.'

She blinks, clearly confused. 'Zoe, I don't understand.'

'You don't have to,' I fume, repeating back the words she had previously used to me. With that, I whip around and stomp off, mad as hell, my blood pressure climbing higher with every step. I hear Angela calling out in a whiney voice from behind me, 'But you can't keep it, if it isn't yours.'

Her words slice through me like a knife but I keep on walking. Although my head is spinning from this latest revelation I'm already plotting how I will put a stop to Maddie's damaging lies, but then I remember that I need cash to pay the window cleaner when he comes tomorrow. Because I want everything to be spick and span for Arthur's arrival, I hurry to the cash machine and furiously punch in my PIN, all the while muttering to myself, 'Those bloody Blacks, what the hell are they up to now?'

When my bank balance flashes up on the screen, I have to grip the keypad to stop myself from crashing to the ground. A £30,000 BACS payment has been made to my account. The reference against it states it is for "medical expenses" and when I click on the payee, the names of M.J. and M.E. Black appear in a red mist of my own making.

CHAPTER 70: MADELINE

I recognise Zoe as soon as I see her tiny shadow peering through the glass of the double entrance doors. I know why she is here. In a town like Stamford, where everyone is connected, rumours circulate swiftly. And by now, she will also have received the money transfer into her account so should have a good idea of what is going on. When I open the door, I'm shocked by how much she has changed in the past month. Her eyes have dark circles beneath them, and her cheeks are pale and sunken. The most obvious change, though, is her huge tummy. She must be having a larger-than-average baby because the rest of her body is as slim as ever. Joe was likewise large for a newborn, weighing nine pounds, three ounces, so it must run in the family.

She glares at me as if she would like to stick a knife in me. We don't say anything, but she pushes by me when I motion for her to come inside.

As she turns to go into the living room, I cry sharply, 'Not in there. In the kitchen.'

With a furious glance in my direction, she charges into the kitchen. I follow her, sighing and bracing myself for what's to come. Once inside, I take a seat at the table and gesture for her to do the same but she shakes her head and remains standing.

'It's unbelievable what lies you've been telling people.' She's visibly shaking. 'About me acting as a surrogate for you.'

'I first had the idea of using a surrogate when we were going through infertility treatment,' I reply calmly. 'Actually, our doctor was the one who suggested it.'

'You and Mike were trying for a baby?' Zoe exclaims, screwing her face up in surprise and something like horror.

'That's right, yes. And while we were successful at first, I miscarried in a matter of weeks. It appears that my womb isn't as accommodating as yours.' As I speak, my covetous gaze finds her stomach.

After giving me a chilly look and covering her stomach with a protective palm, Zoe remarks, 'I'm sorry about the miscarriage, Maddie, but you do know you're not getting your hands on my baby. Arthur is all mine. Nobody else's, and if you continue to spread any more of these vile lies, I'll—'

'You'll what?' I'm on my feet, towering above her and staring her down.

'I'll go to the police,' she mumbles nervously, lacking conviction.

'He's not all yours though, is he? You're forgetting that he's also Joe's and is, therefore, our grandchild. As such, we have rights.'

'You don't have any rights,' Zoe scoffs, her eyes darting to the door as if she's already thinking of escaping. 'And you have no proof whatsoever that your son is the father. Even if you did, it wouldn't get you anywhere.'

I respond calmly, *too calmly*, 'You're quite right, Zoe. But consider the amazing life we could give Arthur.' The terror of what Mike and I are doing hasn't fully registered with me yet. All I can think about is getting my hands on Joe's son.

'He can have a wonderful life with me,' she argues stubbornly.

'How?' I ask scornfully, arching both brows. 'When you lack money and a secure future. You don't even own your own home.'

'Money isn't everything,' she disputes, tears streaming down her cheeks.

'Think what you can accomplish with thirty thousand pounds, Zoe. You could travel. You've always wanted to do that, haven't you? You could even open your own hair salon. Give Angela a run for her money.'

'If you think you can buy my son for thirty thousand pounds you are very much mistaken,' Zoe cries, jutting out her chin.

'What concerns me is that you seem to think you have a choice in the matter.'

Her eyes widen at that and she gulps apprehensively. Our gazes drift at the same time towards the door as we hear it click open. Then, there's the soft tread of footsteps as Mike walks into the room.

Zoe's eyes fill with terror when she takes in my husband's guarded expression. His cold and detached gaze slides over her, not seeing her. This is not what she's used to from him. A little voice in my head whispers that she must know by now that something terrible is about to happen.

Ignoring me, she fixes Mike with curious eyes, 'What's going on?'

Her eyes track his predatory movements as he circles her, moving closer and closer, before warning her, 'Expect a slight scratch.'

Because her eyes are on his, pleading to be saved, she doesn't see the needle. Only feels it. By then it's too late . . .

* * *

Zoe blinks and her paper-thin eyelids flutter open as she looks around the room, unsure of where she is. We're in the living room, although it can hardly be called that anymore, as Mike and I have converted it into a makeshift operating theatre that includes a drip stand, a bed on wheels, a baby monitor, and a stainless steel table with a variety of needles, blades and scalpels arranged according to size. My OCD had got the better of me and I couldn't resist rearranging them. Tomorrow, everything will return to normal and our beautiful home will once again be just that.

Panic sets in when Zoe realises what she's got herself into and where she is. She tries to get up only to find that she is strapped to the bed and can't move her arms. She starts to scream at that point, but I wave a warning finger at her and inject her in the arm with a stronger dose of midazolam. This will make her sleepy and compliant without her losing consciousness. She will also be able to talk.

'It's okay,' I tell her, pulling down my face mask so that she can see my entire face, 'you're in safe hands. I'm very good at my job.'

'Maddie,' she begs, the medication making her eyes hazy and unfocused. 'Why are you doing this?'

I narrow my eyes at her, muttering, 'I told you I took my revenge cold.' Mike then reappears in the room dressed in blue scrubs and latex gloves. Sweat collects on his forehead but when he nods to confirm that everything is okay and we're "good to go" my heart finally settles in my chest. He even gives me a ghost of a smile. When he clicks a button, the sound of opera fills the room. This will drown out any unwanted screaming.

'I can't believe you're doing this,' Zoe groans, eyes flitting accusingly between Mike and me.

'We're the Blacks. We can do anything we like,' I say cuttingly. She's too focused on following Mike's movements to retaliate. When he picks up a gleaming metal scalpel with a sharp edge she writhes against the restraints and cries, 'No, Maddie, please, don't let him cut me open.'

'You won't feel anything. You've already been administered an epidural injection.' I pat her on the arm as I would any of my patients, to reassure her, but I can't help feeling like none of this is real. I could be watching an episode of one of my husband's favourite US medical dramas.

I try to comfort Zoe as her body tenses and her eyes bulge with fear, saying, 'What? Did you think we would perform a caesarean section without giving you an anaesthetic? We're not monsters, Zoe.'

'You're insane,' Zoe sobs. 'You won't get away with this.'

'Watch us,' I growl, biting down on my bottom lip.

'Like Mike and I got away with having an affair for years under your nose,' Zoe mocks, revealing that she hasn't done fighting yet.

'You're just saying that to get back at me. It's not true,' I hiss, but when I see Mike's eyes widen in panic, as if it *were* true, a part of me dies.

'He pursued me for years before I gave in to him,' she taunts. 'And when we were in bed together, he used to laugh at you and call you frigid.'

'You're lying,' I stammer, my body going limp with fear. Nevertheless, I can't pretend that Mike hadn't previously used that word to describe me.

'Of course, she's lying,' Mike declares fiercely, deeply offended.

'He even told me he loved me,' Zoe persists doggedly.

'No,' I respond, shaking my head, but I am seeing the truth in her eyes and dishonesty in my husband's. 'You would have told me. Said something.'

'Because best friends tell each other everything, right?' Zoe is scathing.

'That's enough,' murmurs Mike, casting a menacing glance at Zoe which is intended to shut her up. It doesn't work.

'He even promised to leave you, but of course, he never did.'

A shudder rips through my body, and I snap tersely, 'It's all lies.'

'Ask him,' screams Zoe, her voice hoarse.

'Mike?' I swivel my head to look at him, wanting to be convinced, but he continues to avoid eye contact with me. Tears sting my eyes and blur my vision as I implore once more, 'Mike, tell me it isn't true. Not Zoe?'

'It isn't true,' he growls, bringing the scalpel over to the bed. My body cringes with disgust and my face twists in agony as I realise that he *is* lying. He lied about Gabriella and now he is doing the same with Zoe.

'Do your job, Madeline,' he barks, gesturing towards the bed and Zoe.

I jump at his tone and obediently begin to cut away Zoe's clothes with a pair of scissors but I know his aggression is just a front for his dishonesty. As the atmosphere around us tightens, I have never felt so alone. This leads me to whisper quietly to Zoe, so Mike cannot hear, 'How could you? You were my best friend and I trusted you.'

'Yet, here we are now,' she laments, struggling to keep her eyes open.

'Here we are now,' I murmur softly in agreement as she drifts off, unable to fight the sedative any longer.

CHAPTER 71: ZOE

Darkness. Drifting. Slipping. Sliding. The room trembles and tilts until I feel as if I'm falling. Rain thuds against the windows as something is wrenched from my stomach, leaving me emptier than I've ever felt before. I hear a baby wailing somewhere and a mother's tears followed by the unimaginable words, 'He's here at last. My secret son.' I crane my neck to follow the sound, but I can't lift it high enough, so my neck falls back onto the pillow.

There's a scrape of a knife, whispered words, a sense of pressure and hands fumbling around inside me. I can hear the vibration of noises all around me. The tick of a clock. The thrum of classical music. A single cough. I feel oddly numb when the echoes fall away and everything slows.

Blurred faces hover above me until I find myself gazing up at Chris. My eyes move over his face, his mouth. I want to reach out to touch the dusting of freckles on his cheeks and nose but I recoil instead when he barks, 'I know what you did, Zoe.' I then capture Gabriella falling and hitting her head on the cobbles after she screamed, 'You're not fit to wipe her boots.' I relive the moment the sonographer told me, 'He's a little thug,' when I found out I was carrying a boy. Then I'm back in the maternity unit with Lela, warning me to, 'Expect a slight scratch,' just as Mike did before he injected me. Lastly, I'm with Maddie in the restaurant when she raised her glass and declared heartfeltly, 'To my best friend who I love as a sister.'

It's the regrets that keep me company in the drug-induced melancholic blackness. I should have kept my son a secret and not disclosed my pregnancy to anyone. Not Angela. Not Maddie. Had I possessed the courage to move away where no one knew me, I might have saved my child. And myself! Why had I ever allowed the Blacks back into my life after what their son did to me? They were superficial, materialistic, entitled and overprivileged, just as Chris warned me they were, which made them dangerous and untouchable. I ought to have realised that revenge ran in their blood.

The one thing I do not regret is telling Maddie about my affair with Mike. She deserved to have the smugness wiped from her face after everything she had put me through. And to think that the enormous guilt I've carried around with me for years had been negatively affecting my mental health. When I had accused Mike of being relentless in his pursuit of me, I was telling the truth. The sex was so fantastic that I was powerless to resist him. I had been obsessed with him, addicted even, and would have done anything to please him, including lie to my best friend. I'm relieved, though, that I didn't tell Maddie everything. Not every secret is meant to be shared.

I can still picture her yelling at me, 'You killed my son,' when she first discovered Arthur was Joe's. And then, as I think back to the night of the assault a flash of memory stirs within me as I belatedly recall getting out of bed afterwards and throwing a coat on over my nude body. White stars flash across my forehead like small rockets taking off as I realise that I chased after Joe, trailing him down to the river, where I once again accused him of raping me. He responded cruelly with vile remarks, 'An old hag like you with wrinkled skin and sagging tits? As if? It's no wonder Chris left you. You're a loser and a drunk. Everybody says so, even Mum.'

I shoved him then, much in the way I had Gabriella, wanting him to shut up. Tears blinded me and I was inconsolable; maybe I was still high. But when he lost his balance and stumbled down the river bank, looking fearful, I tried to grab him. Honest, I did, but he slipped through my fingers and landed in the water with a giant splash. Before I could decide what to do, Joe disappeared under the water. All that was left were a few bubbles.

My throat constricts in horror as I realise that I was the one who was captured on the security footage, not some random stranger. Trauma has a habit of blocking out our worst memories. Although I had been in a drug-induced state at the time, my mind scrambled with confusion, those memories of what really happened now return to haunt me. It was me, *Lovely Zoe, Godmother Zoe, Best friend Zoe, Slut Zoe*, who pursued Joe that night. Had I subconsciously known this all along? Is that why I deleted the tapes? Rather than admit to myself what I had done, I'd pushed all recollection of my dreadful crime to the back of my subconscious mind. Only now, when I'm about to leave it, does it decide to spill out, like rotten, stinking garbage. Maddie was right to accuse me of killing her son. And there I was thinking that having an affair with my best friend's husband was the worst thing I had ever done.

I'm pulled back into the room by a strained voice, leaving the horror of that night behind me, only to be thrust headfirst into another. It's Maddie. She's rocking something in her arms as she comes to stand by the side of the bed. When she recognises that my eyes are open despite being glazed, she unwraps the bundle to proudly show me the newborn baby — a boy with dark hair, dark eyes and sculpted cheekbones — he looks just like Joe.

Stunned into helplessness, I reach out with one hand to touch my baby, but it just falls away. For me, everything is a struggle. But not for Maddie, who, when she removes her mask to smile manically at me, seems somehow different. She appears happier and more complete than I've ever seen her, even after Joe was born. Motherhood suits her.

'You didn't think for one second that I wouldn't allow you to see our boy Arthur? I wouldn't be that cruel, Zoe. I also want to thank you for sharing him with me, like I did with you when I had Joe.'

CHAPTER 72: MADELINE

Seventeen months later

Down by the river, it is sticky and hot. On a day like this, the sky is a dazzling cloudless blue, and even the water appears clear and inviting for once. We are under the shade of a huge weeping willow tree whose low branches softly stroke the sun-dappled grass. From where we are seated on the river-bank, we can see medieval church spires and the town bridge. Our picturesque setting is framed by its three attractive stone arches.

Everywhere I turn, sunbathers are sprawled on the grass as a result of the August heatwave. Bare-chested, partially sunburnt men swill beer from cans while families with chil-dren enjoy picnics. Elderly couples, who find it difficult to rise from their knees, greedily hug the park benches. The aroma of fish and chips from the Riverside Fish Bar perme-ates the air. Older kids frolic around doused in sunscreen while small dogs chase them, yapping eagerly with their tongues lolling out. Dachshunds, chihuahuas and liver and white spaniels are commonplace. Majestic swans glide past us on the river and bow their necks as if welcoming guests to one of the royal palaces.

The rest of us catch a glimpse of our younger selves — which we can never have back — when young couples, in and out of love, lie flat out on the grass, exposing too much flesh and occasionally kissing.

I think of Joe and Gabriella then. How can I not? Three days after Joe entered the water of this very river, he was discovered floating face down in it. By the time the rescue team pulled his body from the beer-coloured water, they were unable to determine his gender, race, or age. The Welland had absorbed most of him. What skin was left had clung to his bones like wet paper bags. Bloating had rendered him unrecognisable, even to his family, who wouldn't want to have identified him in the first place . . . least of all me, his grief-stricken mother who hadn't slept a wink in the seventy-two hours since he had gone missing. This was nothing new. I'd spent whole years of my life fretting over my adored son.

As Joe's mother, I had always emphasised to others that he wasn't to blame for his mental health condition. Mike and I searched hard for an explanation for his disturbing and challenging behaviour, and we insisted on having him evaluated for antisocial personality disorder, but deep down I knew better. Joe was born bad. He had even been described as a "pathological liar" by his therapist. It was my closely guarded secret.

As for my other "secret", Arthur is such a cheerful, happy child. Nothing like Joe at a year old. If I'm being completely honest, when Joe didn't get his way, he could be difficult, sulky and defiant. Arthur especially enjoys feeding the ducks, but unlike his father, he doesn't try to grab them or frighten them. Again, he is very unlike my son in that he is loving and kind.

As I watch Mike fling Arthur above his head, tickle his stomach, and make him laugh nonstop, my breath catches in my throat.

'Arthur, come to Mama,' I cry, holding out my arms, eager to be engulfed by his warm, wriggly body that smells of milk and talcum powder.

Mike throws me a mischievous look, all dark playful eyebrows, and the dimpled smile I fell in love with all those years ago as he brings our baby over. When Arthur gives me a chubby-cheeked grin, I ruffle his thick dark hair and scoop him into my arms, slotting him on my hip. The resemblance to Joe is striking. But I also see his mother in him. Soft cheeks. Quick smile. Giggles galore. I stand for a while, filling my lungs and shielding my eyes from the glare of the sun, as I think of Zoe. Late at night, when everyone else has gone to sleep and the house is silent, her words torment me. Of course, I will never believe her outrageous lies. My son may have been many things, but he was not a rapist. He couldn't have been. *Could he?*

But then again, who would ever have imagined that Mike and I were capable of carrying out such a heinous act of murder, especially when you consider that we'd each taken the Hippocratic oath to "do no harm". What hope was there for Joe with parents like us? Though there was no other way of getting our hands on baby Arthur, I'm not inhuman and I struggle most days to come to terms with what we did to my former best friend. But she was never going to quietly give up Joe's son to us, was she? Even though Mike and I have wordlessly decided to never discuss it again, I can't stop myself from reliving the nightmare. At least Zoe didn't suffer. Since I'm an expert at what I do, as I've already stated, I let her pass away quietly and painlessly with a pentobarbital solution — a substance used in assisted suicides. Her heart and brain function shut down within minutes of being administered the fatal dose. But first, I let her see her son.

Everything was meticulously planned of course. While Zoe was counting down the days to Arthur's arrival I was purchasing a first-class one-way plane ticket to Australia, notifying her landlord of her intention to vacate her rental property, and her boss that she wasn't intending to return to work after having the baby as well as hiring a removal company to store all her cheap and ugly household goods; afterwards making sure to spend a certain amount of the £30,000 in her bank account each month. It was so easy to make someone like Zoe disappear because she was alone, had no close relatives, and only Mike and I as friends. Her body was a different story, however. That's where Mike's skills as a surgeon came into their own. It was heartbreaking to see Zoe's lifeless body being dismembered piece by piece but it had to be done. If a whole body had been dumped in the hospital's anatomical waste bin, suspicion would have been aroused, and we would have been looking at a murder enquiry, but small parts, like organs and limbs were commonplace.

Poor Mike, it must have been ghastly for him transporting Zoe's bagged body parts in his car and then having to root around in the underground clinical waste section without being seen. Only after the last of the body parts had been taken away for incineration were he and I able to breathe again. When people like Angela, who is quite the friend these days, ask about Zoe, I always respond with, 'She's having the time of her life in Australia. She has a job now and has even nabbed a new man for herself. I wouldn't be a bit surprised if she doesn't stay out there permanently.'

Because I don't desire my husband in the way a woman should, I never could understand Zoe's sexual attraction to men. I was only six months into my marriage before I realised that sex disgusted me. Therefore, intimacy is something I prefer to avoid, but Mike and I have come to an arrangement. I will continue to ignore his affairs as long as he is discreet, again assuming the women are of legal age. It's not as if I can fulfil his desires. But despite everything, Mike loves only me. And that's enough. His being around for our son Arthur is the only thing that matters.

Even though I felt more duped by Zoe than I did Mike when I learned of their affair, I'll never forgive him for having a sexual relationship with her. The hurt went deep. She was meant to be my closest friend, and I completely trusted her, whereas he was just a man. I'll never make that mistake again. Another of my husband's mistakes is recuperating in the hospital. Gabriella's parents maintain regular contact with me as though I matter to them more than I have any right to. Because of the brain damage, it's unclear how much of a recovery their daughter will make, but at least she is cognizant even if she cannot yet speak. I wonder what mysteries she might reveal regarding her accident when she does. The police investigation as to whether she was assaulted and left for dead or if her head injuries were caused by an accidental fall are still ongoing.

Mike's and my eyes clash as he motions for me to hand Arthur back so that he can put him in the buggy. I don't want to give him up, but I have to, so I let Mike take him. I keep a careful eye on my husband while he secures Arthur. He likes to be in charge of the buggy and always pushes it when we're out together. How my alpha-male husband has evolved in the last year. He's much more hands-on with Arthur than he ever was with Joe. He even changes nappies these days. Unheard of back then.

His five o'clock shadow feels scratchy on my skin when he brushes a stubbled cheek against my face. Kissing the top of my head, he whispers into my hair, 'Time to go home,' and we both turn as one, the buggy in front of us, the river behind us, and our family's future ahead of us.

THE END

ACKNOWLEDGEMENTS

The subject of best friends is a popular one in the psycholog-ical thriller genre but *The Godmother* is my first attempt at writ-ing about the subject. I have to confess that I enjoyed myself immensely, although the last few chapters were the hardest to write. Many of us have walked away from friendships during our lifetimes, mostly because these relationships felt toxic or one-sided, but that doesn't mean we ever forget how much those people once meant to us or the secrets we shared and continue to honour. Zoe and Madeline are very different women but each of them has a dark side. Sometimes Zoe was the severer of the two and other times it was Madeline. I loved that about them. Neither were all good or all bad, just like the rest of us.

Female friendship is important to women but a true best friend is hard to find. We've all heard stories of best friends who have been caught cheating on one another's husbands or betraying each other's secrets, which is why *The Godmother* resonated so much with me. That's not to say most of us would ever go as far as the characters in this story. Whilst writing it, I often pondered who out of the two women I would want as a friend. The answer was of course, neither, but that didn't stop me feeling sorry for them at times or even identifying with their individual plights.

Once again, I've set this book in my hometown of Stamford, so for those of you who are local to the area, you will likely recognise popular landmarks. If you've never been, I definitely recommend a visit. It's a lovely Georgian town, known for its private schools, old dusty bookshops, antique auctions, stately homes, afternoon tea, quaint shops and cobbled passageways. *The Sunday Times* once voted it "Britain's Top Place to Live".

I would like to dedicate *The Godmother* to two of my own dear friends who bear absolutely no resemblance to the characters in this book. Sue Whittaker is an extraordinary person. Not only is she a natural horsewoman, but she is also a lover of trees as well as animals, which you don't see every day. Though humble and unassuming, she finds everyone and everything else fascinating. As for her extroverted husband James, who has his own sword and a giant magical bog oak, I hope he gets around to writing his fantasy story one day. Excelsior! I'm very grateful to have Sue and James in my life and love visiting them at their horsey home in Norfolk.

I also want to say a massive thank you to everyone at Joffe Books for all their hard work in getting this story ready for publication. They have been an absolute pleasure to work with. Go Team Joffe. As always, special thanks go to Kate Lyall Grant, Joffe's publishing director.

If you are not from the UK, please excuse the English spelling. Oopsy daisy, it's just the way we do things across the pond. Apologies also for any swearing but this is down to the characters and has nothing to do with me. Lol. The same goes for any blaspheming.

Now for the best bit where I get to thank my lovely readers for all their support, especially all the bloggers and reviewers. You know who you are!

Your loyalty and friendship mean everything. As do your reviews. ☺

THE JOFFE BOOKS STORY

We began in 2014 when Jasper agreed to publish his mum's much-rejected romance novel and it became a bestseller.

Since then we've grown into the largest independent publisher in the UK. We're extremely proud to publish some of the very best writers in the world, including Joy Ellis, Faith Martin, Caro Ramsay, Helen Forrester, Simon Brett and Robert Goddard. Everyone at Joffe Books loves reading and we never forget that it all begins with the magic of an author telling a story.

We are proud to publish talented first-time authors, as well as established writers whose books we love introducing to a new generation of readers.

We won Trade Publisher of the Year at the Independent Publishing Awards in 2023. We have been shortlisted for Independent Publisher of the Year at the British Book Awards for the last four years, and were shortlisted for the Diversity and Inclusivity Award at the 2022 Independent Publishing Awards. In 2023 we were shortlisted for Publisher of the Year at the RNA Industry Awards.

We built this company with your help, and we love to hear from you, so please email us about absolutely anything bookish at feedback@joffebooks.com

If you want to receive free books every Friday and hear about all our new releases, join our mailing list: www.joffebooks.com/contact

And when you tell your friends about us, just remember: it's pronounced Joffe as in coffee or toffee!

ALSO BY JANE E. JAMES

HER SECOND HUSBAND
NOT MY CHILD
THE SON-IN-LAW
THE GODMOTHER

Milton Keynes UK
Ingram Content Group UK Ltd.
UKHW040120170324
439511UK00004B/119

9 781835 264133